SWEPT AWAY

Also by Julie Tetel Andresen

And Heaven Too

Lord Laxton's Will

MacLaurin's Lady

My Lord Roland

Simon's Lady

Sweet Sarah Ross

Sweet Seduction

Sweet Sensations

Sweet Surrender

Sweet Suspicions

Tangled Dreams

The Blue Hour

The Temporary Bride

The Viking's Bride

SWEPT AWAY

JULIE TETEL

ANDRESEN

HELIX BOOKS

1997

AN IMPRINT OF

WINDOWS ON HISTORY PRESS, INC.

Helix Books

Copyright ©1989 by Julie Tetel Andresen

ISBN 0-9654499-0-4
(Previously published by Warner Books/Popular Library,
ISBN 0-445-20922-4)

Printed in the United States of America

10 9 8 7 6 5 4 3 2 1

SWEPT AWAY

CHAPTER I

*L*ast night I dreamed I was on board ship again. In my dream, I was not a mere passenger, tucked invisibly away in my berth. No, I was on deck, alone at the bow, at one with the craft. I stood behind the proud figure head; I was her human counterpart. Our hair was unbound, streaming behind us, guiding the ship west as it knifed its course through the turbulent waters. My feet were planted firmly on the heaving planks of the main deck, while hers slid down the curve of the prow to straddle white horses raising their crests in the troubled sea. I felt no more discomfort from the ceaseless rocking than she.

It was night. The full moon, a bright eye in the limitless carpet of stars overhead, showed us the way. It cast its white light across the ink churning endlessly before us, promising us that journey's end was always just beyond the next swell, and then the next. In my heart, desperate hope warred with deep despair that sea would ever meet land. So torn was I with emotion that I was transfixed at my place behind the figure head—unable to give up, unable to turn back. My waking self wished for this dream and feared it; my dreaming self hoped for and doubted the end of it. Thus my entire being was set awash in a never-ending tidal flow of wish and fear, desire and despair.

Yet my emotions are hardly the point of this tale of survival. In any case, at the outset of this adventure, these emotional depths had not been plumbed. Nor had I, in fact, during the whole of that abbreviated crossing, ever once roamed alone the deck of the *Judith*, or communed there with the figure head. As for my status, I was at first considered much less than even a passenger, for I was a woman unescorted, and one who had not been expected on board, at that. Now, the evils attending a woman traveling alone are well known to everyone.

However, by the time I had boarded the *Judith* at Plymouth, I was quite experienced in the world's evils; and although I no longer held the high rank or privileged position to which I had been accustomed, I saw no reason to behave as if the world owed me less respect than I had formerly commanded. I might mention that I have never been a timid soul. A common sea captain and his ragtag crew certainly did not intimidate me. I was impervious both to their frank stares and to their curious, sidelong glances. As we got under way, it seemed that my stomach was impervious, as well, to the pitch and roll of the ship at sea. I was rather pleased to discover that I was an excellent sailor, with only an initial squeamishness that I quickly conquered.

Once I had my sea legs, I did not hesitate to circulate on deck as often as possible. I was fascinated to find that the crew performed an amazing variety of tasks: the shortening and lengthening of the sheets according to fair winds or foul; the regular and equitable distribution of the food (or "grub," as the crew so colorfully referred to the boiled beans, salt pork, and apples we ate); the constant check for loose nails in every corner of the craft; the frequent changing of the colors; and the manning of the guns. Although the *Judith* was a merchant ship, no craft took to sea without a cannon or two—"chasers," they are called, or "murthering pieces." As it is my nature to seek purposeful activity, I kept an eye on the cannons, seeing to it that their touchholes were always reamed and that the tackle was always properly rigged around their bases, which were set, rather cleverly, on swivels.

As the days passed, I found more and more to do. Several of the crew, not understanding my excellent managerial abilities, had the temerity at first to remonstrate with me when I explained what I wanted done. With patience and a firm "That will do!" I was usually able to quell resistance. Thus, I fancied I had made my presence felt on deck by the time the coast of Portugal came into view. (I might add that we had skirted the coast of Spain without incident. In this year of 1688, England and Spain were still engaged in their ceaseless quarrel.)

I was assured of my effectiveness on deck by Mrs. St. Charles, a fellow passenger whom I visited daily in her berth. In one of our chats, she commented upon the liberties I took with the seamen and expressed surprise at my success. She said that seafaring folk generally considered having women on board ship unlucky.

I protested at once.

Mrs. St. Charles laughed, a little greenly, from her bunk, for she did not have a sailor's legs or stomach. "Yes, my dear Marie," she said, permitting herself the use of my given name, although I hardly knew her at all. She had said early on in the voyage that she could have been my mother and seemed bent on treating me as a daughter, which struck me as very odd. I had lost my own mother so very long ago that I was quite sure I did not need one now, and besides, I had the distinct impression that I was mothering *her*.

"Women and pigs and ministers," she continued, "all of them unlucky."

"Nonsense!" I replied, blinking at this highly unlikely assortment.

Mrs. St. Charles laughed again, weakly, at my indignation. It cost her an effort to maintain a conversation, but I knew she enjoyed my company, while I enjoyed being needed. In addition to which, she was my sole source of below-deck information. "But a woman is unlucky only if she is carrying an empty pail," she added, "while ministers, no matter what, bode foul weather."

That last made perfect sense to me. Although I hoped that I was a good Anglican, all the ministers I had ever met were a sanctimonious lot. "But pigs?" I wanted to know.

Mrs. St. Charles shrugged. "I wasn't told the reason. The most curious superstition of all is the one regarding hares and rabbits—or so Mr. St. Charles told me just last night, after he shared dinner and a pipe with the captain. It is the worst sort of bad luck to see them, Captain Hawkins said, and they are never referred to except as 'furry objects.' The captain would not even pronounce the word 'rabbit'— he traced its outline in the air with his finger."

When I laughed at this absurdity, Mrs. St. Charles frowned a little. Shifting uncomfortably on her hard bunk, she glanced up at me and asked, "Have you never before heard any of this?"

"How could I have heard of these odd beliefs?"

"I thought you must have been on a dozen sea voyages already!"

"No, this is my first one," I was happy to inform her. "Why should you think that?"

"Because you seem so very comfortable on board and so very busy! Why, the captain was saying last night to Mr. St. Charles that you were—" she broke off.

"Most helpful?" I suggested.

"Ah, those were not his exact words," she hedged.

"You need not spare my feelings, ma'am!" I said. I had absolutely no good opinion of Captain Hawkins, save for his competent sailing of the *Judith*. "That idiot of a captain," I informed her, "spoke to me —only once, I can assure you!—of my assistance to the seamen. 'Bullying,' I think was the way he so quaintly phrased it! Well, I put him straight on that score! But if I press you now, it is only to know that my efforts have been duly noticed!"

"Oh, my, yes! They have most definitely been noticed!" she replied at once. However, she was still puzzled about my apparent seafaring knowledge, and so asked, "But, perhaps, your father taught you something about the sea—?"

Her husband had been a colleague of my father's in the War Department. Oddly enough, my father had booked a berth on this particular voyage months ago, and it was Mr. St. Charles who had arranged to have me take his place. "My father was an army man," I reminded her, rather shortly.

"Ah!" was all she replied, and left it at that.

"In any case, I am happy to have learned of these superstitions," I continued without hesitation. "In the unlikely event I should feel some strong impulse to pronounce the words 'rabbit' or 'hare' to a crew member or to carry an empty pail on deck, I shall firmly repress it, lest I be cast overboard as an ill omen!"

"You, cast overboard, my dear? No, there has been no talk of *that* among the crew for several weeks now!" said Mrs. St. Charles.

I was pleased to see a little more animation than usual in her wan face.

Although no strange impulse ever came over me to say the word 'rabbit' or to carry an empty pail, I did have a rather extended incident with one crew member.

After the ships left Lisbon—the *Judith* was in a fleet of seven, all bound for various destinations in the New World—we headed south to Tenerife, in the Canary Islands not far from the coast of Africa. It had been May when we had first left England, and the winds had been fresh. It was now June, and agreeably warmer.

At Lisbon, there had been a change in the crew, as well as a new owner for the ship—a Mr. Winthrop. The owner and his crew were also English, although what they were doing in Portugal I didn't know. Neither did I formally meet any of them. Nor did I understand this midvoyage transfer of ownership, the details of which, cloaked in rather mysterious terms, were presented to me by Mrs. St. Charles.

However, since it did not make a straw of difference to me, and Mrs. St. Charles could rarely get two facts in the correct sequence anyway, I did not pursue it.

All I knew was that with the new crew had come a livelier shipboard atmosphere, and suddenly I found myself with ever so much more to do. I was thoroughly enmeshed in ship life now, and not at all sorry that there were still weeks and weeks of it ahead for me, before I was to dock at the Colony of Massachusetts in August. That our ship was to make a wide sweep of the Atlantic, around the Caribbean Sea to Jamaica, and then up the Florida coast, in order to reach the American colonies, did not then overly concern me.

With the warmth and the new crew and all the things to do, I was happier than I had been in many a week. The pain of the losses I had recently experienced seemed to ebb just a little. One day, upon my rounds, I chanced to see a rigging rope on deck that seemed to be hopelessly entangled with another, and the two were further tangled around a water barrel. Well, since this was obviously no good circumstance, I called to the nearest deck hand, who looked to be rather idle at just that moment.

"You, sir!" I said. I always called them "sir," no matter how dirty or unkempt, and sure enough, after I had called out again "You, sir!" and he had turned toward me, I could see that he was every bit as gray and grizzled as most. I recognized him as one of the new crew picked up at Lisbon.

After I nodded to his answering look of inquiry, he stepped obediently toward me, but I caught how the look on his face changed from mild inquiry to the cheekiness that I had encountered before. I foresaw no difficulties with him.

"Yes, sir, I have a job for you," I said when he came close enough to me to stand in the shadow of my bonnet. He was of a height with me, for I am tallish for a woman. "These ropes here," I said, gesturing with my parasol to the snarl of twine, "are in need of sorting out."

"I'm the whipstaff, ma'am," he said by way of an answer.

I was used to these impertinent, irrelevant replies. "You are what-ever you please, sir. Allow me, to direct your attention once again to the tangled ropes. You will be happy that I have done so when the evening comes and it is time to trim the sails."

"Do you know what a whipstaff is, ma'am?" he asked, his tone all humility, but I caught the trace of a smirk on his face.

"I have not the faintest idea, sir," I replied, for there would be no point making myself seem ridiculous, if he challenged me on the point, "but I know crossed and crisscrossed ropes when I see them and know what they mean, for I have been on board ship for more than five weeks now—six, after Tenerife."

"Have ye now? But, five weeks or no,' I take my orders from him," he said, cocking his head over to a man who stood slightly above us on the poop, who I took to be the new quartermaster, also with us since Lisbon. That man, whose broad back was toward us, seemed to be fully engaged with a long glass, compass, and charts, and was giv-ing instructions to the flag boy who regularly climbed the mainmast to hoist the series of colors by which the ships in the convoy commu-nicated with one another.

"Do you?" I answered quite pleasantly. "And what is your name, sir?"

It was Thomas.

"Now, Thomas," I said patiently, for I had learned that patience with these seamen was all, "do you wish for me to bother the quar-termaster with this simple task while he is so busily engaged?"

The seaman hesitated a moment, as if in surprise, then indicated, in rather blunt terms, that he would like to see me try my hand with "the quartermaster."

I was not so easily fooled, nor was I some green young thing to be thrown off my stride with such language. We stood there for the next twenty minutes or more, discussing the ropes. Thomas went so far at one point as to threaten me with bodily harm. I was unimpressed. Eventually I wore him down, which was always the way it was when I had to discuss some idea with a seaman. The army men refer to such battles as a "war of attrition," and it is my belief that my tactics worked so well on board because these seamen, used only to Greek fire and cannonballs, were not familiar with the strategy.

The outcome had been clear to me from the start. Thomas was presently untangling the ropes and muttering, quite fearsomely and indistinctly, under his breath. I was unmoved by it, and I knew from experience that I should stand by him until the job was done, to set a good example for the next time. When he had finished, I did not hesitate to point out that he could save us a good deal of time in the future by not engaging in so much discussion.

At that, a thundercloud clapped across his ragged brow, and it looked as if Thomas would lose his temper in earnest. Then, just as suddenly, his rage passed. Cheeky man that he was, he smiled somewhat toothlessly at me. Then he broke into an extraordinary little speech.

"No, ye can't do it to me, missy," he said, shaking his sunburnt, wind-weathered head. "No, ye can't sour me spirits, not when I'm aboard such a pretty wench as the *Judith*. Why, look ye here, straight up the mizzen, and ye'll see as beautiful a yard of canvas as ever a man could lay eyes on. With the mainmast stepped amidship and with the stout chain for a mainstay, ye'll not find another such a lass, dressed as she is in her topgallants, royals, staysails, and spritsails. Her mortars have a free range abeam and forward she's hoy rigged as neat as wax, her tonnage perfect. Aye she's the bonniest bomb ketch in all the world, I'll warrant!"

I understood hardly a word of this apparent praise, but I had let my eye travel up and lose itself in the dozens of great sheets of squares and triangles, pulled taut by a miracle of rigging. Just then, in the blink of an eye, the wind ceased its push against the canvas, and the sails fluttered, dimpling momentarily, with the sound of a flock of birds taking flight. The next second, a puff of air came to fill the sails, making of them sheets of beaten silver with the dents of the smith's hammer in them. Then, hardly had my eye captured that image, before up off the water came a great Atlantic gust to swell them to their most majestic curve. In response, the *Judith* keeled gracefully leeward and then surged forward, sailing fast, the wind abeam, suddenly free and alive and happy to skim the surface of the world.

Until that moment, I had always objected to the pronoun *she* applied to ships. I objected no longer and would have said, as no doubt Thomas would have phrased it, that I liked "the cut of her jib."

We stood there, in that brief moment, silent, in mutual appreciation of the *Judith*'s beauty. I was encouraged to think that our shared poem of wordless sympathy had created an odd bond between us, that Thomas and I had reached an understanding.

I was later disabused of that notion. It was some time after we had turned west and were plunging, in all our glory, toward the Caribbean Sea. I was particularly keen on seeking out loose nails in those days—my eyes are particularly sharp. I was pointing out just such a one to a passing hand, and tapping the head of the nail with the ferrule of my parasol, when I chanced to look up at nothing in particular and spied Thomas. He was on the quarterdeck on the edge of a knot of crewmen, gesturing first in my direction and following that with a heaving motion, as if casting some imaginary bundle overboard. The men found this pantomime highly amusing. I was sadly disappointed in him.

The quartermaster, as I believed him to be, came up to the men just then and must have easily sorted out the topic of discussion, for he turned almost immediately in my direction. By this time, I was standing straight up, one hand on my hip, the other on the handle of my parasol, which was now stuck straight in a floorboard. I returned the quartermaster's regard unflinchingly.

I had certainly noticed him, as had every other crew member and passenger on board. Or rather, I had noticed him noticing me on several occasions, after my initial encounter with Thomas, as I was going about my business on deck. This man did not strike me as one of the ordinary crew, although he wore, like the rest of them, the leather jerkin, plain collar, and pantaloons shoved into the top of his three-quarter boots. But despite the fact that he had kept an occasional eye on me, he had never been in my immediate vicinity when I had seen some important job to be done, and so I had never exchanged any words with him.

Regarding him now, in that brief, frozen moment, I was aware of one important difference between him and the other men. It was not his snapping blue eyes, or the mass of uncut black curls tied back carelessly, or his lean, rugged face. It was, rather, that he was years younger than the old salts surrounding him.

The next moment, he turned his back to me, made some comment to the men to which they grinned appreciatively, and dispersed them to go about their duties on a laugh.

I had it in mind to mention Thomas's and the quartermaster's impertinence to Captain Hawkins—not that that low-minded man would do anything about it—or perhaps to Mr. Winthrop himself, whoever he was. As it happened, the opportunity to speak with the captain or the owner of the ship did not immediately arise.

Mrs. St. Charles fell ill, or so she complained. She had never been strong, so I could not distinguish an appreciable difference between her state of relative wellness and the one of which she now complained. It was difficult for me to understand, since I had always enjoyed such a strong constitution and had seemed actually to *improve* in health as the journey progressed. Nevertheless, after Tenerife, Mrs. St. Charles insisted that she was dreadfully ill and that I nurse her. I obliged her, reasoning that one did the job where one was needed most.

Mrs. Arbuthnot, one of the six female passengers aboard (including Mrs. St. Charles and myself) also seemed to think her presence was required in Mrs. St. Charles's minuscule berth. Mrs. Arbuthnot was a loud, vulgar woman with whom I would have had nothing to do in London, but I was not in London, and so had to suffer her, on occasion. She had an overbearing disposition and an enormous figure (which made me feel, by comparison, almost demure and petite—no mean feat!), and given this, there was not room in the berth for both of us. Mrs. St. Charles preferred me. Mrs. Arbuthnot, loud as she was, was *all* talk and no action.

When the steady diet of broth and apples boiled to mush I fed Mrs. St. Charles by hand seemed to have revived her a bit, I returned to deck, curious to see what depredations in the ship's life had occurred as a result of my prolonged absence.

Then it happened.

We had hit our share of foul weather—summer squalls, a spitting sky, even the doldrums. I had somehow erroneously imagined that the closer we came to that dangerous place known as the Spanish Main, the worst we could expect to encounter before Jamaica would be buccaneers or a Spanish warship, for England and Spain were mightily contesting their territories in the New World.

Instead, mid-June and still many days yet from the nearest scrap of land in the Caribbean Sea, we were hit with a terrible gale that roared out of the east. For four days it tore at the *Judith*, and beat it so badly that the seamen had to cut down all of her higher buildings. Her rudder was sorely shaken, as well. When the storm abated, it took two days for the convoy to communicate again. All of the seven ships were still intact, thank God, with no loss of life, though three of them were as badly crippled as the *Judith*.

We poked along for another day, hoping to have stayed on some kind of course, but another tempest howled out, this time from the west, and we were swept along like spindrift, once again, on the awful seas. I had now nearly lost my sea legs and stomach, but Mrs. St. Charles seemed to need me now more than ever, so I made every effort to provide what comfort and succor I could. Then, as if not enough had yet happened, a third frightful gale screamed out of the north and battered the ship for three days. Rain pounded on the ship's deck with the hammers of the devil's anvil. I was quite as sick as I had ever been, though not as sick as the other women; and in one of my dizziest moments, I imagined that the ships that held our human lives and precious cargo had no more substance or control than seven little corks being shaken violently in a huge bowl by an angry child.

When this storm mercifully abated, the fleet had been blown, for all anyone knew, to Cape Horn. On the first clear night, rapid calculations were made. It seemed, miraculously, that the combined effects of the different storms had canceled one another out: we were practically in the same position we had been when the first one hit, only much farther west—a net gain. Another two days passed before we learned that some further miracle had saved all seven ships. Of course, they had suffered, and the *Judith* more than most. Her topgallants and royals had been amputated and her beauty was irretrievably marred, but she had gotten us through, alive. That first day after the last storm, when every bone-tired seaman and maltreated passenger climbed unsteadily up onto the main deck, I stood portside, clutching the *Judith*'s weather-scarred rails for support. To my own surprise, I hugged them fiercely.

The few hours of blessing and quiet relief quickly passed. That night, far past the last bells, the boatswain's pipe shrilled out, rousing the few passengers from their exhausted, storm-tossed slumber. We were informed of the worst of bad news—the *Judith* had developed a leak. A man had been slung overboard to stop it as best he could with a sailcloth, and the pumps had been put to work. Eventually, however, it had been decided that the leak was so extreme that we could not keep to her any longer, and she was taking on water so fast now that we had to abandon her immediately.

The boy who came around, lantern in hand, cheeks flushed, to rouse me from my larboard bunk, recommended that I gather together whatever I could carry without assistance.

And for the rest of our worldly goods—?

The boy shrugged.

Fully awake now, I was aware of the frantic activity on the main deck, above. The crew was trying to salvage the cargo. I felt the panic in the air, but I am extremely capable in such circumstances—as recent events in my life had shown—and saw nothing for it but to manage, to *do*.

I dressed. I made my hair presentable. I affixed my bonnet, even though it was night, reasoning that the dawn would surely come (I have always been an optimist). I threw a shawl around my shoulders. I packed what valuables were at hand into my tapestry bag. I had no access to the things stowed in my trunk; and although I possessed little of true worth these days, it still disturbed me to think that what remained of my former wealth would go to its grave at the bottom of the Atlantic in the hull of the *Judith*.

I picked up my parasol, and with a last glance around the cramp of my berth, prepared to leave. Some prescience prompted me to stash in my tapestry bag the corked bottle of water held by a leather thong to the shelf above my cot.

I knew exactly what needed to be done. I went down the busy, narrow gangway to Mrs. St. Charles's room. She had a habit of collapsing onto her bunk with her hand pressed to her heart whenever the slightest disturbance on board occurred. I was not surprised to see her condition.

I consider it a great failing of character when a person, generally a woman, falls apart at the least little thing—not that one is compelled to abandon ship every day of one's life. Abandoning ship is not, after all, as commonplace as crossing the confusions of Piccadilly Circus on market day. On the other hand, Piccadilly Circus does present its real hazards, and I have always been amazed by the numbers of people who have failed to master the negotiation of market day traffic, which is probably due to their lack of skill with the parasol in a crowd. But I digress.

Mrs. St. Charles was quite helpless with fear, and Mr. St. Charles was equally helpless over his wife's helplessness. In five minutes I had the situation well in hand, and was leading her up to the quarterdeck and then onto the main deck, where all was in truly magnificent and *quiet* confusion.

No noise could be heard save for the grunts of heavy effort, the occasional call of direction from a low and booming masculine voice, the shoving of great casks and cartons along wood—heavy boxes containing weapons, iron bars, textiles. Not all the trade goods could be saved, but enough perhaps to avert economic disaster for the new owner and his investors.

Lanterns lit the labors. They were hanging askew, giving visible form to what all of our feet could feel: the *Judith* was listing badly. Speed was of the essence. Cords holding in place what I recognized as wherries were hacked, and these boats were lowered by block and tackle into the water.

I made sure that Mrs. St. Charles, who was now swooning; was put in the first wherry. This was accomplished with great ease, for her swooning form offered no protest to the real and gripping terror that a conscious body might have felt at being rappeled down the length of a ship into a small boat in the middle of the ocean in the dead of night.

Judging from the low, unresponsive sky above, it was somewhere past midnight, although I could not have said for sure. I worked hard over the next hour, I would say, organizing the rest of the ladies and overseeing their individual lowerings into the same boat with Mrs. St.

Charles. Mrs. Arbuthnot, for instance, fully conscious, was lowered into the boat in a much, much noisier and more laborious fashion than had been Mrs. St. Charles.

I debated with several of the male passengers who declared that I, too, should be in the boat with the ladies. Mr. St. Charles claimed loud and long his responsibility for my being on the *Judith* in the first place and insisted that I take my place next to Mrs. St. Charles.

To which I said, roundly: "Nonsense!" I pointed out, quite reasonably, that there were only nine seats on that boat, and that thus far, five women were in it already and only two men. I would make the sixth woman, and there would be only one more seat left for a man. I won the argument handily by pointing out that I, personally, did not want to be there when Mrs. Arbuthnot counted up the ratio of three strong male protectors to six helpless women and had a fit of hysterics.

Mr. St. Charles acknowledged the logic of this, reluctantly, and I strongly suspected that he had been trying to hoodwink *me* into taking his place. I had gotten Mrs. St. Charles into the boat. Mr. St. Charles would have to accompany her the rest of the way.

There was still much to do. I was helping with the unpacking of the cargo and unloading bolts of cloth from large hampers I had found and hoped to save. Thomas happened to cross in front of the corner of the deck I had chosen to crouch in. I stopped him with a hand on his arm. He turned to me, a look of exaggerated surprise transforming his grizzled visage into that of a grotesque gargoyle, and barked, "Get into one of those bedeviled boats, missy!"

I waved this away with a quick, "We certainly don't have time for one of our wrangles now, Thomas! Tell me instead how many hours are left before our mainmast is sunk below the surface of the water!"

He paid me the compliment of taking my question seriously. "Five, six hours, at the present rate," he answered. "She's been taking on water for about that length of time now, and we're still reasonably afloat. In the first hour or two, it looked as if we might have been able to save her. . . .”

"Five or six hours?" I repeated and calculated. "Almost dawn."

"Seven, eight hours, if we're lucky," he continued, "but the more water she's carrying, the quicker she sinks. It goes faster toward the end."

"Say, six and a half hours, then, and we'll be fine," I said. "There'll be enough light by then for the other ships to see our distress flags, before they're swallowed by the water. The others will be on the lookout. They know how badly we were damaged."

"They might not be looking soon enough, or in the right direction," he replied.

"They'll eventually see all of us in our little boats. They have long glasses, after all."

He shook his head again and preserved an eloquent, fearsome silence, but I caught on.

"Trying to frighten me, Thomas?" I queried, and shook my head. "You'll not do it to me—not while the *Judith* is still partially afloat!"

Thomas smiled his cheeky smile and said, "And such a pretty name she had, too. She may as well have been called the *Atlantic*. Did ye hear of that ill-fated ship? It's said that the ocean opened its mouth and swallowed her up, exclaiming 'there shall not *two* Atlantics be!' But it's bad luck for me to be standing here talking to a woman when a ship is sinking." Before turning to go, he wagged a severe finger at me: "Get off this ship, missy, and I'll have no arguments from you!"

"I will," I assured him pleasantly, and went back to my task of sorting through the cloth.

Not too much later, the *Judith* lurched. I was aware, of course, that she had been steadily sinking by imperceptible degrees, but with one lurch I felt her lower as much as she had the hour past. I was not a heroine or a martyr. I had done what I could. So had most of the crew, judging by the general decrease in the activity around me.

I emerged from my corner and looked around for the nearest life boat to which I could attach myself. The booms and riggings were dancing crazily around my head now, and I narrowly missed getting hit by a thick beam of swinging wood. When I got to the spot where the first longboat had taken the principal passengers, I noticed all the life boats were gone.

I admit to a slight leap of panic. Fortunately, I remembered the nook below the poop where the smallest of the wherries was moored. I ran back there, clutching my tapestry bag and several bolts of cloth in my arms. A weaving lantern casting its drunken, wavering light across the lurching ship showed me that the boat was still there.

I ran up and leaned against it at the exact moment a pair of hands reached up to loosen the cords.

I whirled around and looked up into the face of the quartermaster. There was a fierce blue blaze of anger in his eyes.

CHAPTER 2

The first words the man ever spoke to me were hot and fiery. His voice was that of a gentleman; his words were not. "Faith, woman! What the plague are you doing still aboard? I would have thought that even *you* would not have been so damnably idiotic as to—"

I broke into this very promising but highly time-consuming imprecation with real exasperation: "Don't you start in with me, too, sir! There's no time for it!" Seeing him eyeing the bundle in my arms malevolently as he loosened the thick knots of cords holding the boat in place, I swiftly continued, "And I can see very well that the boat, tiny as it is, is big enough for both of us *and* my cloth, so don't try to keep me or it out, for there's not another Johnnie boat available, as I am sure you are well aware!"

By the time I had finished, he had already unlashed the boat from its dry dock. Next, he heaved it, with a deep grunt, over to the upended side of the ship and the rail, where he had already rigged the pulley and ropes to lower it.

He did not say another word, but took the cloth from my arms and shoved it into the bottom of the boat on top of a leather case, just missing a hat. He shoved me ungently to the rail, took the long rope ladder slung from one of his broad shoulders and hoisted it over the side of the ship, then lashed it to the brass cleats that studded the rails at regular intervals. That done, he proceeded to lower our boat with his gear and the cloth into the water; and when he heard the first splash of wood on water, he let the ropes drop with a heavy thud into the little boat, swung a leg over the rail, and secured his footing on the rope ladder.

He reached over and swung me over the side with him, so that my entire backside was pressed against his front, and we began to descend the rope ladder together, one of his arms on the ropes, one around my waist. Both of my hands were on the ropes, and I was desperately clamping my tapestry bag under my arm. It felt suddenly a leaden weight with all that I had loaded into it. As we descended thus and were about halfway down the interminably long side of the ship, the *Judith* gave another sickening lurch. The man paused to keep his balance and mine, then, very slowly and carefully, put his foot down the next rung of the ladder, and the next.

During this entire time, which might not have lasted more than a minute or two, he had never seemed to hurry, though he worked with a certain intensity, and he did not speak, save to murmur, "Easy," "There now," "That's it," "Good girl," "You've got it."

When his feet touched the bottom of the boat, he unwrapped my fingers from the ladder, since they were still somehow clutching the rope sides, and sat me down on a cross-plank at the bow. He sat facing me, and when I looked over at him through the dim murk of the night, I saw him nod his head at me, once, as if in approval. He picked up the oars and began to row around the pathetically tilted prow of the *Judith*.

I reflected that some men are very capable in a crisis.

Sitting erect, I noticed I was trembling from my recent exertions. Since I have never had any use for dwelling on what-ifs or horrors-that-might-have-been or narrow-escapes-from-true-perils, I focused my attention on the immediate future. I found good reason for hope, and this produced a beneficially calming effect on me.

The long, rhythmic oar strokes in midnight waters were also curiously calming—or reassuring, perhaps—and by the time we had rowed over to the other boats to join this diminutive fleet, my sensible, rational self was restored.

My companion had done a rather precise job of rowing abreast a boat filled with seamen, so that he could converse with them. When I discovered that this boat also contained Captain Hawkins, I surmised that my companion must have remarkable night vision. I peered through the dank, cold mists swirling about the black surface and hardly made out the lumbering bulk of the captain and several of the crew. I also gathered from the exchange that my companion knew a deal about seafaring himself, as a quartermaster would, of course, and had some rather pertinent observations to make about our chances for being spotted by one or the other of the remaining ships in our convoy.

We rowed on, passing the line of boats, which had been tied, one to the other, in much the fashion of elephants tied trunk to tail. I had seen engravings of such once at an exposition of the East India Company in Mayfair.

"We're at the end of this parade," my companion informed me as he rowed, "bringing up the rear."

We happened to be passing just then the boat directly tied to the captain's, which was inhabited by Mrs. St. Charles, who was sobbing softly, but still audibly, and Mrs. Arbuthnot, who was venting, albeit in suppressed tones, her feelings on Atlantic crossings in general, the *Judith*'s crew in particular, and something obscure about her mother having been right.

I never had much of an opinion of Captain Hawkins or his crew, but only a ninny such as Mrs. Arbuthnot could have laid the cause of the *Judith*'s present distress at their door. Of Mrs. Arbuthnot's mother,

I can have absolutely no opinion whatsoever. The probable style and demeanor of the woman who bore and raised such a daughter require no comment.

Several more long strokes took us past now the third boat in the procession. "That," I replied with conviction, in reference to our relative position in this 'parade,' "is most excellent."

I felt, rather than saw, my companion grin. I needed no further encouragement. "I'll have you know that Mr. St. Charles was of the opinion that I should take up one of the seats in that boat," I continued. "Can you imagine it?"

"With difficulty."

"That was a rhetorical question, sir," I kindly informed him. "As if I would succumb to such a ploy, which I am sure I never would! No, I must say that I am well satisfied with the present arrangement—or, indeed, any arrangement other than the one that would have put me in that boat!"

"I thank you," said the deep voice opposite me.

"Why, take the longboat we are now passing, for instance," I continued, ignoring this impertinence. It was the first of the two longboats that held the crew. I had no fear of offending anyone in either of them with my comments, for I could tell by the general tenor (however subdued, given the present circumstances) that they were indulging themselves in a very nasty substance known as Blue Ruin.

I realized that I had done Mrs. Arbuthnot an injustice, so I appended, "Although I do not think that Mrs. Arbuthnot would be as rowdy a companion as these sailors will be over the next few hours."

"Next few hours?" came the reply. "You, ma'am, are hopeful."

The oddity of conversing with this disembodied voice never once occurred to me. "Yes, I am," I said. "And I agree with what you said to Captain Hawkins—that there was every likelihood that the *Minion*, or the *William and John* or the *Swallow* would be on the lookout for us."

"And there's as much likelihood that they won't spot us at all, won't see the *Judith*'s flags before she is wholly sunk under the water, and won't even come looking for us for another day or two."

I considered this. "Another day or two is not a disaster," I decided. "After three or four, I think we may begin to worry."

"This is a reasonable attitude," my companion agreed. "Do I understand that you are not going to subject me to the vapors or hysterics, but only to bolts of cloth?"

"You understand that perfectly," I retorted tartly, quite unamused. "You never know how the cloth may come in handy, and in any case, I should think the owner of the merchandise shall thank me kindly for any bit I could salvage! And in addition to not irritating my companions with unproductive displays of feminine emotion, I am quite capable of doing many effective things!"

"Then, tie our boat to the next," he recommended, putting down the oars in their locks. We had passed the fifth and last boat, and were now in our position at the tail. "I would lean over and do it myself," he said, "except for the fact that my gear and your cloth are not properly stowed, and I fear capsizing us with any unnecessary movement."

"Very well," I replied, "I am happy to do it." I began to grope for the rope.

"It's lashed to a cleat under the plank you're sitting on. Don't shift your weight too quickly," he instructed me. "Yes, that's right. Now, unwind about five feet of it. That should do it. You can uncoil more later, if you need it. Now, turn and find the ring attached to the stern of the boat in front of us."

I found the rope and unwound it with no difficulty, but when I turned and reached out into the void for the ring, I found nothing. I turned back. "I can't find it. Shall I call to the person in the back of the boat?"

He muttered something, most likely an oath, under his breath. "It's the supply boat. There's no one aboard."

The swirling mists had gathered into a dense, deep-night fog, thereby muffling all the sounds around us. Mrs. St. Charles's sobbing could not have been more than twenty or thirty feet away, but it sounded as if it came from the bottom of a well. The sounds of the easy camaraderie of the gin-swilling sailors came as if from a distant tavern down a long, deserted street.

"I'll have to row a foot or two forward," he said. "I'll try not to ram the back planks, but watch that you don't jam your fingers in the stern, and tell me when to stop."

"Stop," I said a moment later over my shoulder to him. My fingers felt a cold metal ring and fastened on it. "Got it."

"Good. Do you know a slip knot?"

I assured him that I knew many knots.

"Then make one."

"I'll make two, three, for good measure."

"Make a dozen, if you care to, only leave us at least three feet of rope slack between. Now, cleat the remaining rope firm beneath your seat."

I performed these offices neatly and, I would hope, with some efficiency. "Done."

"Very well," he said.

Silence fell and settled in. He shifted slightly on his seat and stretched out his legs before him, so that his boots almost brushed the hem of my skirts.

I began to feel the chill and wondered how I could have thought for a moment that a shawl would be sufficient covering in the middle of the Atlantic in the dead of night. Perhaps I had succumbed to a bit of the frenzy myself. I shivered.

"Drink?" came the question.

It took me a moment to perceive the flask held out to me. I hesitated, not knowing what was in it.

"It will do you good," said my companion.

I took the flask and did what I had seen the seamen do—took the requisite "swig." After my tears had stopped, the shreds of my throat had ceased burning, and my stomach had come back to order, I felt the warmth of the whiskey down to my toes. I handed the flask back. "Thank you," I gasped.

The fog became denser. The sounds, never distinct, receded, or perhaps the inaction after the last hours and, indeed, days of frantic activity, had done everyone in. The seamen could either have been in drunken oblivion by now, or stone sober and contemplating what the next few hours would bring. Mrs. St. Charles, I reckoned, was in a merciful state of exhausted nerves. Mrs. Arbuthnot had, apparently, spent herself.

Of my companion, I could determine almost nothing. He shifted every now and then, as I did, and seemed to be generally awake. I, too, was wakeful and watchful, although, heaven knew, there was nothing to see—only a still, wet, cold void to experience.

My wakefulness did not last. An odd sort of slumber that one slips into when one is cold, visited me for the next few hours. I nodded in and out of consciousness, both an irritation. It was the kind of repose that leaves one crabby—an afternoon nap one did not mean to have. The constant, gentle rocking of the boat in the water kept me lulled, however, and I achieved an unsatisfactory suspended state between wakefulness and sleep, where I hovered.

An undetermined time later, some sound or movement jarred me from this unrestful repose. I cracked my eyes and perceived a faint rose and gold glowing behind the grey mists on the horizon, struggling to penetrate the fog that still enveloped us. Then, I perceived the man seated not three feet away from me. I noticed he was not wearing the common garb of the sailor, but was now habited in the costume of a gentleman: jacket and knee breeches of a smart, naval-blue velvet, lace collar and cravat, white silk stockings, and polished half-boots. I had a memory of ruffles pressed against my back and velvet about my waist as we had descended the rope ladder.

My first thought was simply that our minds ran on parallel tracks: in anticipation of changing ships, as we were no doubt about to do, we had both thought to present ourselves at our best. I had chosen for the occasion my grey merino with point lace at collar and cuff—not a dashing ensemble, but highly proper.

Then I noticed, groggily, what he was doing. It seemed an odd sort of activity. He was pulling toward him the rope that had tied us to the supply boat. Since I was sitting between him and the boat in front of us, it must have been that odd sliding of the rope past my ear that had awakened me. I then heard a whoosh behind me and had the most unexpected sensation of a heavy, wet brass ring sliding by my arm and into my lap. I sat bolt upright, all senses awake now and alert.

I looked across to my companion in stunned disbelief. He was holding in his hand a metal ring to which was attached a rope—the rope that I had tied to the back of the boat in front of us.

His words were harsh and very deliberate. "Do not make any sudden movements, I beg of you."

I held his intense gaze a moment longer. Then, slowly, I turned my head to confirm with my eyes what every other sense had already told me.

We were, indeed, adrift in the middle of the Atlantic Ocean, entirely alone, with no sight of the shipwrecked *Judith* or any trace of the other five boats anywhere on the ever-lightening horizon.

It is not entirely accurate to say that we were adrift. I looked down into the water. It was moving past us very quickly. A wet tangle of seaweed floated past. No, *we* floated past *it*. I perceived that we were moving along at quite a swift pace, and inexorably west. We seemed to have been caught up in an extraordinary current, and it was sweeping our little Johnnie boat ever farther away from the *Judith* and the convoy.

I looked back at my companion. It had taken but a fraction of a second for these new, wholly unexpected circumstances to register. My companion was still staring down at the metal ring he held hooked on two fingers in front of him, as if he, too, were just then absorbing the full dimension of our present situation. For the first time, this close to him in near-daylight, I received the full impact of those blue eyes. They were just then rather stormy, menacing, and highly, unmistakably expressive.

I quickly sprang to my defense. "But, just look!" I said to his unspoken accusation of my handiwork of the night before. "My knots are intact and securedly tied!"

"All three of them, in fact," he answered, low and angry, shaking the metal ring at me, "but the ring is not secured to the boat in front of us!"

This was an unarguable observation. "Yes, but look again!" I said, stung by his injustice, as I leaned over to peer closely at the offending object in question. "Look at the screws on the plate that should have been holding the ring to the stern planks! They're rust-rimed and filled with little bits of rotted wood. It's not my fault that the fittings fell apart!"

"*Not your fault*—!" he began. "Faith! How many times have I secured a rope only to tug it once, hard, at its fittings?"

"I wouldn't know, sir," I replied, coldly.

He shot back at me my words of the night before. "That was a rhetorical question, ma'am! It's automatic for a seaman . . . it's *second nature* to him to check for rotted fittings at the time he secures his tackle!"

"It is *not* second nature for me to do so, and you told me nothing of it!" I replied. "While I like to think of myself as a reasonable person, capable of accepting blame when it is due me, I submit that *in this instance*, it is most certainly *not* my fault—entirely!—that we find ourselves now in this predicament!"

"*Predicament*—!?" He followed this exclamation with a succinct,

"*Faith*!" No word in the English language could have sounded more vile.

"Yes, predicament," I said, trying to preserve what I could of my calm. "Let us not make a piece of work over —" the word *nothing* touched the tip of my tongue, but I swallowed it, just in time. I had just claimed to be a reasonable person, and it would have been wholly unreasonable, just then, to have dismissed our circumstances as *nothing* "— over an admittedly difficult situation! Let us try to sort this out with the good sense I know we both possess! You, being the superior seaman, can perhaps tell me where we are headed!"

At that, he tossed the heavy wet ring back into my lap with a gesture of contempt. He leaned back, carefully, so as not to rock the very flimsy means of our possible salvation, and grasped what he could of his leather case, which was lying under the bolts of cloth. He slid it along the bottom until he could catch the handles with the tip of his boot. Then, with a fluid movement, he slid it under the center thwart on which he was seated so that the case lay before him. It was a neat maneuver.

Bending down, he opened it and extracted a sextant, lifted it to the heavens, and squinted through it. He tried several different positions, his eyes straining for stars. At length, he put it back in the case and latched it with an angry flick of his fingers.

"Too much daylight," he said. Then, cocking a brow with a challenge that belied the pleasantness of his voice, he said, "And if you tell me that I wasted time falsely accusing you while the sun slipped up over the horizon, I shall wring your neck — and with great pleasure."

I have always known when to hold my tongue. I let a moment pass and was rewarded for my forbearance when he said, thoughtfully, "But where we are? I don't know. Many miles from where the *Judith* has gone down, I'll warrant. The charts I have with me," he said, gesturing to the case at his feet, "are as worthless as the *Judith* at the moment. But I do know where we are headed: the Caribbean Sea!"

"What a great piece of luck!" I said to this. "That is where we wanted to go, isn't it?"

"Ah, but *exactly* where is an entirely different matter," he said sardonically, "the central issue being when—if ever—we reach land."

I did not hold the precise map of the New World in my head, but I was fairly certain that it made a long, unbroken, vertical landmass— the coastline varying considerably, of course—with the Caribbean Sea composed of an intricate chain of islands, large and small.

"We are bound to come to land," I said to this, "eventually, no?"

"You, ma'am, are very sanguine," he replied, "as I've remarked before."

"I *am* hopeful," I said, "especially at this rate, which must be— what, eight or ten knots," I suggested tentatively, for I was conversant with some of the conventions of sea travel, though not with those concerning ropes and fittings and rotted wood.

"Faster, even, I warrant," he replied, gazing out with a professional eye over the waters, trying to estimate our speed. "We're light. Double it. Eighteen or twenty knots, I'd say, and we've probably been adrift for some hours already." He paused, then said on a laugh of wry irony, "We could cover several hundred miles today—better than we've done in the past two weeks."

"And the day before the *Judith* went down, I remember the captain saying that we were within five days of the port of Santo Domingo, meaning that there are a number of islands to the east of there that are even closer to us now."

"Many hazards lie between us and land," he said slowly.

"You need not try to scare me," I began, and then broke off suddenly when a sickening thought hit me. "Sharks," I said. I looked about the surface of the early morning water for ominous signs. Aboard the *Judith* I had not given these terrifying creatures a second thought. Now, effectively in the water, I gave them my full, horrified consideration.

"The barracudas are worse," my companion informed me—somewhat unkindly, I thought. "But they might not be the worst of our problems. I'm thinking of the Spanish."

I expelled a relieved breath. The thought of *human* predators did not frighten me. Not that I did not have a healthy respect for the Spanish, but they walked on land on two legs, like me. I was rather more concerned about creatures that moved about in water with fins—particularly dorsal fins.

I forced myself to look straight down into the water that flowed at the sides of our little boat. I saw nothing but water, then I tossed my gaze right and left and had the impression of water within water. I had the odd thought that we were in a wide street of water in the middle of an ocean—one with its own predetermined course, much like a river on land.

My companion interpreted my look of puzzlement. "We're in one of the currents," he informed me. "That much I do know. But which one—?" He shrugged. "It's too much to hope that we're in the Florida current. After the storm, we had blown so far south that we wanted to make sure we did not slip into a current that would lead us to South America. We were heading for the north equatorial current the day before we abandoned ship. With luck, that's the one we're in, or one of its parallel tributaries." He stopped there abruptly. "Let's hope it's the Upper Antilles that await us, and not the Lower."

I did not ask him why he expressed that particular hope. I was rather taken with other thoughts. "But how is it that we find ourselves alone in it? Why were not the others caught up in it? Or might they be out there, simply not within sight?"

"I've been wondering that, too," he admitted, scratching a dark, now-stubbled chin. "We were the lightest of the lot, the farthest out from the *Judith*. For all her ineffectiveness, she just might have shielded the other boats from the current." He shook his head. "I don't know."

My optimism buoyed to the surface again. "Well, then, for all you know, we might be *better* off than our fellows from the *Judith*," I said, much struck. "At least we are moving, and moving *west.*"

To this he merely grunted inarticulately, then reached down into his case again and withdrew, this time, a long glass. He snapped it open, put eye to lens, and swept the glass along the horizon. "Nothing," he said, snapping it shut again. "Depending on how you look at it." Then, with the shadow of a smile, "Nothing. No convoy, no Spanish, and no sharks."

I reached out my hand for the long glass, and he placed it in my palm. I opened it and peered through the tiny aperture. I, too, saw nothing: nothing but the immense curve of the earth, the desert of dark-blue sunlit water and empty sky.

This magnified void was overwhelming. I closed the long glass and looked about me at the tangible reality which had shrunk to two bodies in a boat, a leather case, a tapestry bag, and three bolts of cloth.

I handed the long glass back. He stored it in an inside pocket of his coat. Surrounded by the vast void, suddenly feeling its immense weight, there was nothing more to say. We sat, thus confined to the space of our boat, borne along in the strange and strong ocean current.

Hours passed. The sun climbed. I was thankful for my bonnet and parasol. My companion donned his hat before midday. When the sun was at my back, I handed the parasol to him. He accepted it, wordlessly.

After a while, a clump of seaweed floated by, then another. I held out my hand to scoop up the next tangle of yellowish weed to pass us. I caught a wet, sticky mass and peered down at it a moment, curiously. Then my heart leapt.

"Land!" I cried, excited. "Land!" I handed the weed over to my companion. "Look, it's a tiny crab! About the size of my fingernail! We must be near land!"

He shook his head. "Sargasso weed," he said. "It's gulfweed, all right, but it and that crab, the Little Wanderer, can be found thousands of miles from shore." By way of consolation, he added, "You're not the first to build false hopes."

Time passed. Later, I was about to put my hand out, lazily, to touch a passing creature, amorphous and jellylike in appearance. My companion batted my hand back with one word: "Poison."

After that, I fell to contemplating the endless expanse of water. My bones melted into the planks of the boat. I imagined that I felt the water directly as we were carried along in the current. At times it was as hard and fibrous as muscle tissue as we cut through it; at others, it was lean and corrugated, almost bony, like ribs. At one moment, I saw coquettish, swirling ripples all about me, as if I wished to be dressed in watered silk. My eyes blinked away the sweaty drops that fell from somewhere, possibly my brow. My eyes swam with sweat, with the strain of a glaring, hostile sun. I had the giddy, rather glorious sensation that I was a child, back in my father's library, that the water beneath me was his writing desk, and that my whole body was a fingernail, scratching and peeling away at its waxed polished top. I had loved to do that when I was five years old, and had always received a slap on the wrist from Nanny.

Such imaginings were uncharacteristic of me. A dim realization penetrated my brain: I was delirious. "Water," I said. My voice croaked and cracked.

The wide blue bowl of water surrounding us absorbed this fractured word, dulled it, and swallowed it, without a ripple.

"Water," I said again.

My companion had just then been looking through his long glass. At the sound of my voice he closed it, rather deliberately, and regarded me steadily. I was appalled by the picture he presented me. He had stripped off his jacket. His fine ruffled shirt clung to him, soaked in sweat. I could not have been in better shape, for I saw the keen eyes in his lean, brown face narrow from question to concern.

I shook my head. "No, it's not what you think." My voice croaked slightly. "I *have* water. With me," I said, reaching into my bag. "Here."

That was all either of us needed. Just the sight of a full bottle of fresh water revived us. We rationed it judiciously. Thereafter, the afternoon did not seem so hot, nor the sun glancing off the water so merciless. We were borne relentlessly on, never losing the current. Nor did the current let up, for even a moment.

The sun was completing its arc. I tried not to think ahead to the freezing chill of night, after the burning heat of day. I had faced east the entire day, my back toward our destination. I looked up over my head and tried to lose myself in the translucent azure and pink streaks of the late afternoon in the tropics. My companion had already closed the parasol and laid it on top of the cloth. The air was noticeably milder, tranquil. I felt a warm, balmy breeze fan my cheeks. It smelled good. I looked down at the water. It was bluer, more crystalline. I thought: *This is almost pleasant.*

I wondered whether my senses were threatening to leave me again, whether the sun had truly stroked me. The next moment, I realized that there was a good reason for my sense of well being.

He said, "Land." It was a statement.

I made the effort to look over my shoulder. I saw nothing.

He leaned toward me and handed me the long glass, then put his hand on my shoulder. "That way," he said, nudging me west and north. I put the glass up to my eye and then down again. I did not need it.

If it were an illusion, it was a very tenacious one that grew before my eyes. What had been a speck rapidly became a spit of land, and then I realized that we were bearing down directly on an island— something much more substantial than a bar of sand.

My first impression of the island was that it was resting like a water lily on the swelling bosom of the waters. The heaven was kind above our heads, and the sun was keeping a jealous eye on my vision, slanting tempered rays on the vegetation that I could now discern. I fancied that here nothing withered; things were only warmed into life.

Suddenly, the current stopped. I cried out in frustration. We were caught in an eddy that swirled us in a circle and then seemed to want to take us north. Instantly, my companion manned the oars and furiously rowed over the pattern of surface waves that wanted to keep us from the bay of the island. He battled for many long minutes. The best I could do was to encourage him with a spirited: "You can do it!" "You've almost got it!" "We're there! Just one more pull!" Just when I thought his energies were flagging, that he had exhausted his strength, we curtsied over the last, wide wave and found ourselves at a standstill in the motionless waters of the bay.

We exchanged a wordless look that spoke volumes. Without further ado, he picked up the oars again and rowed us uneventfully across the placid bay. It was an exceedingly beautiful, shallow lagoon with what I believe were patches of coral, in fans of colors—lovely purple, red, and blue, some feather-like, light orange, or shiny jet black. The water was so clear I could see red and yellow sponges, flowerlike anemones, black-and-gold-striped fish, blood-red starfish, and paddling turtles lumbering amiably by.

Soon the boat ran aground on the sand. My companion leaped across me and the remaining hem of water and dragged the boat part of the way onto land. He threw the rope with the metal ring into the sand with a definite thud, and then held his hand out for me to alight.

There seemed quite a lot to be said at this juncture. However, such simple-minded thoughts as, *What are we to do now?* or *Shall we ever get off this island?* or *Are we truly bound here alone and together?* did not occur to me. As I accepted his extended hand and stepped out of the boat onto solid ground, I had thought of something much more immediate, much more fundamental, and that was, "I do not believe that we have been introduced. I am Miss Sedgwick. How do you do?"

CHAPTER 3

My companion turned swiftly. His eyes were momentarily hard and penetrating. The most unwelcome thought assailed me that he had recognized my name and knew of the horrid scandal that had led to my father's demise. The next moment, however, he was bowing and I could no longer read his face. "Winthrop. Adam Winthrop," he answered. "How do you do."

I was completely surprised, for a number of different reasons, first among them being that I had determined Mr. Winthrop to be an older gentleman with whiskers and a paunch. "Mr. Winthrop?" I echoed. "You are the owner of the *Judith*, then?"

He straightened and looked down at me. "Yes, I am the owner," he replied, adding with a quirk of a smile, "or, rather, the former owner."

"You may believe that I am sorry for the *Judith*'s loss!" I said in genuine sympathy. "She was a lovely ship."

"Thank you," he said to this. "I, too, was sorry to lose her." He bowed again, gracefully, and I thought, to my further surprise, that I detected some humor in the depths of his eyes before he lowered them.

How he managed to affect such a carelessness about his loss, I could not guess, but this swift change in his mood caused my worst fear to pass. I was convinced that I had misinterpreted Mr. Winthrop's initial reaction to my name, that he could not possibly have heard of the notorious Major General Sedgwick. Although I am not given to strange fancies, as I have said, almost any wild idea is bound to occur to a person arriving on an unknown island somewhere in the Caribbean Sea. It would have been grossly unfair to have had that scandal follow me halfway around the world to a deserted island.

But was it truly deserted? Discovering the secrets of the island seemed to me to be the first order of business.

I acknowledged Mr. Winthrop's bow with a slight bob and a nod of the head. That was all that the present setting, which was indeed very beautiful, but not quite *correct*, seemed to require in the way of courtesy. (We were, at that moment, standing ankle-deep in the sand.) "Well, Mr. Winthrop, all is not lost," I said by way of consolation, "for here we are, safe and sound, with a minimum of hardship. And not too badly circumstanced, if I do say so. Shall we have a look around?"

"If I discover that we have landed on Antigua, Barbuda or Guadeloupe, I will agree with you that we are not too badly circumstanced," he said dryly. "Otherwise. . . ."

"Oh, were you headed for Antigua?" I asked.

"Santo Domingo," he replied. "Our first stop. Still some miles to the west, I reckon. And you?" he asked. "Jamaica?"'

"No, a place called Boston," I said, perhaps a little distastefully. "Have you heard of it?"

He laughed. "Yes, I've heard of it, but why the sour face? I also hear it's not the worst place in the world."

I tilted my nose. "From seafaring men, such as yourself, perhaps," I said, not attempting to disguise my feelings on the subject, "but from all *other* reports I've heard, Boston is a rude, barbarous place, with no society fit to frequent!"

My companion swept his arm out across the vista of the beach and sea. "Behold—civilization."

Behind me was the whole of the Atlantic Ocean. Before me stood a vast tropical forest, beautiful and terrifying. "Yes," I conceded, "you do have a point. On the other hand, I'll not cavil. It is enough just now to find myself on terra firma—*any* terra firma. Shall we not explore our present piece of the earth?"

Mr. Winthrop assented, very reasonably, to this. He went back to the boat and attempted to drag it wholly out of the water and onto dry sand. It was extremely hard work. It was the end of a harrowing night and day for both of us. In addition, Mr. Winthrop had had to exert a great deal of energy to get us out and over the strong pull of the current. I could see that he was worn and weary and probably as hungry as I now felt myself. I went over to help him, but was effectively useless. He suffered my presence next to him for the barest second, then shot me a frown of impatience, and waved me out of his way.

"I can imagine that you are thinking," I said to him, as he bent, grunting with the effort, into his task, "that you would have done very much better to have been stranded on an island with a man rather than a woman."

Finished, he stood up and brushed his hands of the wet sand. He slanted me an unreadable glance. "No, Miss Sedgwick," he said blandly. "I am not thinking that."

"It is just as well," I said, satisfied. "Although I am not at all strong, I do have my uses—as I have already proven, by having the bottle of water handy, when we needed it most! And if you had not been in such a hurry just now, I could have unloaded both our gear and the bolts of cloth, to have made the load lighter for you!"

He acknowledged the justice of my remarks by uncramping the muscles in his shoulders and back. "Sure, now. On to exploring. Follow me," he said, and proceeded to take a few steps down the beach.

"One moment," I said. "I shall leave my shawl here, but I wish to take my parasol and tapestry bag."

Without stopping, he called back carelessly over his shoulder, "Take the bolts of cloth, too, if you wish it."

"No, I shall leave them here for now," I said reasonably. "They are too heavy."

"So I should think." He kept walking.

"Do you not wish to take your coat, Mr. Winthrop?" I inquired.

"I hardly think so," he answered, still walking.

"Your case, then?"

Without missing a step, he replied to that with a negative gesture.

I watched him take several more steps away from me. *Begin as you mean to go on!* I thought to myself. Then, aloud, in clear, round tones, I said, "Mr. Winthrop, I do not think that I wish to go in *that* direction."

Sure enough, his feet stopped, then he swore. I heard every word, distinctly.

"Sir!" I reproved, as I had every right to do.

His back remained toward me, broad-shouldered and tense. Then, slowly, deliberately, he enunciated, "Miss Sedgwick." He did not perform the courtesy of turning around to face me. "You may come with me or stay here, as you please."

He plainly did not understand. I have never been a woman to accept without question a man's presumed leadership or authority. I had more experience with his sex than he realized. The matter demanded clarification. "Mr. Winthrop, let me explain: we shall deal together *much* better if you understand that I have been married!"

At that he turned around, an extraordinary mixture of expressions chasing across his face. His face was, I had noted earlier, very expressive. He queried, experimentally, "*Mrs.* Sedgwick?"

"Ah, no," I said, hesitating. "Sedgwick is my family name." Then, with a touch of defiance: "My father's." Mr. Winthrop continued to regard me steadily. After my dramatic disclosure, I felt some explanation was in order. "Edward—Mr. Lipscomb—and I were married such a very short time, you see, that it did not seem quite *fitting* to retain his name."

This subject had captured Mr. Winthrop's apparently quixotic attention. "How long—er, how short a time were you, in fact, married?" he asked.

"Three months," I said.

He considered this. "It took Edward an entire three months to initiate a divorce?"

"Certainly not, sir!" I retorted, frostily.

"Thought not," he said, shaking his head. "Probably didn't have the guts."

I was unamused. "If you must know, Mr. Lipscomb died—tragically!"

"Oh, you cast him adrift in the middle of the Atlantic, too?" came the reply.

"Of all the—! Let us put this matter to rest! It was most certainly *not*—or, rather, not *entirely*—my fault that the ring fittings were rotted! So, if you wish to lay the whole of this episode at *my* door, let me tell you that—" I broke off, realizing that this line of argument was quite beneath my dignity. I mastered myself, with effort. I said, coldly, "If you must know, Edward died while crossing a street."

"Sounds more like him," Mr. Winthrop observed, nodding knowledgeably. "Poor Edward!"

My bosom swelled. "The drunken driver of a chicken cart ran him down!" I said, indignant, almost beyond words.

"Faith! A chicken cart?"

"And a very large cart it was, too—fully loaded! Crates were strewn all over High Street, and traffic was subsequently held up for the rest of the day! You cannot imagine the uproar I beheld when I arrived at the scene—more than an hour later. It was still pandemonium, although the officer on duty informed me that the rumor which was circulating—that Edward had been squashed by an entire tray of chicken crates—was a complete exaggeration! It seems that only one crate landed on him, but glanced him, most unluckily, at his left temple. He died instantly!"

Not a muscle moved in Mr. Winthrop's face, but I had the distinct impression that the abominable man was going to laugh. I composed a suitably crushing retort and would have delivered it, imperiously, except that the image of the crates of squawking chickens, gawking passersby, lunging horses, and over-turned wagons rose unbidden to my mind. The incident seemed suddenly so incongruous and so *distant* that I managed to say, "It is *not* funny!" and was pleased that my voice did not quaver.

He wisely did not comment on Edward's tragic death. Instead, he remarked, "So Mrs. Lipscomb was a blushing bride of a mere three months."

"Miss Sedgwick," I insisted, and stated firmly, "Eve Marie Sedgwick." I quickly passed over this. "Actually, I have only ever been called Marie. And as for 'blushing'—I can hardly have been said to be *that* at my age!"

Neither did he comment on my given names or my age. He said merely, "You are a widow, then. Recently?"

"Recent enough," I temporized.

He was now appraising me openly and very thoroughly.

"Recent enough to still be in half-mourning," he said, in reference to my dress.

It so happened that, given my coloring, grey became me very well, and I wore it gladly. In point of fact, I was still entitled to the black of full mourning, for Edward's accident had occurred a spare three months ago—just a few weeks before I had boarded ship. As long a time had elapsed since he had died as in the whole of our married life. It did not now seem possible.

I had been happy enough in my married state, but never blushing, for I had deferred marriage until the advanced age of four-and-twenty. I had chosen to marry Edward for the simple reason that, as a matron, I should have greater freedom in public to do precisely what I wished. That was the only reason, as far as I could tell, why any independent, intelligent female would choose to subject herself, in private, to the whims and petty tyrannies of a husband. That, of course, and the brute economic fact that my father would give me no access to the portion my mother had left me if I were not married. But Edward had died, and I was not overcome with grief. Was I still in mourning? It was a hard question to answer. In mourning for what? For whom?

"Yes," I said, truthfully enough.

But I was not in mourning for Edward. His death had come at the beginning of our fourth month of marriage, within a fortnight of my father's arrest, a week after my father's heart failure. I had heard the details of Edward's accident from the attending officer, of course, but I had never quite rid myself of the notion that Edward had died from shame, or from cowardice—or from whatever one would call the inability to hold one's head up in the face of disaster. He had not been able to *outface* the scandal—and, of course, the fact that my father had died before he had been able to clear his good name was not going to have helped Edward's career any, either.

I am a great believer in the strength of the will, and I had thought that I had had enough for both of us. I had not counted on Edward's will to die. Thereafter, I was conveniently packed off to some distant Puritan relatives in the New World with the blessing of well-meaning headquarters staff officers who were, no doubt, as happy to be rid of my embarrassing presence as had been my relatives, none of whom truly wanted anything to do with me. Upon leaving England, I had shed my black dress and my wedding ring, along with the name Lipscomb. I reassumed Sedgwick, reasoning a scandal-tainted name to be better than that of a coward.

Mr. Winthrop knew none of this, of course, and was disinclined to probe further. He nodded his head once, as was his manner, and with an extremely gallant sweep of his arms in my direction, said, "Where you lead, I shall follow."

Prettily said, but I could play that game, too. His gallantry was spurious, at best. Thus, I could not resist the deliberately provocative inquiry, "Are you *sure* you do not wish to take along your coat or your case?"

"I am quite sure, ma'am," he replied, his voice grave, but I caught the glint in his eye.

"Very well, then," I said. "Shall we try *this* direction?"

He fell into step beside me. Of course, I had had no alternative but to propose the *opposite* direction from the one he had originally taken. It was truly six of one, half-dozen of the other: either way we looked, we saw the beach stretch far and away, only to curve out of sight. It seemed equally logical to go in either direction, at least as far as the curve, to see what, if anything, lay beyond.

We made our way down the beach, finding the shallowest sand possible. A green screen of dense foliage crowded to the very lip of the sand. I had heard that such forests in the east Indies were called *jungles*. The forest we beheld might properly be referred to as a jungle of the West Indies. The stately trees, darkening forms in the lengthening shadows, rose up against a sky streaked with the red and orange fires of an approaching sunset. Birds fluttered among the foliage, their songs punctuated by occasional chattering calls that elicited equally exotic rejoinders. Vines laced and draped the whole, making the jungle weep, and the little bay to our left shone like mother-of-pearl. The air was warm and exquisitely clear.

It was well that our first moments on the island began with such beauty and peace.

Conversation moved on to impersonal topics. Food was uppermost on our minds. We discussed at some length the possibilities of penetrating the jungle growth for fruits or berries, but I vehemently dismissed it. Although it was still only late afternoon and broad daylight where we walked, we could see that one foot into the growth, it would be as dark as night.

"Snakes," was my definitive argument against.

Mr. Winthrop laughed.

I made clear to him my aversion to any living creature without legs.

"Ah, yes, the sharks," he remembered. "Now snakes. How about spiders, then?"'

"Spiders do not bother me," I said with impeccable logic. "They have legs."

The foray into the jungle was deferred until the morning.

Which led me to another uncomfortable thought—the night—but I did not allow my mind to dwell on that one, either.

We straggled on down the beach. At one point, Mr. Winthrop picked up a long stick, one of the many pieces of driftwood that we passed. He withdrew a pocket knife from his trousers and whittled the tip into a sharp point, all the while walking and talking, before veering off to skirt the hem of the water lazily lapping the white sand.

He stood contemplating the water. Then, he kicked off his half-boots and peeled off his stockings and rolled his once elegant breeches above his knees. He waded straight out into the water, stick-spear raised in hand. Intently, he surveyed the water around him, without moving his legs or agitating the waters.

While he fished, I permitted myself the leisure to study him. I had not previously *really* considered my companion. Now, however, with my fate so linked to his, I took stock of him.

I was not at all a man-hater, despite what I have said about Mr. St. Charles, Captain Hawkins and his witless crew, poor Edward, and my father. I had found, however, through life that few persons of the male sex were to be depended upon.

Thus, I let my eyes rest on Mr. Winthrop as he stood knee-deep in water. What did I see beyond a broad-shouldered man in a lace shirt with untidy hair surrounding a rugged, deeply tanned face, and an arm raised with stick-spear in hand? I could not say. Dispassionately considering him, I was pleased by his hard, muscular physique (my survival, after all, was closely dependent on his). Was he handsome? I dismissed the question as, frankly, irrelevant; but recognizing its irrelevance, I answered, tentatively, that black hair and blue eyes are always an attractive combination, even on such a hard, angular, unhandsome face as Mr. Winthrop's.

Presently, he lunged his stick into the water and withdrew it, a speared fish on its tip. Grinning broadly, looking very happy with himself, he waded out and up to me, planted the stick in the sand, causing the fish at its tip to quiver, and pronounced, "Dinner. "

"Dear me," was all I could think of to say. "Must we eat it raw?"

"I'd as soon fix a fire later and eat then," he said. "I'd like to see what's around the curve first. We can come back for the fish. Or do you wish to eat first?"

In the face of such consideration for my wishes (you see, it never does to let a man *unquestionably* take the lead), I determined that I was far more curious than hungry. It was true that we had not eaten since the evening before, but I had never been precisely *thin*, and could easily skip a meal or two without undue suffering.

Mr. Winthrop stuffed his discarded stockings in his pocket and picked up his half-boots in one hand. We continued on to the curve. The landscape changed abruptly at that point. Instead of flat jungles, the side of a dramatic mountain, still thickly vegetated, rose abruptly to the heavens, while its spur was thrust into the sea. We scrambled over the rocky crumbles of the heel of the mountain and proceeded around the curve.

We beheld a truly glorious sight. A pure gold beach curled out before us, like the wide, thick tail of a magical dragon. All shone gold, and surely it was far more magnificent than the combined treasures of the New World gold that had irresistibly drawn the Spanish to these shores. Even the water, kissed by the setting sun, sparkled gold, and was alive with golden flying fishes that I had heard about, named gilt-heads. Sea mews and cormorants swooped and whirled and wheeled in an evening sky streaked gold. The massive, silent mountain of dark-green velvet rose up off the wide beach, much like the lining of a jewel box, opened to display the gem within.

We tacitly agreed to take one step down this beach, then another, then another. We were bathed in the golden sunlight, warmed and nourished by it. All hunger pangs fell away. We exchanged a glance of wonder, but we did not speak. The glint of gold stunned me, blinded me by its beauty.

Mr. Winthrop suddenly put his hand on my arm. His fingers closed over my wrist, communicating to me all his tension. Then he stopped. I felt his body stiffen. When my gaze penetrated the golden light, I stopped and stiffened, too.

Coming toward us, still at some distance, was a flock of the largest, most extraordinary, most terrifying birds I had ever seen. They were of different sizes, but the largest was as large as any man I had met, and they did not strut in the manner of other birds—they *walked*!

I blinked in disbelief. Then it came to me. They were not birds at all; they were human beings, wearing a variety of brightly colored feathers. As my eye decomposed the mass, I perceived that not all of them wore feathers, and the longer I regarded this procession evi-dently coming toward us, the more ordinary they appeared. I cannot describe my profound relief.

Mr. Winthrop did not, evidently, share it. His grip on my arm did not lessen.

"I doubt it wise to make a run for it," he said, low.

He started walking again, propelling me forward with him. His gait was very slow, very wary. I must say that I did not regard the sit-uation as seriously as I supposed Mr. Winthrop did. Now, I am not foolhardy and can recognize imminent danger as well as the next per-son. Nevertheless, by the time this procession came close enough for me to distinguish individual faces, I had completely recovered from my initial, erroneous impression that here was anything out of the ordinary, and I wondered how my eyes could have so deceived me.

Mr. Winthrop had stopped. I continued a step farther. The hand still gripping my arm restrained me. I looked up at him.

His eyes were grave and serious; his rugged, sunburnt face was closed. "You are with me," he said.

I strained to understand his meaning.

"You are with me," he repeated, low. "We are together—not to be separated."

I took him to mean that some horrible, unspeakable fate might await me, a woman, if I were not regarded as belonging to him. I am not, as I have just said, foolhardy. I perceived the wisdom of this. I nodded my understanding.

Nevertheless, I saw nothing before me to inspire profound fear. Far better, I reasoned, to meet a group of human beings on the beach than a terrifying flock of birds! Perhaps this meeting was even a stroke of good fortune. Once we had made our friendly intentions known, surely they would wish to help us.

The procession approached. I had yielded to the pressure of Mr. Winthrop's fingers, which he did not remove from my arm, and had stopped. I felt it a courtesy. It was their beach, after all.

I had heard many tales of the savage inhabitants of the New World, and I was not at all surprised to see for myself what a lot of twaddle those stories were. To be sure, the men and women (they were close enough now that I could distinguish the difference) coming toward us were oddly dressed—or rather, undressed—but they struck me not so much as wild beasts but as children, in costume. And who, after all, has not seen a Frenchman mincing along the streets of London? I need speak no more of fine feathers and odd birds!

The procession stopped within yards of us. As I gazed in wonder over the bronzed faces and bodies and glossy black hair, I perceived two more figures coming up the beach behind them: a man, the largest of the group, awe-inspiring in size (even for me), wearing the most elaborate feathers on his head and holding a spear; and at his side, a diminutive woman of indeterminate, but visibly advanced age. Her hair and person were unadorned.

Inspiration, like an enchanted, golden sea mew, touched the brim of my bonnet and instructed my next moves. I shrugged off Mr. Winthrop's arm and strode forward, my tapestry bag still clutched under my arm. It was my intention to approach the ancient, diminutive woman. My parasol proved useful in passing through the people standing between us. I did not even have to apply the ferrule to anyone's back or side (which was just as well, since their bodies were, for the most part, naked), and I must say that here was the perfect occasion for the skillful use of a parasol in a crowd.

I was not, for all of that, rude. Never think it. I murmured, "Excuse me," "Pardon me," "Allow me," as I passed through, and smiled and nodded in thanks and understanding as the crowd, not unexpectedly, fell away. I made my way through the throng without any difficulty whatsoever. I had no cause to feel particular triumph in my smooth passage. I am not a petite woman, as I indicated earlier, and these people were not precisely large. In fact, I felt like Mrs. Arbuthnot among them. Then, too, one always feels a tremendous advantage in public when fully clothed.

Without impediment, I reached the woman. I thought it would be impolite to look directly into her face, so I curtsied before her, laid my tapestry bag at her feet, opened it, and withdrew my silver-chased comb and brush. I held these objects out to her, offerings to the woman who could be none other than the mother of the chief.

Since I am rather vain about my hair, I had traveled with two sets of combs and brushes; and when, upon abandoning the *Judith*, we had been instructed to take our most precious hand-held valuables, I had naturally taken both sets. So, I could easily spare one, and I thought that the chief's mother would be pleased with the silver set, it being more valuable than my ivory one.

She did not immediately take my offerings. As my arms became tired, I chose to look into her face. It was moonshaped, with high cheekbones, and very plain. She had hardly a trace of gray in her thick black hair, but I read in the deep lines of her face her advanced age. I also read there her puzzlement.

Well, nothing could be simpler than to show her my intention. I took off my bonnet and began to unpin my hair. I wished to show her the use of the comb and brush, so that she might enjoy them herself.

Hardly had I gotten the first pins out before I heard a collective gasp behind me. I whirled around to see that the entire procession—I estimated their number at about fifty—had turned in our direction and fallen to their knees. Thinking that I had committed a great breach of etiquette, I, too, fell to my knees, with my hair streaming down my back in great disorder, unfurled to my waist, the pins hastily palmed and the comb and brush still offered before me, in supplication.

What should happen next but that the old woman and her son, the chief, I supposed, also fell down on *their* knees! These were strange customs! I feared that I did not quite comprehend. I looked back over my shoulder at Mr. Winthrop for some direction in the matter. He was regarding me with blankest astonishment. Now, many people had regarded me in just such a fashion (not, of course, because I am in any way extraordinary looking. While I am not exactly repulsive, neither am I a raving beauty). Usually I would receive such a stare as a result of a perfectly commonsensical action I have taken. I had considered that, in offering to the apparent matriarch of the group some nice gift, Mr. Winthrop and I might be treated kindly. It was not an outrageous assumption to make.

Nevertheless, Mr. Winthrop was looking quite amazed. He, out of everyone, I noted with some irritation, had *not* fallen on his knees. In any case, when he intercepted my gaze, he shook himself slightly and made his way over to me. Of course, he had a much easier time of passing through the procession than I had had, since everyone was on their knees. In any case, when he reached my side, he raised me by the elbow to my feet, then helped the old woman rise and placed the comb and brush in her hands. She accepted them. After that the chief raised himself, and the four of us stood there a moment The others, for some reason, did not rise.

I racked my brain for something to say and, figuring English to be of no avail, said the first thing that came to mind that might be of some mutual benefit: "*¿Habla español?*"

This produced no change in my interlocutors' stone blank expressions.

Mr. Winthrop, however, had something to say to this. "Do *you* speak Spanish, ma'am?" he asked in an undervoice.

"Why, no, Mr. Winthrop," I admitted. "But I thought that since the Spanish have traveled so extensively in the region, we might have been able to communicate with these people. However, I think you have found the weak point in my approach. Do you, perchance?"

"In fact, yes," he replied.

"How fortunate, then!" I said. "Did you learn it while trading in Spain?"

"No, rather, I spent the last two years in a Spanish prison," Mr. Winthrop said, "and so I cannot vouch for the purity of my Castilian." His face had assumed a pleasant social mask, but his voice was very low and determined. "However, that experience, and my general knowledge of events in this region of the world, compel me to ask you, Miss Sedgwick, not to spoil the most brilliant piece of diplomacy I have ever witnessed by reference to a nation of people who can be nothing but enemies to these Indians."

This was hardly the moment to pursue these rather startling disclosures and, needless to say, I was diverted by his high praise of my actions, which certainly tempered his implied censure at my attempt at Spanish. "Oh, do you think my idea for a gift was a good one?" I said. "It seemed like the very thing to do! Though I am afraid that I do not quite understand what has happened here."

"At a guess," Mr. Winthrop replied, "I would say it is your hair."

My hair is a very distinct shade of red. I am rather proud of it, actually. I looked about me at the two copper-colored Indians before me and the group, still on its knees, watching us intently, behind. It could have been my hair which had caused them to gasp, for they might never have seen any the precise color of their skin before. Yes, I could see that it might strike them as something important—a sign of some kind. How could l have been other than pleased?

"Perhaps you are right, Mr. Winthrop," I said to this, "but is it not extremely discourteous of us to be standing here, speaking English in front of them, when they evidently do not understand a word of it?"

I turned back to the old woman and made the appropriate gestures, demonstrating to her how she was to use the comb and brush. I showed her the pins in my hand and made elaborate motions, showing her how to pin up her hair. At length, I succeeded in communicating something, for the woman eventually broke into a smile and began speaking (I supposed that the gibberish that came out of her mouth was human speech) rapidly to the tall man at her side.

The chief pronounced several long, guttural phrases. The people on their knees rose and formed a circle around us. For some reason, it was not until that moment that I felt a frisson of fear. It passed, however, when the chief turned and moved in the direction from which they had come. He motioned Mr. Winthrop behind him, then me, then the old woman. The rest of the company was to follow in a mass.

"Mr. Winthrop," I whispered forward. "How is it that you go *before* me? It is my hair that captured their attention."

"Ah, Miss Sedgwick," he said, sotto voce, "I must suppose it was because I was the only one not to go down on my knees!"

I thought that one over and could not prevent myself from whispering in return, "How very vexatious!"

I saw his broad shoulders shake slightly and shot him a dark look.

We proceeded to the end of the beach, then turned into the forest. So filled was I with thoughts that I hardly noticed my surroundings, added to which the path was narrow, allowing very little to be seen. I used all my attention to keep the branches and foliage out of my eyes, although Mr. Winthrop attempted to keep my path clear as he made his way through the brush. The old woman was immediately behind me, crooning some weird melody.

We arrived at an immense clearing. Huddles of huts rambled all over in what might have been a very loose and large circle. From what might have been the center rose a carved pole, thrusting heavenward, around which curled smoke, indicating a fire. I was cheered by the prospect of food.

We were not to eat—at least, not immediately. By this time, I was feeling the full effects of an empty stomach. Events had taken on their own momentum, so that when the chief took Mr. Winthrop by the arm, and the old woman had taken me by mine and led us through the clearing, I had no ability to register what the village looked like, or even to have a very exact impression of its layout. As we made our way, strange thoughts collided with one another in my suddenly tired brain.

However, the worst did not happen. Mr. Winthrop and I were not separated. We were led to the same place—a hut on the outskirts of what looked to be the village proper.

We were motioned inside. We entered and stood looking at one another for a long, astonished moment. We heard the chief and his mother retreat, calling out all sorts of incomprehensible things to their people. Their calls were excited, presaging something to come. I was hoping that it would, in fact, be dinner. In the meantime, however, it occurred to me that this hut was to be temporary shelter. Perhaps the chief and his mother were making us guests for the night.

From the way Mr. Winthrop's eyes narrowed as he glanced around the tiny abode, I would have guessed that he had come to the same conclusion I had. His eye then fell on me for a fraction of a second. He tossed his half-boots and stockings in a corner, then abruptly, without a word, quit the hut.

Just like a man! was my involuntary thought. *Never at home!*

CHAPTER 4

*H*e came back, of course. He had nowhere else to go. Some few minutes later Mr. Winthrop's form darkened the door of the hut. He did not enter, nor did he speak. He merely leaned against the door frame, looking out.

The hut was at the farthest edge of the settlement, on the selvage of the clearing. The door of the hut opened to the west, allowing the very last of the dying rays of the sunset to hobble into the tiny, enclosed space. Most of the feeble sunlight was blocked by the dense jungle that impinged so closely upon our hut. Mr. Winthrop was looking straight into it, and his back was set in rigid lines. He was, apparently, not inclined to discuss the difficulties that quite possibly attended us in our immediate future.

I deemed it well and good that each of us should keep his own counsel at just that moment, and so I continued about my task, which was the repinning of my hair. Fortunately, I had kept all the pins in my hand and still had the other comb and brush set in my tapestry bag, which was now opened on the hard-packed dirt floor of the hut, next to where Mr. Winthrop had so carelessly tossed his footwear. I found myself on that same dirt floor, for it was impossible to maintain either my balance or my propriety when manipulating pins and brush and a really unwieldy mass of hair. I had had to kneel down and sit unceremoniously upon my heels.

Hardly had I pinned that last curl in place before two men, most likely sent by our hosts, appeared in front of Mr. Winthrop at the door. I immediately rose and stepped next to him. At first glance, the two envoys seemed to be more fully dressed than any of those people we had met on the beach. On second glance, I realized that, in point of fact, they were not wearing any more *clothes* than any one of this tribe we had seen so far. Male dress consisted solely, as far as I had been able to discern, of a breech cloth. The impression these men gave of being more fully dressed derived rather from the fact that their faces were painted in a startling fashion, they were wearing several bracelets apiece on their upper arms, and they were carrying rather magnificent spears with carved wooden handles as tall as they were. It all seemed rather official and, I must admit, festive.

These two envoys communicated, expediently, by means of a few simple gestures, that we were to follow them. Mr. Winthrop fell in behind one of them—again, without a glance in my direction. I was beginning to suspect that Mr. Winthrop was, at times, rather rude.

The second man gestured for me to fall in behind him. I hesitated, debating briefly whether I should need my bonnet, since the occasion seemed to call for more formal attire. I was not given the opportunity to fetch it (which rather vexed me, in that I had just then decided that I would feel better with it), for my escort took me by the arm in a grip that would have been plainly unfriendly to have resisted. We stepped in behind Mr. Winthrop and his escort.

We were led through a maze of huts. Since I did not yet have my bearings and night had rapidly fallen, as it does at these latitudes, I still conned no real notion of the plan of the village. There seemed, to my amazed and very travel-weary eyes, to be at least one hundred huts, or more, scattered haphazardly across the clearing. Presently, we found ourselves at what must have been the village square—a rather vast circle, in fact, whose perimeter was defined by huts much larger than the one we had been led to. This clearing within the clearing was, I gathered, the village green, although goodness knows, it was not green, nor was a blade of grass anywhere to be seen.

Instead, in the center of the circle rose the pole I had espied earlier. I saw now that it was a very large, excessively ugly statue, carved of wood, rather crudely, as if an unskilled sculptor had taken the trunk of a thick tree and simply hacked away at the top half to produce the face and torso of a fierce-looking man. Or could it have been a bird? It was difficult to decide, for the hooked nose could have easily been a beak. (I did not care to contemplate the lower half of the statue.) The general effect was of overwhelming bad taste. I most certainly did not approve of it.

Opposite us, on the other side of the offensive statue, in front of the largest of the huts, a large fire was burning. I was heartened to see and smell that it was devoted to the cooking of food—our food, I hoped —apparently, the evening meal. Blue plumes of smoke rose and disappeared into the deep purple gloom of the night.

Ranged in a semicircle around the fire was an assemblage of people, three score or more, gaily dressed, but more opulently so than our escorts. I was bedazzled at first by the wink and gleam of bright yellow jewelry on smooth, deep-copper skin in the firelight. In the center of the semicircle could be found the chief, so I presumed, and his mother (the woman to whom I had presented the comb and brush) seated on large wooden chairs.

We were led across the central circle and presented to the chief and his mother, who regarded us with a good deal of regal *hauteur*. Mr. Winthrop did not so much as sketch a bow (I was not surprised), while I attempted a curtsy, but was not allowed to complete the gesture, for we were led to the edge of the circle composed of those people standing around the chief and his mother, where we were bade to sit. More accurately, I should say that we were *shoved* into a seated position.

As little as I liked finding myself, once again, in a highly uncomfortable position on the ground, I was rather pleased by the fact that at the moment Mr. Winthrop and I were seated, all the others who had been standing in the semicircle also sat. I took this as a sign of our status as honored guests. Now, not everyone present at the gathering sat. Our escorts, for instance, did not. Out of the corner of my eye, I noted that they had stepped behind us and were standing there immobile, one hand on their hips, the other holding their spears at a right angle to the ground. Thus they were to remain for the entire evening—a noteworthy feat of self-control.

Another group of folks, who had been standing just out of my sight behind the first group, had sprung into action. There were many more working than feasting. I was heartily relieved to see that their activity involved the distribution of food. As this group scurried to their serving tasks, I had a moment's leisure to survey our surroundings more thoroughly. I studiously avoided regarding the lower half of that hideous statue in the center, but as my eye roamed over those objects which caught the light from the fire, I noted that my offering of comb and brush lay on a metal plate at the base of the statue. I thought that this, too, must be meaningful, and was pleased. I caught Mr. Winthrop's eye and nodded my satisfaction. He returned my look, his eyes impassive his mouth unmistakably grim. Evidently, he did not, at the moment, share my satisfaction.

Actually, mine did not last. The serving of the food was interminably long. Each separate dish—and there seemed to be several of them—was put in its own capacious bowl and first taken to the matriarch, who made elaborate gestures, while her son pronounced at length. I must say that I was so hungry by then that I was not attending to the proceedings, and so I do not remember exactly what transpired, or in what order. At length Mr. Winthrop and I received deep wooden plates piled high with an indistinguishable assortment of food, along with a huge chunk of what looked to be a thick, flat, yellow bread.

My stomach was behaving oddly and seemed to want to reject the idea of eating. After the parsimony of water, my famished eye perceived an almost obscene bounty on my plate, and I was so faint by that time that my head was fairly swimming for having been exposed rather contradictorily to the appetizing odors—or, so they seemed to my starved palate. However, I would neither decline to eat nor begin to eat before the others, for fear of giving offense. I would let no physical quirk impinge on my civility.

I was pleased to see that the chief and his mother were served just after Mr. Winthrop and I, and they commenced eating. I felt confirmed in my belief in our status as honored guests.

Initial silence reigned while the first bites were taken. I glanced surreptitiously at our closest neighbors to discover whether there was a particular order to eating the food which I could only distinguish by color. I discovered none, and so—my stomach having adjusted itself to the idea of food—I fell to eating without once considering the oddity that this was the first meal I had ever eaten in public with my fingers. So hungry was I that I hardly tasted the food at first.

The brief opening silence was followed by a hum of low talk among the seated people which gradually increased in volume throughout the course. The servants—surely they were servants, for they wore no jewelry and their nether garments seemed much skimpier than the others'—kept hopping to their tasks. In due course, all those taking part in the feast received a second plate of food. After it was presented, the volume of conversation might be said to have reached almost normal speaking tones.

With this second plate I was most definitely revived, and the food was prepared in such a fashion as to slake my thirst at the same time.

My senses returned. Feeling much more like myself, and given the general flow of conversation surrounding us, I deemed it within the bounds of courtesy to engage Mr. Winthrop's attention.

I turned to him. His hard, angular chin, darkened now by the scrabble of a beard, was etched in high relief by the firelight, which also fell to burnish his thick black curls. These were in wild disorder, hardly contained by the bedraggled ribbon at his nape. Sensing my glance, he turned to regard me. He, too, looked revived by the food, and his face had lost something of its grim impassiveness.

I gave voice to the question uppermost on my mind. "How came you to spend two years in a Spanish prison?" I asked without further preamble.

He answered with a directness that matched my question. "As a prisoner of war," he said.

Mr. Winthrop was, at all times, a surprising companion. "Prisoner of war? I thought you were a merchant."

He shook his head. "Only recently, and as a result of the many long hours I had in prison to contemplate my future. I had only just bought the *Judith*," he explained. "This crossing was, in fact, my maiden voyage with her."

"Oh, wretched luck!" I cried, keeping my voice low, then repeated my earlier consolation that at least we were both still alive and of a piece.

Mr. Winthrop glanced away from me and over to where the chief and his mother were seated. "That remains to be seen," he replied cryptically.

I passed over this remark. "Did you have a sizable investment in the *Judith*?"

"I owned her outright," he replied, with his earlier carelessness. Then, after hesitating fractionally, his blue eyes resting enigmatically on me, he added, a little abstractedly, "However, given the source of the money with which I bought her, there is perhaps something of an ironic justice in her loss."

It was not my business to probe into Mr. Winthrop's financial arrangements. "And the Spanish prison?" I prompted.

"The consequence of campaigning in the Spanish Netherlands with the French." He paused to adjust his phrasing. "In French service, that is."

That was not as direct an answer as he had given to my initial question, but I did not realize it at the time. "You're a soldier, then," I stated by way of asking.

"It's a trade I followed for a number of years. It brought me no great gear or gold, but it's a safer occupation than merchandising, I'm thinking, for, despite the Spanish prison, it never reduced me to such helpless captivity, as you may observe."

I had already determined that Mr. Winthrop judged our present circumstance in worse case than I did. "How came you to serve the French?" I asked, instead of taking issue with the fine point of our captivity or not.

"I am Irish—" he began.

"With a name like Winthrop?"

"My father died just after my birth. Some years later my mother remarried, this time to an Englishman. Robert Winthrop adopted me," he explained. "But my mother never saw the lights of her husband's new church, and so, after Mr. Winthrop died—and with the Dissenters' activities of the seventies, which brought with them the usual wave of anti-Catholic sentiment—I was encouraged to go to Paris, where I was to study medicine. Therefore—" He broke off. "It's a long story."

I understood perfectly. It did not concern me, after all, and he had already told me enough to satisfy my curiosity. I now understood his black hair and blue eyes and the faint lilt in his voice. Further disclosures were entirely unnecessary.

"Medicine and soldiering seem somewhat contradictory professions, when all is said," I observed, by way of allowing a turn in subject.

He smiled faintly at that. "Yes, but a little knowledge of the medical arts goes a long way on the battlefield."

A major point in Mr. Winthrop's story still eluded me, however; for, given my father's rank and Edward's profession, I carried in my head the various campaigns of the last ten years on the Continent. "But it has been four or five years since the French left the Netherlands," I said.

Mr. Winthrop looked at me then. His deep blue eyes registered a remarkable array of emotions: surprise was there, and a wariness, too, both reactions tempered with a humor I could not interpret. "The French left when Marlborough arrived in Flanders," he said simply. He did not observe that it was unusual that I, a woman, should be so well versed in foreign affairs.

"Then, how came you to be held prisoner in Spain within the last two years?" I asked.

He did not immediately reply. After a brief pause, and again, with a strange mixture of emotions which, unaccountably, included that same lurking humor, he said slowly, "You don't want to know."

He had a point. In all probability, I did *not* want to know, and, furthermore, it was none of my concern. I would press him no more. "At least, in the course of your various adventures, you managed to learn Spanish," I said, shifting back to neutral ground, "which would ordinarily serve a merchant well in the New World—"

"And the two years I spent in a Spanish prison showed me a side of the Spanish character which I found anything but admirable," he interpolated.

"You must have learned to speak French, by the by, no?"

Mr. Winthrop grinned. "I had as much success with French as I did with the medical books," he replied without the slightest trace of discomfort.

"Nevertheless," I said, "knowledge of French and Spanish is a fair sight more useful than ancient Greek. *I* possess the ability to scan a line of Homer with relative ease. My father believed in this training, even though I was a girl, and I cannot help but think, just at the present moment, that the benefits of a classical education are vastly overrated! I know no *practical* language—other than English, of course, which does not seem to be of much use in this setting!"

A smile of genuine amusement lit Mr. Winthrop's eyes, then they narrowed slightly. "Your father had you taught?" he asked casually.

I shook my head, tossing off the question. No more did I wish to speak of my past than did Mr. Winthrop. "That was a long time ago," I said, dismissively.

He, too, let the topic pass. "Before you married poor Edward," he said (provocatively, I thought) by way of reply.

"Before I married Edward," I said, and repeated firmly, "But that, too, seems a very long time ago now." I was not about to allow his sly comment about Edward to go unanswered. I could be just as provocative as he.

I began to eat again, very daintily, as I cast my eye about the strange assemblage. "Do you not agree with me that it is a festive occasion tonight, Mr. Winthrop?"

He allowed his eye to scan the scene. "Sure, now, Miss Sedgwick, it's a festive occasion, with everyone in their finery."

"Just what I was thinking!" I approved and added sweetly, "Now, aren't you sorry you did not bring your coat along to complete your formal attire, as I had earlier suggested?"

Mr. Winthrop slanted me a glance. "Coat or no, Miss Sedgwick, the soldier and not the medic in me feels an overwhelming desire to wring your neck for having brought us to this pass," he said pleasantly.

"Unfair!" I replied promptly. "And if you dare *ever* to blame me again for the circumstances of our having been cast adrift, I shall—"

I was not permitted to voice this promising threat. "However, since you may also have saved our lives a while back on the beach," he interrupted, "and just might be regarded in something of a special light by our present company—" he made a minimal gesture, encompassing the circle of feasting "—our hosts would not pardon me your death, for I fear that I could never make them understand the degree to which you are irritating!"

Mr. Winthrop, I noted, had a genius for back-handed compliments. "Oh, do you indeed think I saved us earlier?" I asked, rather pleased. "Very possibly."

I considered this. Since I have never been one to make a virtue of necessity, I shook my head. "The occasion called for some display of goodwill, after all, and these are a hospitable people. I think they mean to help us. They are honoring us with a feast. They have dressed up." For evidence, I held up my hand, displaying a piece of bread onto which I had placed something that looked green. "And the quantities of food! Why, this dish alone, for instance—"

"We might have been the food," Mr. Winthrop interrupted again, this time in a voice carefully devoid of expression.

I blinked at his extremely odd phrasing. "What on earth do you mean?" I asked, very reasonably.

He replied with one word: "Cannibals."

"Nonsense!" I said briskly.

To this Mr. Winthrop said nothing. During the prolonged space of silence, I felt my stomach fall like a stone. I had to remind myself that I was among savage Indians about whom I knew nothing. I looked suspiciously at my food. I had actually been enjoying it. My gorge rose, and a wave of nausea threatened to overcome me. I struggled a dizzying moment to keep my dinner and my reason.

Fortunately, my good sense won. The food was distinctly *vegetal*, and I had seen with my own eyes that the meat portion of the meal was fish, for they had been scaled quite elaborately before the chief and the matriarch. Still—

"How came you to think of . . . of cannibals?" I asked.

"Reports of cannibalism have circulated since the earliest voyages of Columbus," Mr. Winthrop informed me. "The Caribales, or Cannibals, if you prefer, are to be found in the Lower Antilles."

I had a stray memory of the hope he had expressed earlier in the day, while we were still adrift in the boat, about our not being in a current that would take us to the Lower Antilles.

"And do you think we are in the Lower Antilles, Mr. Winthrop?" I asked cautiously.

"I sincerely hope not, Miss Sedgwick."

Well. I had no intention of dying for a good many years, but I realized the hazards of travel: shipwrecks, sharks—even the Spanish. Cannibalism was a turn I simply had not considered—and was entirely unprepared for. But then who, after all, could *prepare* for such an eventuality? Mr. Winthrop had known of the danger, though, and if he had been worried that we had fallen into the hands of the Caribales, I could well understand his earlier reticence.

I turned the matter over in my mind, examined every human feeling I commanded, and relied, once again and heavily, on my extreme good sense. It came to my rescue. "I do not think I believe you," I said. "That is, it is not that I do not believe *you*. Rather, I do not believe the reports! Why, I have heard many stories about the Indians of the New World, and I must say that, from what little I know so far, half of them do not seem to be true!"

"You are not the first to doubt the reports of the Caribales," Mr. Winthrop replied. He looked at me again, his eyes reflecting the gallows humor of his next words. "However, those Europeans with firsthand experience of the stories would no longer be among us to confirm them!"

Needless to say, I was *not* amused, and I refused to consider our case hopeless.

To my small, controlled silence, he said, "What, no panic, Miss Sedgwick?"

"I cannot panic when I do not know the outcome," I said coolly. "And what, after all, if we have washed ashore in the Upper Antilles?"

"Then we may find ourselves among the Arawak," he said. "They are peace-loving and friendly, so I have been told. However, I never anticipated meeting either group, and fear that I have spent my time studying the strengths and weaknesses of the Spanish, as the greatest enemy."

This struck me as pure prejudice. "Worse than the Caribales?" I asked, frankly astonished.

"Much worse," Mr. Winthrop replied on the ghost of a laugh, "given that my jailer was one Don Pedro." He did not elaborate, but merely shook his head. "Death is death, and the Spanish have been merciless dealers of death in the New World."

Despite what he said, I would have felt better just than to have been the prisoner of the merciless, death-dealing Spanish. The Caribales did not even seem *human*. But where, in fact, were we? Among the Caribales, or the Arawak? Was it even chances?

"How are we to know whom we are among?" I asked.

Mr. Winthrop did not think the question worth answering. He merely glanced at me, his brows raised meaningfully.

As if by way of demonstrating an answer to my question, our escorts came around to face us just then, and somehow we knew that we were to rise to our feet. We did so. I stood and looked my escort straight in the eye. He returned my stare. *No*, I thought, *here is no cannibal. Change the color of his skin and his mode of dress, and you will see yourself.* The thought comforted me until we were brought face-to-face with the chief and his mother.

We stood there, Mr. Winthrop and I, in front of them. Their faces were copper masks, betraying nothing. Neither did they say anything, which was quite unnerving. Then they clapped their hands, once. I felt myself being drawn backward by the elbows, toward that hideous statue, I supposed.

We were shoved to our knees. I had become insensibly aware of the throb of drums off to one side of the circle. I had noticed, too, a strange, dry, rasping sound, as if rice were being shaken in a box. The drumbeats had become more insistent, the shaking, rasping noises more intense. The fire was close by. I could still smell the remains of dinner. I fought against every horrible image associated now with the meal.

To steady my thoughts, I stole a glance at Mr. Winthrop. His attention was fixed a little to one side. Following the direction of his gaze, I noticed a beautiful young girl, very evidently in the first blush of womanhood, her skin burnished bronze in the firelight, walking very ceremoniously, not quite strutting, toward the seated regal couple. She was bearing my present of the comb and brush on the metal tray. She must have come from behind us, from where I had seen the comb and brush placed at the base of the statue.

My eyes fell a moment on the metal tray, then widened considerably. I suddenly realized that it was fashioned of gold. Then my eye swept the assembled company and reappraised the glint of the jewelry I had earlier noticed. If my eyes were not deceiving me, these Indians were bedecked in *pure gold*.

The girl presented the tray to the matriarch, then withdrew to the side. Immediately thereafter, as if from nowhere (although I believe it was from behind the two regal chairs—let's call them *thrones*) sprang several dozen dancers, both women and men, into the circle between us and the regal pair. The dancers wore wreaths of flowers and feathers on their heads, and strings of shells on arms, hips and legs, which jingled incessantly as they danced. They seemed to be holding rattles in their hands—the instruments, I now realized, which had earlier produced the rasping noises—and their necks and arms and ankles were laden with gold. It was all color, lithe movement, and gentle shaking, and it was almost entertaining.

After the dancers came the warriors. The pounding of the drums became pronounced. After a while, it felt as if they were being beaten in my very head. I must say that I did not find the warriors as entertaining as the dancers. To begin with, they were wielding smooth but serious-looking sticks in executing what looked to be ritual combat; second, they punctuated their movements with truly blood-curdling shouts and cries; and third, as they performed, they came ever closer to where Mr. Winthrop and I were still, rather ignominiously, on our knees in front of the statue—what I was beginning to think of in terms of a sacrificial altar. The heat from the fire was too close and seemed to touch me personally.

Abruptly, it all stopped—the movement, the music, the cries. The warriors had halted not two feet in front of us. The sound of the drums pulsed in my ears for long, resounding moments afterward, but all before us was motionless, silent—and *expectant*.

The warriors fell away to clear a path for the chief and the matriarch, who were descending upon us. The matriarch held high above her head the golden tray on which were displayed (what I had hoped would be) my peace offerings. The chief, I was profoundly sorry to see, held a very wicked-looking spear. He raised it meaningfully above his head and began to intone in fearsome accents.

From behind me, a hand grabbed at the knot of hair I had pinned at my nape and pulled my head far back. When the drums began to beat again, slowly, gathering speed and force by infinitesimal degrees, I closed my eyes against the coming horror.

I hope it is clear that I am not a coward. In closing my eyes, I intended nothing of craven behavior. Rather, for my last moments on this earth, I preferred to control my own images. So I closed my eyes against the hot, heavy, foreign night surrounding me to see in my heart snowy London nights, sharp and exquisite, cold, clear, and pale; with the moon and stars cut out with silver scissors. That is what I wished to hold in my mind's eye when the end came.

For my last word, I breathed, almost without knowing it, "Caribales."

A moment passed. No agonizing death came. Nor, alternatively, was I blissfully released from this vale of tears (although I have never held with those who think life a heavy *burden*). Instead, what I heard next was Mr. Winthrop's voice replying to my statement, very softly, "Arawak."

I cracked one eye. The first sight that greeted me, given the position of my head, was the tropical night sky. Both eyes opened wide. It seemed to me, in the split second that had bridged certain death into life, that the night had blossomed. The sky was no longer foreign and oppressive, but very, very beautiful. Great silver flowers studded the purple velvet above. I thought that if I stood up and reached high, I could pluck one of those star-flowers and fold my arms around the fat moon. In that one very beautiful moment of life, I felt my pinched Northern soul expand, just a little.

I rolled my eyes cautiously over to Mr. Winthrop, and saw that instead of being submitted to some unspeakable death, *he was being shaved*. I caught his eye and thought I spied an extremely ill-timed twinkle in their blue depths.

"I needed this," he said, evidently referring to the shave.

I was not yet sufficiently acquainted with Mr. Winthrop's whimsical turn of mind to be anything other than thoroughly angry. My voice low, quivering with suppressed wrath, I said to him, "I may never forgive you, Mr. Winthrop, for having completely spoiled for me what is apparently a very gentle rite of welcome!"

Mr. Winthrop was unrepentant for having just scared me half to death with his wild tales of the Caribales. "Let us just call the score even, if you please, Miss Sedgwick," he replied.

I certainly had no adequate rejoinder to *that*. In any case, my attention was completely diverted to my own situation. I felt the pins being taken from my hair and the heavy fall released down my back. Then came a vigorous and rhythmic stroking of my curls, most probably with my very own silver-chased brush. Those few moments had allowed me to recover sufficiently to be now quite irritated as I saw my hair pins placed on the golden tray and borne off by a servant.

Now, I had presented, by my own free will, the gift of the silver comb and brush, but I was not disposed to giving away my hair pins, for I did not possess another set. However, since I was on my knees, and a strong hand held my head while several dozen warriors with heavy sticks stood not two feet in front of me, I did not think it wise to protest that my hosts had traded a thought too freely on the generosity of their honored guest.

Hours later, after the welcome ceremonies had ended quite anticlimactically and we had been duly escorted back to the hut, I was roused from an uncomfortable slumber by Mr. Winthrop's hand on my shoulder.

I lay on a grass mat that had been rolled out for me by my escort. Mr. Winthrop's mat had been placed next to mine, but Mr. Winthrop had chosen to alter the sleeping arrangements slightly by taking up a position with his head just outside the door. Before going to a sleep we desperately needed, we had put together a plan for departing from the village, which centered mainly around the idea of catching an hour or two of sleep, then regaining the boat on the lagoon, in which had remained the compass, quadrant, sextant, and chart. Once we had determined exactly where we were, we would set out with the earliest tides for the nearest European settlement. He could then go his way, and I go mine. It was extremely rude to leave in the dead of night like that, after having been so hospitably fed and feted, but I was not inclined to take the dictates of civility that far—at least, not when the remotest chance remained that our hosts were fattening us up. . . .

The plan, though bold, was easily contrived—owing to the simple reason that none other presented itself to us. I must suppose it was because we anticipated reaching a European city within the next day or two that Mr. Winthrop chose his particular sleeping position.

Thus, we were not, from a purist point of view, asleep under the same roof. I appreciated his tact. In contemplating my immediate future after this quite extraordinary interlude, I was rapidly coming to realize that the *propriety* of the adventure would consist chiefly in not recounting *everything*.

As I was saying, when Mr. Winthrop's hand touched my shoulder, I was instantly awake, though surely not thoroughly refreshed. I rose fully dressed, donned my bonnet, shoes, and stockings (which, you can imagine, were very much worse for wear), gathered my tapestry bag and parasol, and followed Mr. Winthrop, who was also, by then, dressed and shod. He took my hand.

The moon was still fat and full. He gestured with his head toward the path by which we had come to the village. I think he had taken special note of it, and had been planning our departure from the moment we arrived, for he did not hesitate in our silent progress through the town, while I was completely disoriented. He even had the presence of mind to have noted the water source and refilled our water bottle. He found the path on the first try and plunged down it, ever silent, still holding my hand. Our progress was made with deliberate haste and very efficiently. Not one branch slapped in my face, nor did I stumble over a root or log, so carefully did he lead me through the forest.

Sure enough and none to my surprise, really, we regained the golden beach, now bathed in silver moonlight. Thereafter, it was easy to retrace our steps. We rounded the heel of the mountain, walked down the beach that curved around toward the lagoon, passed the now limp impaled fish (our intended dinner of the night before), and arrived at the rowboat.

Suddenly, the exertions of the past hours caught up with us. The sight of the little boat, bobbing on the shallow waters lapping the hem of the beach, made my whole body cramp in anticipation of folding myself into it. I felt incredibly tired, and suspected that Mr. Winthrop might have had reason to feel weary, as well.

His next words confirmed my suspicion. "But it's a rowboat," he said, half to himself, as if he had conveniently forgotten that the means of our escape would be fueled by the power of his own muscles.

Tired though my body was, my thoughts were in excellent order. (Crisis appears to stimulate my intellect to its highest abilities.) "No, Mr. Winthrop," I cried in excitement and triumph, "it's a *sail* boat!"

He gave me a look that needed no interpretation.

"No, I have not lost my wits," I said, calmly and reasonably. "I have remembered the bolts of cloth that I had the great foresight to save from the sinking *Judith*—which, I might add, you have *not* yet thanked me for. We have more than enough material for sails!"

In the starry darkness, I saw his face light up. "Excellent, Sedgwick!" he approved heartily.

My idea seemed to have given us both new life, just as the bottle of water had revived us the day before. Mr. Winthrop now reached eagerly into his case and withdrew his tools of navigation. He put the sextant to his eye.

"Upper Antilles?" I asked, almost certain of the answer.

He nodded simultaneously to my question and replied, "Not far off Montserrat or Nevis, if I'm not mistaken. To the east, no doubt." He lowered the instrument, then rummaged a moment in the case before lifting out a chart. "But, how far off is the crucial question." He strained his eyes over it for a few moments before giving up the effort, since the starlight was too dim. He paused a moment, peering again into the darkness of his case, then said, "For your saving of the cloth, I accord you first-mate status," he said. "I brought some matches. So you decide, Sedgwick. Should we use them to study the chart now, or instead waste equally precious time in waiting for the dawn?"

I was not about to waste further precious time arguing with him

over my supposed status or his authority to confer it on me. A simple
"thank you" for the cloth would have sufficed. Instead, I bent my
mental energies to the problem at hand. I looked up and down the
beach, remembering that the lagoon lay equidistant between the
beach stretching north (the route we had not taken the afternoon
before) and the beach stretching south that curved to the larger bay
where we had first met the Arawak.

"We cannot sail out from here into the lagoon," I said, thinking
aloud, "for then we shall meet with the current taking us north. West
is the direction we probably want to go. So we shall need to pull the
boat around one end of the island or the other, depending on which
direction it is best to sail off from, no?" I said.

He nodded.

"In the interest of saving our energy, then," I continued, "it seems
best to light a match so that we choose the right direction on the first
try. On the other hand, it seems unlikely that one match will suffice
for a proper study of the chart, and I would surely hate to waste them,
in case we should find it necessary to build a fire before we reach a
European port."

"One match will suffice," he said to this. "I have cannon matches
—slow-burning."

"Cannon matches?" I replied. "Of all the things to think of, since
you surely did not anticipate saving any cannons!"

He shrugged. "But useful in the present case, you'll admit, and they
were at hand. I, like you, gathered what I could that seemed most fundamental and was light weight."

It was decided. He lit one of the cannon matches with a flint. I held
it and the chart while he performed the necessary calculations. He
murmured a position which meant not a thing to me, then began
stroking his beardless chin thoughtfully.

"How did they do it?" I asked in reference to the motion of his
hand.

He looked up, laughter reflected in the light of the burning match. "A shell," he replied. "They used a damned shell. Razor sharp."

"Sir!" I remonstrated at his language.

"Best damned shave I've had in a long time, too," he replied, just to annoy me, then continued, rather more seriously, "Although this island is too small to appear on the map, we're evidently north and east of Montserrat. I propose we go south, as we did last evening, to the larger bay, to gather wood to erect our sails. Then we can shove off—with luck, just at dawn."

He stripped off his half-boots and stockings, then picked up the rope with the ring that had anchored the boat and began to pull it in the water. He was careful to walk where the water was shallowest.

I, too, stripped off shoes and stockings, and waded just far enough into the fresh waters to lay these articles, along with my tapestry bag and parasol, next to my shawl in the bottom of the boat with the other gear. I then insisted that I take a turn pulling this unwieldy load, so that he could conserve his energy for making the masts and sailing the craft. When he protested with what I suspected to be rather misplaced gallantry, I pulled rank.

"First mate's privilege!" was my argument.

Thus we lumbered down around the curve of the bay. Our progress was, nevertheless, quite steady. In time, the remaining stars, reluctant to leave, blinked and went out. The eastern sky, embracing the whole of the untrammeled horizon to our left, was a colorless blank. Then, it began to flush rose. It promised to be, in perhaps another hour or so, an opalescent dawn.

We negotiated with some difficulty the heel of the mountain, at the curve of the island. Not only were there large, slick rocks for us to climb over, there lay submerged equally large boulders on which the boat could splinter. We could afford neither leaks nor time for repairs. Consequently, covering those few yards of coastline seemed to take hours.

When we had rounded the coast and had a view of the bay and beach spread out before us, Mr. Winthrop passed me the rope for my turn to pull. Having completed this maneuver, he looked up and out in front of us. He uttered, low, a single, vehement word.

I, too, looked up at what had prompted Mr. Winthrop's unseemly language. This time I did not reprove him, for I saw that his oath had been fully justified.

CHAPTER 5

"Do you think our kind and generous hosts of the evening before have come to wish us a good voyage?" I suggested. Yet even as I spoke the hopeful words, I doubted them.

Toward us came a great quantity of Arawak. Although this scene had already been played, I was aware of some subtle difference between the group we had met the evening before and the one this morning. I could not immediately put it into words.

Mr. Winthrop, however, instantly grasped the difference. "My acquaintance with local customs is slight, but I do not think that bows and arrows form a part of Arawak departing rituals."

That was it, of course—the difference in the aspect of the two groups. The one the evening before had been armed casually, with a spear or two. This morning, they were all men and all equipped with bows and arrows.

"Do you think they are still friendly?" I asked, although the looks on their faces, even at the distance of fifty paces, were anything but hospitable and welcoming.

"Nothing for it but to find out," Mr. Winthrop said. "I'll try to establish some terms."

With that, he took the rope from my unresisting hand, clearly affirming his leadership on this occasion. He stopped stock still, then looked at me intently, his voice grave. "I have a plan," he said. "You wait here. Don't move until I motion for you with my hand. I won't make an obvious gesture, so be on the watch. When I give you the signal, I'll be counting on you to know what to do."

"Yes, of course," I replied with great confidence.

"Good woman, Sedgwick!" he approved. "You won't let me down."

"Indeed, not," I assured him earnestly.

Of course, I had not the vaguest notion what he meant. I had the good sense, however, not to spoil his concentration by asking senseless questions or by having him worry about my ability to carry through on my part in the coming drama.

He proceeded to take several steps forward down the beach, toward the Arawak warriors, boat in tow. At exactly half the distance between me and the Indians, Mr. Winthrop stopped. Then, slowly, very deliberately, he unbuttoned what was left of his dress shirt and peeled it off to expose a broad expanse of muscled chest. He tossed the lace and silk chemise carelessly into the boat, then stooped down to retrieve several objects therefrom, probably from his leather case. It seemed his case contained no end of interesting articles, for the next thing I knew, he had thrust both a sheathed dagger and a pistol into the waist of his knee breeches and had pocketed some other smaller articles, which I could not distinguish from my distance. He resumed his approach toward the warriors, who, at his movements, had stopped.

Mr. Winthrop presently arrived in front of the group, which had taken up a position some ten feet from the lip of the water. Mr. Winthrop slid the rope through his hand until he could grasp the dratted brass ring that was the cause of all our difficulties of the past twenty-four hours. He weighed the ring in his hand a moment. Next he tossed it, half defiantly, half challengingly, but full well precisely at the very bare feet of the chief, who stood detached from the group at center front. The ring landed at the tips of the chief's toes.

I am a stalwart person and so made no outward reaction to this gesture, but I winced mentally at the thought of what might have happened had Mr. Winthrop inadvertently hit the chief's foot. It was not a pretty image. Even if I had known then that Mr. Winthrop was the perennial horseshoe champion of his village throughout his boyhood, I would not have been less anxious. It certainly can happen that a ring toss champion can lose his nerve and precision if, at the toss of one ring, his entire fate might be decided.

However, this was but the beginning of Mr. Winthrop's display of boyhood expertise. He found a piece of driftwood and tossed it some distance from himself. With a fluid movement, he unsheathed the dagger at his waist and hurled the knife so that it hit the wood, dead center. He strode across the sand to his projected target and, holding either end of the wood down with his feet, bent over to retrieve the knife from the wood with his teeth. Still standing on the wood, he adroitly flipped the knife around in his hands. Then he flipped it behind his back and under one leg, although this action was less adroit (but his slight mishandling of the knife would only have been seen from the back, where I was). Then he flipped the knife again into the air so that it stuck, *thwack*, in the wood between his feet. I gathered from this series of maneuvers that Mr. Winthrop had wasted a serious portion of his youth perfecting his game of mumblety-peg.

What came next was very strange. Mr. Winthrop bent his body down and twirled around, crouching quite close to the ground, all the while emitting strange yelping noises. At first, I thought he had gone quite mad. Then, I saw that he had a purpose. He was slipping things from his pockets into his hands, but I could not quite see what he was doing, since he was twirling the whole time and making these very distracting noises—which must have been the very idea behind these odd actions. At the same time, I noted, he was gathering objects from the sand and pocketing them.

Then, without warning, he stood up, yelping and crying in a truly blood-curdling manner, and to my (and, I must suppose, everyone else's) profound shock, he crossed two sticks above his head, clicked them together twice at each temple, and suddenly his hair was on fire!

But, no—I realized the next second that what he had done was to take two cannon matches and place one behind each ear. He must have concealed his flint in his palm behind the two sticks, and with that set the matches to flame. I must say that he made it look like magic, and it was most effective, but a little overdone for my taste. I would have to speak to him later about this waste of two more of our precious supplies.

Before I registered that thought, however, he had embarked on his finale; apparently, he had saved the best for last. Hair aflame, yelling loudly, he tossed a shell into the air, whipped the pistol from his trousers, and rather spectacularly exploded the shell midair with a well-placed bullet. He stood, one hand on his hip, the other holding the smoking pistol high in the air, bare-chested, legs spread, feet planted squarely in the dazzling oyster white of the beach, the flares on either side of his head flickering and wavering, then extinguishing.

The morning's entertainment was over.

A moment of utter silence reigned, then the Arawak men erupted into animated conversation. They were evidently impressed by Mr. Winthrop's physical skill. I believe that such displays operate as a universal means of communicating among men, even from such disparate island tribes as the Arawak and the English. While I do not normally admire masculine sporting prowess, I had to admit that, in this instance, Mr. Winthrop's performance was awe-inspiring. I reserved judgment of what, if anything, it would gain us in the end.

While his Arawak counterparts were in open, animated discussion, Mr. Winthrop, standing his ground upstage (shall we say) on the beach, signaled to me. I did not know what to do. Fortunately, the options were few.

I ran to the boat. Once there, I looked over again at Mr. Winthrop for further instructions. He continued to gesture, minimally. It seemed, quite incredibly, that he wished for me to plunge into the water and swim away. I shook my head. He gestured again. I reinterpreted. This time, I reached into our two cases—my tapestry bag and his leather one—and grabbed what I could of our meager possessions. I clutched these articles, hiding them within the folds of my skirts.

That was all I had time for. The Arawak warriors had arrived at an agreement. The chief had moved away from them to stand at the same distance from the water as Mr. Winthrop. The rest descended upon me, running and yelling. My heart quailed. This, surely, was my last. I knew a moment of extreme anger against Mr. Winthrop. In that half-second, I thought that his activities might have been some secret masculine ritual, at the end of which came a feminine sacrifice.

Then, in a flash, I understood what Mr. Winthrop's gestures had indicated: that I was to take hold of something long and thin. I grabbed my parasol from the bottom of the boat and thrust it ferrule-end out, threatening, menacingly. This produced no effect whatsoever on the Arawak warriors bearing down on me, unchecked. I thought, again, that this was my last.

However, my instincts must have gotten the better of my (quite faulty) reason, because by the simple expedient of stepping out of the way of the men hurtling themselves toward me, I managed to save myself from an ignominious dunking in the water. The object of their stampede was not my valuable self, anyway—it was the boat. A half dozen or so lifted it onto their shoulders, while the others raised their bows above their heads and shook them exultantly against the sky, dawning rose and gold.

While the warriors carried the boat aloft toward the chief, Mr. Winthrop crossed the beach to where I was standing.

"What the plague did you think to do with that ***?" he demanded impatiently, with an uncomplimentary epithet referring to my parasol, as he reached my side.

"I thought that is what you directed me to pick up," I said.

"I meant the *musket*, woman!" he snapped.

"What musket?" I asked.

"The one I had stashed in the boat on top of the cloth," he answered. "You must have seen it."

Now that he mentioned it, I did recall having had many hours to eye it the day before as we sped along in our Atlantic current, but I had not fully registered its presence on board. "Certainly I saw it, but since I do not think in terms of muskets—"

"Or rotted ring fittings either!" he interrupted, quite irrelevantly, as far as I was concerned.

I was *not* going to rehash that old ground, and so I continued, quite reasonably, "—I cannot imagine what on earth you expected me to do with the musket."

"*Do? With a musket?*" he echoed. Then, "*Faith!* I thought I could count on you!"

"You can!" I protested. "Do you mean that you wished me to fire on them?"

"No, but you might have held them at bay, or scared them off," he said.

"Oh, that was the plan, was it?" I said. I considered it. "You, on your end, reducing them to speechless wonder. I, on my end, scaring them. Not bad."

"It was . . . it was *damned* good!" He was really angry.

"Not *that* good, surely," I said coolly. Just to irritate him, I unfurled my parasol and snapped it against the rising sun. "I doubt that one woman threatening three dozen men and more with a musket would have been very effective. And what if, in my ignorance, I had fired it by mistake and actually *hurt* somebody? Or worse! And even if I could have held them off while you ran to the boat, it was not as if we could just have rowed away, simple as you please. They have their bows and arrows, and without our sails, we would have been pretty easy marks."

"I still had several bullets left."

"You would have *killed* some of them? I queried, quite incredulous.

"I was planning on firing them into the air."

A pithy, "Ah," was all I needed to say to that.

"It was worth a try!" he retorted hotly.

It was manifest that in laying the foiling of his plan at my door, Mr. Winthrop was expressing more his general frustration in our present circumstances than his anger in my inability to have carried through on whatever he thought my part should have been. As for our present circumstances, they were materially worse than before, since we were no longer in possession of our boat. Our fates were suddenly bound together, now more than ever. This was no time for a break in the ranks. I understood his frustration and shared in it.

"Your plan was as good a one as anyone could have contrived in the moment," I offered in a soothing spirit, "and impeccably exe-cuted! Quite spectacular, in fact. I compliment you!"

I regret to report that Mr. Winthrop's reply to my praise was not as politic as my approach. It is also unprintable.

So much for the soothing spirit. "Your antics were so truly *capti-vating*, in fact," I pursued, knowing when I have been unfairly attacked, "that I feel quite sure our friends the Arawak now wish to keep us *captive*, as a result! I think you may have found your true public! So, in any event, it seems quite unlikely that your plan would have secured our departure!"

Fortunately, Mr. Winthrop had no time for a verbal reply, for I had seen out of the corner of my eye that the chief, along with two other men, had been approaching and were now upon us. Nevertheless, I read in Mr. Winthrop's quite expressive face his doubts for the ultimate success of his bold plan. By a series of hand motions, we were bade to follow the chief, and, just in case we misunderstood, two escorts (I do believe they were the same two from the evening before) planted themselves at our backs. Since our boat was being borne off in the opposite direction from the water, we had no other choice but to follow the chief, our host, back to the village.

The sun had been climbing in a sky that was now extravagantly blue. I was acutely hungry after the exertions of the evening, and most tired. My existence had been too precarious for too many hours running for me to object strenuously to *not* casting off once again in shark-infested waters surrounded by a few planks of wood. From the way Mr. Winthrop shrugged and accepted the chief's lead, I guessed that neither did he find another day's rest among the Arawak completely out of place.

"What do you think awaits us now, Mr. Winthrop?" I asked in a whisper as we trailed across the sand.

He looked down at me. His anger had passed. The blue eyes in his swarthy face registered a lingering irritation, however, now tempered with an extraordinary mixture of resignation and laughter. "For me, at least, another good shave," he replied.

Now, here was a perfect example of Mr. Winthrop's whimsy. Although I attributed this character defect to his Irish heritage, I could not, at the moment, criticize him for it, for this mention of creature comforts struck a chord in me. My hair was feeling itchy and tangled under my bonnet. At least, in returning to the village, I might be able to retrieve my hair pins. Among the things I had grabbed from our bags was, of course, my comb and brush. In one hand I was still fiercely clutching them in the folds of my skirt, along with the remains of our other possessions; in the other hand, I held my parasol.

On the return trip to the village, I experienced very different thoughts from the ones I had the evening before. No longer was I filled with expectant apprehension or profound worry over my possible fate. This time I was concerned with recruiting my forces during a day of rest (still hoping that Mr. Winthrop and I would find a way to leave the island on the morrow), and to this end, I thought to enjoy my surroundings. With our escorts stolidly behind us and our host leading the way, we found the path that would take us to the village. It was wonderfully lush and green and smelled of a heavy, exotic perfume. I peered closely into the dense growth and fancied I saw long-tailed, brilliantly plumed birds fluttering from branch to branch. I allowed my eye to roam all around as we trod that winding, uphill path. It inevitably fell on Mr. Winthrop's back (need I say that, once again, he *preceded* me) and then to his legs, where it stopped.

The remains of his formerly elegant knee-breeches were torn at the back of his left thigh to expose a nasty gash, which had dripped blood down the back of his calf. The wound itself looked clean and had already begun to clot, but I could see that it would need tending and that I would have to be the one to do it. And I knew exactly how he had acquired it.

Presently we passed two wide-open spaces on either side of the path that I had not noticed on our first arrival, which had been at dusk, and then we were at the village proper. This time, I could judge the approximate plan of the village because that hideous statue rose above the tops of the huts from what must have been the center. In relation to that statue, then, we were entering at the southwest edge of the clearing. The village—or town, as I could now, in fact, see—was much, much bigger than I had estimated the evening before, and could easily have contained well over several hundred huts.

Still following the chief, we took several steps around the outward curve of the village, in the direction, I judged, of the hut to which we had been led before. After a few steps in that direction, Mr. Winthrop stopped dead in his tracks. This unexpected action not unnaturally produced a minor collision—me with his back, and our escorts with mine. I was jolted and, therefore, lost my footing.

Mr. Winthrop quickly steadied me by turning in my direction and placing his hands on my shoulders. It was an intimate embrace, in the filtered shade of my parasol, and he did not immediately release me. Instead, holding me against his length, he said, "I have an idea."

"Your ideas leave much to be desired!" I said.

Looking deep into my eyes with a twinkle in the depths of his own unmistakably blue ones, he said, quite outrageously, "Not at all. However, speaking of desire, I believe this idea to be even *better* than the one I had on the beach."

I must say that I was quite shocked at the implications of his words and actions. "Mr. Winthrop!" I reproved, low. "Are you quite sure that this is the time or the place?"

"Miss Sedgwick!" he mocked in return. "None better!"

Imagine my surprise. I would not have thought that broad daylight and the company of three Arawak warriors were the usual inducements for a man to think of lovemaking. And if I was half as disheveled as Mr. Winthrop had become in the past forty-eight hours (and he had become, despite his shave, mightily disheveled—though not in a wholly unattractive way, I had to admit, fleetingly, during this strange embrace), I could not imagine that I had inspired in him any overwhelming lust.

In fact, lust was not uppermost on Mr. Winthrop's mind (men are such quixotic creatures), for he continued, immediately, "Watch this!"

Mr. Winthrop, still holding me in a rather possessive, protective grip, with one arm across my shoulders, entered into an elaborate conversation with the chief, who had of course stopped and turned when he had realized that Mr. Winthrop was no longer following him.

Mr. Winthrop shook his head and gestured—meaningfully, I would suppose—and seemed to be making rather obvious allusions to my hair and his show down on the beach. Mr. Winthrop pointed to one of the huts and made a wide, swinging motion with one arm.

Oddly enough, it seemed that the chief understood something of what Mr. Winthrop meant and began to speak rapidly over our heads to our two faithful escorts. One word could be detached from this chaos of human sound, and that was *caney* (or so I would write it if an English mouth were saying it). Mr. Winthrop nodded vigorously, and continued his end of the gestural conversation, and to my great surprise, the chief also nodded, as if in agreement. Then, we doubled back on our initial direction into the village, took a quite different path, and proceeded to wind our way toward the center of town.

It was alive with the sounds and movements of people engaged in their daily activities. Women moved briskly to and fro, carrying baskets and bowls and jugs; children skipped and squealed in clusters in the paths and alleys; old women squatted in twos and threes at the doors to various huts, or crooned to babies who cried from within. All was color and movement. As we made our passage, our presence was naturally perceived, but no one actually stopped to look at us. Perhaps that was their way of not being rude, and I had the strange sense that Mr. Winthrop and I were, somehow—welcome.

Not quite at town center we stopped in front of a rather large, round hut (I had noticed by then that all the huts were round). The chief gestured to Mr. Winthrop, again with the word *caney*. Mr. Winthrop, his face very grave, appraised the hut at leisure, made some rather distinct gestures, then nodded approval. The word *caney* was uttered several more times, and we were ushered in.

The interior was much larger than the hut we had occupied the night before. However, the relative size of the space was not the most remarkable difference between the two dwellings. Rather, what was striking in this interior were the two sets of thick posts, suggesting four corners, which touched the perimeter of the circle. They not only held up the greater expanse of this larger roof, but also were attached to two netlike slings, each perhaps eight feet long or more. In addition, a variety of household utensils, such as bowls, dishes, pitchers, trays, mortars, and hollowed-out gourds, hung from the rafters and the walls, while on the hard-packed dirt floor were spread a number of mats. Against one portion of the wall was erected a contraption that resembled, most remarkably, my nanny's grandmother's loom, which I had seen in use several times when I was a little girl. In turning back around toward the door, I was pleasantly surprised to see a wooden chair. It was rather smaller and less ornate than the thrones in which the chief and his mother had been sitting at dinner, but a chair nevertheless. There were no windows, but the door, facing due south, allowed in sufficient and agreeable daylight.

There was more talk and more gestures, then the chief and our two escorts withdrew. This time, Mr. Winthrop did not quit the hut. Instead, he and I were left facing one another in wordless, almost breathless, silence.

To break what I felt was a most awkward, highly charged moment, I closed my parasol and propped it against the wall. Then I said briskly, "First things first, sir! Let me attend to your wound."

It appeared that Mr. Winthrop did not realize he had hurt himself. "Wound?" he echoed.

"Yes, the one you inflicted on yourself on the beach when you flipped the knife under your leg. That was the only aspect of your performance that was not up to the rest!" I said. "Of course, there was also the matter of the cannon matches, which I had at first thought a wanton waste, but since we have returned to the village anyway, I now think that the spectacular effect was well worth it!" Without pausing, I continued, in a most businesslike fashion, "Now, given the inconvenient location of the wound, I think you will have to lie down on the floor, if I am to dress it properly. I notice that there is a pannikin of water—let's hope that it is fresh. To bind the wound, I thought to sacrifice my lace collar. It's the neatest piece of accessible cloth I have left anywhere on my person. I hope you don't mind?"

"Lace on my thigh is no worse than the prospect of yellow-and-green-flowered sails," he replied to this, by way of assent and not without humor. He stretched himself out quite obediently, face-down, on one of the mats.

I sank to my knees and began my ministrations. I placed those articles I had surreptitiously folded into my skirts on the floor next to me. I had the wooden cup of good water at hand; my eyes and fingers were on the gash. I began daubing the back of his blood-streaked leg with the wet lace.

"Speaking of sails," he said, "and if we are to point out each other's lapses from good taste, I do wonder, with all the ells of plain cloth I had on board, how you came to choose two flowered bolts and a blue stripe!" This mild reproof he followed with the comment, apparently taking a leaf out of my book, "And, as for manners, ma'am, I note that you have *not* thanked me for having negotiated these most improved living quarters. I figured that all my heroics on the beach should have won us something!"

I was concerned at just that moment by the nasty, jagged look of the wound, which suggested to me the dangerous possibilities of infection and fever. At that comment, however, I smiled. "Very true, Mr. Winthrop!" I said, and cast my eye around the hut we were to share for the next few hours—or until we could get our boat back. "It is a vast improvement—in relative terms—and I thank you for these comforts. Now, out of curiosity, mind you, I would like to know—just what *are* those things?" I asked, nodding my head in the direction of the enormous slings stretched between the two pairs of posts.

"Those are sleeping nets," he explained. He twisted his head back around to look at me. That glint of humor, which seemed always to lurk in the depths of his blue eyes, surfaced. The Indians call them hammocks, I believe," he informed me. "These are the first true Indian hammocks I've seen, but European sailors have picked up the custom from the red man and use them as comfortable, space-saving bunks. The nets are in widespread use on ships. You'll have a chance to try one tonight."

"Tonight?" I said, returning his regard. "Do you think we shall still be here?"

"I think we shall be here for the next day, at least," he said evenly. He gestured with his head toward the door. "You see those two men out there?"

"Our escorts?"

"Guards, more like."

"Guards?" I repeated cautiously, but the implications had already crept up on me and were beginning to surround me.

"I do not think we are going to be allowed to go," he stated simply.

"Why not? It does not make sense."

"That," he said, "is just as much a mystery to me as it is to you. I do not think they mean us any harm. However—" he trailed off, as his gaze strayed again to the door, and he shrugged slightly, indicating his puzzlement.

"But, what makes you think that we are to be kept here, against our will?" I asked. "Our Arawak hosts, though rather strange, have been—in another and equally strange way—friendly."

"I agree. However, those men stationed just beyond our door now are the two who stood behind us at the evening meal and were posted to guard us during the night. I was suspicious already last night, and that is why I waited until they fell asleep at the watch before waking you to make our way back to the boat."

"Why didn't you tell me you thought we were being guarded?" I asked, a little indignantly.

"Because I was not entirely sure then," he replied easily. "And although I do not know why, I am sure now that they intend to keep their eye on us, to prevent our escape."

Since I could discard one horrible possibility that would not befall us as captives of the Arawak (as opposed to the Caribales), thoughts of self-preservation were not, at the moment, uppermost. Rather, it was at that moment—at that *very* moment—that the realization of the true situation at hand began to flood over me. I just then glimpsed the consequences of the past several days—how it was that my life was now thoroughly and most unexpectedly intertwined with that of a man I did not know.

I have already mentioned my brief, ultimately tragic marriage to Edward. I could not have endured a man who tried to rule me; and although I did not really wish for a man who would let himself be ruled by me, I considered the latter option the lesser of the two evils. So, practical woman that I am, I sought a man who would be shaped to my wishes and found Edward. However, not even in a year of circumspect courtship and three months of life together as man and wife did I feel quite so close, so *connected* to him as I did at that very moment to the man who was stretched out next to me, half naked (really, there is no other way to describe his state of undress), my hands on his private flesh. It was a profoundly disturbing realization.

"I see," I said, rather slowly and distractedly, while Mr. Winthrop was slanting his remarkable blue glance at me, perhaps judging my reaction. Unfortunately and most inadvertently, I must just then have applied too much pressure to a particularly sensitive spot in his wound, which I was still mechanically wiping.

A flash of pain crossed his face. I jumped back from him on my knees. "I'm worried that you might have gotten some sand into the wound to irritate it," I said quickly. "But I have a jar here that I grabbed from your leather case," I said. "It looks to be a pomade of some kind. Perhaps it is a medicinal ointment?"

"A brown jar?" he asked.

I affirmed this.

He expelled a long breath. "Yes, its a salve against infection." He then laid his head back down across his arms.

I began to apply the salve as gingerly as I could to the tenderest part of the wound. For all my care I heard him groan, perhaps in pain.

"Sedgwick, you've done it again!" I heard him say into his arms in an odd, muffled voice. "Although you don't perceive the practical differences between a parasol and a musket, you've redeemed yourself with the salve! I never know from one minute to the next whether you are going to have me killed or save my life!"

This man was in no pain. He was laughing outright!

"I have every intention of keeping you alive," I said rather stiffly, keeping to my task. Finished with the salve, I wrapped the lace around his leg and secured it with a neat bow. I was still attempting to absorb the myriad implications of my immediate future with Mr. Winthrop when a shadow fell across the door to our hut.

I looked up and felt a distinct relief to see there a small group of women. They were evidently beckoning to me.

CHAPTER 6

ive women stood at the door, all young, one bearing a large basket on her head. I rose and crossed to greet them, a look of inquiry raising my brows. "May I be of some service to you?" I asked. Although I knew full well my words were wasted, I deemed the effort at politeness to prevail over the possibilities of comprehension.

That effort, too, was wasted. Their attention was not on me but fixed on Mr. Winthrop who, behind me, had also risen. I saw, with some astonishment, that the women were standing on tiptoe to catch a glimpse of him beyond my shoulder, since I was blocking the door. Their eyes were popping slightly and their hands were clapped over their mouths, covering what could be nothing other than giggles.

I thought their behavior not only undignified but completely strange. I turned to regard Mr. Winthrop. "What on earth do you think has caused this reaction?" I asked him, unable to discover the source of their mirth.

"I wouldn't know," he replied, but his answer was somewhat distracted, for *his* attention was caught on the first young Arawak women that he had seen close up in daylight.

"Perhaps it's my dress that has caused them to stare."

His un*dress, rather!* I thought indignantly. However, it was not as if these women had never seen a muscular, bare-chested man before. As for the clothing covering these particular Arawak women—

"*Whose* dress is causing *whom* to stare?" I shot back, unable to suppress my indignation.

Mr. Winthrop glanced over at me, his eyes dancing. "I think it is the lace tied so incongruously to my leg," he offered, thinking nothing of the kind.

"We shall agree that it is the lace on your leg," I said at my most formal, "and close the subject of Arawak dress as one unfit for conversation."

"Certainly," he said, with a deep and formal bow at extreme variance with his evident delight and amusement, "for now I am relieved of all need to comment on the obvious."

There was no time for more. At that, I was pulled bodily by both arms from the hut (or caney, if we are to speak appropriately) with a babble of high, tuneful voices filling my ears. I had no time to fetch my parasol, only just enough to throw one last, expressive glance over my shoulder at Mr. Winthrop, who was watching these proceedings with evident, entertained interest.

I was pulled farther down a path that wound among the huts. It was gentle pulling, not entirely against my will, but since I was rather bewildered—they were earnestly trying to explain to me whatever it was that was going on and, quite predictably, failing to communicate *anything* whatsoever—I was able to stumble along with them only by means of their hands on my arms and at my back, dancing around me, prodding me ever forward. They were so gay and excited and happy about whatever it was we were doing that I felt no fear at all, and allowed myself to be swept along through town in this extraordinary fashion. Indeed, I had no choice *but* to allow myself to be swept along through town in this extraordinary fashion.

We quickly arrived at the town limits—on the other side, that is, from where we had entered previously. We followed a path along what must have been the north end then, and passed by several enormous cultivated fields, where neat rows of strange-looking plants were sprouting out from carefully spaced large, round heaps of earth. Away off down several of the rows I could see men at work with—and now I was truly surprised—what looked to be hoes.

I was gesturing toward these fields and plants and receiving (how could I have expected otherwise?) entirely unintelligible replies. Eventually, however, I seemed to make myself understood, and words meaning nothing to me, such as *maize* and *batata* and *manioc,* were insistently and incessantly repeated, as if after the tenth repetition I would be more likely to understand them than after the first. Of course, I *did* understand that they were naming the plants for me, but their names did not enlighten me in the least. I wondered, idly, whether I had tasted any of them the evening before, and began to feel my hunger all over again.

More to the point in this new view of life among the Arawak was the realization that they practiced neat and extensive agriculture. Now, in truth, I should not have been at all surprised. Every Arawak man, woman, and child I had seen so far had been well-fed—not plump, but visibly and pleasingly round. The bodies of the young women I was with, for instance—But, again, I digress.

We passed through the cleared fields and arrived, eventually, at the jungle. There was a path. The women plunged me down it, skipping merrily, and we entered a web of flies and mosquitoes and were immediately swallowed in a dozen different shades of tropical green. The jungle we entered was not so overgrown as I would have anticipated, but still quite wild, and I guessed that the path must have required constant recutting and clearing. I inhaled the fragrant air, which was unlike any I had ever breathed. It was laden with a strange perfume—a blend of logwood flower, pimento, and aromatic cedars.

Before my eye could dwell on the beauty of the bushes flaming scarlet and orange, before I could admire the vivid flowers thrusting spiky lobster claws from the emerald floor into our path, before I could register the constant calling and chattering of jungle life, I needed to establish one essential piece of information.

This time, I made myself clear on the first try, by the simple gesture of snaking one arm through the air parallel to the ground and accompanying the gesture with a hissing noise. The women instantly grasped my meaning, and nodded sapiently. It is my belief that women the world over easily understand such things.

I was reassured by their response, which consisted of clapping their hands in front of them imperiously and stamping the ground (with their bare feet, no less. I was still, relatively more safely, shod). Then they raised their arms above their heads, snaking their arms as I had done mine, hissing and chanting something. If that was a charm against jungle serpents, I was an instant and zealous convert to Arawak magic. I would also have liked to have had to hand my parasol, for despite Mr. Winthrop's recent maligning of the utility of this article in a crisis, I thought that it would make an excellent serpent-chaser.

After that, I relaxed into the luminous beauty of the jungle, an enormous and melodious poem of color and light. Several twists and turns took us deeper into the bush. At one point, I thought I heard what sounded like a nearby rain, but it did not fall on us. We continued. At length, we reached a watery glen. I stopped, still.

The glen was hushed of the chatter of the jungle. The only sound was that of the rush of water. Above us a river, confined between two hips of ridges mantled in a virgin green vestment, piled up behind two enormous boulders. A smooth, muscular arc of water plunged some ten feet between them to cascade brilliantly down into a boiling froth at the bottom. At the end of the spill of water foamed a pool of the purest, most limpid water I had ever seen, wreathed by slick, mossed boulders. The pool lay in a half-shadow.

The women drew me to the end of the path, which was marked by a little watercourse that descended like a flight of rock steps and disappeared into the pool. I stopped at the steps to look down on the liquid crystals splintering over the nearest rocks. I peered into the pool. It must have been very deep at its center, for there was no sign of any current. A wind rustled the leaves of the palms above, but did not ruffle the water's surface. The mirror image of the green cliff, clad in ferns and bromeliads, plunged into the depths. A large fish coasted just below the surface.

I was suddenly aware of the peace and shelter of the small, enclosed area. It was not until I no longer felt them that I became aware of the warm winds that had been blowing over me since we had first stepped onto the beach of the lagoon. The trade winds had followed us from the beach to the town and from the town into the jungle, only to stop at this enchanted glen.

I felt great charity toward these charming women who had brought me here to share their most lovely piece of the earth. This mood was quickly dispelled when they began plucking, quite rudely and incomprehensibly, at my dress. They pulled at the neckline sufficiently to pop one of the buttons that ran down the back. Now, the neckline itself was already ruined by my having earlier ripped the collar off, and this once-serviceable grey merino was forever ruined by such a series of travel stains that I would never again be able to wear it in fit company. But to have it ripped in such a strange fashion was really rather offensive.

Then I understood that they meant to undress me! It was difficult to know whether to be relieved or angrier still.

"What *are* you doing, ladies!" I exclaimed in my most imperious voice.

They might as well have answered, "Why, ma'am, popping all the buttons off your dress!" for they had just discovered that the back of the dress was closed by means of buttons, and it was at this moment that I realized that there was not a button or tie or fastening of any kind to be found anywhere on their garments.

"We're popping them off, one by one!" they seemed to say over and over, "and a very good game it is, too!"

There were twenty buttons or more, and each one as it popped caused them to exclaim with laughter. The buttons soared and hit the ground or glanced off a leaf or flipped one or the other of them in the arm or leg or stomach. As I have said, these women were young, but understand that they were not girls.

By the time I had finished my own exclamation of, "Stop this nonsense immediately!" my dress was effectively ruined—my *one* dress —and if it were not for the fact that I saw the young women busily seeking the gleefully popped buttons in the shrubbery, as if that were a further aspect of the game, I would have been well and truly angry.

As it was, by the time all the buttons were gone, they realized that there was another layer of clothing below. You cannot imagine the reaction *that* discovery provoked. They stripped off my dress and began to babble all the more excitedly among themselves over my chemise and underslip, then began to point at the water and some articles in the woven basket. *At last*, I understood that they were inviting me to bathe.

Now, here was a welcome thought, and the thought was mother to my sudden desire to plunge into that clean, clear water, this most enticing of baths with a free-flowing shower.

Catching the fun, my own imp got the better of me, and I laughed inwardly in anticipation of what their reaction would be when I lifted my underslip to show them white clothes below. I can assure you that their reaction was all that I would have hoped. They were reduced to a most gratifyingly undignified astonishment.

In the midst of all this silliness, I discovered that the women were also circumspect. When I was to divest myself of my underdress and white clothes, the woman who had been carrying the basket unfurled an enormous rectangle of cloth—it looked and felt to be a smooth, finely woven fiber, perhaps flax—and draped it in front of me, apparently for modesty's sake. I certainly appreciated the gesture, for displays of nakedness, even before women, were not entirely to my taste.

Along with the rest of my clothing, I shed bonnet, stockings, and shoes. When my simple cottons lay in a heap on the ground and I was wrapped in the cloth and ready to slip onto the water, I was handed a wooden bowl of some sticky, syrupy, putrid green substance that was, evidently but mysteriously, supposed to accompany my bath. I accepted the bowl with what I hoped was a look of inquiry rather than disgust.

I received no answer. The woman had turned her back to me, for my privacy, I realized, and had seated herself on the ground. The other women had picked up my clothes—dress, chemise, underslip, white clothes, shoes, stockings, and even my bonnet—and had taken them away as they headed down a secondary path that seemed to curve around the glen.

With nothing further to guide me, I hung my towel on the nearest branch and, wooden bowl in hand, waded into the pool, which was every bit as delicious as I had anticipated. I splished and splashed waist deep for some minutes, simply enjoying the clean after the bodily accumulation of salt, sweat, dirt, and sand of the past days. I sniffed at the bowl in hand and was surprised by its pleasant scent. I scooped a dab of the gooey green glue and rubbed it experimentally on my forearm. It made my skin a little shiny, but otherwise seemed to have no effect—at least, no adverse effect. Perhaps this substance was intended to clean the scalp! I tried a dollop at one temple, massaging it in, then tilted my head onto the water to rinse it off. My scalp felt wonderfully clean, and the tangles seemed to have fallen out of my very knotted tresses.

Need I describe how I spent the next half hour or more? It was glorious—the water fresh, my hair clean, feeling like a heavy skein of silk down my back, my skin scrubbed. The woman (my serving woman? my guard?) still sat, her back to me, straight and impassive. I had no desire to leave the water just yet, and in any case, my clothes had not returned.

I had not previously known exactly how to propel myself in water, so, staying to the edges, I stretched myself out on top of it with my arms above my head and fluttered my feet.

I paddled into a hidden corner of the pool where lay patches of sun. Here, the cascade was no longer visible, and the sound of its rushing water was muffled by baffles of mossy rock. The dappled green of the glen cradled me. I lay watching the silent sky above, filigreed through the swaying leaves. It was of a blue so intense that I had to close my eyes against the wonder of it. The radiance of the moment so far surpassed my imagination as to paralyze it.

You who know only the North, do not know color or light.

I floated for long minutes until the thought came to me: *This is paradise*. I sat up with a swirl of water. This was a wonderful and terrifying paradise, whose wonders and terrors I had not been left to face alone. That thought was both comfortable and uncomfortable.

At length, I emerged onto slick boulders on the opposite curve of the pool from where sat the woman accompanying me, still with her back to me, still immobile. Perhaps she was sleeping. On a boulder, I sat like a lizard, sunning. I mused and dozed and dreamed. My bones melted. My reverie lengthened.

Suddenly I was roused by the sounds of the returning women. They had been gone an extremely long time—so long, in fact, that my hair, as I sat on the boulder, was almost completely dry. At the sounds of their voices, I waded back into the pool, piling my hair on my head to keep it from rewetting, and glided with long strides through the water. I climbed up the opposite bank, caught the large towel from its branch, and had wound it around me by the time they had reached the end of the path and were standing in front of me.

They first handed me my slip, then my chemise, then turned modestly around so that I could dress in privacy. I noted that my undergarments smelled very sweet and clean, as if they had been washed and sun-and-wind dried. I accepted these garments gratefully, donned them, and then, by way of gesture, asked for the rest of my clothing.

No matter what gestures I employed, neither my shoes and stockings nor my bonnet were forthcoming, but I could live without those. After some gesticulating, I did manage to retrieve my white clothes, but my dress was nowhere to be seen. The woman with the basket had already taken up my towel and the wooden bowl and had begun to return down the path that led to town. I began to be very suspicious. Five women had brought me here. One woman—the one with the basket—was already on her way back. Only three women remained, and they began to coax me and prod me and were finally reduced to *pushing* me down the path with them. It seemed the fifth woman was in possession of my clothing. It seemed, furthermore, that I was to return to town and parade there in broad daylight *in my chemise and underslip*.

I had the whole of the return journey to contemplate this new and very unwelcome state of affairs. It was embarrassing. It was degrading. It was humiliating. It was *indecent*. And it was wonderfully comfortable and cool. I could not imagine what Mr. Winthrop would have to say on the subject when he next saw me in our caney, to which I was now heartily reluctant to return.

He had nothing at all to say about it, for, upon our return to the village, he was nowhere to be seen, either in our caney or in town. As a matter of fact, I realized that *no* man had been seen in town during the day, either going to the pool or returning from it. The only men I had seen that morning had been far away in the fields, effectively out of sight. Not even the oldest of old men were there, squatting on the ground or napping in the shade.

The town itself was occupied solely by women and young children, and from the extent of business and industry in town—weaving, pottery, preparation of the food, care of the children—it seemed that *all* the women must have been in town. This meant that all the men must have been out tilling or hunting or doing whatever it was that Arawak men did, Mr. Winthrop with them. Could this be a regular part of daily life, I wondered?

It took but a moment's reflection for this strict separation of the sexes to strike me as an extremely *reasonable* way to conduct a society. Although the women in town were constantly occupied, I found the town peaceful, with quiet rhythms which were no doubt as pleasant for the mothers as for the children. I thoroughly enjoyed the rest of the day, which was broken by several small meals. I was given no tasks to do, so I simply strolled about the town (constantly accompanied by two women at my back) in my underclothes, my hair unbound. Although my parasol which I had fetched drew some notice, no one took the least interest in my state of undress. Of course, there was more than one reason for that.

Since there are a variety of moral lessons to be derived from this tale of exceptional adventure, this is perhaps the moment in my narrative to mention that some of the young women in town—not the girls, mind you, but the *women*—appeared in public half-naked. Yes. I mean, quite unambiguously, that some of the young women (and, I must say, *well-developed* young women) wore nothing above their waists except thick armbands of gold, layers of necklaces of gold mixed indifferently with necklaces of shells, and large, looped earrings. Lest anyone think that I am not reporting this strange custom accurately, allow me to remark that it is highly unlikely for one's eyes to mistake when a woman's torso is clothed, and when it is not. Although I might add the further testimony, if any is needed, of Mr.

Winthrop's interest in this custom, I do not wish to waste words with an exact description of his evident, albeit unexpressed appreciation of the particular examples of feminine nakedness that he had seen earlier in the day at the threshold of our caney.

I repeat that not all of the young women were thus exposed. The Arawak children—both boys and girls—went completely naked, as far as I could tell, until about the age of five. This was quite shocking in itself, but it paled against what I considered to be the nakedness that really *mattered*. Nursing mothers, I noted, were wrapped in rather elaborate halters. However, I also saw many a young woman who was not tending an infant and who was fully clothed.

Now, "fully clothed" is apparently a relative concept among the Arawak. An Arawak woman's skirt, for instance, is not distinguished one from the other, as it is in England, by quality of material, cut, and amount of decoration. The material was on every Arawak woman the same, and all the cloth was equally bright and quite beautifully colored in vivid shades of red, yellow, pink, orange, or saffron. Rather, the Arawak woman's skirt (the dress is called, in Arawak, a *nagua,* I later learned) is distinguished entirely by length. There appeared to be three lengths: midthigh, knee, or midcalf. After some observation, I noted that the longer the skirt, the more gold jewelry the woman wore. This was not difficult to interpret, and must have indicated class; the respective tasks of the women seemed to bear my hypothesis out. The chief's mother, for instance, was fully clothed, her skirt fell to midcalf, she wore an enormous amount of gold jewelry, and she did absolutely nothing except croon weird melodies. I easily understood this correlation.

What puzzled me, however, was the fact that several curvaceous young women who wore long skirts and quite as much jewelry as the chief's mother were nevertheless only *half* clothed. This meant, then, that the question of bodice covering was *not* correlated with the apparent ranks that existed among the Arawak. A particularly beautiful and extremely shapely (though I was no judge of Arawak standards of beauty) young woman of high rank caught my eye almost from the first. She had long, black hair which she wound with gold thread, large, sloe eyes, and was very proud of her carriage, from the way she swished her long skirt about her hips to the way she thrust forward her very naked—Well, I hardly need to elaborate.

It so happened that this young Arawak beauty was also laden with a Spanish galleon's worth of gold, and she reminded me of that hateful Miss Castleragh, whose father was commissary general just below my father's command and who had never liked me. She had been wearing what looked to be her mother's entire jewelry box that evening at the gala military affair at Hounslow Heath honoring King James's newest high-ranking appointments, unfortunately, from the Irish commands. That night my father had been accused of having sold British naval secrets to the Spanish for fifty thousand pounds.

I shall never forget the vulgar glitter of Miss Castleragh's jewelry that night, or the wicked gleam of malicious satisfaction in her eyes when they fell on me only moments after that stunning denunciation was made in front of some three hundred guests. I must say that this proud, strutting Arawak woman looked to be cut from the same cloth as Miss Castleragh. Although I was willing to allow for prejudice on my part against the Arawak woman on account of her chance similarity to Miss Castleragh, my initial judgment of her was not proven wrong by subsequent events.

In any case, it occurred to me that this (how shall I say?) *unseemly* mode of undress for the young women was perhaps the reason behind the strict separation of the sexes during the day. Now, if that were the case, an easy solution to the problem would be simply to cover the young women so that the men could go about their work undistracted. Perhaps there was a shortage of cloth in the community, which consideration led me to think of the three bolts I had saved from the dying *Judith* and a very good way to improve the moral tone of the community.

About that cloth—it was uppermost on my mind when I ambled onto the main town square or, rather, circle. Upon my return from the bath, I had been pleased to find that my tapestry bag and all of its contents had been deposited in the caney—not, however, Mr. Winthrop's leather case, or the bolts of cloth. I had been wondering how to communicate my desire to recover the cloth. When I arrived at the main circle, however, I did not have to rack my brains further, for the bolts of cloth were completely unfolded and festooned between the huts that formed the focus of the circle: long, wide, yellow-and-green-flowered and blue-striped garlands, quite horrifically decorating the tribal village! I had never seen *anything* in worse taste. I decided then and there that if the Arawak wished to do something useful with the cloth in addition to properly covering some of the young women, they might do very well to cover that hideous statue in the center of the circle which, now that I had a good look at it in broad daylight, was quite, *quite* obscene. I had every intention to suggest such a scheme to the chief's mother at the earliest opportunity.

That opportunity did not immediately arise. At the end of what was, for me, a rather pleasant though somewhat fretful day, since I was still eager to leave the island without further delay, I was drawn into the preparations for the evening meal. This occurred just as the sun was setting in an explosion of oranges, yellows, and violets, and there was still no sign of men in town. However, when the moon came up full and luminous, as if it were perched on the other end of a see-saw, the men returned.

This evening I inevitably noticed an important feature of Arawak dining that had escaped me the evening before: the men and women were separated again, just as they had been during the day. The chief and his mother were seated side by side, as I had noticed the evening before, but now I saw that the men sat on the chief's right, the women on the chief's mother's left. I realized that I must have been seated on the men's side at the feast the evening before. I was almost offended, after the fact.

This seating meant that I did not have an opportunity to speak with Mr. Winthrop when he returned to town. In fact, I did not immediately perceive him in the throng of men on the opposing side of the circle, and so I missed his initial reaction to my state of dress, which I had forgotten about anyway. Halfway through the meal, however, I felt someone's eyes on me, and when I looked up and met Mr. Winthrop's gaze, I thought for one horrifying moment that I, like some of the other young women, was missing my bodice. I looked down hastily and was reassured that my chemise was in place, the drawstring securely tied between my breasts. When I looked back over at him, he had directed his attention, discreetly, elsewhere.

The dinner was, again, very tasty. This evening I was not as ravenous as I had been the evening before, and so I attributed my enjoyment of the meal to the fact that it actually tasted very good. The vegetables were succulent, the fish done to a turn, and all the dishes were every bit as copious as they had been the evening before. Either they always ate that way (which made me think that Mr. Winthrop and I had been less honored guests than I had initially supposed), or the feasting (in our honor) was continuing. The dancers came out again, then the warriors, and I found it ever so much more enjoyable from the sidelines than I did when I had been on my knees in the midst of it all. However, each particular step performed by the dancers and warriors seemed to be repeated into a rather boring monotony, so that I must say that I lost interest, after a while. Still, it was better being bored than scared witless.

At length, the feasting was over and I was escorted back to the caney. Mr. Winthrop was not inside, and so I chose to stand at the door, leaning against the rough jamb, bathing in the silver moonlight. I was glad I did so, for as I peered into the surrounding darkness, I did perceive the forms of two men crouching in the shadows of another caney nearby. Mr. Winthrop had been right: we were being guarded. Then another furtive shadow slunk around another nearby caney, but I was too absorbed in my own thoughts to really care. I was wondering, in fact, given the strict separation of the sexes during the day, whether Mr. Winthrop might not be housed elsewhere for the night. Although our separation would make our eventual escape together more difficult to plan and execute, it would certainly relieve other, perhaps more *fundamental* problems. I deemed such a separation quite probable, even desirable.

That comfortable conclusion was routed when Mr. Winthrop suddenly appeared before me, his leather case in hand, his silk shirt on his back, half-buttoned. He stood in front of me, saying nothing at first. He ran his eye over my chemise and underdress with one quick, almost imperceptible but comprehensive glance. When he looked back up, I could not read his eyes. Then he took my wrist lightly but firmly between his fingers, and led me inside.

"No show of disunity just now," he said very softly into my ear. "The guards are watching. Come in compliantly."

I did so. We entered the soft blackness of the caney. He immediately released my wrist and spoke low into my ear, "There does not seem to be any way around it," he said in evident reference to our sharing of this roof. "I cannot risk so much as poking my head outside tonight. We're being watched very closely."

He placed his leather bag over against the wall where all the utensils were grouped, then came back to the center of the caney, where I was still standing.

"I got my case back, as you see, but I haven't found the boat yet," he said, murmuring low into my ear. He put his hands lightly on my shoulders, directing me to seat myself on the mat. Sitting himself down, cross-legged, a foot away from me, he continued on the question, "Have you, by any chance, seen it in town?"

"No, but I didn't look for it, either," I said.

"You would have seen it, I think, if it was here," he said idly. "It'll turn up sometime." Then, as if losing interest in the whereabouts of the means of our escape, he remarked, "I wasn't allowed within a hundred yards of the town limits. What did you do today?"

"Mostly, took a bath," I said.

"So did I."

"Oh, in the pool in the glen?"

"Glen? No," he said. "In a river."

I considered this. "They even have separate bathing places?" I wondered aloud.

"Sure, now, separate everything," he said to this. "You cannot imagine the ruckus that was raised when I set foot in what must have been the women's garden. Faith! I didn't understand it, but I got out of there fast. In any case, the bath did me good. Got a haircut, too, in the bargain."

I peered over at him closely. The moonlight that crept into the caney was dim, but it was sufficient for me to see that his hair was in every bit as good an order as mine. I had noted earlier in the day that the locks at his temples had been singed by the cannon matches. (I had, of course, been too tactful to mention it to him, since the trick with the cannon matches was really his most spectacular idea.) These damaged locks had now been cut, and his hair had a scent reminiscent of the green syrup I had used on mine, though different—with a masculine appeal. It was tied back in a short braid. I could see that he was clean-shaven, too. His shirt was open and the delicate lace fell incongruously against the hard muscles of his chest.

I could have shared quite a lot of observations with him just then, but I suddenly remembered that I was wearing only a chemise and an underslip, so I drew away, a little hastily, to sit back on my heels.

"And your wound?" I asked, as impersonally as I was able, under the highly personal circumstances.

"They put something on it," he said. I heard a note of indifference in his voice. He did not think much about his wounds. "Herbs or something. I don't even feel it. They took your lace. I have no idea where it is."

"Probably the same place as my dress!" I exclaimed, low, with indignation.

To this observation, he wisely did not comment.

"They have taken my pins, too—and your hair riband," I continued, "not to mention the bolts of cloth and the boat! They take entirely too much upon themselves, I'm thinking!"

"I'm thinking that they're in a position to take whatever they want," he replied. "And they definitely want something from us—but what?"

"Perhaps we will discover it better in the morning," I suggested, hinting that it was time to end this intimate whispering in the dark.

He was not disposed to retire. Understanding my hint, he shook his head. "No, not yet. Speak to me, Sedgwick," he said simply. He withdrew the knife and pistol he kept in the waistband of his breeches and placed them behind him on the mat. Then, stretching his length out and propping his elbow on the ground, head in palm, he went on, "After a day listening to that gibberish, I welcome the sound of your voice—no matter what nonsense you might have to say for yourself."

"No matter what nonsense I might have to say for myself?" I repeated in a voice dangerously calm.

"Well, how much sensible conversation could I expect from a partner who does not perceive the differences between a musket and a parasol? And it *was* rather maddening to have seen my brilliant plan foiled in such an idiotic manner."

"Well! Now we are at the heart of the matter, I suppose!" I said in a harsh, low whisper. "Your plan was very ingenious, I'll grant you that, but its ultimate value was far more in the realm of good entertainment than effective diversionary tactics! And as for the musket and the parasol, I take leave to tell you that I will not now—or ever—aim a firearm at a human being who is not in any way directly threatening my existence. And I must say that, so far, the Arawak have been kind and welcoming to us, despite the fact that they are holding us against our will—although, in all fairness to them, they might not know what our will is! But to blame me entirely for the unusual situation in which we now find ourselves is beyond what is acceptable, and I won't have it! Besides, you don't know—*you really don't know*—whether or not we are better or worse circumstanced at present than any of the rest of the crew and passengers from the *Judith*!"

I felt, rather than saw him, smile. "Aaaahhh," he said to this tirade, "music to my ears."

Talk about taking the wind out of my sails! "You are a provoking man!" was all I could think of to say.

"And you a provoking woman," he retorted lazily.

We had veered toward improper ground here, so I shifted the subject immediately. "Well, if I had known you were wanting to chat, I would have brought the chair over. I do not find sitting back on my calves and heels all day particularly comfortable."

"I would fetch it for you now," he offered with spurious gallantry, "save for the fact that I do not wish our movements within to draw the attention of our guards—and there are still two of them out there, in case you had not noticed. We are not well enough acquainted with their customs to risk drawing even closer observation. Little as I like the present arrangement, I would like it far less to be separated or have the guards move in with us!"

I was so strongly in agreement with him on this score that I really had nothing to say beyond a heartfelt, "Very true!" Besides, I had not really wished or expected him to fetch the chair, thoughts of which prompted me to contemplate my next few days without proper furniture. "What I wouldn't give for my next meal to be taken at a table and for me to be seated upon a chair," I said, "with a linen tablecloth thrown in for good measure!"

I heard him chuckle, as if from far away. "Tables and chairs?" he echoed, consideringly. "I could live without them, if I had to. No. But what I wouldn't give right now for a blood-red steak and a pint of stout," he mused. He paused, as if in reflection. "And the sounds of a tavern," he added after a moment. "English voices. The jests, the singing. Even the curses would sound good."

"The click of carriage wheels, as well, and the clip of horses' hooves outside," I said, adding to this. "Or just the very street—*any* street, cobbled or clean." Suddenly, the entire tableau of a London street sprang, full-blown, in my mind's eye. "The men and women," I continued, "all of them fully dressed! The traffic, the bustle, the store windows, bowed so beautifully and brimming with wares. Why, even the sound of church bells, marking the quarter hours. I am not sure I realized how much I missed them until this very moment!" A wave of pure homesickness washed over me.

We sat, the two of us, in the dark, on the dirt-packed floor of a caney somewhere in the Caribbean, swimming in our memories, lost in reflection. The mental image of the outline of the Houses of Parliament wrapped in a fog at dusk caused me a particular pang, although, in all honesty, that building had no good association for me in the wake of the nightmare of the scandal that was the indirect cause of my present predicament on this Caribbean island.

"Away with such thoughts," my companion said abruptly. "We cannot afford to indulge them."

He was right, of course. We would make ourselves sick and ineffectual if we pursued thoughts of home. "Look for the silver lining," Nanny always used to say.

"I could learn to love this weather," I offered.

"While I," he said, following my lead, "could easily accustom myself to a life without church bells. It was not until you mentioned them that I realized how little I missed them." He paused in reflection. "No time. No schedule. Just the sun and the moon and the stars." He began to sound almost dreamy. "No churches, either." He laughed, as if to himself. "And no religion, no politics."

Since he had mentioned the subject of religion and politics, I ventured the comment, "But with James, an avowed Catholic, now on the throne, wouldn't you be better circumstanced in a return to England than you were when you left to take up with the French?"

He looked up, directly at me. "The Irish will always be the enemy in England," he said with a degree of blunt truth.

"You are not *fully* Irish," I suggested.

He shook his head. "But I'll never be Anglican. In any case, James is narrow-minded and vindictive, and, like all the Stuarts, essentially a wrong-headed man. He'll never keep the throne. The English will be inviting William of Orange to come from Holland to rule before the year is out."

As outrageous as it seemed, I recognized that his statement was not completely implausible. However, in the wake of my father's scandal, I had not been closely attending to the shifting political winds in my last few weeks at home, and so did not know how shaky James's throne was, or was not, at the moment.

"Having campaigned against the Spanish in the Netherlands should nevertheless serve you well, if you decided to return," I said, all the while assuming that we would, indeed, return.

He shrugged. "I've had enough of following the fife and drum, and I have a long-ingrained aversion to red coats." At that, he grinned.

"Not a soldier at heart?" I queried.

"Nor a medic, but a man does what he must," he replied and left the subject. "And you? What do you miss least?"

I knew the answer to that without further reflection. "The eyes staring at me," I said.

He did not immediately seize this topic for discussion, and when he did, he surprised me with his approach. "Was it bad for you?" was the question he posed first.

"Worse than you can imagine," I replied with brutal honesty. In the dark of this caney, I knew the impulse to explain, if only a little. It is such a *relief*, after all, to unburden oneself. "All because of a vicious rumor against my father—and without the least shred of proof!"

"No proof?" was his next question.

The money my father was supposed to have pocketed as a bribe had never been uncovered. The paymaster general had been put on the case to discover in any bank or investment house the incredible sum of money reported in Major General Sedgwick's possession. Not a piece of silver or gold had been found in my father's name—not a note or scrap of paper to confirm the report.

"Not the least shred of proof," I repeated, "and within days after he was denounced before all of his colleagues and peers, he died of heart failure, and so was no longer around to defend himself against the ugliness!"

A silence fell. It lengthened.

"Do you doubt the report, then?" he asked, almost conversationally.

I would not answer that. Unfortunately, my father had suffered financially—grievously so—in the wasted campaigns and commissions of Charles II, who had been succeeded by James a scant three years before. Thus, my father was believed by a good many people, once the denunciation was made, to have wanted to recoup his losses. However, many *others* had lost personal fortunes in the general disarray of the military during the Restoration, and many of them had been present at the gala at Hounslow Heath. It was from *that* quarter of government officials that I suspected the strongest belief in my father's culpability had come.

"So far from thinking my father guilty of any wrongdoing, I think it was rather the . . . the *adventurer* who started the ugly rumor who had the most guilt to cover! For, what else could a man be who had roamed the Continent all those years, as my father's denouncer was said to have done!"

To this, Mr. Winthrop merely chuckled softly.

I perceived the extreme insult of my words, but it was not a topic on which I could speak with any moderation. Thus, when I attempted to make amends with the words: "Excuse me if I insult one of your kind!" I sounded a little haughty and very ungracious.

Mr. Winthrop must have understood my emotions, for he took no offense. "Oh, you think me an adventurer—a bravo for hire, perhaps?" he inquired indifferently. "I've been called worse, I assure you!"

"Not a thief, a liar, and a murderer, at any rate!" I retorted, keeping my voice soft and in as much control as I could. "Which is what *that* man is for having stolen my father's reputation, for having lied about the facts, and for having precipitated my father's death!"

Again, he made no immediate response to these disclosures. Then, "Don't be forgetting, Sedgwick, that I was a soldier for many years and became a trader after that, and have been all of those things— murderer, liar, and thief."

I had no wish to insult Mr. Winthrop gratuitously; and although I had not directly alluded to who my father was or what he was supposed to have done, I was reassured that in his response to my accusations, Mr. Winthrop's voice had registered a note of kindly and discreet understanding.

After a moment, he asked almost irrelevantly, "And, poor Edward? What line of work was he in?"

"Mr. Lipscomb," I said coolly, "was in the foreign service. I need not hide the fact from you that he specialized in peninsular affairs, as it happened."

"Ah, sure, now," he said softly, as if he suddenly understood something.

"And you?" I asked, wishing to put this topic behind me. "What do you miss least about England? Or, alternatively, what do you like most about our island?"

I could feel his eyes on me in the dark. "Do you really want to know?" he asked, this time with a somewhat dangerous note, I thought, in his voice. I sat back away from him, on my heels. Then I saw him shake his head. "I'll tell you later. For now, Sedgwick, to bed," he said. He rose at that, in one graceful movement. When I did not move, he pulled me up off the floor by my forearms, then released me immediately.

"My legs protest such seating arrangements," I said weakly.

His response was light: "You may just have to get used to it. It's early days yet." He did not elaborate. Then, he instructed, "On your sleeping net, the long sides fold over as covers."

He did not help me into the net but retreated to his side of the caney. I climbed awkwardly into this most ridiculous bed. For a few moments afterward the net swung gently. Although I thought this a perfectly barbaric way to sleep, I found it comfortable enough, once the swinging had subsided. I pulled the flaps of the net over me, although I was not at all cold.

I heard Mr. Winthrop climb into his sleeping net and stretch out, sighing. His sigh was laced, oddly enough, with contentment. "I'll keep looking for the boat tomorrow," he said, and continued with a remarkably dissonant array of observations, "Maybe we'll be able to shove off the day after. By the by, that underdress becomes you—a vast improvement over that miserable grey frock, even at its best. The

Arawak don't want us to leave—of that, I'm sure. I wish I knew why. Good night, Sedgwick."

I have already noted Mr. Winthrop's flair for the left-handed compliment. Suspended in the air, surrounded by my fate, I began to think Mr. Winthrop a rather remarkable person, considering that he was a man.

CHAPTER 7

I quickly discovered that Mr. Winthrop was not the only remarkable person in town.

My second day among the Arawak was much like the first, save that I made no trip to the glen. Again, I spent the day exclusively among women, and again, I was given no tasks to perform. With the run of the village (that is, always with two women at my back) I had really nothing better to do than to watch and observe them at work.

They were very industrious, scrupulously clean—as were all the Arawak—and quite beautiful, viewed collectively. I attempted to decompose the mass. At first, they were totally indistinguishable one from the other, with their black hair and eyes, and moon faces. Of course, I had already noticed that they could be differentiated by the various lengths of their skirts, their bodice coverings, and the varying amounts of jewelry they wore. After that, I began to perceive that one young woman had, in addition to gold loops in her ears, a gold stud in her nose (I found that singularly unattractive). Another woman was fat, while a third had a small scar on one cheek. Their noses came in different widths, as well, and so, by the end of the day and the evening meal, I had come to see rather greater individuality than I had first perceived.

Miss Castleragh's copper-skinned double, the beauty with the haughty ways and all the gold jewelry, crossed my path on several occasions this day. On one of these, she gave me a look that would have passed at any English fete or rout or ball as "giving me the cut direct." On another of these, she actually stopped in her tracks and ran her eye over me, appraisingly, critically.

She even addressed some words to me (incomprehensible, of course), but to my profound amazement, her voice reminded me forcefully of Miss Castleragh's. Perhaps it was only the effect of an overactive imagination, for I imagined, as well, that she said to me the very words that that hateful Julianna Castleragh had said only moments after my father's denunciation. "Mrs. Lipscomb," she had breathed, sweetly, falsely, "what a dreadful turn for you! How can you bear the shame?"

"Easily," I replied with bravado. "I can more easily bear true shame than support these wicked lies."

"But, all the money your father lost last year . . ." she said suggestively, but did not finish the phrase, as if, by the very mention of the fact, she had proven his guilt. She continued without a pause, "And it now becomes clear why he planned his trip to the New World. Why, my father was telling me of it just the other night, marveling that the major general should choose just this moment to be away from London for such an extended period!"

"If you know so much about it, then you will also know that the trip," I replied, angry that his private movements should have been so widely known and discussed, "has been planned for ages and had the full blessing of the duke of York and the Office of Ordnance."

To this she merely smiled and prophesied, "But I do not suppose he will be taking it now, with or without anyone's blessing. And Mr. Lipscomb?" she queried, going in for the kill. "How shall he take the news? Shall he be able to retain his seat on the parliamentary committee and his general direction of the —th Foot, I wonder?"

Toward the end of Edward's courtship of me, Miss Castleragh had decided to let her roving eye fall on Edward. Her reference to him just then had positively *slain* me, for I knew that she had informed all of London that Edward had married me instead of her because I was the major general's daughter, and her father was the lesser-ranked commissary general.

"Mr. Lipscomb," I replied with what would become awful irony, as I looked around for him (he was nowhere to be seen), "will be as unaffected by this as will be my father."

For some extremely odd reason, it was just at that moment in our conversation that I had a vision of Edward standing at the door to my father's library, holding a large, flat packet in his hand. I saw that it was decorated with a variety of franks that looked foreign, probably Spanish. When I had asked him about it, he had answered evasively.

I shook my head clear of all these reminiscences. There was no reason to remember that disastrous evening, my father, his booking on the *Judith*, Edward, the flat packet, or how right Julianna Castleragh had been on all counts.

The very next moment, the Arawak woman moved on. As her hips swung away from me, I dubbed her The Proud One.

For the most part, as the day unfolded, I familiarized myself with the general run of female society. It was extremely orderly. The greatest numbers of women seemed to be occupied in hand labor: pottery-making, tilling the women's garden, and the messier side of food preparation—the gutting of the catch and the grinding of the meal. From the short length of their skirts and the complete absence of jewelry, these must have been the laborers. Then came the women who seemed to perform "inside" tasks: tending the children, weaving, basketry. They seemed to be, in short, the "bourgeoisie." These were also the ones who had served at dinner.

A third group must have corresponded to the petty nobility, for I recognized among them those who had been seated around me at the meal the evening before. From that group had also come the women who had accompanied me the day before to my bath. Their faces were open and friendly when they saw me strolling about the town, but they made no effort to communicate with me (which might have been due to the fact that I could not have understood them, anyway) or to make any other kind of contact with me. The Proud One, need I say, belonged to the highest echelons of Arawak society, called in Arawak the *caciques*, and seemed to spend most of her day preening and dancing idly to music made by her handmaids.

The evening meal was, again, copious and delicious, the dancing diverting. I exchanged several meaningful glances with Mr. Winthrop across the circle. This evening, however back at the caney, Mr. Winthrop was not disposed to intimate confidences, as he had been on the evening before. In fact, he scarcely glanced at me when we were alone together. When I heard him climb into his sleeping net, I discovered the reason for his reticence. As he stretched his length out, he breathed three words which told the story of his search for our boat, and they were: "No luck today."

The next day passed *exactly* as the one before, in that I found on this third morning a fresh frangipani flower at the door to the caney, just as I had the day before. Yesterday, I had paid no attention to it. This morning, as well, I chose to ignore it. I would have asked Mr. Winthrop about it, however, he was up and out of the caney before dawn and out of town for the day with the rest of the men. By evening, I would have forgotten entirely about it.

On this third day, with nothing productive to do, I must admit that I was becoming bored and frankly irritated and dissatisfied. It was all the more irritating to me to be kept from useful activity because with my high sense of purpose, I saw very, very many ways to *improve* this village.

Added to which, the dinner and evening's entertainment was the same, and while they were still so fresh and exotic that they should not have failed to fascinate me, I was most unreceptive to the charms of this primitive life. I found myself increasingly anxious to be gone from this island.

Mr. Winthrop evidently shared my anxiety. This evening, after the dinner feast, he got to the caney before me. When I came in he drew me by the arm to him, then let his hand fall.

"We've got to get off this island, Sedgwick," he said. His voice held a certain urgency.

"Did you find—?" I began.

He shook his head before I could finish the question about the boat. "They've hidden it. They know I'm looking for it." Then he repeated, on that same note of determination, "We've got to get out of here. Something is brewing."

I had already determined that Mr. Winthrop viewed our situation among the Arawak in worse light than I did, but I was not going to argue with him about the urgency with which I now felt we should leave this island—and perhaps for other reasons than he had fashioned for himself. So I said nothing, simply nodded wordlessly.

"However, I've seen their canoes," he said, "and I know where they keep them. They haven't let me within a dozen yards of one in the past two days. But today I shook off my guards for a while and found where they store them. I have devised a plan for us to get away in one of the canoes tomorrow night."

"You have?" I answered in real relief. His voice sounded confident, and the words, "I've devised a plan," had a nice ring. It sounded excellent.

What I thought, I said. "Excellent."

"You're with me, then?" he asked.

"Oh, yes," I said immediately.

"I've studied the charts and don't expect that we will have to be on open sea more than three or four days," he said. "Can you make it?"

"Oh, yes," I said again, a little less immediately. A thought inevitably occurred to me. "Incidentally, what is a canoe?"

In the dim light of the caney, I saw the white flash of teeth in a grin. He answered my question directly. From his explanation, I gathered that a canoe was essentially a tree trunk, hollowed out by means of burning. This sounded even less promising than a rowboat as a means of transporting oneself across unknown, but certainly shark-infested waters. I advanced this well-considered opinion. Mr. Winthrop pointed out that we would not be completely adrift in the waters of the Caribbean Sea for there were paddles to go along with the canoe. As first mate I, too, would have rowing privileges.

"Well, then, how can I refuse?" I said to this.

"How, indeed?" came the response.

He then told me of his plan. I found two flaws. "You mean *steal* one of their canoes?" I asked, in reference to the first flaw.

"Scruples, Sedgwick?"

"Well, it does seem rather mean to steal one of their canoes, especially after knocking our two guards unconscious with a large rock," I countered, very reasonably, by the way of mentioning the second of my objections to his plan. "There are bounds of courtesy, after all, Mr. Winthrop. We would do well to respect the minimum."

Mr. Winthrop paused. After a moment, he said, very casually, "You need not accompany me, Sedgwick. You are free to stay here."

This argument was particularly compelling. "Then let us agree not to hit them very *hard*," I said to this.

After that, we discussed the particulars, determined our two courses of action for the next day, and set our escape for midnight the next night.

And then something happened to me (the most natural thing in the world) that transformed our relationship to the Arawak.

The fourth day began exactly as the first two, except for the fact that when I arose, I was conscious of feeling now distinctly bored and irritated with what, no doubt, lay ahead of me during the day, added to which was the anxiety of the proposed escape. I was glad to have at least one task to occupy me, and that was the surreptitious filling of our precious water bottle, along with the collecting of whatever other vessels of liquid I could find to take with us. I had pretty well abandoned the idea of finding my dress before we left. As for my hair pins, I had consigned them to oblivion.

Exactly as on the other days, a scarlet frangipani blossom lay at the threshold to the caney, but the sight of it this morning provoked me most unreasonably. I supposed now that there was some significance attached to the gesture, and this, too, for some reason irritated me, added to which I did not even like the flower's oppressive perfume. Being an eminently reasonable woman, I should have guessed the cause of my irritability, but I did not, for this singular experience among the Arawak had disordered my sense of time. And even if I had guessed it, I would not have been able to predict the consequences of it.

So it was that I was escorted for a second time to the glen for a bath. Although it had been hot the days before, the trade winds blew incessantly to cool a body; and despite the dirt everywhere in the village, it was not at all dirty, really, or even dusty. Thus, neither was I particularly dirty or dusty. Nevertheless, the idea of a bath was *particularly* welcome just then.

To the glen I went, accompanied this time by only three women—two acting as handmaidens, one as the servant. The prospect of the fresh, clean water caressing my skin cheered me the entire way. As before, we arrived at the end of the path; as before, I was handed a towel; as before, I disrobed—this time, of course, with much *less* clothing to discard.

My chemise, underdress, and small clothes in a pretty heap, I slung my towel over the nearest hanging branch and had my toes poised over the water purling across the slick stones, when a wild series of shrieks right at my back rent the air. I grabbed the towel to me, my heart hammering, and whirled to see all three women holding up my garments and exclaiming with an excitement that crackled as a bolt of lightning.

It took me a moment to sort out the source of their transports. Then I saw in the center of my small clothes several flecks of blood. My time of the month had come. (The reader must excuse my extreme indelicacy at mention of this purely personal and, indeed, private matter, in order to understand everything that ensued and the role into which Mr. Winthrop was forced. The reader will also begin to appreciate how one's moral sense can go awry when one is removed from a proper setting—which will go a long way in explaining some of my actions, much later. But, again, I anticipate.)

My immediate thought was: *Thank goodness I did not discover this in the midst of the Caribbean Sea in a dugout tree trunk in the company of Mr. Winthrop!* (At this point, you see, I still retained all sense of propriety.) My second thought was: *The bath will be positively divine!*

Although their excitement over my present condition was somewhat prolonged, I thought, and disproportionate to the routine, even mundane event which should have concerned no one save myself, I had no thought beyond taking my bath. The rather vague thought was forming in the back of my mind that there would be time enough this afternoon to collect the cloth necessary to take care of my condition during the next three or four days at sea. Assuming the women would wash my clothes, as before, I turned to immerse myself in the water.

I was hauled, abruptly and quite ungently, away from the water by my elbows. However, if I was astonished by this rude action, the looks I apprehended on their normally cheerful faces when they turned me toward them were of blankest horror. An excited babble and excited gestures indicated that I was not to go in the water. This, of course, was directly against my wishes at the moment, and so I tried to shake them off, to make them understand that there was nothing I would rather do just then than to have my bath.

I will *not* recount the indignity of being propelled down the jungle path, away from the glen, by three Arawak women who were much stronger than they first appeared. (I did put them to the test, too. I would have been a match for two of them, but I could not wrest away from three.) *Neither* will I recount what it was like to travel through town wrapped in a mere towel. I had almost become accustomed to parading in my undress, but appearing in public—even a public composed solely of women—in nothing but a large piece of cloth tried my customary good nature to its very limit and beyond. *Nor* will I deign to describe the precise events that occurred once I had been dragged (there is no other word for it) through town to a hut where I was to spend the next three days in seclusion.

With my great respect for verbal restraint, I will limit my discussion to remarking that this hut, placed in a far corner of the town, just beyond what I perceived as its outer circle, was the only Arawak structure I had seen that was square and not round. It was also very small. It nestled in the shade of a scarlet frangipani tree (you can imagine the feelings of revulsion that I experienced being surrounded by *that* scent for the next few days!), and its floor was laid with palm fronds.

The matriarch had been called, and in her presence, I was pushed upon that thick mat of leaves, covered with nothing but my towel, while another cloth was laid upon my head and my face was smeared with a red paint. When I first attempted to wipe it off with the cloth on my head, it was made clear to me that my hands would be bound behind my back if I attempted such another action. I did not. I was also not allowed to leave the hut for any reason whatsoever, and my food was pushed to me regularly over the threshold. This food was most definitely *not* up to the standards of the feasts. It was bland and tasteless and mushy.

As the final indignity, three women guards were placed in a circle about ten feet from the door of the hut, and the guard was changed around the clock, so to speak.

I had *three entire days* in which to reflect on the savagery—nay, then, the *barbarism* of these Arawak and their customs. I also had three days in which to fret about Mr. Winthrop, the proposed escape, my long-term future, the profound differences between a parasol and a musket, and the sober truth of checking for rotted ring fittings. As for company, the rackety cheeping of a bottle-green hummingbird inside the hut and the ceaseless *co-kii, co-kii* of tree frogs outside did *not* improve my mood. By the time my confinement was over, I had concluded that Mr. Winthrop was long gone from the island. As for my own fate, I only hoped that he would have the decency to alert the English authorities in Jamaica of my plight on this godforsaken island. Barring that, I was prepared now to make it known to the Arawak that I would be leaving this island myself *under no uncertain terms*, even if I had to swim away.

At sundown of the third day, I was bade to rise and leave the hut. I squinted into the west. The last sullen streaks of sunset scarred the sky, like bleeding wounds. I was greeted by the same five women who had attended me on that first day. They bathed me now, head to toe, with a cloth and a large bowl of water. It is a comment on my condition that my gratefulness overrode my embarrassment at this intimate washing. I was also given my own chemise, underskirt, and small clothes. Such, again, was my condition, that after a scant week among the Arawak, instead of feeling only half-dressed, I found these undergarments the height of modesty and good taste. My hair was brushed until it gleamed, and a wreath of yellow buds (they resembled flowering nightshade) was set upon my head as a crown. By then, the color in the sky had been drained, leaving the clouds a smoky blue.

I was escorted back to town center as the now-familiar purple of the night sky enveloped us and slowly blossomed with its riotous bouquet of star-flowers. I was hungry for real food and apprehensive now about what strange custom the Arawak could possibly inflict on me next; deeper down, I was even a little sick with fear, given the stunning éclat with which my women's courses had operated on the Indians. I wondered what role they intended for me. Thus, when we emerged to a full view of the sweep of the circle, I was almost overjoyed to see Mr. Winthrop standing a few feet out from the semicircle of men, legs planted as a warrior's spears in the ground, arms akimbo, his face grave and impassive.

As I embraced this scene, I felt scales fall from my eyes. I was seeing Arawak society—*really seeing it*—for the very first time. Perhaps one (and the *only*) benefit of my seclusion was that my disjointed impressions of what had been going on around me in the few days I had spent among the Arawak before my seclusion suddenly fused together into a coherent whole. I no longer saw the Indians as stage players whose actions were to me at times quaint, at others incomprehensible, but whose essential "play-acting" was in no real doubt in my mind.

As I look back on it, I had expected either that the Arawak would eventually throw up their hands and take low bows for their performances, signaling to me that the play was over and I could go home, or that I had only to penetrate a few feet beyond that part of the island I had seen and I would find the "wings" backstage which would take me out onto a "real" city street.

In this arresting moment of insight, I understood that this was *not* a play, and that Mr. Winthrop and I were not mere spectators. We were integral participants in this drama—for while it was definitely not play-acting, it was most certainly dramatic.

Who has not had the experience of walking into a room full of people and immediately seizing the meaning of the currents and countercurrents flowing among those gathered? Such was my experience the night of my father's denunciation. Although I could not have guessed the enormity of the public humiliation I was to suffer, I knew that some mischief against my father was afoot—had been for days—and was coming to a culmination of some sort that evening. Such was my experience this evening, coming upon the assembled Arawak of rank and nobility. Not one sign or signal from anyone present alerted me to the complexities of the present situation. Perhaps it was the furtive glances from the women who attended me that suggested something was brewing. Perhaps it was my stray memory of Mr. Winthrop's allusion to it several evenings before. Or, perhaps, it was the single, direct, and unmistakably malevolent regard from The Proud One that confirmed my sense of foreboding. I guessed at a glance what was at stake (human motives are not, after all, so difficult to read), and that Mr. Winthrop and I were directly involved.

In the center of the circle, as I have said, stood Mr. Winthrop, looking almost magnificent: his hair unbound, his face bronzed, his torso naked, his breeches ragged but of a piece, his body unadorned—a man of flesh and muscle.

Next to him stood an Arawak warrior. I had noticed him from my idle observations of the previous evenings: strong and seasoned, rough, and with a look about him that indicated single-minded zeal. He was also usually laden with as much gold as The Proud One. This evening, however, he wore no jewelry—only paint and pride. I also noticed for the first time two vertical marks on his upper left chest which looked to be welts. I suddenly recalled having seen these markings on other men, as well—our two guards, for instance.

I had privately named this militant warrior The Dissenter, after the Protestants in the North who, while they had been unjustly persecuted in the wake of the end of Cromwell's stern, repressive Protectorate, nevertheless had continued to make things uncomfortable for *everyone*—including, for instance, Mr. Winthrop, who had really nothing to do with the issues dividing the Dissenting Interest and the Church. This Arawak warrior looked to be the type to stir up the same kind of senseless trouble, albeit on a smaller scale.

I was not entirely surprised when I was led to a position of honor and seated next to the chief's mother. Behind her throne stood The Proud One (could she have been the chief's daughter, after all? I had often entertained that possibility, but somehow, I still did not think so). Then The Dissenter left the center of the circle to approach us. I had a sudden, visceral intuition that he was the one who had left me the flowers at the door of our hut. With a penetrating regard at me, he bent to lay an elaborate shell necklace at the matriarch's feet, just inches away from where I was sitting.

Then Mr. Winthrop, remarkable man that he is, followed The Dissenter's lead and laid a similar shell necklace at her feet. How he contrived to have a shell necklace on his person just then I did not know. As he bent gracefully down to offer the matriarch his token, he, too, looked over at me briefly. His face was swart and lean, his blue eyes rendered cobalt in the firelight. I saw in their depths a gleam of something I could not quite define.

"One of these necklaces will be yours," he said to me, low, almost on a whisper.

I must have looked as puzzled as I felt, for he continued, "There's no time to explain. I intend to carry through on my part here. But you have a part to play, as well. Don't fail me again."

I opened my mouth to speak.

His whisper cut my words off clean. "I mean it, Sedgwick," he said, with an odd quiver in his voice. Perhaps it was nerves. "You had better choose your actions carefully, or I can no longer be responsible for your future among the Arawak. However, I'll do my best to spare you indignity."

He held my eyes steady for the briefest of moments, then rose and regained his place in the center of the ring, next to The Dissenter.

Although the moment was fleeting, I had time enough now to recall the regards The Proud One had cast at Mr. Winthrop during the feasts on the previous two evenings. I had thought nothing of those flirtatious looks then. Now, however, they took on monstrously significant proportions. So, The Proud One wanted Mr. Winthrop and, so it seemed, The Dissenter wanted me. I would have bet both shell necklaces just then and thrown my ivory comb and brush set into the bargain that Mr. Winthrop had guessed all of this, too.

I realized, then, with amazement, that what I had heard in Mr. Winthrop's voice and seen in his eyes had been laughter. This man was not afraid—he was *enjoying* himself. And God forbid that in his enjoyment he should lose me to The Dissenter!

Then the drums began to beat with a slow, painful throb, suggesting that Mr. Winthrop's laughter could not possibly last.

CHAPTER 8

The sultry moon slanted its white light down on the two men, standing tall and fearless, facing each other in the center of the circle. The fire crackling behind them was at once warm and fragrant. It cast its revealing light over their resolute faces, leaving the surrounding circle of Arawak peers and me in mysterious shadow. In the long silence between drumbeats, the restless trade winds could be heard to rustle through the thatch of the caneys with a dry, grazing wheeze. The same breezes made the branches of the trees in the surrounding jungle sway and groan, like spirits of darkness. On them wafted as well the aromatic scents of sea and cedar.

The heightened, eerie effect of the setting at first seemed at variance with what was to come, for it all started conventionally enough—or so it seemed. Two long sticks were thrown into the circle—one to The Dissenter and one to Mr. Winthrop. They were the kind of stick I had seen on my first evening among the Arawak, when the warriors had performed their ritual combat. This evening, I guessed that Mr. Winthrop and The Dissenter were to perform something of the sort, although I did not question how Mr. Winthrop might have learned the combat ritual in so short a time. I had simply accepted the fact that he was extraordinarily adept at pointless displays of physical agility.

As his opening move, Mr. Winthrop caught his stick with his left hand, while The Dissenter caught his with his right. A rapid mental review of Mr. Winthrop's previous physical displays confirmed to me that he was decidedly righthanded. I had to admire his very subtle gesture, a cue of dexterity sent to his opponent, however unconsciously received by the latter. Mr. Winthrop apparently believed in pressing advantages when and where he could.

He caught the stick in his left hand, as I said. Then he twirled it (with an unnecessary flourish, I thought, but he is given to such stylish embellishments) before catching it, with a smack, in his right hand, now gripping the instrument firmly with both hands. He raised it above his head, keeping it parallel to the ground, where it smarted against The Dissenter's stick, also held horizontal, as the salute to this ritual combat.

Or so I thought. It did not take many minutes before I understood that this was no ritual combat of prescribed moves and counter-moves. As the sticks thunked against each other continuously and with intention, I studied more closely the faces of the two combatants. Mr. Winthrop looked absolutely calm, but purposeful. On the other hand, The Dissenter's eyes were aglow with a most ferocious emotion and his lips were curled and *sneering*. Since I had not spoken with Mr. Winthrop during the past three days, I could not know how he had inspired in The Dissenter such a deadly hatred.

Then, a wave of furious activity erupted before my eyes, and all speculations ceased. My entire attention was riveted on the action in the center of the circle.

The two men had squared off against each other, had tested the other's skill. Mr. Winthrop had matched The Dissenter thrust for thrust, counterthrust for counterthrust, and then some. Suddenly, The Dissenter feinted (as I believe the maneuver is called in the art of fencing) and, in the next split second, aimed unmistakably for Mr. Winthrop's face. My heart jumped to my throat before Mr. Winthrop, swift as thought itself, countered with a check. They disengaged, but crossed sticks again almost without pause for breath.

In the first moments, The Dissenter had been on the defensive. Now, he had taken the offensive and was driving Mr. Winthrop back toward the fire, ever closer. I worried that Mr. Winthrop had miscalculated, had spent himself too early, and would soon find his bare feet braised on embers. Then I realized that his initial offense had been a very good defense. Since he did not know the conventions of this encounter, he had wisely chosen an aggressive stance. His maneuvers had been unwieldy at first, while he learned the steps and the gestures. Now, as he was being driven backward by The Dissenter, I saw that he was, actually, gaining confidence, becoming surer of foot and hand. Time after time he leapt nimbly aside from The Dissenter's stick, evading or checking some brutal blow, and countering with one of his own. He was not yet panting, and the only emotion to replace the calm resolution on his face was, now and again and incredibly, a smile of satisfaction when wood met wood, first high, then low, then right, then left.

The Dissenter's face reflected no similar positive emotions. His sneer had hardened into a mask of fury. He was evidently maddened and frustrated by his opponent's elusiveness. Then something distracted Mr. Winthrop's attention. He had allowed himself to be driven too close to the fire. It might have been a spark jumping out from the flames that touched his bare calf; I could not tell. Whatever the reason, his guard fell for a fraction of a second. The Dissenter saw his opening and landed a blow broadside on Mr. Winthrop's torso with murderous force.

Mr. Winthrop staggered. He almost fell directly into the fire. My heart fell from my throat to my stomach. In that next split second he righted himself and saved himself not only from the fire, but also protected the other side of his torso from an equally crushing blow that was coming toward him. It was a miraculous maneuver, but he had suffered. His face was transfigured with pain. Beads of sweat started on his brow. The sinews of his muscles stood out from his back and shoulders and arms, as if strained. In that second of agony he remained, incredibly, on his feet.

I felt winded, suffocated. My heart, apparently dislodged from its customary place, flew out of my body to beat in Mr. Winthrop's breast. I throbbed with his pain; my chest felt racked and broken. My forehead broke out in moisture. I fought for air. When I regained my ability to breathe, I willed Mr. Winthrop my breath.

After some dizzying moments, Mr. Winthrop seemed to have recouped. He had his second wind. He also changed tactics. It was his footwork. He created a pattern of steps that had just enough of the incalculable to keep The Dissenter off balance. It was as if The Dissenter's blow had wakened him. Mr. Winthrop was suddenly made of steel and set on wires. If it had not been his original intention to harm The Dissenter, he had changed course. He now had The Dissenter on the run. He was playing with him, luring him into a mistake.

The Dissenter made a crucial one. Mr. Winthrop gave him a deliberate opening. The Dissenter took it. It was irresistible, in fact; Mr. Winthrop had left exposed his cracked ribs. Just as The Dissenter was lunging in to deal what he must have felt was the final—even fatal—blow, he found his stick whirled from his grasp and himself on the ground, unhurt but helpless, gazing up at Mr. Winthrop's face. Mr. Winthrop was smiling, but not pleasantly.

The Dissenter's shock was profound. I guessed that he had never experienced such a humiliating defeat. How he had been thrown he evidently did not know. Neither did anyone else, for the circle of onlookers was as mute as a grave.

Mr. Winthrop further amazed his opponent and his audience by placing his foot on one end of The Dissenter's stick, lying harmlessly on the ground, and levering the other end of it with the tip of his own, so that it flipped up in the air, much like a pickup stick. Mr. Winthrop caught it, again with his left hand, and tossed it to The Dissenter, who had now risen onto his elbows. With a theatricality wholly character-istic of him, Mr. Winthrop stepped back a pace, gracefully, and said in English, "Get up. Get up, man." He was winded, but his voice did not lack force. "We're not through yet."

This command needed no translation. The Dissenter rose, slowly. With a nod, Mr. Winthrop indicated that the combat was to resume.

The effect on the Arawak audience equaled the shocked roar fol-lowing the announcement of my father's treason at the military gala at Hounslow Heath. After their dead silence at The Dissenter's fall into the dust, the Arawak cried and shouted a wild babble. I was sure they had never seen the like, but I could not judge whether their pro-foundly emotional cries conveyed signal approval for Mr. Winthrop, deep scorn for The Dissenter, or encouragements to The Dissenter to make the most of Mr. Winthrop's foolish generosity.

Mr. Winthrop was to prove his action anything but foolish. He evi-dently had a purpose: to whip his opponent, to drub him. Unmindful of his injury, Mr. Winthrop had himself in icy control. He never gave an inch, but beat The Dissenter back, back, back, away from the fire. It was furious. It was awful. When Mr. Winthrop had The Dissenter where he wanted him, he attacked with a series of blows that left The Dissenter defenseless. With a savage thrust to his right upper arm, Mr. Winthrop rendered The Dissenter incapacitated. The Dissenter's stick fell now, definitively. His arm hung limp, as if dislocated. For the final humiliation, The Dissenter himself collapsed in a heap at the very end of the semicircle of men who ringed the circle. Mr. Winthrop had exiled The Dissenter—sent him, literally, to the margins of the soci-ety. It was final. It was cruel. It was amazingly effective.

Mr. Winthrop went back to the center of the circle. It was only then that I saw the toll the fight had taken on him. I almost rose then and rushed to the center, to lead him away, when—out of nowhere and with no warning—a dog ran into the circle and jumped high onto Mr.

Winthrop's back, practically onto his shoulders. I thought, at first, that it was a mistake—that a cur had run into the village. When no one moved to help him, I thought that he was being punished for having so humiliated one of their tribesmen. Slowly it dawned on me that Mr. Winthrop was passing a series of tests.

Mr. Winthrop, for his part, was not waiting for any help. He must have known beforehand what was in store for him this night. Instantly he sprang into action. As he turned to identify this new foe, I saw his blue eyes flash with fury and new pain. I nearly fainted from sympathetic pain myself, but fought for consciousness. Mr. Winthrop needed me.

Perhaps I did swoon during this most savage episode, for I cannot describe what happened. I have a vague memory of a nightmare of snarling teeth and growling jaws and vicious paws clawing at human flesh. Somehow water had been strewn into the circle, creating mud, in which man and beast slipped and slid.

An eternity of time passed. Mud and blood now freely spattered the center circle where Mr. Winthrop was fighting for his life. Then it was over. Two forms—one man, one beast—lay motionless on the ground.

My heart must have reentered my body then, for I felt it fall from my throat to lodge again in my breast, where it stopped, cold.

When Mr. Winthrop rolled over and staggered slowly to his feet, my heart began to beat again, erratically and painfully. He put his toe to the body of the dog and rolled it over. I winced and turned away. Before I did so, I glimpsed the beast's mangy carcass, the belly slit and gaping from neck to hindquarters.

The effect on me and every other witness was stupefying. I recovered enough to understand that Mr. Winthrop had not slit the dog's body with his bare hands, as I supposed the Arawak might have thought he had done. Attuned now to every movement that he made, I noted that Mr. Winthrop slipped something from his palm into the pocket of his once elegant breeches, now rags. It must have been his pocket knife, and it had saved him.

As he continued to stand over the corpse of the dog, without fainting or otherwise showing any weakness, I slowly let out my breath. Surely it was over now. I mustered my forces to rise and go to him, thinking this to be my part. I was forestalled, once again, this time (mercifully, I thought) not by another wild beast, but by the chief himself.

My thoughts of mercy were short-lived. The chief had risen from his throne and had crossed to Mr. Winthrop, still standing alone in the center, his eyes sapphires in a dirt- and sweat-streaked face. I thought with every particle of my being that Mr. Winthrop was going to be richly rewarded for his performance. Once again, I was wrong —dreadfully wrong.

Spear in hand, the chief walked up to Mr. Winthrop and regarded him face-to-face. He said something, long and low, to which Mr. Winthrop did not respond. Instead of making any move that l would have been able to interpret as congratulatory, the chief went over to the fire and with the tip of his spear spread a path of burning embers on the ground in front of Mr. Winthrop. My senses simply could not absorb the evidence that Mr. Winthrop was supposed now, after everything he had already suffered, to walk across those live coals.

Only now that the memory has been mitigated by time and immense distance can I force myself to write the words: *Mr. Winthrop walked over the coals.* Gone was any trace of his earlier smiles; his face was wrenched in pain. He was sweating profusely. I felt he was doing this for us. Such were my feelings of identification with him that I would have gladly changed places with him and borne the physical pain; I surely felt a mental pain equal to his. I felt as if I had been lowered with him into a volcano and was experiencing the mental anguish of this primitive trial by fire. But it was not merely mental. The soles of my feet whimpered in sympathetic agony.

Then it was over. Mr. Winthrop stood (he was still standing, my amazed eyes informed me) at the other end of the path of fire. My hands and heart and feet were wrung. I had nothing left to feel for the final act. I was not pained, or horrified, or otherwise moved when the chief placed his stone spear into the fire, held it there until it glowed, then stepped up to Mr. Winthrop and traced two lines, diagonally, across his left breast with the red-hot tip. My body, already seared, felt the scorch down to my blistered feet.

Then there was noise—human noise. It might have been wild cheering, but my hearing had been numbed, along with every other sense. Mr. Winthrop had passed all tests. My dazed mind vaguely registered the idea that he had been branded for life as an Arawak warrior. Almost in spite of myself and my feelings of total revulsion at this initiation ritual, a clamor of joy coursed through me to realize that he had done it—that his pain had not been for nothing.

I looked across the circle at him. His eyes were fastened on me. When they began to glaze and he wavered slightly, I knew this time, and unmistakably, what my role was to be. I grabbed the shell necklace he had placed before the chief's mother and threw it over my head. Then I propped myself on my own wobbly legs and conquered my very queasy stomach in order to make haste to his side. I did not care at the moment what I was *expected* to do, or what Arawak manners were in this instance. I knew only that I wished to save him from sinking to his knees from pain and exhaustion or, worse, from falling on his face, and possibly undoing in Arawak eyes what I deemed was a superhuman feat of power and endurance.

I arrived at the moment his knees buckled. I quickly flung one of his very dirty arms across my shoulder and leaned my entire body into his side up to his armpit, so that I might bear his entire weight. Unfortunately, I had arrived at the side that had received the murderous blow from The Dissenter's stick. The low, animal groan of pain that rattled out of his mouth told me that he was in worse shape on the inside than he had shown on the outside. I think, by then, he had lost most of his consciousness.

The chief looked down at me, an expression of utter disbelief on his face, as if no Arawak woman had ever intervened in a masculine initiation ritual, which I am sure she had not. However, that had nothing whatsoever to do with me, so I returned the chief's regard with my most imperious stare and pronounced, managing a polite smile, "Mr. Winthrop belongs to me, so I will take him along to the caney now."

The chief did not, nor could I have expected him to, understand. He replied, at length. There was no way of knowing, of course, but I believe his reply was entirely tangential to my statement.

Before I had made the fraction of a movement to leave the circle, dragging Mr. Winthrop with me, the chief had recovered enough to have issued a series of commands to his warriors who, at my first movements, had descended upon me. It was no contest. They easily wrested Mr. Winthrop from my arms and, with shouts and cries, hoisted him high above their shoulders. They began to run with his swooning body out of the circle and, indeed, in a direction that would take them out of the village.

Naturally, I ran after them, calling, "Bring him back this instant!" and "Don't you *dare* do him further harm, you savages!" and "I have never in my life been so outraged as I am at this very moment!" and stronger invectives, which mightily relieved my feelings, but otherwise had no effect on my auditors. In fact, before I had gotten very far, I was physically restrained from pursuit by a tangle of feminine arms. Well, at that, I will admit (and there is no use denying it), I was transported into quite, quite, *quite* undignified behavior—which also won me nothing.

I began to yell again, "Bring him back! Bring him back this instant!" And bethinking myself of all that I had lost from the moment of setting foot in this village, I added, "And while you're at it, you may as well return my cloth to me—all *three* bolts, mind you!—and my hair pins!"

In the next frenzy of minutes, I did, almost miraculously, succeed in communicating the idea that I wanted my cloth back, for I suspected that Mr. Winthrop would need it. I also succeeded in comprehending that Mr. Winthrop would be delivered in due course to our caney.

I was not, for all of that, particularly relieved when, in fact, some time later, several Arawak women appeared at my door with the cloth. This delivery was followed soon thereafter by a group of warriors, who deposited Mr. Winthrop at the threshold. It was then, when I had to practically drag him inside myself, that I realized what the men had done with him. They had evidently taken him to the river and cleansed him of mud and blood and sweat and grime. His hair and knee-breeches were still damp.

I laid him out on the long mat in the center of the caney upon which he had, only a few nights previous, lounged so easily. I had fashioned for him there a make-shift bed and pillow out of some of the cloth. With other lengths, I wound a brace around his torso, so that no sudden movement on his part would further damage his broken ribs. He was heavy and mightily injured.

It was dark in the caney. Outside, the night sky had already bitten a slice out of the luminescent moon. I needed little light, however, and depended wholly on the tips of my fingers to find his wounds, wash them lightly, and rub them with a thin film of the salve against infection in that precious brown jar. Outside, the drums beat—in celebration of Mr. Winthrop's success, I must suppose—and the odors of a roasting fish and sounds of happy Arawak permeated the air. All hunger, all emotion in me, were swept aside. There was only the man and his body stretched out before me.

I rubbed from the bottoms of his burned soles to the nape of his neck, where the dog had first gripped him. Bent over him, I worked long minutes until my back ached and my fingers were stiff. I hoped that the pain I was absorbing into my body came from his. At last, I had done what I could. I sat back on my heels to survey this man—my one link to civilization, my one chance of survival. So intertwined had our two existences become that, in truth, seeing to his care and comfort just then seemed tantamount to ensuring mine.

He was breathing deeply and evenly, but from his increased and fretful twitching, I determined that he was profoundly uncomfortable. The fluffs of cloth I had tried to make into a mattress were woefully inadequate to soften his pain. I had no choice but to pillow his head and bruised shoulders in my lap. This seemed to comfort him. To give myself something to do, I gently stroked his hair and massaged his temples with one hand. The fingers of my other hand strayed to the two diagonal marks on his breast, where they lingered. I was prepared to sit thus, silent and motionless and waiting, for the rest of the night.

I did not have long to wait—at least, it seemed like no time at all before Mr. Winthrop's eyes fluttered open.

"Mr. Winthrop?" I whispered anxiously. I instantly withdrew my fingers from his breast and temple.

"Sedgwick, is that you?" he asked, raising his head a little and straining his eyes through the darkness.

I assured him on this point.

"Glad to see you here again," he said, a little groggily, then closed his eyes again and let his head sink back into my lap. "Very glad."

Good manners always serve, no matter how extreme the circumstances. I was pleased that Mr. Winthrop had seemed to remember this. I could do no less.

"Thank you, sir," I replied, in good form. "You may believe that I am pleased to be here, too."

At these words, he opened his eyes, made an odd, wrenched sound, and clutched his broken side. "Sedgwick, have a care. It hurts when I laugh."

I worried that he was delirious. I thought it best to humor him. "Yes, quite so, Mr. Winthrop," I said, seriously.

At this, he clutched his side again. His hand rested on the cloth. "What's this?" he asked.

"Our cloth. I retrieved our cloth," I said, rather pleased to be able to report this. "I've made you a brace."

His hand traveled around the brace, then returned to press experimentally at the broken ribs beneath it.

"Tell me the worst, Sedgwick—" he began.

I held my breath. I did not know the extent of his internal injuries, but they could well have been massive.

"—did you bind me in the yellow flowers or the blue stripe?" he finished.

He *was* delirious, I decided. "The blue stripe," I lied. I feared that in his obviously deranged mental condition, be would be distressed at thoughts of a dressing of yellow and green flowers.

He nodded, apparently satisfied, then attempted to move his torso. He winced at the effort and grimaced, but not precisely in pain. "I think you've overdone it," he said with reference to my careful swaddling. He tugged at the binding, as if wishing to undo it.

"Oh, no, sir!" I replied, a little alarmed. "Please don't! You've several broken ribs, no doubt, and who knows what else!"

"I've had broken ribs before, Sedgwick," he informed me, "and know that mine aren't broken now."

"It was not for lack of trying!" I exclaimed. "I think The Dissenter was trying to *kill* you."

"Who?"

"The Dissenter—your opponent this evening," I explained. "You know—the Protestant Dissenters who, after all, were the indirect cause of your departure from England."

Mr. Winthrop made another strangled noise and clutched his side again. "I *warned* you, Sedgwick," he said.

"I had already named him before this evening," I said, suddenly realizing with delight the justice of this appellation. "And extremely farsighted on my part it was, too. The name became especially apt tonight, since this Arawak was trying to run you out of town. Happily, he did not succeed."

"I have a name far more apt for him, I assure you."

"Which is—?" I queried, interested.

He shook his head. "One syllable—unmentionable. In any case, his Arawak name is Duid." He did not pursue this subject. Instead he asked, "How long have I been out?"

"I don't know," I answered, truthfully enough. "Not very long, considering. . . ."

He paused to listen to the sounds outside. "The drums have stopped," he remarked. He inhaled, but the effort cost him. "I can smell the tobacco. The men are still up, smoking."

"Oh, is that what that odor is?" I asked, a little surprised. "The other night, I smelled something that reminded me of my father's library after a meeting. Only the odor here is—I don't know—fresher, smoother. It actually smells very good. I didn't know the Arawak knew of tobacco."

"The Indians grow the stuff," he informed me. "You must have known that."

If I had, I had apparently forgotten it, or really not thought about it, since tobacco was as far removed from my life as, well, women were from men in daily Arawak society.

"I should be there now," Mr. Winthrop was continuing, on a note of regret, "smoking with them. I was not allowed to partake two nights ago, when they first brought out the pipe. Tonight was probably my night."

"I feel sure they are smoking in your *honor*," I replied, by way of consolation.

"Very probably," he agreed, almost indifferently. He looked up at me then. His eyes traveled first to the crown of flowers on my head, then focused on the necklace at my throat. He reached up with a stiff hand and touched the shells. "Very probably," he repeated, "now that the chief's mother has given you my necklace."

"She did not exactly *give* it to me," I said.

He frowned, as if trying to remember the sequence of events after the chief had branded him and the initiation rites were over. "But, you're wearing my necklace, and you are here," he said, letting his hand drop from my throat.

"Actually, I *took* the necklace," I said, "before I ran to your side to catch you."

Mr. Winthrop covered his eyes with one hand. With the other he clutched his side again. "Oh, Sedgwick!" he almost whimpered. "You are too much!"

I felt his brow for a touch of fever but registered none.

"I didn't want to take any chances," I explained, very reasonably.

Mr. Winthrop raised an arm to touch the shells again. "Chances?" he asked.

"Well," I hedged. "Yes. That is, I was worried for a moment that I might end up in The Dissenter's caney."

"But instead you are here, and we are together."

"Yes," I said. "Back where we started."

Mr. Winthrop paused. Then, very deliberately, he said, "But not quite *exactly* where we started."

While he let those words sink in, his hand fell from my necklace and grazed my breast. The contact was inadvertent, I must suppose. Nevertheless, I felt a tingle of excitement.

Before I had a chance to recover, he was saying, "Sedgwick." His voice sounded a little weak now, and pained. "My head aches, and my forehead feels on fire. I think you were stroking my brow before. Do it some more. It seems to ease the pain."

How, in truth, could I refuse him this simple request after all he had just gone through? Was it not uncharitable of me to suspect that his voice was not as weak as it sounded nor that his head ached as much as he claimed it to? It was true that he had saved me from The Dissenter's caney and that the dispute over me would not even have arisen had not my women's courses announced to the entire village that I was (let us say) eligible for breeding—which is not to say that I was the sole reason for the contest between Mr. Winthrop and The Dissenter. Yet, although I did not think Mr. Winthrop a man to take unfair advantage of a situation, I could not quite rid myself of the idea that I was just now being *had* by him.

I laid my hand on his remarkably cool brow and began to massage his temples, very gently. I realized then the vast difference between comforting a man who was unconscious and tending one who is in full possession of his senses. I, personally, found the contact anything but soothing.

To relieve the fullness of the charge I felt, I diverted our attention to the place on his body farthest from me. "Your feet," I said, conversationally, "are not as badly burned as I might have thought. I did wrap them in strips of cloth, though, smeared with the ointment. I hope they do not blister too badly or, worse, develop infection."

The movement of his head in my lap was a nod. "I had been preparing for the coals," he replied.

"You knew what was coming?" I asked, incredulous.

"Not the details, but I had gotten the general idea," he said, speaking now, truly, with some effort. "I had been advised to make calluses on my feet, and so I have been walking over rough bark and stones for the last three days. I gather that the Arawak men develop the calluses for the occasion over a period of years, while I—"

"—will not be walking for some days to come!" I said, quite indignant at the trial he had been forced to endure.

"I'll be walking tomorrow," he stated flatly.

I was not, at the moment, going to argue the stupidity of that statement. "Exactly who advised you about the trial by fire?" I asked, seizing on the more relevant topic.

"Some of Duid's rivals," he replied.

"His rivals?" I queried, highly interested.

"The man has his enemies," he explained. "As the son of the former chief, now dead, he would."

This surprised me. "*Former* chief's son?" I repeated. I began to understand the chip he wore so ceremoniously on his shoulder.

"Something like that," he said. "But, then again, not quite. I thought I understood that his fall from power had something to do with his *mother*'s death, but perhaps I misunderstood."

Diverted by this mention of the female line, I asked, "Could The Proud One possibly be his sister or some other relation—or, even, his betrothed? You see, I've always seen them as two peas in a—"

"The Proud—?" he broke into this. "Ah, yes. *Her.*"

I heard the lurking smile in his voice. "For whom you also have a different name, I suppose?" I said, frostily.

"In fact, yes," he replied. The smile in his voice had surfaced to become a positive *leer.* "But, no. The, er, Proud One is betrothed to the chief's son, Ajijeko, who is away now on a long hunting expedition. She's not native to this island. She belongs to the tribe of the Paressis."

"Oh!" was all I could say to these disclosures. I did not ask him how he had come by the information but queried instead how it was that anyone chose to *warn* him of what was coming.

"That was easy," he replied. "Within twenty-four hours of setting foot in this town, I realized that I had a sworn enemy in The Dissenter. You can figure that one out yourself, if you care to. My first day on the hunt, the chief denied me a bow and an arrow. I could understand his caution in keeping a weapon out of my hands. So, what I did was to whittle a sling shot. Then I rigged it the next day with a thong made out of my bootlaces, which I retrieved that night from the caney."

"You are now going to tell me that you are an excellent shot with the sling," I interjected, drily.

He glanced up at me. "Let's just say that I killed more birds with fewer stones than the Pri . . . than the *Protestant* Dissenter," he replied. "I won some friends among the other lads when I showed them a few of my shooting secrets."

"But *why?*" I could not refrain from asking. "Why enter into such a senseless competition with him—the son of a former chief, no less?"

He shrugged his shoulders. "It's hard to explain, Sedgwick." He sighed a little. I could feel his pain and his tiredness now. His eyes were fixed on the blackness in the far corner of the caney. "Perhaps he thought a quick way to retrieve a measure of his former position was by beating the outside man and winning the redhead. As for me, I gathered that an engagement between us was expected by the others, so I openly confronted him in the woods with the sling shot. He repaid the compliment by challenging me in town."

"He was trying to *kill* you! What if you hadn't bested him, and he had really gone after you? What would the chief have done?"

"Nothing, no doubt."

"*Nothing?*" I echoed. "And you went ahead and challenged him, knowing that?"

"It's the price you pay," he said simply.

Men! What nonsensical creatures! "But The Dissenter has all the more reason to wish you dead now!" I pointed out.

"And if flowers keep turning up at our door in the morning, that murderous desire can easily be reciprocated," he returned without hesitation. Apparently Mr. Winthrop did not miss much. He rolled his head up to look at me. "After tonight, though, I have won the chief's protection. Now, my death at Duid's hands would not be treated with impunity. He'll think twice."

"However, if The Proud One—engaged as she is to the chief's son—keeps making those eyes at you," I commented, tit for tat, "and *you* reciprocate, I am sure that the chief can withdraw his protection from you at a moment's notice."

Mr. Winthrop was still gazing up at me, an unreadable expression lighting his eyes, and said (provoking man that he is), "You finally noticed that, did you? But there was never any future in it, for I only involve myself with women to whom I can actually speak."

"The gallant cavalier?" I rallied him, in an attempt *not* to be affected by the implications of this particular passage. "Yes, indeed," I said, hiding behind light sarcasm, "soldiers are well known for turning women's heads with pretty phrases."

"Sure, now," he agreed easily. "The most flowery being: 'Hmm, love? You awake?'"

All right. I laughed.

"How can you joke at a time like this?" I asked him, shaking my head over this unexpected, though immodest, humor.

"Who said I was joking?"

Through the dimness, I saw points of laughter in his eyes. I certainly had no reply. I could scarce credit the look, for I could hardly think of a less likely moment for a man who had been through all he had been through to be thinking of *that*.

It seemed he was not thinking of it, after all. Next he said, somewhat incongruously, "That reminds me. Scratch my back."

"Does your bandage itch?" I asked anxiously, helping him as he attempted to turn himself over.

"No," he said, a little shortly. "Just do it."

I fully felt now the racking pain of his body for he groaned deeply while turning. I attempted to arrange the make-shift bed more comfortably for him, but I did not fully succeed. The effort of turning had clearly cost him.

I began to scratch his back lightly.

"Scratch vertically down my back," he said, "and draw blood."

"Dear me! You are most certainly joking *now*, Mr. Winthrop!"

"No, Miss Sedgwick, I am not." His voice was audibly wrenched with his bruises and burns. "Draw blood," he commanded.

Still, I hesitated.

"I might have spared myself the cracked ribs if I had had these marks earlier," he said. His voice had become groggy. "Yes, the marks will assure my position among the men on the morrow. Do it, Sedgwick." His voice was now faint, though the command still came through, and it trailed off to nothing when he added, "Be sure to draw blood."

"What on earth are you talking about?" I asked of these strange requests.

I received no answer. I realized, after a space of silence, that he had fallen into a swoon, or at least an uneasy sleep.

Stretched out now beside me, it took a great effort on my part to fulfill his odd request. I was only glad, when breaking his skin, as lightly as I could, that he was now—at last and mercifully—beyond feeling this fresh pain inflicted upon him at his own request.

CHAPTER 9

I would have expected to have awakened the next morning with Mr. Winthrop's head still in my lap. I did not. Instead, when I cracked my eyes open the caney was empty, and I was stretched out on a mat, cramped and highly uncomfortable, my wilted crown of flowers at my side. By the dimness outside, I judged it to be unconscionably early. I could not imagine how or why Mr. Winthrop had left my care. I certainly did not think that he could have *walked* away on his own.

I could hardly give the matter consideration, however, for that horrible morning noise outside jammed all mental operations. This loud, terrific racket occurred every morning just before sunup. This morning, for the first time, I was in a position to discover just what caused it. I stumbled to the door and looked out in time to see the sky momentarily blackened by hundreds of hawks, scolding all lie-abeds to rise. Although I am extremely good-tempered in the morning, I found this noise to be rather trying, and I must say that a gentle cock-a-doodle-doo offers a far more civilized awakening.

Despite the cacophony, there I was, witness to a Caribbean dawn. I stepped out of the caney and took a few steps around it, to face east. The town was on a plateau halfway up a hill, with a wide view of the horizon. From behind the tops of the trees of the jungle surrounding the village there flashed vertical shafts of silver light thrusting into the light coral dawn. Then came the first magnificent wedge of fire, and the coral deepened so that the entire village glowed orange. I could feel the warmth right away. The earth was still turning around the sun—or the sun around the earth. I cared not which. The trade winds blew as steadily as ever. It was the beginning of another perfect tropical day.

This was the first morning that I actually anticipated *enjoying*. As I had said to Mr. Winthrop not too many days before, one could easily accustom oneself to the wonderful weather of the island and to the food. I had not had a proper meal for some days now and was looking forward to eating my fill of the extraordinarily succulent fruits that abounded on the island: guava, I believe it is called, and fruits tasting remarkably like wild soursop and custard apples, along with fruits of unpronounceable names that sounded like *planata* (or some such thing) and *pawpaw* (or *papaya*—I could never quite determine which pronunciation was correct). And the fish—how I longed for some grilled fish! In fact, if I never tasted another slice of red meat, it would not be too soon.

However, this morning, and despite my hunger, thought of food was not the main component of my anticipation. Rather, I admit, it was the discovery of the extent of the impact among the Arawak of Mr. Winthrop's success the evening before.

I was not to be disappointed. Since I predicted that he had had a rousing success, I performed what I could of a morning's toilette before circulating in the society from which I had been banished during the previous three days. My primping consisted chiefly of washing myself with the fresh water we were continuously supplied in our caney, vigorously brushing my hair and braiding it, and finally, smoothing down my skirts and tying the drawstring of my bodice, which had loosened during sleep, and fixing a button or two which had come undone.

Before quitting my abode, I picked up my parasol, which had served me so well. It made me feel a little more complete, along with my shell necklace, which I now wore very proudly, and I still retained enough of my sensibilities to know that if I exposed my skin to too much sun, I would be frightfully freckled forever. I had no access to a mirror, so I could not have said, for a certainty, what condition my skin was in. (Incidentally, I recommend to all ladies that, at some point or another in their lives, they go without a mirror for some extended period of time. It is a refreshing experience not to be burdened with appearance—indeed, it is a *relief*). I was now ready to sally forth.

How much more pleasant it is to have all eyes staring at you when the looks are openly admiring, rather than derisive or scornful or hateful! I received such admiring glances—and yes, even smiles, some shy and some more strongly equalizing, as if to say, "Welcome to our community. You are one of us now."—in my stroll through town that morning.

And quite a pleasant walk it was, too—one which I was not quite disposed to ending. However, after one complete turn through town, I felt that I would render myself rather ridiculous if I kept it up, and in any case, it was still very early. I felt, suddenly, as if I were at liberty to do whatever I chose, since I no longer had two guards at my back. And because there was still time before the distribution of the morning meal, I decided to return to my caney to begin to implement those home improvements that had occurred to me in the long watches of the night as I held Mr. Winthrop's head.

Before I made it back to the caney I was accosted, very congenially, by the four women of elevated station who had previously accompanied me to the glen and who had guarded me at the women's monthly hut. They were all smiles—very pretty smiles, really—and I immediately named them Sylvia, Margaret, Rose, and Lily. (I was to learn later that their names approximated the appellations Silver Star,

Promised to a Man across the Water, Forest Flower, and Second One—this last name resulting from the fact that the young woman was the *second* daughter of a prominent family who had no sons. I thought the name demeaning. Later on, I had a talk with the mother of Lily—or Second One, if you prefer—about why it was that daughters deserved respect equal to that accorded sons, but I am sorry to say that that particular conversation did not flourish. It might well have been due to the fact that I did not, at that time, command all the fine points of Arawak grammar, which were not only tricky, but very, very strange.)

Sylvia acted as the leader of the group. She was also the only one of the four to wear a bodice covering. She took me by the arm, and the five of us proceeded to make our way to town center, to the very scene of Mr. Winthrop's triumph the night before.

On the way, Sylvia addressed all manner of comments to me. She was animated and very gracious. I was sure that she was saying all that was proper and kind. I responded at her conversational pauses with, "Yes, Mr. Winthrop really did do a very fine job, did he not?" and, "Dear me, I did have a few *uncertain* moments for him—not that I had any doubts about the outcome!" or, "Why, thank you very much. I shall be sure to tell him that the next time I see him."

Which, of course, made me wonder exactly where Mr. Winthrop was, for I was not to see him that evening or night, or for quite a few days after that. While I was able to glean quite a lot of information about Arawak life over those next few days, I was not quite able to extract the particular information about Mr. Winthrop's whereabouts. I did gather that he was in company of several other Arawak warriors, on a hunt, or some such thing. There were even moments when I worried that he was being put through some more hideous initiation rites—ones too grisly to be exhibited in public, if one could even imagine such. However, the bright, openly friendly faces of my female Arawak counterparts somewhat dispelled my fears.

I was now given tasks to do. Or, rather, I *demanded* to have tasks to do. I began with the weaving, but soon became bored. I was later to discover an activity that both interested me and satisfied my sense of civic duty. I was not, like the matriarch and some of the "noble" women, content with inactivity. I had always been extremely engaged and busy in London. I had never been concerned with the plight of orphaned children or the really scandalous condition of such institutions as Bedlam. Rather, devising standards of the flow of traffic in Londontown and city beautification projects had always been my *forte*, let us say. I will not bore the reader with a list of my civic accomplishments, for it is really a very long one and a matter of public record, anyway. In the meantime, however, I was still trying to master the techniques of Arawak weaving. I used the loom provided me in my caney, which I took out every morning in order to weave in the group that included Sylvia and her entourage. Since I was not fully absorbed by this task, I quickly hit on the really *brilliant* idea of teaching my four women friends how to speak English.

Now, I cannot imagine how these savages thought of such a thing, but almost immediately *they* decided to teach *me* Arawak! I do not flatter myself to say that I was rather quick with it—and with no great help from my teachers, really, for the giggles that erupted from Sylvia, Lily, Margaret (particularly, that ninny), and Rose when I repeated what they said to me did *not* produce an atmosphere conducive to learning. I ignored their discourtesy and kept right on talking, naturally.

For all the excellent progress I was making in communicating with the women among whom I was now living (though not permanently, I hoped), I was heartily glad when I finally spied Mr. Winthrop among the males at the evening meal. It must have been a week or so after his initiation, and I was pleased to see that he was walking with no difficulty. I assumed that his feet had healed. I was highly desirous of speaking with him when he returned to our caney, later that night.

I had expected him to be pleased to see me. At the very least, I had expected him to *greet* me, for heaven's sakes. However, when he entered the caney, he looked anything but pleased. He was, apparently, in one of those "moods" that afflict all men from time to time. (Men are not—nor could we expect them to be—as steadfast as women.) If it had not been for my innate sense of the social graces, Mr. Winthrop would have taken to his hammock without so much as a "Good evening, Miss Sedgwick."

I had thought that the first thing we would discuss upon his return would be our escape. We had not truly been together since the night before I had been dragged so ignominiously away from the glen before my second bath. On that night, we had devised our escape in a canoe. I wondered if, in the meantime, Mr. Winthrop had, perchance, located our boat.

In any case, when he entered our caney that night and saw me standing in the center, he subjected me to a hard, wordless stare, then flung himself into his hammock.

"And a pleasure it is to see you, too, Mr. Winthrop!" I said, as evenly as I was able.

From the blackened depths of the far side of the caney, Mr. Winthrop answered me with a curt warning, "Don't, Sedgwick. Not tonight."

Can you imagine it? Here I had not seen him for days now—the only person on this island with whom I could really communicate—and he was dismissing me! I really did not think I should tolerate it. At the same time, he might have been dead tired from whatever he had just spent the last week doing. Or perhaps his feet did still hurt him. I longed to ask him about their condition, but in that brief moment of silence, I felt that some new element had entered the air of our caney—a kind of crackling; certainly, a disturbing tension that I had not previously noticed when we were together. It did not seem quite *right* just then to make any reference to his body, nor could I quite plunge in to the topic of our escape.

I chose a middle ground. "So, Mr. Winthrop," I said, as if he had not just bitten my head off, "I hope you like what I have done to our caney."

There was a small, taut silence. Then he shifted his weight in the hammock such that I think he must have crooked his arms and clasped his hands behind his head to prop it in a raised position.

"What have you done to our caney?" he inquired with a sigh.

"I hope you noticed the curtains at our door," I said, ignoring the implications of his long-suffering voice. "I think you will see that they make a very attractive effect in the daytime. I have also found a way to make a broom, and have made several for the other ladies. They think they are very amusing but rather practical, as well, and I have shown them the proper way to sweep out their caneys. I think the brooms will go a long way to cutting down on the dust in town, as well. And outside our caney—well! I am rather pleased to have found just the right plantings to go on either side of our door—a judicious mixture of shrubbery and flowers."

To these disclosures Mr. Winthrop made absolutely no comment.

I plunged cheerfully on. "On the subject of beautification, I have devised a variety of plantings that shall grace the town center. I've had improvements in mind for that space for days. Now, the matriarch—her name, in case you did not know it, is Great Arawak Mother—well, she obstinately *refused* to cover the lower half of that hideous statue with our cloth (not even the blue stripe!), and so I proposed to her the idea of planting a series of small bushes in a circle around the pole. She thought it extremely odd, but did not refuse me outright. So, you see, what I have in mind is for the bushes to grow. Over time, they would eventually cover—"

"Sedgwick," Mr. Winthrop broke into this, "we are in the middle of a *jungle*."

"I know that," I said to this irrelevant remark.

I thought I had heard the faintest trace of humor in his voice, but his next rude words dispelled that impression. "Then don't speak to me of *planting* things," he said almost bitterly.

I had a mind to tell him that I very much enjoyed gardening, but I did not think him worthy, at the moment, of that information. "Perhaps you would rather have me speak to you of the boat," I said coolly, coming straight to the point.

"Boat?" he echoed, as if he had forgotten it entirely. After a lengthy pause, he added, "When I find it, I'll let you know."

I certainly know when a conversation is at an end—and without a *word* about where he had been, what he had done, or what he proposed for us to do! I had many fascinating things to tell him, but I was not going to continue to attempt to make conversation with a boorish man in a foul humor. Without another word, and with as much dignity as one could achieve in climbing into a net suspended four feet off the ground, I took myself to bed. I lay awake for a long, long time, and it was my impression that Mr. Winthrop did as well. I must say that the atmosphere that night was anything but easy, pleasant, and companionable.

So the rhythm of the next few days was established; and the days stretched into weeks. (I know that because this interval was long enough for me to have spent another three days in the women's hut.) I began to feel, in fact, very *uncomfortable* with Mr. Winthrop, and we communicated little. However, the less I spoke with him, the more I spoke (and was able to speak) with Sylvia and the other ladies.

About The Proud One, I learned that she came from the Paressis on a neighboring island. She was here, of course, to become acquainted with her future in-laws while her betrothed, Ajijeko (otherwise known as First Warrior), was away doing whatever it was that would make him worthy of being chief. I was not entirely sure when Ajijeko was to return or how binding Arawak betrothals were. Given The Proud One's obviously roving eye and her evident interest in Mr. Winthrop (which had only increased after his triumphant initiation),

I hoped that First Warrior's return would come soon and that Arawak betrothals were binding.

The Proud One did her best to disconcert me. She did not succeed. The more proficient I became at Arawak, the better able I was, whenever I chanced to cross paths with her, to hold my own in any exchange that might occur between us. She pretty well turned up her nose at me most of the time.

As for Mr. Winthrop, he was now occupying a position of honor on one side of the chief (Arawak Father), in the capacity of the chief's newly adopted spiritual son. I did not know how long that honor would last—perhaps only until First Warrior's return. The vanquished Dissenter had to suffer the humiliation of the end place on the male side. He continued to look malevolent.

In any case, Mr. Winthrop's evidently elevated status at the evening meal could be observed by all, The Proud One included. After some weeks, she condescended to stop and speak with me.

"Well, Miss Sedgwick," she said, for openers.

(Of course, she did not use those words. It seems quite pointless to transcribe the Arawak ones. The reader will understand that, henceforth, I am faithfully conveying the content of all conversations conducted in the Arawak language.)

"So, Foreign Born," she said (as long as I am professing to accuracy), "I notice that your man has returned."

I thought her choice of the word *man* quite vulgar. I did not know then that the Arawak word means "man" as well as "betrothed" and "husband." Looking down my nose at her (I was half a head taller), I replied, quite pointedly, "But First Warrior has not, I notice."

To The Proud One's slight surprise that I should allude to this piece of Arawak gossip, I pressed my advantage. "You are engaged to him, are you not?'

"I am engaged to the chief's first son," she informed me.

Gone was my advantage. She might as well have said that if Ajijeko did not return, she was entitled to Mr. Winthrop. "At the next moon, I will marry the man who is the chief's first son," she elaborated, "and who does not bear fresh marks of another woman."

I did not fully understand her reference to "fresh marks," but I felt as if I had been slapped in the face. Before I had an opportunity to frame an adequate reply (words do not normally fail me in English— my first thought was, in fact, *And if that isn't Julianna Castleragh all over again!*), The Proud One swept off, with the merest glance over her shoulder in my direction, as if to say: *Mr. Winthrop might well be mine someday soon!*

Mr. Winthrop's mood had become progressively fouler as the days and weeks had passed, so that I was sorely tempted to call back to her to say that she was welcome to him. I refrained.

Incidentally, The Proud One's Arawak name is Alluring Eyes. Clearly, the Arawak aim for truth in naming. For the record, Mr. Winthrop was known as Blue Eyes, while my name was not Foreign Born but rather something akin to The Beauty.

What a charming people, the Arawak!

They are charming and hard-working, and little given to rest or respite. We must have been among them for five or six weeks, at least, before we were given a holiday. I never did understand what the occasion was, but it seemed to have something to do with some god or another and an elaborate ceremony in front of that hideous pole the night before.

On the morning of the holiday, I decided to explore. I had no idea where Mr. Winthrop had gone, for he had arisen before me and, as usual, had left the caney without a word. I had not been outside of town much, and so I decided to follow a new path that wandered down the mountain, away from the jungle. At every turn I faithfully performed the ritual against snakes and was pleased that it seemed to work.

It was high noon when I emerged from the dense growth that

crowded the path all the way down the mountain. I saw before me a wide lagoon on the northeast corner of the island where blue herons walked stiffly in the shallows. Suddenly I was waist-deep in mangrove bushes. A fluttering activity squawked and bustled over and above these bushes. Birds, as numerous as sparks when a horseshoe is thrown in the forge, were everywhere. I had, apparently, discovered an enormous rookery.

One species in particular caught my eye. They were small and black but had an unusually wide wingspread and a red pouch under the beak. They lazily soared on the air currents, gliding beautifully out over the water. I watched for several minutes while a group plummeted, grabbed fish, and soared upward again, having barely touched the water. I wandered farther down the path, toward the water, my eyes fixed on these aerial gymnastics.

My eye caught the movements of one bird in particular. I stopped near a clump of scraggly, wind-swept cedars to watch. The bird was cruising majestically, hovering over the water and the other birds fishing. Then he chose to terrorize one bird in particular much smaller than himself, of course, and when this smaller bird dropped his prize, the bigger one snared it, secondhand, before it hit the water.

"Bully!" I called out to him in disgust, resuming my walk. "Pirate!"

Hardly had I taken another step when, from behind one of the trees, a strong hand reached out and deftly caught the bodice of my lace chemise. Suddenly a man's hand was clapped over my mouth, while his other landed at the neckline of my bodice, with the knuckles of his fist lodged between my breasts.

I looked up quickly and was assailed by a wild, contradictory jumble of emotions to discover that it was Mr. Winthrop who held me thus. I was vaguely aware that the drawstring of my chemise had loosened and that one or two of the buttons had fallen open. Before I could look down or repair the damage, much less utter a protest at this manhandling, Mr. Winthrop said low into my ear, "Not another peep out of you, Sedgwick, and no sudden movements."

My eyes blazed an answer to this. I attempted to convey the message, *I have heard those words from you before!* I was thinking of the morning that we had awakened to discover that we were cast adrift in an Atlantic current. However, this time, the circumstances were *quite* different.

So was his response. His blue eyes chuckled roguishly in return. Instead of tossing a wet brass ring into my lap, he continued to hold me in a rough grip. He cocked his head over to one side and rolled his eyes in the same direction, whispering in my ear now, "Look."

I looked. What I saw was most unexpected. Hopping toward a wooden cage, evidently whittled and fashioned by Mr. Winthrop himself, was one of the small, black birds with the little scarlet pouch.

"I'm trying to catch him," Mr. Winthrop explained, "and don't want him scared off." His tones were barely audible and tickled my ear.

My reply to this was inarticulate, since his hand was still over my mouth.

"Can I trust you not to scold if I unmuzzle you?" he asked.

I nodded vigorously. He lifted his hand experimentally from my mouth. When I did not immediately launch into what I thought of his behavior (which I had half a mind to do), he let his hand up all the way.

"Your *other* hand, sir," I whispered harsh and low. He complied. I twitched my bodice into place. "Thank you. Now, why do you wish to capture this fellow?"

He shrugged slightly. "It's a change from killing them, I suppose," he replied. "I'd like to study him."

"How do you know it's a *him*?" I inquired reasonably, objecting to the idea that every animal is male until proven otherwise.

"That much I've observed, for I've been here most of the morning,' he replied, with a provocative twinkle in his eye. "See what happens to his pouch when a hen passes by."

I had somehow not noticed that I was still standing stock against Mr. Winthrop's muscled chest and that his hands had been placed on my shoulders.

"Must I wait to see quite like this?" I asked, attempting to shake myself from his arms.

He countered my puny effort to free myself by tightening the steely bands of his arms around me. "Why, yes," he said, as if much struck by this idea. "Good of you to suggest it."

At that, he shifted his weight slightly and leaned back into the tree, still holding me. It was then that the quality of his embrace changed, from one of wishing to prevent me from scaring off his prey to one of a quite different intention. It was not *altogether* unpleasant.

Nevertheless, one of us had to observe the proprieties. "Sir, please unhand me," I said firmly, but attempting not to raise my voice.

"Why?"

Unwisely, I thought this impertinence deserved an answer. "Because I was just passing by and came upon you and your snare entirely by accident."

"But I," he said, "am an opportunist, you see. And what a pleasant accident it is that you fell right into my hands." He considered this, then added, "Not at all unlike the entire accident that brought us together here on this island."

"My point exactly!" I said. "We are just two people who have been, by an accident of fate, thrown together, and I fear that the past weeks we have spent with each other have been . . . have been . . . that is to say, I feel rather strongly that—"

"You feel rather strongly?" he interrupted. "That sounds promising."

"I feel rather strongly that we should take a care to observe in the strictest fashion the moral tone a man and woman would in England!" I finished, with emphasis.

"How dull!" he said to this. "Again, why?"

"Because . . . because,"—here I ridiculously groped for an adequate reason—"because we may find our boat any day now, in which case we would be off for the nearest European port, and at which point we would part company."

"Yes, that is very true," he agreed, straight-faced and quite seriously, as if he did *not* have me trapped between his legs. "Then, again, we may never find that boat. What then?"

"What, then, indeed!" was all I could think to say. I was feeling thoroughly flushed now. It was a *very* warm day, after all. I tried another tack. "Well, it is perfectly obvious that, were we in England, we would probably never have met, and if, in the unlikely event we had, we would not have had anything to do with each other."

"Too true!" he said with unflattering alacrity. "And it is equally obvious that we are *not* in England now, and not likely to be soon."

"Yes, and speaking of our present surroundings, allow me to point out that during these past weeks your sensibilities may have been strangely affected by—"

"My what?" he interrupted rudely.

"Your sensibilities," I repeated.

"That's what I thought you said." He laughed.

I ignored this and continued, "—that your sensibilities may have been strangely affected by these *unseemly* surroundings—"

"By these *what* surroundings?" he interrupted again, this time on a note of incredulity.

"Unseemly, sir!" I repeated. "As if it is not perfectly obvious—and has been so from the start!"

"The only unseemliness I have seen is you parading in your underwear in front of me," he said.

"I had absolutely no choice in the matter," I replied stiffly and quite accurately.

"Which does not, in the least, alter its general effect."

"I am far *more* dressed than many of the women," I argued logically.

"But I do not share a caney with any of them, and they are not wearing my necklace," he said, putting his hand to the shells at my throat.

"And what does that have to do with it?"

"Everything," he replied. "I'm a man, like any other."

"Necklace or no, many of the women—the young women—in town are half naked, while I am not!"

"You seem to have an exaggerated sense of the 'unseemliness' of Arawak life. As you well know, men are not allowed within ten feet of town proper during the day, and at the evening meal are strictly separated from the women. Hardly could I imagine a society less set up for 'unseemly' behavior, as you might call it."

Strangely enough, he seemed to have a point; and up until this moment, he had *not*, despite his avowal to the contrary, been behaving quite like any other man in a similar situation. However, I was not ready to concede any of this. "If that is the case, then how do you explain the most unseemly eyes that The Proud One—Alluring Eyes—has been making at you?"

"You mean Eyes Downcast, do you not?"'

"No, Alluring Eyes," I corrected immediately.

"I suppose that depends on your interpretation of the Arawak word referring to the slant of her eyes," he said.

"Aha!" I said, wildly diverted now by this turn in subject. "I knew, in the end, that this discussion would have something to do with *her*. As for the interpretation *Eyes Downcast,* I do not suspect the Arawak of irony!"

"You rise so beautifully to the fly, Sedgwick," he commented to this, "and are never more alluring yourself than when you are angry."

This remark had been calculated to anger me in earnest. "You should certainly know by now what counts as alluring," I fired back, "given the many alluring looks she has gratified you with of late!"

"While you have not," he replied. "But I've already told you that neither she nor any other example of alluring Arawak femininity could hold a particular appeal for me."

"You are joking!" I said to this.

"Why do you never believe me?" he complained.

"For one," I said, bethinking myself of my grievance against him in the last few weeks, "if you are referring to the fact that you wish to *communicate* with any woman with whom you might think . . . with whom you might contemplate . . . that is, any woman in which you might be *interested*." I finally said, "I notice that you have done precious little communicating with *me* of late!"

Our faces were inches apart, and I had a good view of the emotions that chased across the lean, unhandsome features that so unexpectedly formed an extremely attractive whole. From the look that had come into his eyes as they rested on me while I worked through the tangle of that last remark, I would have said that he had completely forgotten about not scaring off the bird he had been waiting the whole day to capture. He shifted his weight again, and I seemed to melt into him.

To this, he said, not attempting to mask his humor, "You are obtuse."

"I am not!" I said, indignant now, trying ineffectually to pull away from him. "You have not addressed a civil word to me in days!"

He shook his head. He moved his hands at last. "Not merely obtuse, but also an idiot. You cannot imagine why I have not?"

"No," I said simply, "I cannot."

"Which makes you—in addition to being an obtuse idiot— entirely adorable," he said to that.

I was used, by now, to Mr. Winthrop's turn for the outrageous, left-handed compliment. This one affected me powerfully, for while I had been called by men a great many things in my life, I had *never* been called "adorable."

With his head, he gestured to the mangrove bushes and said, rather allusively, "Our nest was thrust upon us *before* the courtship. An awkward circumstance, you'll admit."

I would, but that did not explain why he would not speak to me in the caney. "If you are referring to us getting to know each other, I might point out that we've had many evenings together in the past several weeks to talk, to converse, and to . . ." I trailed off here, but he did not press me to finish.

"Many long, *long* hours together, I'll agree," he said.

"But something has held you back," I said slowly, thinking back over those hours. So close to him now, I became aware of a tiny space inside him that he was guarding. The phrase that came to mind was "regretful reluctance." Even when put into words, I did not understand it.

He shook his head, declining a direct response. Instead, he continued, "First things first, and trust comes first." Then, with a very roguish smile, "Besides, like other creatures, I need the open air to offer my love."

"You are offering me your love?" I asked, suspicious.

"Every inch," he said.

That was plain enough. Should I have been shocked? I confess I was not. Remember that I had been a married woman and knew about such things. However, as I stood there, my partially bared breasts against his chest, my length pressed to his, my legs caught intimately between his thighs, I began to think that something essential had been missing in my marriage to Edward.

"Sir!" I said. "I think you are being vulgar."

"I hope I am not obscure," he replied, with an irresistible twinkle in the depths of his blue, blue eyes.

"Not at all," I said with a quiver in my voice which I hoped was interpreted as shock, rather than some less modest emotion. And in a paradoxical sense, I realized that he was conducting himself with a strange delicacy. "I thought you took the soldier's approach to love."

"You think a number of false things about me," he replied. His voice had a curiously serious tone that was belied by the gleam of humor and something else again in the depths of his eyes that effectively took my breath away.

"Do I take it that *this* forms a part of the courtship?" I queried.

"You are very obtuse and very idiotic," he said, "and very adorable. I'm an opportunist, as I've said, and the opportunity is now."

And that was all he said. The next moment, he bent his head to bridge the remaining few inches between us and nudged me into a kiss. Obviously, this was not the first time I had been kissed. I admit that I had never thought kissing a particularly interesting pastime. With Edward, for instance, handsome as he was . . . but I do not wish to bore the reader with those details (for they are, indeed, boring). It occurred to me, the moment Mr. Winthrop put his lips to mine, that my previous experience in kissing had not fully prepared me for this—or for any other of the extraordinary and new emotions I had experienced these few scant weeks in his company; most particularly, the ones I now felt in his arms.

His hands slid down my arms to catch my hands. He bent his arms at the elbows, lifting our hands, joined now palm to palm, slightly in the air. All our fingertips touched; I felt my heart split into ten separate pulses to beat in each individual fingertip. Then my heart flew to my lips to return the insistent beat of his.

A moment later, he placed my hands on his shoulders and slid his down my back. With his movement, I could feel the play of muscles beneath my pulsing fingertips. A streak of fire went down my spine. He smelled so clean, so scrupulously clean, as was the Arawak way— salty and fresh and smooth-shaven—that I was no longer sure where his body ended and mine began.

"You may certainly take it that this forms a part of our courtship," he said, not quite lifting his mouth from mine, but kissing each corner. This was followed by a soft kiss on my temples and another at the pressure point of my neck. "To which you may begin to respond at any time," he said, returning to his original point of contact.

Dear me, I thought, my knees buckling, I thought I had been responding. "You want more?" I asked, a little dazed.

"Much more." His teeth caught my bottom lip and his tongue ran along the inside. I might well have been obtuse and an idiot, but I did not mistake what he wanted and was happy to give it to him, with abandon.

It was so very, very natural that I did not once stop to think of my wanton behavior in kissing a man so deeply and so thoroughly—a half-naked man to whom I was not married, to whom I was neither betrothed nor had any immediate possibility of being pledged to. I merely savored the strange Caribbean elixir foaming through my veins, an intoxicating mix of gentle trade winds scented with salt and cedar, miraculously soft sunlight and deep pastels, the taste of papaya on a man's lips, the memory of bared flesh and flexed muscle joined to its touch, the grainy, gritty feel of sand underfoot, the strange squalling and calling of birds and the sweet chirp of tree frogs indistinguishable from Arawak cries coming toward us, the slip of bodice over breast, the spark of soft breast to muscled chest, the contact of thumb to nipple, the lifting of an underskirt—

Wait. The sounds of Arawak cries coming toward us?

Suddenly they were all around us—a dozen Arawak or more—crying out, jumping up and down, and generally making themselves obnoxious.

Mr. Winthrop raised his head and looked down at me, his sapphire eyes stained black. "Banish these folk!" he said with profound irritation. "Why can we never be rid of them when we want?"

CHAPTER 10

*I*magination has a way of playing tricks. In that moment when we became aware we had an audience, my desire for continuing in amorous congress with Mr. Winthrop raced ahead. His words must have operated on my admittedly deranged sensibilities with the force of magic. I believed they *had* been banished.

Now, where were we? Oh, yes. I looked up at him.

He looked down at me.

His really beautiful blue eyes were stained black with desire. I had never seen such a look in a man's eyes before—certainly never a look that had been inspired by the sight of me.

Our audience faded away to nothing. He ran his eyes over my dishevelment. A tiny blaze lit their depths. He raised a hand and wiped a bead of perspiration first from my brow, then from between my breasts.

"Sweating is the body's way," he whispered into my ear, "of weeping with desire."

These words produced a wave of emotion down to my toes. I raised my fingertips to the moisture at his neck and across his shoulders. "Cry baby," I returned.

"When you talk like that," he said, touching my ear with his tongue, "I take no responsibility for my actions."

He bent to kiss me again. I raised my lips willingly. The kiss was dark, dizzying, delightful. If I had been holding back before, I did not do so now. I realized then that in the past minutes, hours, days, even weeks now, in such close proximity to this man, I had come to think about him constantly, covetously, to desire him in the most *inappropriate* way (some would have called it wicked). He ran his hands down my bodice and opened it fully. I allowed my hands to roam at will across a lean, magnificent body with no soft flesh, one that had saved me, had protected me, and now desired me. It was a blunt, brazen, unabashed seduction, and I did not know who was seducing whom. Then he lifted my skirts and pulled me toward him fully. When my knees and stomach began to dissolve, I realized then who was lord and master of the situation. I even *welcomed* him, hailing him as my conqueror.

Now, in truth, none of this happened. Not the loverlike words, nor the embraces. But a moment had passed since we had perceived our Arawak intruders, and my love had groaned his irritation into my ear. He had straightened me up, and the next thing I knew, he was saying to me, gruffly, "Pull yourself together, Sedgwick!"

He meant it literally, of course. I was a wreck—and, in my swamp of emotion, quite irritated myself, but not so much at the interruption now as I was with Mr. Winthrop's quick recovery and unloverlike words. As I hastily set my dress aright, it crossed my mind that perhaps men were able to turn on and off their emotions and desires more easily than women, and did not indulge in such wild fantasies. (I was to learn later that I was wrong.) At the time, however, it seemed most unfair.

Perceiving now, out of the corners of my eyes, the spears that were being waved all about, I asked, "Have they decided to kill us *now*, after all this time?"

One young warrior quickly dispelled my fears. He, like the others behind him, was painted atrociously over face and chest. He was addressing Mr. Winthrop and had been doing so for the past several seconds. Out of the rapid, excited jumble, I made out the words, "Come quick! No time to lose! It is of the utmost importance!"

The young warrior gestured up the path to where Arawak Father was standing, also ferociously painted and bearing his spear. He stood in company of more warriors. The Dissenter was not among them. "You see them? They are waiting for you! Bring the Beauty—" at that, he gestured to me.

Mr. Winthrop glanced at me, his brows raised humorously.

"If you *dare* reinterpret my name—" I threatened ominously.

His warm glance reassured me, although his words did not. "Thatch of Fire seems most appropriate," he replied, all innocence.

The young warrior would have none of this byplay. "Bring her with you, or leave her here! We care not which! But *come*!"

"I am coming," I stated.

"Then, let's go!" repeated the young warrior with insistence, addressing Mr. Winthrop directly, apparently by name.

My attention was instantly caught. "*What* did he call you?" I demanded of Mr. Winthrop.

Mr. Winthrop had the audacity to grin. "Don't ask," he said.

"I thought your name was Blue Eyes."

"Is it, now?" he retorted with something closely resembling a smirk. Then he grabbed my hand and fairly pulled me up the path.

Explanations of the urgency of the occasion came from all directions in a babble of voices and information.

"It's them!" we were told.

"The monsters!"

"Yes, the monsters from across the sea!"

"The devils who are made of metal, not flesh and blood!"

"The devils who hold sticks of fire in their bare hands!"

I had not perfectly grasped the situation by the time we had reached the others awaiting us halfway up the mountain, at the spot where the path was swallowed by the usual jungle growth of palms and outsized ferns which doubled as trees. Nor was I to be better informed once we had arrived at Arawak Father's side. Instead, Mr. Winthrop and I were treated to what I would call a severe lecture on our behavior by Arawak Father. Actually, *I* was not directly addressed, since Arawak men and women do not speak to one another in public. In any case, Arawak Father concluded his remarks with the stern observation that (I interpret liberally): "Such public embraces, my son, are not permitted in Arawak society. In fact, they are considered to be in the worst of bad taste. But we will excuse you two on the grounds that you are not True Born of the People, that you will not indulge in such uninhibited displays again, and that we have very much more important events with which to occupy ourselves."

So much for the unseemliness of Arawak ways!

Arawak Father proceeded. He spoke always with authority and dignity, even when he had the least extraordinary thing to say. "We must make haste," he intoned. "Follow me."

His words might have been measured, but his actions were not. The group of us—about twenty warriors or so, Mr. Winthrop, and myself—did make haste up the rest of the path. As we fairly ran, more explanations, brief and halting, were given.

"They have come in their canoes," we were told by one or the other of them. "Their great, spiked canoes, draped with cloth!"

I had begun to understand the situation—rather clearly, in fact. So had Mr. Winthrop. Odds ran even that we were soon to be in a very difficult situation.

We were taking a path that skirted the village and headed deeper into the jungle, farther up the mountain. Mr. Winthrop protested. "No, I've got to stop in town first," he said.

They shook their heads. "No time! No time!" they chanted.

"My glass," he explained. "My telescope. I've got a telescope in the caney." Seeing their incomprehension, he turned to me: "Dammit, Sedgwick! *You* explain it!"

"Big eye," I tried. "Far eye. See far." Then, to Mr. Winthrop, I said, "You're right. We *must* find out who is approaching. Do you think we are soon to be saved?"

He looked down at me, an enigmatic, inscrutable look in his eye. "That depends on what we are to be saved *from*," he said.

He did not dwell on the point, however, for he was determined to retrieve his telescope before taking any step farther into the jungle. Between the two of us, we managed to convince the group that we needed the telescope.

The detour was quickly effected. Arawak Father and his group of warriors continued on into the jungle. Our group followed us. The sight of warriors running through town in broad daylight certainly turned the heads of all the women who had remained there on this day of rest. By the time we had retrieved the telescope from Mr. Winthrop's leather case, had found a clearing at the southeast end of town, and Mr. Winthrop had climbed a tree in order to look out to the sea, we had collected into our group every woman and child within a hundred yards of town proper. It had turned into a gay and noisy crowd. The air was full of expectation—and even, curiously, delight.

Mr. Winthrop held the long glass to his eye for a brief, considering moment. Then he lowered it slowly, and turned to look down at the crowd gathered round the tree.

"The enemy," he concurred, seeming almost pleased, "in one form or another."

He climbed down. I stretched out my hand for the long glass, and without once considering the indignity of what I was doing, scrambled up the tree for my own view.

With the naked eye, I could see a great red ship, still far off, drawing slowly, majestically, toward the island, by way of the southern bay. At its present rate, it might be able to cast anchor and send its wherries to shore in the next several hours. With the long glass, I could discern from this great distance the glint of brass cannons mounted on the prow above the curving beak-head. I could not quite make out the seamen on board, but I did not need their dress or demeanor to confirm what Mr. Winthrop had already discovered. Soaring above the mainmast fluttered smartly the gold and crimson banner of Castile.

"The Spanish," I breathed, as I descended from the tree into Mr. Winthrop's outstretched arms.

"Not necessarily," Mr. Winthrop replied. "They might be, as well, pirates or buccan-hunters sailing under false colors."

"Pirates or buccaneers?" I repeated tonelessly, only now perceiving the potential gravity of this situation. "And if so, what are we to do?"

"The same thing in all events, we are to defend ourselves against them," he said to me, placing me on the ground. His hands lingered at my waist before he turned back to the crowd, which was evidently awaiting his next words. "Show me what it is in the jungle that is so important, Brave One," he said to the warrior-spokesman.

Brave One was more than happy to comply. The group turned as one to race through town (trampling some of my careful plantings in the process—much to my irritation!) to a path on the far side I had never before followed. A few of the women, inspired, perhaps, by my example, accompanied us into the jungle. Such mixed groups were extremely rare in Arawak society, and the acceptance of the presence of women in the group attested to the unusualness of the situation.

The jungle immediately swallowed us. I knew by this time that the denseness of the forest opened into a loosely connected system of dells and great clumps of creeper-hung trees; that it was always and ever a vague, steaming, antediluvian world. It was a rain forest, of course. It had just rained and would rain again soon, such that raw, spongy,

rain-sodden soil underfoot percolated with little rivulets of water, collecting and swelling and running together. We penetrated ever deeper
into the forest, climbing slightly; crossed ankle-deep riffles of water
and small rocks; and continually slashed our way through the growth.
So accustomed was I to the surroundings that, from the trilling
squawks around me, I could now spot the green plumage touched
with shades of orange and brilliant blue of the parrots, which would
make them such an ornamental pet in England but which rendered
them nearly invisible in the vivid forest canopy. Crowded in this
world I knew to be birds, bats, toads, lizards, insects, tree frogs, and,
yes, even snakes, but as we crashed through their kingdom, I was no
longer afraid or horrified or otherwise negatively affected by their
presence. I found the dense growth and the life that dwelled within
reassuring, almost comforting, in the sense that I knew it to be our
surest protection against the intruders soon to land on our shores.

Then we stopped. We seemed to be at the densest part of the jungle,
that part where a bewildering variety of trees support in their crowns
a whole world of air and parasitic plants that live almost entirely out
of touch with the ground. Up there, one hundred feet above our
heads—in bright sunshine, as now, or heavy rain—were rich, teem-
ing colonies. To that height vines and scrambling plants aspire, and
from it the extraordinary plant—what the Arawak called *kaklin*—
sends down its hawserlike roots. These kaklin roots are more like veg-
etable probes and hang straight down from the topmost branches of
the forest trees. This spot in the jungle was draped in these roots,
ranging in diameter from the size of a man's finger to as big around as
a man's forearm. When they reached the ground they seemed to take
root again and begin to grow in girth. I had no bearings whatsoever
and could not have found my way out of the jungle alone to save my
life. It was my general impression, however, that we had traveled
toward the southwestern tip of the island, and found ourselves near a
cliff.

The Arawak, both men and women, knew to a turning the pathway where they were. They were already bending over a strange mound of earth and uncovering what looked to be a natural pile of roots, old leaves, branches, and trunks of decayed trees that had fallen haphazardly.

Soon this mound was undone, and the Arawak stepped back from it to allow us a view of what it was they so ardently wished us to see. Since he was (*as usual*) standing in front of me, Mr. Winthrop stepped forward first and looked down into what was evidently a pit.

He stopped still, then stepped back as if stunned, or somehow blinded. "So *that's* it," he breathed in accents of awe. "That's why they have wanted so desperately to keep us!"

I had thought, not without good reason, that it was my hair and its perhaps magical associations that had caused the Arawak to wish to keep us. However, a vain thought exists only to be pricked and deflated, so I, in my turn, stepped to the edge of the pit and looked into it.

I, too, was stunned by what I saw. In fact *blinded* is the correct word. Even in the muted lights and shades of the jungle—or perhaps because of it—the gleam and glint of the contents of the pit momentarily hurt my eyes.

I was gazing down into a pit at least fifteen feet in diameter and perhaps as many feet deep, filled with *pure gold*. At first, in my amazement, I saw merely an undifferentiated heap of gold. As my eye adjusted, however, I saw that the mass could be decomposed into objects to be worn, such as bands, rings, bracelets, necklaces, pendants, circlets, crowns, and even masks; objects to be held, such as bells, scepters, tridents, wheels, and shields; as well as objects to be admired, such as shells and parrots. The longer I looked, the more I was able to discern. Some of the objects were decorated with jewels—red gems like rubies and green ones like emeralds—and here and there gleamed points of silver.

It was a treasure so vast, so immeasurable, that rumor of it might well have spread to the greedy ears of the Spanish. I now understood the sense of urgency that had spread through town, that spurred the warriors, that charged this corner of the forest. It was the kind of energy that surrounds the doors of furnaces, or coffins of rich men, and attracts all those seeking heat and riches and possible death. I wondered whether the Spanish, with their noses trained for gold, could *smell* their way to this hidden spot.

I looked at Mr. Winthrop, who was standing next to me, immobile. He was lost in thought. Feeling my gaze on him, he looked up from the pit and met my eyes, gravely.

"Now we know," he said slowly. "Now we know what we're doing here."

I agreed with Mr. Winthrop's unspoken conclusion. In the past hundred years and more, the red man of the New World had not been particularly successful in defending his treasures against the rapacious appetites of the white man. No doubt the Arawak had reasoned that Mr. Winthrop and I might be better able to defend them against the wiles and stratagems of the next hostile invasion from our own kind.

"Yes, now we know. It's a fortune worth protecting by seizing whatever meager defensive measure might come their way," I said, a little sadly, thinking of the well-built, well-armed Spanish ship just off our shores.

"A fortune worth dying for," he stated, looking up and around at the intent and proud, brave and resigned copper faces circling the pit, returning his regard. "And, more to the point, it is a fortune worth killing for," he added, evidently thinking, as I had, of that same well-built, well-armed ship sailing straight for our unarmed, unprotected island.

"They will kill for the fortune," I pointed out, "only if they know —or suspect—one is here."

"A pertinent point," he acknowledged. "The question is, then, do they have prior knowledge of the treasure? Do they merely suspect it? Or, is this a chance stop? If the latter is the case, then we might do well to lie low and not advertise our presence at all."

"You mean they might come and go without ever knowing the island is inhabited?" I asked, heartened by this idea.

"That's one possibility," he said, "and the easiest one to plan for. I've got to know first what this treasure represents—whose it is, where it came from."

At that, he turned toward the group, which was watching silently, waiting patiently for him to speak. Even Arawak Father's eyes rested on him. Speaking aloud for all the group to hear, Mr. Winthrop addressed several questions to Arawak Father.

Arawak Father took a breath that filled the cavity of his chest to its proudest swell. He stepped away from us, toward the edge of the golden pit, and planted his spear in the ground. Despite the imminence of the crisis, his story unfolded in slow and measured words thusly:

"Before the White Devils came to our land, the Arawak and our cousins the Taino and the Siboneyan and the Guanahatabeyes and the Paressis lived peaceably among ourselves. I do not speak of the Caribs," he said with great dignity. "I never speak of the Caribs. They call themselves brave men." Here he shook his head. "We call them savage beasts.

"But I do not speak of the savage beasts," he continued, "I speak only of The People: of the Taino, the Siboneyan, the Guanahatabeyes, and the Paressis. There was no fighting among us." He paused. If it had been anyone other than Arawak Father, I would have interpreted the gleam in his eye as one of humor. He continued, dignified and straightfaced, as before. "No fighting, save for the usual disputes over fishing rights, women, and which man from which tribe was the strongest. In the time of my grandfathers and their grandfathers, women might be carried off, men might die, honor might be lost, but only through pride or lack of skill—never through treachery. The gold of one people was never taken by another people. Now, however—"

Here, emotion choked his voice. He began again. "Now, however, the White Devils with the sticks of fire have come. They have driven the people off their islands. They have carried off our women and killed our men. They have taken our gold, as well. And always through treachery. It is not the treachery of their sticks of fire. No. It is the treachery of their words. Their words are not like the people's words. Their words never sit still. Always their words are blown away on the wind. They have a sheaf of leaves upon which they etch their words. They open the sheaf one day and pronounce the words and their meanings. But this sheaf is magical, treacherous. When it is closed, the etchings do not rest on the leaves. They are imbued with the evil spirit and move from one leaf to the next, so that the next time they open the sheaf, the etchings mean something else. That means that more women are carried off, more of our men are killed, more of our gold is taken.

"Some years ago, The People came together at one of our councils. It was after the fifth moon—about this time of year, when we complete marriage contracts, trade, and feast together. The Paressis had suffered much that year. Not only was much of their gold taken, but their silver reserves, coming from the men in the south, was found and taken, too. We could not allow that to happen again to one of our cousins. We had to act. We decided that Arawak Island should be the hiding place of our collected gold reserves. This island is the least known, the least on the pathways of the White Devils. It was good. When next it was the Siboneyan who were attacked, the White Devils found nothing. Nothing! To be sure, their evil spirit's anger was unleashed with a fury on the Siboneyan. Their villages were burned, their warriors killed, their women ravaged—but, again, I do not speak of the actions of savages. The Siboneyan heritage and treasure was saved for the coming generations. The White Devils know now there is nothing for them on that island, and they will never bother it again. Our Siboneyan cousins have begun to rebuild themselves.

"All the Zemis—the spirits—have told Great Arawak Mother that the White Devils were coming to Arawak Island. There had been many signs, many portents, most of them evil. However, when The Beauty and Blue Eyes appeared on our shores in their canoe, we realized that the spirits also knew how to smile on the Arawak and their cousins. The Beauty, with her hair the color of the Great Ancestress of the Zemis, was most obviously sent by Her. The Beauty brought with her Blue Eyes, a man with the White Devil's body and thinking. Blue Eyes passed all of our tests, and now possesses the Arawak's soul. It is good."

Arawak Father said nothing more.

Mr. Winthrop had been listening to this recital without moving a muscle or making any other outward movements. I knew enough of him now to know that such was his attitude when he was devising a plan. Although I suspected that Mr. Winthrop had the tiniest, most niggling doubt that Arawak Father had overestimated the smiling favors of the Zemis, he, of course, betrayed nothing of it.

We both knew that the sum of the sophistication in our possession included the instruments of sailing, one musket, one pistol, three bullets, and several cannon matches. The main core of Arawak warriors counted several hundred, and there were several hundred other men who could be summoned to duty. Still, all their spears and bows and arrows were no match for even poorly armed Spanish. Mr. Winthrop and I had, nevertheless, understood the gist of what was at stake here for the Arawak, which was nothing less than their honor and lives. Neither had we any doubt about what our supposed role was to be in preserving both.

Mr. Winthrop shook off his immobility and asked a final question.

It was haltingly framed, but Arawak Father understood it immediately.

"Could the White Devils know of our treasure?" Arawak Father echoed. "Certainly. They have captured many of our warriors, tortured them, sold them into slavery, and worse. They could have been told of the wealth stored here, by one or another of The People who was not able to live up to the memory of his mother and his mother's mothers. I cannot say. I will not say."

Mr. Winthrop considered this information. He held Arawak Father's eyes steadily for another few moments, and then came his calls to action. The first act, needless to say, was to artfully recover the pit.

There were approximately three alternatives available to explain what the Spanish ship was doing skirting our shores, and we were to prepare as well as we could for all three contingencies. The first was to clear everyone out of town and into hiding places in the jungle. A group of warriors was sent down to town to accomplish this. In the case that the Spanish were merely stopping off on the island by chance, and landed on the southern bay, if they found the path that led to town, it would be best for them to find a town that at least *looked* deserted. They might even be tricked into thinking that it had been abandoned, perhaps even some time ago. Instructions were given to make the town look as abandoned as possible.

However, if the Spanish had come with a purpose, difficulties immediately arose. One lone *large* Spanish galleon could be counted on to have aboard several hundred men. What they lacked in sheer numbers, however, being overpowered by the Arawak warriors two to one, they more than compensated for with fire power. The Arawak had had enough experience with the Spanish to know that.

Thus we prepared for perhaps many days of hiding, of eluding Spanish soldiers who might take to the jungle in search of the treasure. Elaborate plans were devised for the guarding of the treasure, with watches posted, reinforcements designated, and reinforcements of the reinforcements assigned. Arawak Father stayed at the pit to guard it. I imagined that he would not budge from it until either the Spanish were no longer a threat or he had been killed.

Mr. Winthrop had given me tasks to do in town and with the women. I fulfilled them. All was frenzied activity in those hours of the mid-afternoon.

At one point, I met Mr. Winthrop on a path. Strangely enough, he was wearing his lace shirt. He was in company of several men; I in company of Sylvia, Rose, and Lily.

"What," he demanded hotly, "is that?"

"You see very well," I replied, "that it is my parasol. I thought I might need it."

Instead of making any irrelevant comments, he merely grunted, then grabbed me by the arm and said, "We're on our way to the look-out. They should be landing soon. Come."

Hand in hand, followed by a mixed group of men and women, we ran to the wooded crag in the mountain that jutted out over the southern bay. When we got there, to our astonishment and initial relief, we beheld empty waters, an empty shoreline, and empty land.

Mr. Winthrop discussed the situation with several of the men. They came to no easy agreement. Perhaps the ship had circled the island, missing it entirely? It had not seemed so from the direction of her sails the hour before. Mr. Winthrop withdrew the long glass from inside his shirt and scanned the southern and eastern horizon. The western horizon was blocked by the mountain.

Then a look of dawning horror crossed his features. He turned to me. "Can it be?"

"Anything is possible," I replied wisely, without a clue as to what he might mean.

More discussion ensued. The warriors maintained that the Spanish could not have headed around the *western* portion of the island. There were too many rocks. Mr. Winthrop countered by arguing that the Spanish were not afraid of rocks. Furthermore, the shallow waters there were both a disadvantage and an advantage for them. If they weighed anchor far enough out, they could send boats in to the rock and wade to the island. Half a ship could be unloaded, and one hundred Spaniards might be on land in under an hour's time.

There was still an hour or two of daylight left. We were running now, about ten of us, back to the treasure. Mr. Winthrop was experienced in the ways of the jungle and darted this way and that, moving in zig-zag fashion ever west, alerting the groups hidden at various places of the potentially new, more pressing danger. We reached the treasure, ran past it even, to climb a small hill, still densely forested, just beyond.

We were, as I had suspected, far to the west and the south on the island. Before us unrolled the blue waters of the sea, dancing with sun guineas in the late afternoon. With the naked eye I could just discern a smoky blue shape, perhaps the outline of another island. Below us dropped a cliff several hundred feet down. It was not quite sheer, but extremely steep and tufted at intervals with clumps of trees growing almost at right angles from the rock. At the bottom of the cliff was a bay, cramped and rocky, not as hospitable for sailors as the wide sandy sweep of the southern bay.

Despite this evident drawback, at the mouth of the bay stood the Spanish galleon, miniaturized to a toy by the distance, but no less fear-inspiring for all of that, even with its sails furled. Its deck swarmed with men, in the choppy waters bobbled Johnnie boats, and already on the sandy verge of beach stood what must have been the captain of the enterprise and three of his men.

Mr. Winthrop's muttered words were all that was appropriate. He recovered from his anger, then bade us lie down on the ground—the six men and four women—to flatten ourselves from view. Mr.

Winthrop withdrew the long glass from inside his shirt and eyed the situation.

I stretched out next to Mr. Winthrop and laid my parasol next to me. Our faces were almost touching.

"I would like nothing more than to hear you say that you have a plan," I whispered. (My precaution was quite unnecessary at this point. The Spanish were too far away from us to hear our words, just as we could not hear them.)

His profile was grave, but when he lowered his long glass and turned toward me to answer, I saw laughter light the depths of his eyes. "We could send *you* among the Spanish, Sedgwick—armed with your parasol and your best intentions, of course! They wouldn't last a day on the island!"

Mr. Winthrop evidently thought this remark amusing. "I have not imperiled your existence for several weeks now, sir!" I said with perfect truth. "And at this very moment I find your whimsy *quite* inappropriate!"

Still smiling, he turned back to peer through his long glass. His sight was trained at the very foot of the cliff in the center of the group of sailors. He paused a long moment before replying, without any embellished language whatsoever.

"For once, you are right, Sedgwick," he said in a toneless voice that told its own story. "They have a map."

CHAPTER 11

Mr. Winthrop laid the long glass in my outstretched palm. "See for yourself," he invited.

I put the instrument to my eye and peeked just over the ridge of the cliff and straight down, onto the tops of the heads of the four men standing on the beach, several hundred feet below us. I had a perfect view of the curling sheet of parchment being held by four pairs of hands. I could not quite determine the outlines of the map from this distance, but I could tell from the way they were turning and tilting it and positioning themselves with respect to its coordinates, gesturing first to the bay, then up the face of the cliff, that they had an excellent idea of the exact spot of the treasure.

Who had drawn the map and how the Spaniards had come to have it in their possession were not questions that could be answered. It was enough that someone—some Indian, captured and tortured—had drawn it, and drawn it with complete accuracy.

I lowered the glass and looked back at Mr. Winthrop. He was issuing instructions to the others, who were lined up away from us in a row on their stomachs, peering, in their turns, over the edge to the danger below.

When Mr. Winthrop had finished and turned back to me, I handed him the long glass with the words, "They know it's here, and they know where it is."

"Yes," he said, accepting the instrument. He allowed his eyes to roam over me intently, rather gravely, very slowly. They traveled down the length of my unbound hair, which fell in a wild tangle down my back. They strayed to my bare feet, then to the backs of my calves, which were exposed, since the hem of my underskirt was hitched under my legs. They wandered back up to my bodice, which was gaping open slightly in this prone position. I did not move or otherwise attempt to cover myself from this intimate scrutiny. The time for false modesty had long passed. His eyes lifted then, lazily, to my face, to touch my mouth and rest upon my eyes. He did not have to tell me his immediate thoughts, for they were writ plain enough in the desire in his eyes.

"Have we no hope to stop them?" I asked quietly.

"We'll be able to hold them off," he replied directly, "for a while."

He had turned his length toward me slightly. We were lying a breath apart. He did not touch me. He did not need to.

He continued speaking: "The first party of men will scale the cliff. We—even just the few of us here—can easily rid ourselves of them. The cliff face is in full view of the wherries coming ashore and the anchored galleon. It is doubtful whether they will continue to storm the cliff face once they lose four or five men to us."

"We could wait until each reaches the top before we get him," I suggested. "Those waiting below need not know that we are here, and we could capture them one by one."

Mr. Winthrop had already thought this idea through and discarded it. "Several hundred is well beyond our capacity to successfully capture. In any case," he said, shaking his head, "they will have decided to signal when they reached the top. The treasure stands not twenty yards away, behind us. It would be a matter of minutes between the time they reach the top, then signal that they have located the treasure."

"Shall we hold out as long as we can, then?" I asked.

He nodded. "As long as we can," he affirmed quietly. "Depending on how many men we are able to stop initially, I would predict that most of them will decide to regain the ship and land again at the more welcoming southern bay. They'll comb the island for the treasure. They'll burn what they have to and kill whom they meet. They will not stop until they have the treasure loaded on ship. Very few things could, or would, stop them."

"The Spanish give no quarter?" I asked.

"No quarter," he replied.

"But you were released from your Spanish prison in one piece," I said, searching for a glimmer of hope in this hopeless situation.

He smiled, almost wistfully. "Not if Don Pedro had had his way," he commented.

"Your jailer?" I asked. I recalled the name from an earlier conversation we had had on the subject.

"My nemesis, more like," he said. "Or I was his. We had a long history. I was captured after sinking one of his boats, the *Encarnacion*, four years ago, not far from Amsterdam."

"If that is the case, how *did* you manage to be released?" I asked reasonably.

"A trick of fate—a piece of information that fell into my hands. An accident." He shrugged. "I'm an opportunist, remember? I've been meaning to tell you—" He broke off. Then he shook his head. "No more of that. It doesn't matter anymore. Not now—not in these circumstances."

I saw no reason to probe that last remark, for I naturally interpreted it in terms of our immediate conditions. We heard the shouts of the men below, issuing instructions, determining how best to scale the almost sheer face of the wall of the cliff. We heard a clink and a clatter rather closer below us. We did not need our eyes to realize that the Spanish had already climbed a little way up the cliff and had thrown a rope with a cleat attached to it to grasp the trunks of a clump of trees that grew out of a small ledge about fifty feet below us.

After a long moment, I asked, "Any regrets?" I encompassed in my question the whole of our life together from the moment on the sinking *Judith* that my hands reached up to grasp the last remaining boat and met his.

"Only one," he answered lazily, his eyes on me, unmistakably.

Lying next to him, so close that I breathed with him, I had merged with his thoughts. The actual words we had been exchanging had not formed the content of what we were saying to each other. We were both remembering the sweet, seductive, satisfying kisses we had exchanged earlier in the day on the beach and the sweet, seductive, satisfying final embrace that should have come, but for the untimely interruption of the Arawak warriors—and the Spanish. Having had the foretaste of Mr. Winthrop, I began to feel really rather *cheated* by it all.

We had been one now for many days in survival, and now we were soon to become one in death. "I do have one regret, too—that is, besides the *other* regret," I said without the barest trace of a blush. I explained, "It's your feet."

"My feet?" he returned, pardonably puzzled.

"It was the coals," I said. "You cannot imagine what I felt watching you walk over them."

"Yes," he said, "I can." Incredibly, his harsh, unhandsome face had relaxed into a smile.

"Let me see them," I asked.

He showed me the soles of his feet. They were hideously scarred.

"How *did* you stand it?" I inquired. "I nearly fainted from the very sight of your pain."

"Physical pain," he said, "passes." He considered the question a little longer. Neither of us was averse now to discussing topics that we had deliberately avoided in the past days and weeks—those that had touched too close to our strangely intertwined lives, our very existence, and our future together, which was now, probably, to be brutally short.

"Physical pain passes," he repeated thoughtfully, looking away from me, out into the distance. "I knew it would not last more than several seconds in time."

"But afterwards," I insisted, "the pain must have lasted and been very real."

"It was," he admitted. Then, he gave a little shrug. "But it was not nearly as bad as the mental anguish I experienced during two *very* long and real years in prison. And with Don Pedro for my tormentor. . . ."

At those words, he gazed out over the cliff and down on the heads of the Spaniards, frowning heavily, recalling, perhaps, the worst of bad memories. Then, his expression changed swiftly from painful recall to startled disbelief. He snatched the long glass to his eye and surveyed the ascending Spaniards, then lowered it and turned toward me. His face transfigured by complete surprise, he said, "But, speaking of the devil, here he comes now!" To my look of blankest inquiry, he explained, "Don Pedro is heading this landing party. That must be the *Cinco Llagas*," he said, nodding in the direction of the ship. "Well, well! Don Pedro! It is as if, by very mention of his name, I conjured him! Like magic!"

"Then perhaps you can find other magic words to make him disappear," I said quite practically and with feeling. "I believe that 'abracadabra' is commonly used in such instances."

He looked at me, his eyes dancing now with delight and his own devilment. "Sedgwick, you are right again! There are very many words I can think of to make him disappear! I wonder. . . ."

This time, when his words trailed off, it was not in sad reminiscence. He was considering the possible advantages in the highly fortuitous circumstances that it was a man well known to him who was now scaling the cliff. Mr. Winthrop had gone quite still. He was evidently devising another plan.

For those of you who feel inclined to sneer at the amazing coincidence that brought Don Pedro to the shores of this island and for those of you who would dismiss this meeting between the two adversaries as little more than artful contrivance, allow me to observe that since having lived this adventure, I have come to believe that life itself is little more than a series of coincidences. Open a history book, and you will find random coincidence at work bringing about remarkable events that different, equally random coincidence would have determined otherwise. Although my story makes no claims to grand history, the principles are the same, and the coincidental meeting soon to be between Don Pedro and Mr. Winthrop is *not* the most extraordinary coincidence to have shaped our shared destiny.

"Watch this, Sedgwick!" Mr. Winthrop said a moment later and sprang into action. He rolled over and spoke briefly, but deliberately and with precision, to the Arawak warriors beside him. He took a last look through the long glass, seemed to like very much what he saw, and handed this instrument to Brave One. He then withdrew the pistol from his shirt and his sling shot and bequeathed them to Brave One, as well.

As was now usual for a man of Mr. Winthrop's temperament and talents, he did something entirely unexpected and most remarkable. He went to the treasure pit, rapidly uncovered a corner of it, and began to withdraw a motley variety of gold pieces. He donned rings on toes and fingers and bracelets at ankles and wrists. He shoved armbands up the sleeves of his shirt and slung necklaces over his head to lodge under the ragged lace at his neck. More laden with gold than any Arawak I had yet seen, he grabbed a bejeweled scepter and finally, a golden mask. This mask fit perfectly on his head and covered his face down just below his nose. Its crown was shaped like a bird's crest, also jeweled, and came to an end just at his top lip, at which point a quite outsized and rather hideous golden tongue was fashioned to stick out and over his mouth, covering his lips from view, yet permitting them to move unencumbered. The mask was both eerie and exotic and made him look, from the neck up, like a golden bird of paradise.

As an afterthought, so it seemed, he came over to me, withdrew his pocket knife, and without so much as a by your leave, chopped a length of tresses from my hair and stuffed the curls into his pants. It was so odd and unexpected that I had no chance to protest (nor will I comment on the symbolic significance of the gesture). He dropped the knife at my side.

Then he walked near the edge of the cliff, critically surveyed the strange kaklin roots that hung from the top branches of the forest trees, found one very long, medium-sized root and tugged on it with all his weight. When the root held him, he immediately took five running steps and swung himself out over the cliff, howling a thoroughly blood-chilling cry, and landed on his sure and disfigured feet on a ledge in the cliff no more than one foot wide and two feet long. It happened so quickly that I did not have a moment in which to be anxious or even to shut my eyes against the horror of a slip.

He did not slip. Instead, the great gilt-headed bird stood, hands on hips, feet splayed, to look magnificently down upon the four Spaniards who had reached the little plateau about ten feet below his own minuscule ledge.

"*¡Hombres blancos!*" he intoned fearsomely. "*¡Perros españoles!*" he spat with great scorn. He paused dramatically before rolling the words off his golden tongue, pronounced as a chilling malediction, "*¡¡D-o-n P-e-d-r-o!!*"

As anyone can easily imagine, this entrance and these words effectively captured the Spaniards' attention. One of them was heard to say,

"*¡Válgame Dios!*"

Two others of them were so surprised that they nearly lost their footing. These two poor unfortunates saved themselves from a fall of over one hundred feet to broken rocks below by grasping blindly at the branches of a sturdy bush whose roots, miraculously, held their weight. They eventually righted themselves, never once taking their bulging eyes off the great golden bird with the man's body who seemed to have flown to the ledge above them without the aid of wings.

At the sound of the name *Don Pedro* rolling off the golden tongue of a bird on a remote Caribbean island, one man in particular was powerfully affected.

"Yes, I know your name, *diablo blanco*," the great man-bird said, "and that of your ship, the *Cinco Llagas*."

The man's eyes widened to saucers. This was Don Pedro, then—a tall, handsome gentleman with windswept hair and neat-clipped beard. He was a singularly elegant man, dressed as he was in the characteristically Spanish suit of black taffetas with silver lace. He had abandoned what was no doubt an equally elegant breast-plate, along with a sword, in order to make the climb, and was obviously regretting it, for his right hand went automatically to his left side and he seemed disoriented at grasping nothing but air.

The great man-bird laughed mockingly, witheringly, at this empty gesture. "Your weapons—your sticks of fire, your swords, your lances, your spears from across the sea— will avail you nothing here," he said to them in the perfect accents of their native tongue.

(So clear to me was the situation that, even with my imperfect command of the Castilian tongue, a translator would have been superfluous.)

Don Pedro, rather pale and still visibly shaken, had nevertheless somewhat recovered. He was not going to be so easily taken in. He reached into his doublet, withdrew from the waist of his pantaloons a pistol, and aimed it straight at the great man-bird's heart.

Mr. Winthrop must have been anticipating such a move for he had simultaneously called out in Arawak the word "Shoot!" and Brave One had already raised his sling shot. With one stone and perfect aim, Brave One picked off the pistol from Don Pedro's hand. Mr. Winthrop had obviously taught him well. Mr. Winthrop had furthermore been shaking his golden scepter directly at the pistol all this time, so that in their continuing awestruck confusion, the Spanish might well have thought that the great man-bird who flew without wings had made the pistol fall by the magic powers of his scepter.

The pistol fell from Don Pedro's hand and clattered down the side of the mountain. In the process, it was triggered to explode a bullet which ricocheted noisily for several seconds afterward.

Nothing carefully planned could have been more arresting than the effect of Don Pedro's falling pistol. The Spanish swarming the beach had now stopped still and were looking up, immobile, at what was going forward on the side of the cliff. Even the men continuing to traverse the bay in their little boats seemed to stop and watch the drama of four men and a bird perched so improbably on the side of the mountain.

Nevertheless, Don Pedro's eyes narrowed slightly. He was determined not to be thrown off his guard or scared out of his wits. The man next to him had subsequently raised his pistol to shoot at the bird, but Don Pedro put his hand out to stop him. Don Pedro wished to discover for himself what was at the bottom of this display.

"Who are you in those clothes, O Impostor?" Don Pedro returned with a great deal of skepticism and bravado (one had to admire his sang-froid. It made me realize just *how* ruthless an enemy he might prove to be, if he ever did make it the rest of the way up the side of the cliff).

"These are the clothes," the bird returned, "of the last White Devils to land here."

With those words, Mr. Winthrop ripped off the silk shirt to expose the mass of gold on his chest and arms. The sun, a swollen orb of fiery copper in the waning afternoon, shed its light on the western face of the cliff and glanced off the gold. The Spanish blinked and were bedazzled.

Then, to my (rather immodest) surprise, he stripped off what was left of his velvet knee-breeches and let them go the way of his silk shirt. I covered my eyes. I uncovered them. I was in fact either relieved or profoundly disappointed that he was not naked at all, but rather wore the Arawak male's breech clout under his knickers. He wore his undress so comfortably that I suspected then that he must have worn the Arawak male dress customarily in the jungle but only at the end of the day donned the knee-breeches in front of me. His almost-naked body was bronzed a deep golden-red, was muscled and wolf-hard and quite, quite *magnificent*.

He whipped the curls of my red hair from the waist of his breech clout and shook them high in the air. "And this is what is left of the beards — *las barbas rosas* — of those White Devils!!" My curls, too, he allowed to be carried away on the wind. By the way the Spaniards' eyes followed the fate of those red curls, I guessed that they were giving serious consideration to the powers of the golden man-bird.

However, I could see that Mr. Winthrop had not yet convinced Don Pedro. The Spaniard opened his mouth to challenge, but the golden bird cut him off.

"I see the doubt written on your face, White Devil!" the golden bird spoke. "I will have no more of it!" He made a wide sweeping gesture, expressive of divine anger. Then he began to speak, slowly and in Arawak, as if pronouncing a magic formula. The Spaniards watched, open-mouthed.

What Mr. Winthrop really said is this: "Brave One, do you see the snake coiled in the tree above the man who stands next to the captain? When I shake my scepter three times I want you to shoot the snake down. Use only your pebbles, not the arrows. I want no trace of your handiwork to be seen."

I could not have torn my eyes away from the scene if I had wanted to. The golden bird slowly shook his scepter three times—during which, the look of derisive skepticism did not fade one fraction from Don Pedro's face. Then, with a *whizz* and a *zing*, Brave One's stone hit its mark and to my—and each Spaniard's—complete terror, a pink-and-coral snake some ten feet long fell from its branch to curl around the neck and arms of the man standing next to Don Pedro.

The skin on my back and scalp reared up. I cannot describe the blind terror of the scene that ensued. The poor man wrapped in the snake screamed in the worst fright I had ever heard pass human lips. His terror was mercifully short. He writhed with the creature for only a few horrific moments before he lost his footing and fell, still coiled in the serpent, more than a hundred feet to an instant and crumpled death.

So unexpected and so dizzyingly confusing to the other three Spaniards had been the attack from above that one of the remaining three had looked up, startled, in his turn, and crouched down to ward off a similar attack to himself, but in the process, he, too, lost his footing. He fell to a horrible, bone-crushing death only moments after his comrade.

"*Omnia munda mundis*," the golden man-bird pronounced.

Mr. Winthrop, I remembered, was an occasional Papist. Although I did not hold with ideas from Rome, his use of Latin seemed to turn the trick. I did not look down on the two broken bodies below me, but I fully registered the face of Don Pedro. The sneer had been wiped clean, to be filled now with pure terror. I thought that Mr. Winthrop and his magic words might just pull off this fantastic *tour de force* after all.

I looked over at Brave One, the other warriors, and at Sylvia, Rose, and Lily, who were returning my regard with eyes shining with a joy similar to mine—with admiration, gratitude, and every companionable human feeling possible between people from such two different worlds.

Then, just out of the corner of my eye and beyond the heads of my dear Arawak friends, I saw something move stealthily and afar off on the other side of the jungle. It was a man. With a fresh surge of very new and different alarm, I saw him move toward the edge of the cliff.

In a flash, I recognized him. I had not thought about him all day, had not inquired into his whereabouts or activities. It was a man who clearly intended Mr. Winthrop grave harm —The Dissenter.

I looked down at the weapons available to me. I quickly discarded the idea of the pistol, which I did not know how to operate and which would make a terrible racket, besides an ugly mess. When I eased myself away from the edge of the cliff, I armed myself with weapons much more to my liking.

Parasol and pocket knife in hand, I touched the shoulders of Sylvia, Lily, and Rose, and gestured with my head for them to follow me. They did not question my leadership. We crept through the jungle soundlessly, hurrying. My heart beat so quickly I could scarcely breathe, so afraid was I that we would be too late to stop The Dissenter from doing his worst.

Mr. Winthrop, unaware of the danger that menaced him from above, was relentlessly pressing his advantage.

"You, Don Pedro," I heard him say, "I have spared, but only momentarily! Shall I shake my scepter and sink your ship and all the gold in it I know you and your band of devils have stolen from Tortuga and Cartagena? Shall I?"

Then, to cap Don Pedro's fear, I must suppose, Mr. Winthrop began to recount intimate details of the Spaniard's disreputable deeds. Or so I gathered from Mr. Winthrop's reference to a Doña Domenica in a phrase that seemed to include some form of the word *adultery*. I was no longer attending closely to the tactics of the golden man-bird, but I did guess that it must be a rather horrific experience to hear one's deepest, darkest crimes roll off the golden tongue of a man-bird on a remote island in the Caribbean; and I would not have been surprised if Don Pedro, in his fear and guilt, had quite ruined his lovely suit.

All my thoughts were focused now on the *real* snake in this juggle who, I saw now in my own horror, had possessed himself of a large rock and was now circling around to the edge above where Mr. Winthrop was reducing Don Pedro to quivering blancmange.

Leaves slapping my face, my feet stepping on I cared not what slimy specimen of jungle life, I managed to cut The Dissenter's path off not ten feet from the cliff's edge. I waved Sylvia to the edge of the cliff and motioned for her to flatten herself from view. Lily and Rose I kept behind me, and the three of us stashed ourselves behind a stout tree. I waited, heart in my throat, until the soft sound of breaking branches underfoot was next to me. Then, with a practiced thrust of my parasol, I easily tripped The Dissenter.

He fell to the ground with an audible thud. Then, when he rolled over instantaneously and attempted to spring on his attacker, opening his mouth to yell in the process, I thrust the ferrule of my parasol, lightning-quick, into his open mouth, and planted my foot upon his chest in the tradition of the greatest male hunters, thereby effectively preventing both his scream and his physical rise. I must say that my dexterity was worthy of Mr. Winthrop's best maneuvers, but I did not have a moment for self-congratulation. The large stone had fallen out of The Dissenter's hands and was rolling toward the edge of the cliff. It might very well have fallen to accomplish its aim, save for the fact that my wild gestures (I did not dare speak aloud) alerted Sylvia to the approaching danger. She reached out from her prone position and caught the rock just before it fell. In the same moment, The Dissenter recovered and was easily capable of freeing himself from my certainly flashy, though in truth very flimsy, attack. As he was jumping up in order to overpower the three of us or even kill us with his bare hands (which, from the look of savage hatred that transfigured his face in that split second I did not doubt he was ready to do), I disabled him in the only way I knew to disable an Arawak warrior in the presence of women.

I make no blush to recount that I took the pocket knife and slit the knots of the cords holding his breech clout in place. Since this occurred in the very act of his rising, the cloth fell from his body to expose him in all his manly glory to the very wide eyes of Lily and Rose, who had jumped to my aid.

The Dissenter looked down in undisguised horror at his nakedness, up at the three women, whose sight of him thus visibly caused him more searing humiliation than that which he had experienced at Mr. Winthrop's hands the night of the initiation. Then, with no more than a whimpering squeak, The Dissenter scampered off into the jungle from the direction he had come, before the three of us could lay our hands on him to stop his escape. We let him go, knowing his deep shame would protect him from us far better than any other deterrent at the moment.

By then, Sylvia had arisen and come to us. "It is over," she said with a broad smile. "The two remaining White Devils are descending, frightened and hurrying." She added with a blood-thirsty, unfeminine relish with which I was *much* in sympathy, "Perhaps they will fall, too."

"Let us hope," I said with an answering smile and perfectly unChristian charity. "So. It is over."

Then the four of us fell into each other's arms, partially out of joy, but also partially because, in our profound relief at what had just passed, a wild trembling had invaded all our limbs. I do believe we would have been unable to have remained standing if we had not offered one another this mutual support.

After a moment of emotion, we wiped our eyes unselfconsciously and went back to where Brave One and the others were still lying. Brave One politely passed me the long glass. I peered over the edge to witness, sure enough, the scrambling descent of Don Pedro and the other Spaniard, and a glorious and gratifying confusion among the Spaniards on the beach making haste to shove off.

The golden man-bird remained on his perch, his scepter held high and threatening, suggesting that if the Spaniards did not remove themselves fast enough from the island, he would shake it and some horrible fate would befall them and their ship.

Feet on the ground, Don Pedro took one last look up the mountain. His face was ashen, but when his eyes rested for a fraction of a second on the golden bird, I read in them the tiniest doubt. I saw Mr. Winthrop shake his scepter once. This cured Don Pedro, who then shook his head free of the doubt, closed his eyes, crossed himself devoutly, and began to move his lips rhythmically in what could only be supplication to the Virgin and every saint he had ever offended. It was a very long list, for at least a minute passed before he turned to shout all sorts of orders to the few men remaining on the beach. I could not quite hear his words, but I could well guess what he was saying.

The nine of us lay there. Then, up to my ears drifted the not very loud but *very* dry words, "Sedgwick, do something to get me off here. The ledge is slowly crumbling under my weight, and my feet are killing me."

Yes, I suppose I *did* think by that time that Mr. Winthrop was endowed with magical powers and was capable of flying up to join us on his own.

We had a surprisingly harrowing time of it getting Mr. Winthrop back up from the ledge. I will not stop to recount each spine-tingling detail. Brave One orchestrated the ascent, while I watched the departing Spaniards through the long glass. They did not look back.

By the time Mr. Winthrop had his two maltreated feet back on safe ground, I had seen something through the long glass that had made me gasp.

Without further preamble, I called over to him, "Come quick!" He obeyed, still slung in all his gold, but he had handed his golden helmet-mask to Arawak Father, who had not until that very moment left the side of the pit. He now crossed to the edge of the cliff to embrace his adopted son.

"It's The Dissenter!" I called to Mr. Winthrop, "He's speaking with Don Pedro. He's flapping his arms like a bird and pointing back up to the cliff!"

Mr. Winthrop took the long glass and looked through it.

"By the time Duid learns the Spanish words with which he can explain to them what really happened on the cliff," he said slowly, consideringly, "the Spaniards will have sold him into slavery." Then, peering more closely through the lens, he paused and turned to me to ask, curiously, "What *is* Duid holding about himself? It looks to be branches of some kind, or a bush. I cannot quite make it out."

"Ah, yes," I said. "Well, let me explain that."

Mr. Winthrop listened, puzzled at first, brows raised. I believe that I blushed (but only a little) and held his eyes steady when I described in as delicate terms as possible just how I had disarmed The Dissenter.

When I had finished, Mr. Winthrop threw his head back and laughed. "I knew I could count on you, Sedgwick!" he said, his voice rumbling with humor, his eyes bright. He made a movement toward me as if he were going to kiss me, fully and passionately. I awaited the embrace willingly.

It did not come. Mr. Winthrop had checked himself. Perhaps he had remembered the Arawak strictures against such public displays.

I could not be sure for, in that moment, I saw that he had opened his eyes slightly and that his mood had abruptly changed. I felt not his passion but a cold chill pass through him. He had turned away from me, slightly but unmistakably. He did not say a word, but kept his eyes transfixed on a point just beyond my shoulder.

I whirled around to see what had claimed his attention and saw to my surprise an object that should have inspired my delight but did not.

"Our boat," I breathed, looking up at the strange, European-looking vessel suspended in the branches of some trees. "They hid our boat next to the treasure," I continued, my voice a little dull. "How appropriate." Then, I choked, "Well, isn't that nice?"

"Yes," said Mr. Winthrop tonelessly, "it is. And with their treasure safe, I am sure they will no longer wish to detain us."

CHAPTER 12

The Arawak warriors, also noticing the direction of our gazes, confirmed in deed Mr. Winthrop's words. With Brave One leading the activity, they proceeded joyfully to cut our boat down from its dry dock in the lower branches of the tree. The five Arawak warriors hoisted it on their shoulders and began to make off with it down the path in the direction of town. From there, I had no doubt, they would carry it the rest of the way down the mountain to the southern bay, if we so desired it.

I should have felt far happier than I did. However, there was scant time for reaction to this new discovery, and the let-down I felt might well have been due to the extreme danger that we had just passed through.

Mr. Winthrop had turned away from me and toward the treasure pit. He was already divesting himself of the gold jewelry and beginning to restore it to its hiding place. I watched, rather blindly, as he refused all offer of payment from Arawak Father, who seemed determined to press upon him a great quantity of gold necklaces, arm bands, and bracelets, or, at the very least, the golden scepter. Mr. Winthrop would have none of it.

"My Zemis do not allow it," I heard him tell Arawak Father.

This line of argument naturally satisfied the Arawak leader. It certainly did not fool me. "And what gods might those be?" I attempted to rally him in an aside.

"The ones that suit the occasion in which I find myself," he answered without hesitation.

I sought a topic—*any* topic—to avoid discussion of the discovery of the boat. "The Latin was a masterstroke," I complimented him. "It seemed to convince Don Pedro of your magical powers."

"Indeed, and to think that all those listless hours I spent in catechism should have saved my life."

"Well, you outdid yourself," I said, hardly knowing what to say next. "By the way, what *was* that passage you quoted?"

Mr. Winthrop laughed a little at that. "*Omnia munda mundis*?" he repeated. "'I haven't a notion. It was the most obscure phrase that came to mind just then. I cannot say whether or not it was appropriate."

"It certainly worked for Don Pedro."

"Sure, now, where would the world be if a piece of scripture didn't work wonders for a true believer?" he asked by way of agreement. "And Don Pedro's a pious Catholic."

"To become more pious presently," I remarked. "Your reference to—to Doña Domenica, I think is her name?—was brilliant. Do you think he fears now roasting in hell?"

He laughed more openly now, as a dark shadow passed from his eyes. "The look on his face when I began on his personal life was worth the entire treasure. My pleasure in the episode is marred only by the fact that Don Pedro will never know that it was I, Adam Winthrop, who so humbled and hoodwinked him." Then, changing mood and subject, he said casually, "I didn't know you understood Spanish."

"I don't really," I said. "I understood most of your opening lines in context, and then I did catch the lady's name. That was just at the moment I saw The Dissenter skulking in the woods, so I missed your recital of all his other misdeeds."

"His other misdeeds?" he queried.

"Well," I said, "if I remember rightly, the adultery you alluded to would only put Don Pedro in the first ring of hell. He seemed far too bold a gentleman to have profoundly feared *that*. Did you not need to scare him off with threats of the last ring? It is, I believe, saved for traitors and deceivers, is it not?"

"It is—my recent deception exempted, of course," he said. His eyes had been resting on me. The jungle shadows of sunset had lengthened, so I could not fully read what was in their depths. I thought— although I could not have said for sure—that I saw his uncertain light of regretful reluctance turn to a more positive resolution. He continued, his voice firm and confident now, "I knew full well of his deceit and treachery. In fact, this is what I have to tell you—"

Then, to my frustration, Arawak propriety (in the form of Arawak Father), which did not allow conversation between a man and a woman outside of their caney, prevented further disclosures.

Arawak Father planted himself firmly between us, then prodded Mr. Winthrop down the path in the wake of the Arawak warriors who were still chanting triumphantly through the jungle. Sylvia, Lily, and Rose came to my side, and in best Arawak manners, we waited the requisite amount of time to follow the men, at a discreet distance, back to town.

Every detail of the ensuing evening was perfect. The night sky, a rich cobalt, had never been more beautifully jeweled. It was studded at first with only a few diamond points, then rapidly sequined with starlight. The drums had never beat so powerfully and rhythmically. The dancing had never been so inspired. The food had never been so delicious. This night would live on in Arawak memory for many generations to come.

I was singularly lacking in festive spirit. I had little appetite and took no interest in the great honors heaped upon Mr. Winthrop and me. I hope, however, that I was polite and showed none of my underlying restlessness and dissatisfaction to my hosts, who had been from the beginning kind and generous and strange, although their strangeness seemed rather less so to me now.

From across the town circle, I caught Mr. Winthrop looking at me. I intercepted his gaze. Our eyes held for a fraction of a second, then we both looked away. Although I glanced over at him several more times during the course of the evening, his eyes did not seem to stray again to me, or at least not when I was looking at him.

Our boat, which bad been placed in the center of the town circle, had received a great amount of attention. It had been touched by every inhabitant of Arawak Island. It had been chanted over. It had been rubbed with all sorts of roots and bones. It had been lifted high and carried around the circle at various intervals. It was, this evening, a sacred object.

Given that, then, and to signal the end of this extraordinary day, a select group of warriors was designated by Arawak Father to hoist the little boat high above their wide, muscled shoulders and to carry it down the path that led to the southern bay. The other men, including Mr. Winthrop, followed. The women stayed behind in the village for the mundane tasks of cleaning up from the feasting and putting the children to bed.

I had to assume that the boat was taken down to the bay to be readied for our departure on the morrow.

An interminable amount of time later, Mr. Winthrop returned to our caney. I had thought that my low spirits would rise again in his company, but if anything, his presence caused them to sink further, if such were possible.

We were back, once again, where we had started—but not quite— as Mr. Winthrop had once so rightly pointed out. When he entered the caney, I felt the air crackle and break around me so that it was suddenly difficult to breathe. I had been standing, stupidly, in the center of the caney. At his entrance, however, and without a word, I moved instantly to my side of the small, enclosed space and leaned against my hammock. Without a word, he moved to his, then turned to face me. I could just discern the outlines of his shoulders and thighs in the dim, deep-night shadows and could feel his blue eyes upon me. He seemed to wish to speak. He opened his mouth, then changed his mind.

The boat, now down at the bay, ready for our departure, seemed to hang like a tangible object in the space between us this night in the caney. We would rig it with sails. We would have days of provisions. We would have our charts and our sailing instruments. No doubt we would even receive an Arawak escort through the chain of islands, hiphopping ever west through the blue, blue waters of the Caribbean Sea with the blue, blue Caribbean sky above.

Our boat was more a symbol of the world from which we had come and to which we had to return than the tangible means of our escape. We could have tried to escape anytime these past few days in a stolen canoe, but we had tacitly agreed against such a desperate course. Perhaps there was superstition in our decision: we wished to leave the island in the same vessel in which we had arrived.

"We'll leave on the morrow," he said at last. His words sounded harsh.

I felt regretful reluctance coming from him—a holding back. I could not fathom it but now was not the moment for profound reflection.

"Yes, of course," I agreed quickly.

An uncomfortable silence quivered in the closed caney. I had no wish at the moment to lie down in my hammock. The position would have seemed just then somehow indecent, even provocative—an invitation. Our enforced intimacy and proximity had become most unnatural.

Only cold, impersonal words could decharge the air. I continued, quite practically, with thoughts of our boat and the preparations for making the sails. "For I have given the evening over," I continued, "to thinking of how they should best be rigged," after which comment I described in some detail the excellence of my plans.

To which Mr. Winthrop, rather more experienced sailor than I that he was, said merely and after a brief pause, "Right."

Then he climbed into his hammock and stretched out. "Good night." The words were terse and final.

I have come too far in my narrative to introduce dishonesty into my account. I lay awake for a very long time afterward, unable to think of anything other than the man lying several yards away. Lying there, pleasantly suspended in my hammock, surrounded by the warm, velvet dark, my imagination ran riot. I had discovered earlier in the day—or was it a hundred years ago?—a weakness for his kisses. It was a weakness so secret, so alien to my nature, that I would not fully admit it to myself, save under the cover of night.

And under that cover, my weakness leapt out at me, savage and ferocious, to overpower me. It had its way with me, so to speak, and I indulged in the most prolonged, intimate, shameless fantasy a woman is capable of inventing.

It was to be a *very* long and unsatisfying night that Mr. Winthrop and I spent together in the caney after saving the island from the Spanish and retrieving our boat.

The next morning hardly began in better fashion. Awakened, as usual, by the raucous clamor of hawks at daybreak, I practically fell out of my hammock at the very moment that Mr. Winthrop did. It was an extremely awkward, even naked moment, one I recall with recoil when, on unsteady legs, we faced each other in the raw dawn, our faces as stripped as our bodies, without any of the concealing arrangements of features or shadows across the eyes which in other, more familiar social settings, could mask one's thoughts or feelings. No orderly human sounds or sentences passed our lips to soften the savage moment, to contain the beasts that no longer lived in the wild jungle that teemed just beyond the fragile circle of civilization, but who dwelled within us, in our bodies, barely caged, roaring to be set free.

Mr. Winthrop had but one look on his face—that of the hunter—and its effect on me was nothing less than feeling like his prey. In truth, I cannot imagine that I had any other look on my face but that of brazen *willingness*. Still, the force of the visual contact, so brutal was it, caused me to wobble, step back a pace, and reach out to the object behind me for support. That object was the net of the hammock, and I immediately found myself slightly tangled in its cords.

Instead of producing charming confusion on my part, or a laughing rejoinder at my clumsiness on his part, this small incident nearly undid both of us. I fear that in the course of untangling myself, I bared quite a bit more flesh than had already been open to his gaze any time these past weeks. The entire passage could not have lasted more than ten seconds from the time we descended from our hammocks to the time I had turned back around to face him, my hands free from the trap of the net, my hair tumbling in chaos over my shoulders and back and breasts—the only concealment left to me, since my bodice was gaping open.

I might just as well have been standing completely naked in front of him then. In fact, I had the clear impression that I had been naked before him for days and days now. Naked in thoughts. Naked in desires. As naked as he was to me and had been from that moment on the ledge, perched high on the cliff, when he had stripped off his chemise and breeches to reveal a body of polished bronze beneath, from the width of his shoulders, down his muscled chest, to the taut planes of stomach which tapered to the shape of a flock of eagles in tight formation to disappear into the waist of his breech clout, from which he then tore my copper curls and let them fly from his body into the air.

That was what it came down to then, the breech clout. There was but one layer of cloth between us—the last flimsy, porous, highly mobile line of civilization shielding his body from mine. I believe in that next, eleventh second, he took a step toward me across the caney, from his side toward mine. The look in his eye was set, determined, quite hot, but with a cold fixity for all of that, as if he held me, dead center, in the aim notch of a mighty sling shot or in the sight of his gun.

The drums were beating a magnificent tempo to match beat of my heart. Before the twelfth second passed and he took the next step, his expression had changed and shadows had fallen across our door. Our gazes were locked for another second before Mr. Winthrop tore his eyes from mine and turned his head toward the door of the caney, but not before I had seen the resolution change to something else—a hesitation. A reluctance had surfaced. I did not think that the curious mixture of irritation and relief that crossed his features just then was entirely due to this untimely intrusion.

I myself was quite breathless, as if I had been running hard. I drew air into my lungs to steady myself, then I, too, looked to see who had come to our caney at this unprecedented hour of the morning.

It was Arawak Father, in company of several high-ranking warriors. His presence at our door was entirely unexpected. His words were even more so. "You will not be leaving today," Arawak Father pronounced in slow, measured accents.

Why did my heart leap with an irrational happiness at this statement?

Arawak Father did not look at us, which was just as well, for he, no doubt, would have had to interrupt his beautiful speech with a stern scolding for the evidently unseemly thoughts that had been uppermost on our minds. Since we were, however, in the privacy of our own caney, and thus free to do whatever we chose, he instead aimed his eyes and words high into the ceiling of the caney, such that his intonation encompassed and encircled us, accompanied by the force of the drums beating afar off:

"The Zemis have shown us their ways. They have smiled on us. They brought The Beauty and Blue Eyes, who saved the Arawaks' lives and preserved the treasure and heritage of The People from the White Devils. For this we have spent the long hours of the night past in prayerful thanks. In return we have promised to send The Beauty and Blue Eyes back into the waters, to the west, where they may move among The People to the destination of their Will.

"Great Arawak Mother was told this night that the happiness of the Arawak people was to be doubled on the morrow. It is today. It is so. It is good.

"My first son, Ajijeko, has returned," Arawak Father continued.

It was at this point that the reason for the incessant beating of the drums outside finally dawned on me. I believe that I had been too absorbed in my own emotions to think that the drums, which had never before beat before sundown, had been anything other than an accompaniment to my heart.

"Ajijeko has returned with members of the council. They await us on the beach, as is proper and fitting. They await the commencement of the council. They await the commencement of the feast. They await the commencement of the marriage ceremony that is to be enacted between the highest Arawak and the highest Paressis. It is good."

Here he drew a breath. "It is good. They await as well the arrival of The Beauty and Blue Eyes, who will not leave this day, but who will honor us with their presence at our council."

I do believe that this was Arawak Father's notion of a gracious invitation. His eyes had fallen now on Mr. Winthrop. (He would not have looked at me, or expected me to respond.) I, too, looked to Mr. Winthrop, who did not look at me or consult me in any way whatsoever about the decision to delay our departure by a day or two.

"It is good," Mr. Winthrop replied solemnly, nodding his head once, as was his manner.

Although agreeing with his acceptance, I was not at all pleased by

Mr. Winthrop's high-handedness, but I did not think this was precisely the time to make an issue. The next moment, Mr. Winthrop had quit the caney with Arawak Father without a backward glance. I did not dare poke my head out of the caney for several seconds afterward, and when I did, I greeted now none to my surprise Sylvia, Lily, Rose, and even Margaret, who skipped and danced around me, speaking so rapidly I could not understand them. They pulled me toward town center where, at this early, early hour of the day, myriad preparations were already underway and being executed by the entire female population of the island.

Mr. Winthrop, in company of the caciques, was, I supposed, already heading for the beach. The drumbeats were receding in that direction, as well, suggesting that quite a reception was to be exacted for the returning males.

We women worked hard and steadily the entire morning. I cannot say that it was unpleasant. In fact, it was quite festive, for all the work was accompanied by dancing and song.

My only hope was that the men were working as diligently. They were, as I later discovered. Some were fishing. Some were setting up the ball court. Some were praying and chanting and offering tokens to the Zemis. (I did not count this last activity as real work.)

The women were setting up a dozen mounds of fruits and preparing the batatas and the cassava or manioc and the maize, those strange yellow shafts of grain. We were also very busily occupied in adorning one another. With my combs and brushes, I was in great demand to arrange coiffures. I was inspired this day and achieved many a beautiful result.

In addition, wreaths and garlands of grasses and flowers were woven, necklaces and ankle bracelets of snail shells were strung and jingled agreeably as we worked, feather crowns and mantles were bound in corded knots to form tight, brilliant layers of plumage to be worn later, and hundreds of long, supple green branches were prepared and hung with turtle shells and white stones and laid in mounds in careful plaited patterns, apparently for use later, perhaps as a rhythmic accompaniment to dancing and singing.

Throughout all of this activity, the drums never ceased to beat, nor the fingers to twine, nor the trade winds to blow appetizing odors and the sounds of women laughing and singing about the town. In the center of the activity was, of course, Alluring Eyes, very self-absorbed (I do not fault her for that on her day of days), and therefore not disposed to interfering with my enjoyment of the occasion.

No formal meal was undertaken by the women, but we did nibble here and there, and imbibed a liquid from calabashes that were passed around. It was a mildly intoxicating drink, I noted after several passes, which struck me as all the more unusual for a people whose lips generally tasted nothing other than water, fruit juices, or coconut milk. It was *very* good.

Some time not far past midday, a great masculine shout arose from somewhere outside the town limits. The women shouted as one voice in return, and dropped all that they were doing. We had, in fact, completed everything. We ran in the direction of the path that led to the southern bay and the beach where I assumed Ajijeko and his group had landed, but before we actually descended it, we took a sharp left turn and emerged out on the vast clearing that I had noticed on one of my initial trips into town.

The clearing was more of a plaza. It was, in fact, a grand playing court backed on the broad ends by stout walls slightly taller than the tallest man. Down the center of the court ran a white line about one foot wide, while along the walls that ran lengthwise, red and green lines crossed one another in a pattern I could not quite interpret. On both of the short ends of the plaza, the most elaborate chairs, or *duhos* (*thrones*, I have been calling them) were set. I was not surprised when the women took to one short end of the plaza; the men already occupied the other.

In fact, as we descended the path, I noticed that some men had already taken to the court and were tossing about a medium-sized ball. There was no signal I could discern to mark the opening of the play, but all of a sudden two teams seemed to emerge out of the casual activity on the court. The two sides of spectators began to call out encouragements, applaud the fine shots, and deride the missed ones.

I gathered soon enough that I was watching a game of *batey*. There were about twenty players to a side, and despite these numbers, the action reminded me of nothing so much as of shuttlecock tennis. The ball looked to be hard, but with a bounce, and seemed to be covered with strips of palm leaves. The sides played it alternately. If the ball went over the boundary or remained lying on the ground, it was counted dead, exactly as I had seen it played in tennis. It was a question, then, of taking it in the air or when it was bouncing, the object being generally to keep the ball from stopping. The ball could only be taken with the elbows, shoulders, head, back, or hips, but never with the hands, which, judging from the hooting that accompanied hand play, either inadvertent or deliberate, was considered very bad form. One of the fine tricks seemed to be to bounce the ball against the wall. Other maneuvers involved the red and green lines, but I never did understand precisely the significance of play in and around them. One side eventually won, but I could not have said why.

Once I caught on to the game on the plaza, I had the leisure to survey the ancillary action animating the sidelines. The Proud One was making a delicious meal of the occasion, strutting and preening in all her glory. She was allotted a duho next to Great Arawak Mother, which she graced only a fraction of the time, this being too lively an occasion for mere sitting. To give her her due, she looked quite lovely, even radiant.

The cause of that radiance sat on the other side of the plaza. It was not difficult to identify Ajijeko, First Warrior and The Proud One's intended, for it must have been he who was seated in an elaborate duho next to Arawak Father. He was a well set up man, bronzed and broad-shouldered, though not as well set up as Mr. Winthrop. Ajijeko had returned with several dozen other men whom I did not recognize. Whether or not they were from Arawak Island I could not determine. They all wore the two diagonal welts on their upper left breasts. Neither Ajijeko nor any of his accompanying warriors joined in the ball play, but remained spectators the entire afternoon.

Neither did Mr. Winthrop play. It may well have been due to the fact that he, too, was given a duho for the afternoon, which might have been his signal to sit it out. I noticed that several of his fellows—Brave One, for instance—encouraged him on several occasions to play, but he declined each time, quite graciously, I might add. I suspected that he would have been a natural for this type of sport. Perhaps he had performed enough for the Arawak and did not wish to overshadow anyone else's skill and expertise.

For myself, I needed harbor no such delicate considerations. Thus, when the women took to the court during the course of the afternoon and I was prodded by Sylvia to play, I accepted the challenge. So festive was the event that I did not once consider the oddity of women playing sport in public, particularly before an audience of men. Although the women's play was noticeably tamer, the ball kept low, the men attended to all the action going forward on the court, and responded appropriately to all of the well-placed and missed shots. (However, in the very back of my mind, I could not quite help but wonder whether the attention given to the female game by the male spectators might not have been due to the fact that fully one half of the female players wore no bodice covering. I, personally, felt that that must have been very uncomfortable for those women.)

I make no claims to Mr. Winthrop's physical agility, and I had never before performed in public. Nevertheless, I acquitted myself rather decently on the court. I attempted nothing fancy and was appropriately encouraged by the increasingly raucous sideliners whenever I managed to hit the ball.

I caught Mr. Winthrop's eye once or twice during the course of the women's game. He looked maddeningly calm and self-possessed, as if those few seconds of naked desire had not charged between us earlier that morning. And if he was ready to ignore it—well, then, so was I. We were soon to leave the island anyway, and it was quite fortunate that we had not engaged in any *indiscreet* behavior. And it was not exactly as if I *wished* for his attention, after all. Our enforced intimacy of the past weeks had been entirely accidental. It was not as if Mr. Winthrop was the man I would have necessarily chosen of my own free will with whom to be stranded on a Caribbean island, or with whom I would want to be absorbed into Arawak society. Never think it.

At length, the women left the ball court. I believe that I was on the losing side. The men remained to play some more, while the women, as a group, went to what I called the Enchanted Glen to bathe. Perhaps the men went to their spot in the river to bathe.

The women bathed as a group, but very discreetly, since public nudity (in a relative sense, that is) is not good Arawak form. We formed a circle and paddled about with our backs to one another. It was very ceremonious, quite refreshing, and rather good fun. We emerged one by one to be enveloped in large linen cloths held out to us by attending commoners.

Before I could get back into my clothes, Sylvia, who had already dressed, came up to me wearing a look improbably compounded of mischief and humility. She was evidently hiding something behind her back.

To my question, which translated into something akin to "What is it, my dear?" Sylvia brought her hands around and held out to me a brilliant length of cloth, neatly folded.

"For you, Beauty," she said, her dark eyes shining.

I saw at once that it was an Arawak dress—a nagua—and from the number of folds, I determined that it was a *complete* one.

She continued, "Forest Flower, Second One, Promised to a Man across the Water, and I thought that your present dress—"

Here she gestured with her eyes to my somewhat frayed underslip and chemise.

"—no longer does you justice—"

This statement explained the mischief in her eyes. I had a fleeting memory of Mr. Winthrop's compliment of my underdress, but that was before the weeks of wear and tear on the fine cambric, and in comparison to my grey merino, which I remembered now with a shudder of distaste.

"—and could be improved with the true cloth of The People. Thus, we were moved to ask Great Arawak Mother for permission to weave you a matrimonial-length—"

I had difficulty with the term *matrimonial,* but I do believe that was the word she used.

"—and she agreed! Since I am the only married one among us, I have the deep honor to present this to you."

The humility which now touched the offering of her gift was thoroughly charming. I could not refuse it and, indeed, did not wish to. I framed a reply that I hoped would be all that was appropriate and gracious. I stretched out my arms to accept the gift, but she shook her head. The mischief had returned to light her eyes.

"You must wear it now," she said firmly, "before the festival is over. Yes?"

How could I refuse? The only difficulty we had was over the issue of my white clothes. Sylvia was adamantly against my wearing the garments, arguing that they ruined the lines of the nagua with bulges beneath. I eventually gave in to her on the point. I also experienced difficulty wrapping it quite right and making the correct folds on my left shoulder. Sylvia fixed the fit with an experienced tug and a knot, and my dress was secure.

She surveyed me critically and appreciatively, then, with a nod, said, "The color of the wood flower is perfect. We had all agreed that it would suit your hair and skin best."

Understand that the color of wood flower is *pink*. In England, I had stayed strictly with greys, greens, and yellows. Dressed now in this bold, unexpected color, I felt new sartorial possibilities emerge. (I have an excellent eye for fashion.) It was well that the afternoon was dying and that night would soon be upon us for my initiation into wearing pink.

Back in town, the workers and commoners were continuing with the festival preparations. Immediately upon the return of the women, the dancing began, and continued on into the night. The dances were performed in rows or circles. As usual, the men and women danced separately. Each one placed an arm about the waist of the neighbor, and the leader of each group also led the singing. I did not participate in the dancing (neither did Mr. Winthrop, I noted—but I was not *really* paying attention to him or to anything he did). From what I could determine, the singers recounted bygone events, Arawak conquests, their genealogy, and good and bad seasons they had known. The Dissenter, I believe, was denounced and declared dead to the tribe.

Night fell. The moon rose. The drums never stopped, and this was to last for three or four hours. All was accompanied by wood flutes and rattles.

There was food and drink. The fish was plentiful and perfectly grilled. The fruit was passed continuously, as were the vegetables. I had always enjoyed the Arawak vegetables, and so ate my fill this evening. The calabashes filled with the intoxicating liquor also made their rounds, but I drank very little. (I noted that Mr. Winthrop was rather abstemious this evening—*not* that his behavior affected mine in the very least, although I did notice that he had noticed, with some particular attention, my nagua.)

When the moon was high above in the exquisite night sky, Great Arawak Mother rose from her duho and wandered aimlessly, so it seemed, into the center of the town circle, near the pole—which did not appear to me nearly so hideous as it once had. Perhaps the few sips of the drink I had permitted myself had distorted my perceptions, but the pole affected me rather more *provocatively* than it ever had previously.

Great Arawak Mother began to croon. Her activity did not immediately command anyone's attention. I had discovered that one activity blended into the next, with no sharp dividing lines, giving the day a fluid, graceful character. She crooned for quite a while, so it seemed, before the drums and dancing and eating and carousing eventually ceased. Soon enough, however, as though all Arawak knew their parts, the town circle was emptied of everyone but Great Arawak Mother. She held out her hand imperiously. At this gesture, The Proud One stepped to her side. She was now laden with a heavy weight of gold jewelry, and she alone was the only one so adorned.

The two women stood there, alone, the cynosure of all eyes—one old and wrinkled, the other young and smooth and firm. If this was the prelude to a wedding ceremony, I found it strange and remarkable. Great Arawak Mother held the stage for an interminable amount of time, it seemed to me, recounting all sorts of stories which, after a while, I understood as the history of the Paressis, the people to which The Proud One belonged.

Then, the more I listened and understood of the proceedings, the more I suspected that *Ajijeko* was being given to *The Proud One* in marriage—and *not the other way around!* My suspicion became a realization when Ajijeko came alone to the center of the circle and fell to his knees before Great Arawak Mother, who then pronounced many words over his head, including those that identified him now as Ajijeko of the Paressis.

It appeared—and I had great difficulty comprehending it, at first—that I was witness to a marriage within a *matriarchy*!

I felt the scales fall from eyes yet a second time since living among the Arawak, and I suddenly realized that perhaps many, many more veils could have been lifted, were I to continue to live among these strange and entirely beautiful people.

However, I was still attempting to absorb the quite incredible idea that men could be given to women in marriage. How delightful, but how *very* delightful was that discovery! And, I must say, after my initial delight passed in a joyous wave, I was left with the equally happy notion that such an arrangement was entirely *reasonable*. Of course, the whole day's proceedings now made sense to me. The bridal party, if one could call it such, that we were attending was hosted by the male side, and presided over by the groom's mother—or rather, grandmother, in this instance. I realized now that Arawak Father was not Great Arawak Mother's son. No, he must have been her son-in-law, the husband of her daughter who was apparently dead, and the chief only by default, at his wife's death. I remembered Arawak Father's reference to the tribal ancestress and the memory of the mother's mothers, but none of it had made any particular sense to me. I remembered how the men came first in a procession and Great Arawak Mother came last and began to reevaluate the second position as one of *honor*. I thought now of how the men left town every day, all day, and I suddenly realized that the women *truly* ran *everything*!

I glanced over at Mr. Winthrop. I believe that he was studiously avoiding my gaze. The coward!

Then, Ajijeko left the circle to return with a length of cloth, folded exactly as the one Sylvia had presented to me. Judging from the intense, motionless attention of the onlookers, this was the most solemn part of the ceremony. The Proud One held her arms high, looking up at the sky. Ajijeko proceeded to wrap her in the cloth, as Sylvia had showed me. He fashioned for her first a skirt, over the one she was already wearing, and then a bodice covering.

I hope that it is clear that I am not at all slow, but it did not fully dawn on me until that very moment that the bodice covering was the sign of a married woman! I confess that it simply had not occurred to me before. I felt an entirely new construction shape the relationship Mr. Winthrop and I had shared for the past days and weeks.

I do believe that Mr. Winthrop's eyes were on me at just that moment, but I simply did not deign to return his regard.

CHAPTER 13

*M*r. Winthrop was free to look where he wished. My attention was claimed just then by a tap on the shoulder. I turned and saw Margaret and Lily and Rose, who were smiling shyly.

I knew full well what was expected of me. Without gushing (I am not a gusher), I thanked them for my lovely nagua.

They were charmingly diffident, murmuring all the appropriate Arawak phrases that served for the English disclaimers, "Oh, it was nothing!" and "Do you truly like it?" and "You look very beautiful in it!" and "We wished we could have done something *more* for you!" and "It is a small token of our thanks!"

This exchange went on for quite a while. Since I was, indeed, feeling very appreciative of their gesture, and quite thoroughly honored, I wished to make an exchange gift. Unfortunately, I had nothing equivalently appropriate whatsoever, which was rather vexing, but the circumstances were such that almost anything would do. I decided to go to my tapestry bag and examine the various articles therein with an eye to gift-giving.

I excused myself, reassuring the ladies that I would return. I quickly wove my way through the alleyways, entered my caney, went to my tapestry bag, and began to rummage around in it, abstracting various objects and examining their worth in the light of the moonbeams streaming in. Having selected several items, I was bending down again to choose two more, with my back toward the door, when the source of light was blocked. The air charged through the caney with a crackle.

I stood up and whirled around. I experienced a wave of heart-stopping surprise and calm inevitability as I perceived Mr. Winthrop's body damming the moonlight behind him, his lean, muscular frame blocked in pitch against the white glow.

He took a step into the caney. "Eve Marie," he said. It was as much a statement as a question.

With his movement away from the door, the moonlight spilled back in. It flowed through the center, across the mats, and into the far corners. It eddied up to the tips of my toes.

I took a step back — from the light, from him. This time, I managed not to entangle myself in the hammock netting.

"Mr. Win—" I began, but could not finish. It was very hard to give up this last vestige of civility after everything else I had been forced to abandon since setting foot on this island. "Adam," I greeted him, after a moment.

I felt, rather than saw, his smile. "I agree," he replied, cryptically.

We were both in better control this evening than we had been that morning, silent, eyes locked, fresh from our hammocks but unrested. I knew my next move. "I came to find some gifts to exchange," I said, needing to take a deep breath to steady my voice. "I was just going back out to continue the feast."

He followed my lead. "I came to get my pocket knife. I need to cut some things."

"Well, you caught me by surprise," I said. I tried for a conversational tone. "I was not expecting you."

He shifted ground completely by remarking to that, "You would

have had to expect me at some point." He paused. Then, "Or are you
—like me—thinking it impossible to spend another night together in
this caney under these conditions?"

The drums were still throbbing outside. I wished they would stop.
"*Most* impossible," I agreed.

Even to my own ears, my words sounded heartfelt, as if they had
been ripped from me. My admission at once relieved the situation and
exacerbated it.

He nodded, once, in understanding. "I have a plan," he said.

My heart, which had stopped at his entrance, began to beat again,
somewhat erratically. All his plans to date had been good ones. I took
a *very* deep breath. "You have permission to move to another caney?"
I asked. "That might be considered odd, given everything."

"Very odd," he agreed. "Given everything." Then, he shook his
head and took another step toward me. I stood my ground. "But that
was not the plan I had in mind."

White light illuminated one side of his body, leaving the rest in
darkness. I saw the wisps of black hair escaping the band that held the
curls at his nape form a nimbus around his head. I saw the cords of his
neck join the slope of his shoulder to glide into his powerful forearm.
I saw the ridges of the two diagonal welts on his chest, the frets of his
rib cage, the knot of stomach muscle drawn across the jut of a hip
bone. I saw the angle of the shadow of the valley covered, within the
bounds of Arawak propriety, by a breech clout. I saw a thigh and a
knee and a calf, and then one foot.

The same light that fell on him fell on me and my hair and my
nagua, washed now in the silver darkness to an indistinct glow of
pearl.

"It isn't?" I asked, breathless now.

He merely shook his head and took another step toward me. It
needed only two more for us to touch. I could smell now his Arawak
clean. I could see now, etched clearly, the lines in his face. His eyes had

lowered to survey my new dress. He made no comment. He lifted his eyes, a deep cobalt, back to mine.

"It isn't," he affirmed, taking another step, then another. "We've arrived at the basic need of survival."

He had closed the gap between us. We were touching.

"The basic need?" I echoed.

"The one that goes beyond mere personal survival, that is." He reached up to touch the shell necklace—*his* necklace—at my throat. His eyes spoke eloquently. "But mere personal survival is very dull."

"As for going beyond mere personal survival, allow me to remind you that I have been a married woman," I said with all my dignity, "and am well acquainted with that basic need."

His harsh features relaxed into a smile of genuine amusement. "That I will not allow."

"Are you—could you, in truth, be doubting the *reality* of my marriage?" I demanded, rather *in*dignant now.

"Not at all. It's rather that poor Edward—if I recall the incident correctly—allowed himself to be run down by a chicken cart."

I blinked. "What is your point, sir?"

He did not answer that. Instead, he put his hands on my shoulders. There was an unmistakable chuckle in his voice. "Which incident, combined with the last days and weeks in your reckless, life-threatening company, leads me to conclude that he could not possibly have fully appreciated you. Speaking of which—"

At that, he began to perform an entirely unloverlike task with his hands. I do believe that he was *frisking* me.

"Mr. Lipscomb certainly appreciated all my good qualities," I said, rising to the defense of my late husband while attempting to wriggle out of this strange embrace (if embracing it could be called). "What *are* you doing?" I managed to ask.

"So that my two needs do not cancel each other out, I am searching for concealed knives," he explained seriously as he patted my thighs and hips, raising his brows suggestively when he discovered that I wore no white clothes. "Or your parasol. With you, I never know from which direction my personal survival will be threatened next." He pulled my bodice covering toward him and looked down it. "Not a Spanish marauder in sight," he affirmed straight-faced, as if satisfied for his safety, and restored the cloth to its original position. "Much, *much* better, by the by," he said, gesturing with his head to my nagua.

And before I had an opportunity to respond to *any* of these outrageous actions and comments, he was shaking his head and saying, "While all men might share certain views of a woman's good points, I doubt very much that poor Edward's list of your good qualities intersects anywhere with mine. Then, again," he said, "we're agreed that poor Edward did not have much imagination."

"We are in no such agreement, sir!" I stated as if I were *not* affected by his hands on my body. In fact, my skin, everywhere he had touched me, felt as if it were standing on tiptoe.

"For if he had, he would not have got run over by the chicken cart."

"Which observation makes no more sense the second time around than it did the first!" I said, with far more confidence than I felt.

(Admittedly, enveloped as I was in his presence, and with the vivid memory of the kiss we had exchanged the day before flooding my perceptions, I could no longer judge which observations made sense and which did not.)

"My point precisely," be returned, laughing outright now. He had slid his hands down my arms and grasped my fingers in his.

I was quite hot and confused. "Do you mean to explain yourself?" I asked.

"Enough to say that if poor Edward had been the husband he should have been, I wouldn't have to explain it to you." He tipped my chin up and kissed me then, lightly. "And we'd be a lot further along than this," he added after a long moment.

It was really quite extraordinary, but I think that I was beginning to understand. However, I was not quite ready yet to be submerged in the smell and feel and taste of him. "Are you saying," I inquired, "that you would never be so clumsy as to be run down by a chicken cart?"

"Something like that," he replied, nibbling my ear, "but, you know, I am running out of tricks to capture your maidenly interest."

At that shameless ploy, I broke away from him. "*What?*" I said. "You cannot possibly wish to me to think that your *tricks*, as you call them, have been for the purpose of—that is—"

He broke into this unpromising speech. "I walked over coals for you, my dear," he said simply, then deftly caught my hands behind my back and held me to him. "Can you doubt it?"

"Yes!"

"Then poor Edward was a bigger clod than I thought. And if I left it to you," he said, "I fear that we would be on this island forever."

I was pressed against his length. His arms were around me. My face was lifted to his. I could see tiny flames flicker in the depths of his eyes.

He had made a leading statement. I could no less than follow. "About our boat—?" I queried.

"Yes. Our boat," he said. His voice struck a new note just then. It was as if I could hear the strange regret and curious reluctance leave it to be replaced by a warm resolution. "I have come to a decision about it."

(I was right. He *was* resolved.)

"Which is—?"

He raised a hand to tuck one of my long curls behind my ear. He had his eye fixed on his task, concentrating. "I have something to tell you," he said. "In the nature of a confession." He let his hand fall to my shoulder, which he caressed. He looked back at me, straight into my eyes. "A delicate matter."

My heart was pounding erratically. I was curious. I was intrigued.

I was utterly fascinated. He had me literally and figuratively in the palm of his hand.

"I've already decided when and where to tell you, but it's not here and it's not tonight," he continued, causing a delicious mixture of emotions to run through me at this provocative statement. He was looking at me as though he were kissing me. "I don't want to force you. I need to know first whether you are willing to be mine—tonight, now, no questions."

Was I willing? Dear me, what a question! My unruly imagination had run far, far ahead. But did he truly intend his question to be as naively seductive as it sounded? No matter. Given my interpretation of what he was asking me to decide, I needed but a scandalously short moment to come to a decision.

"Dare you risk your personal survival for this?" I asked, raising my lips to his for my answer. Apparently, my baser self, which was not yet fully known to me, ran to coy femininity. "I may kill you yet."

He smiled his satisfaction and kissed me then, fully. "Try me," he challenged.

I forthrightly accepted the challenge. So, after all the sun and sky and sand and surf and sweat and mud and blood, it had come to this: two mouths, two bodies, two desires, and two very thin pieces of cloth.

About that cloth—soon both pieces were removed. I found his rough, irreverent comment on my lack of white clothes perversely stimulating, as was his equally rough, though highly inventive response to the possible discomforts presented by the mat-covered, dirt-packed floor of the caney.

For the most part, however, words were few. Instead, it was all flesh and muscle and moisture and discovery. I, for instance, had thought that my heart was a stable organ. It had beaten quite regularly in my breast for nearly twenty-five years. It was not disposed to fluttering that I could remember, and it had never moved about in my body. Since being on this island, however, in company of Adam Winthrop, I had noticed it oddly fluttering on occasion. And it seemed to *move*, to travel about in my body, to lodge in unaccustomed places. The night of Adam's Arawak initiation, it had grabbed my throat and throbbed at my temples. It had even left my body to beat in his. At our first kiss, if I remembered aright, my heart had split into ten separate pulses to beat in my ten separate fingertips.

This night, now, I found my heart between my legs. It was *most* unexpected, as well as uncomfortable, and because I was beginning to see that the unusual discomfort could be relieved in only one, very traditional way, modesty compels me, dear reader, to draw a veil across the next series of events.

No. Honesty compels me to delve further into my narrative. I have always considered myself a healthy woman of normal appetite, and so, after my marriage, I had been quite curious and quite desirous — to the extent that it was proper. However, early on, I had lost a little hope, having been so often *disappointed* (any woman will know what I mean) by poor Edward (dear me, I am saying it now, too), and the effects of these experiences should have made me feel violated and a little depressed, if it had not been for my ability to imagine myself to be *somewhere else*. This ability also allowed me to feel just a little smug. (I am being quite honest here.)

Now, in a moral tale such as this, it might strike anyone as distinctly immoral to have been engaged in amorous activity with such a whimsical, unsteady, thoroughly disreputable character as Adam Winthrop — a man, who, furthermore, simply happened to be the one with whom I had found myself one fine day adrift in the middle of the Atlantic in a Johnnie boat. This being the case, I feel it necessary to point out that, technically speaking, under Arawak law and custom, we were *married*.

In short, during the ensuing passage between me and this thoroughly unsteady man — though completely dear and masculine and mine—I experienced what it was to be swept up and away in a passion not wholly unlike the strong Atlantic current which had first brought us together. It was an experience of openings, like the spreading of flower petals to the sun, or the dilating of pupils to embrace the dark, or the stripping of husks from the maize to reveal a spear of golden kernels bedded in strands of silk. Then, as I teetered on the brink of the infinite beyond, my last civilized thought was: this is new, unexpected, and quite, *quite marvelous*!

My first thought afterward was that I felt clean, cleansed, and it took many long moments after that for my heart to regain its customary place and tempo. When it did, I realized that it had not really come to rest at all, but that it wanted to offer itself through my eyes to Adam Winthrop. In that moment of tenderness and wordlessness and defenselessness, I do believe that he offered me his as well.

His first words to me were: "The earth moved."

Dear, dear, *dear* man! "Did it for you, too?" I cooed.

Light and love sprang to renewed life in his eyes. They crinkled. His chest shook slightly against my breast. (We were still improbably entwined in each other at that point, and in my nagua).

I knew these signs. "Does that amuse you?" I demanded, rather incensed that while I should be awash with spent passion, he should be *laughing*!

"No," he said, but I heard his effort to steady his voice. "I mean that I felt the earth really move."

By now he had given over to his humor and was laughing outright, which should not have surprised me, since men—delightful as they are at times (notably ones like this)—are at other times such odd, unpredictable creatures! However, given that we were more or less directly upon that earth, with nothing between it and us but a very thin woven mat, I had the chance, in the next second, to register for myself the objective truth of Adam's statement.

The earth had moved and was moving again! It vibrated, as if cartwheels were crossing cobblestones or barrels were spanking across wooden planks. It rumbled, as if I had put my ear to the stomach of a well-fed and extremely fat old man. When it well and truly *moved* beneath us, we disentangled ourselves hastily enough and rose to our feet. I grabbed my nagua to me.

We stared stupidly at the ground for another moment, as if expecting to read in the dirt some answer to the mystery of this event, but the next rumble cured us of our stupor. In a quick exchange, we decided to consult our Arawak friends about these strange movements in the earth's surface. Since the drums were still beating, signaling that the feasting was still in progress, we were assured of finding someone to answer our questions.

"Although it is just a suggestion," I remarked, as Adam, in his haste, nearly dived through the caney door, "I would advise that you dress yourself." I was wrapping my cloth about me in the prescribed manner.

Predictably, my words halted him. "Good point," he said. "I sometimes forget the difference."

"But our hosts do not." I tugged on the knot at my shoulder, securing it as Sylvia had done. "We would no doubt be summarily dismissed from town if you appeared naked in public."

His toilette took him all of fifteen seconds. "Banished to the jungle?" He considered the prospect. He ran his eye over me, a caress across the caney, and said, "Good idea. I know just the spot."

The earth moved again. I hastened to the door.

"For later, though," he added. "If we—and the island—are still here."

He grabbed my hand and pulled me outside with him. It was strangely comforting to me and wholly alien to my nature to have him touch me with the intimate rudeness of ownership. We made our way to the town center, where the festivities were still at a pitch, although The Proud One and Ajijeko were nowhere to be seen. The first thing

I noticed upon our arrival was that my careful plantings around the ceremonial pole had been thoroughly trampled by the dancing and carousing. However, before I had a chance to react adequately to that, the earth moved again beneath our feet, and my thoughts were rather more occupied with discovering whether or not the entire village would remain intact.

Incredibly but reassuringly, the Arawak did not seem profoundly disturbed by the instability of their world. In fact, I was soon to discover that they would have been disappointed if their grand feast to honor the dual events after having been saved from the White Devils and having concluded an important marriage ceremony were not accompanied by some dramatic sign from above.

Heedless of all Arawak customs, Adam went straight to Arawak Father, who was seated, serenely, on his duho, eyeing the continuing feast with every evidence of satisfaction. Great Arawak Mother was seated beside him, rapt and entranced and crooning.

At our arrival, Arawak Father stood up. "Yes, my son?" he inquired. Though he betrayed no particular emotion, he evidently did not know why Adam should be accosting him.

Adam came straight to the point—that is, as straight as he could, given the limitations of his expressions in Arawak. "Are we, by any chance," he asked, "standing on a volcano?"

The concept of *volcano* took a moment or two to sort out. So did *earthquake*. However, since the earth continued to shift and rumble beneath our feet, it was easy enough to make known our questions and our fears; and Arawak legend, as it turned out, was rich in stories of fire-spitting mountains.

Arawak Father put our immediate fears to rest by explaining, "Arawak Island is not a fire-spitting mountain. It is peaceful and good and bountiful. It only gives life. It never takes it away. In the direction of the Silver Men, however," he said in rather more severe accents (that direction would be south), "the Savage Beasts—the Caribs—

live on fire-spitting mountains. It is fitting and good that this should be so. In the time when the Great Ancestress of the Copper Hair ruled the world and The People were numerous and strong, the earth opened up under the feet of the Caribs and poured fire onto them and their towns. It will happen again to the Caribs, and to the White Devils who now drive the Caribs from their islands. It is good."

He paused. The earth swelled and swayed quite terrifically just then. Arawak Father's face lost nothing of its serenity. "But it will not happen this night. Great Arawak Mother has decreed it."

I confess that I did not *quite* have the same confidence in her decrees as the rest of the Arawak. Adam and I exchanged a wordless glance, confirming our mutual skepticism. The earth rolled again so terrifically that I was sure that Vulcan (or his Arawak equivalent) dwelt below these lands and wielded with ferocity his hammer in his subterranean smithy. The roll continued long enough for me to think that this might well be the last, that the earth must open up now and shoot its fire. It was a further comfort to grip Adam's hand ever tighter, and he returned the pressure.

At that prolonged roll, Great Arawak Mother's crooning abruptly ceased. She opened her eyes. Her gaze fell straight on me. I was surprised and terrified anew by the piercing look she bent on me. She stood up. At a wide, sweeping motion of her hands, the drums stopped for the first time in hours. This seemed significant. Then, Great Arawak Mother began to speak to the sky: "I have heard you, Great Zemis!" she cried in a weird, creaky voice. "I have heard your rumblings. The People are honored by your attentions. Ajijeko has returned, glorious, and has married for the highest good of all The People. The treasure has been saved in the way that you predicted. You have spoken this night of all of this, and I have heard you. But now, what is it that you tell me? Could it be that you withdraw your protection from The Beauty?"

I certainly did not like the sounds of that!

"Could it be," she continued, "that our Great Ancestress should not continue to smile on her daughter? We have agreed to let them go—The Beauty and Blue Eyes—at their will, but only on condition that The People continue to protect them. Now, you warn me of impending danger for The Beauty if ever she is separated from Blue Eyes. I am honored by the warning and, in turn—" at that, she focused her eyes on me "—I warn them." Her gaze remained fixed on me. I made some sign of understanding. "O Great Zemis, you may consider them warned! I thank you! I am honored! I am humbled!"

All was motionless silence for many long moments after Great Arawak Mother finished speaking. Then, quite miraculously, I felt the rumblings deep in the earth fade away and die. I am not quite sure how anyone arrived at the knowledge that the quaking of the earth was over and the danger of a volcanic eruption had passed, but it seemed that the Arawak, of one mind on the subject, had accepted that the communication with the Zemis was over for the evening. They simply went back to what activity had been occupying them before the rumblings. Great Arawak Mother sat back down, closed her eyes, and resumed crooning and shaking her head. Arawak Father had sat throughout, impassive, and so did not have to alter his activities one way or the other. The drums began again to beat. The dancing picked up where it had left off. The eating continued, as did the passing of the calabashes with the intoxicating liquor.

Adam evidently thought it a sign for us to continue where we had left off. He turned me toward him, took both my hands in his, and said, a smile on his lips and a look of desire in his eyes, "I'm not to leave you. Consider me warned. Now, about that place in the jungle. . . ."

The jungle was never so beautiful to me as it was that night. Adam and I, fingers entwined, hurrying, left the town by a path I had not yet taken. It was, Adam informed me, the men's path. I felt an illicit, luxurious wantonness surge through me at this violation of Arawak custom.

It was a warm night, even warmer and steamier and sweeter in the jungle, but the ever-present sound of water rushing and gurgling afar off was insensibly cooling and constantly fresh. The warm, sweet, steamy air itself held an intoxicating freshness, as if all this had never been breathed before.

As the throbbing of the drums receded, the sounds of the nocturnal jungle life increased—a concert of toads and crickets and birds. We passed under regal palms and ferns as large as oak trees which were filigreed against the sequined sky, like outsized parasols. We skirted green pools of grasses and thick clumps of bamboo (as the Chinese call the plant, I believe) and trees bearing flowers that looked like large, pouting tulips. Leaves the shape of artists' palettes entwined and climbed around other plants, growing bigger as they did so, to spread into elephant ears. All was alive and ever young and hot and slow.

We passed a bay of flowers as big as bushes. "Those are impatiens," I said, suddenly struck by the similarity between what was so tiny and delicate at home and this large, spreading, voluptuous flower in the Caribbean. "Although it seems impossible for anything to be impatient in this climate," I mused aloud.

"Only me," Adam returned, "and I'm damned impatient. Ah, here we are."

We had arrived at a small open space in the jungle, as open spaces go in wild overgrowth. In the middle idled a stream that looked little more than a spit and spurt of moisture, one of the jungle's sweating rivulets. The ground looked mossy and soft and a vast improvement over the floor of the caney—which was precisely Adam's idea. He drew me to him and, without another word, began to unwrap my nagua.

"Since being presented with this cloth," I said, reluctant to give in to him so easily, "I have had it off more than I have had it on."

Having unwrapped it to my waist, Adam paused to consider that.

There is something about it that invites unwrapping," he said, but did not seem to want to give the matter further thought. "And very, very satisfying it is, too, to unwrap it. Did you know that the Arawak do not kiss?" he asked, kissing me lightly.

I could only shake my head in response.

"They consider it indecent."

Now that he mentioned it, I had noticed that the Arawak mothers and children did not kiss. I recalled seeing a good deal of nose-rubbing, and cheek rubbed to cheek, but pressure from the mother's lips on any part of the child's body did not seem to occur. Then, of course, there had been the scandal of the kiss that Adam and I had exchanged in view of the Arawak warriors.

"But they are a highly proper folk," I said, reversing my earlier ideas of the unseemliness of Arawak ways and abandoning myself shamelessly to this conversation of light kisses, "and do not know what they are missing."

"Sure, now," he replied, kissing me with equal passion in return. With some very bold, uninhibited gestures, he fully released my nagua and his cloth, and presently we were on the ground—precisely where we had left off before the earth had moved beneath us. It was exceedingly pleasant and soft and a little damp.

"But the lessons go both ways," he said, allowing his hands and lips to roam at will, "and I'm eager to try the Arawak ways."

I, too, was eager, but entirely in the dark. "Arawak ways?" I echoed, a little doubtfully.

He leaned over on top of me to kiss my temples and my eyelids. "Do you know the word *kimali*?"

I did not.

"Or *takwakwadu*?"

Nor that either.

"Then you could not know *kubilabala*."

It was true. I did not.

He laughed a little in my ear and clucked his tongue softly. "Do you women speak of nothing interesting or important?" I understood that for the rhetorical question it was. As for *kimali,* he whispered the meaning into my ear.

"No," I scoffed. "Really?"

"Indeed," he affirmed. "Had you not noticed the vertical marks on the backs of other men in town?"

I had not really looked at any man's back but Adam's. I began to understand. "So *that's* why you had me scratch you after the night of your initiation—to prove that we . . ." I began, but did not complete the thought when I was awed by another realization. "You *did* have lascivious thoughts in mind that night, after all! And to think of all you had just been through!"

"Indeed, I did, and you keep forgetting the reason I was put to the tests," he pointed out.

Ignoring this, I said, "Dear me, though, it seems rather brutal," in reference to this strange new custom of scratching a lover's back. "And the other words? Do you mean to tell me?"

"No, show you," he said.

I was rapidly dissolving into him, but a tiny corner of lucidity remained. "And just *how* do you know these things?" I asked.

He laughed again, a sound which was shaded less with humor and more with passion. "I'll tell you *all* in the boat, when we leave."

"Together," I said by way of question.

"Together," he confirmed. "I heard Great Arawak Mother's warning and do not intend to be separated from you anytime soon."

"And when are we leaving?" I asked.

"Tomorrow or the next day," he said, arranging our bodies in an interesting fashion, Arawak style. Before the passion came to wash over us fully, he murmured, "Or the day after that."

CHAPTER 14

That tomorrow never came. To be precise, tomorrow came; *our* tomorrow did not.

Living in a society reasonable enough to be ruled primarily by women, I should have listened better to the warnings of Great Arawak Mother and her concerns for my future. I did not put much store in her strange and sibylline pronouncements on the evening of the grand feast. Certainly, I had been profoundly relieved when the earth had stopped quaking beneath our feet, but even more certainly I had believed neither that the Zemis were communicating with her nor that her verification of the reception of their message was the cause for the end to those rumblings.

As for her warning that I not be separated from Adam, I had received that quite happily. I had taken it as a blessing, even, and almost paradoxically, as a good omen for our future together; and Adam had responded to it appropriately, reassuring me that he would remain by my side. Still, he had made no promises about how many tomorrows this happy union would last.

And that was the devil of it. In that night of unbridled passion we spent together as Arawak woman and man, we had discussed nothing of our future together once off the island—neither before the earth tremors, nor afterward, during the prolonged, instructive, and highly delightful passage in the jungle. Neither had we thought to discuss it upon our return to the caney very, very much later that night (although we did discover there that the hammock was most likely *not* intended for use by a bridal couple). The only words we tasted on our lips were the sounds of each other's names; and to give both of us our due, neither had asked the other for anything beyond what the moment had demanded and offered. We had thought then, of course, that many tomorrows stretched before us.

Thus, when all of Great Arawak Mother's vague apprehensions for my future (one which did not include Blue Eyes) suddenly took shape as cold reality, I had to regret not having thought to demand from him a clarification of his intentions toward me. If I had only heeded Great Arawak Mother's warnings! But how could I have suspected that the cause of our separation would come in such innocuously familiar form? How could I have *truly* known the very next morning, a little before dawn, only half-wrapped in my nagua but fully wrapped in Adam's arms and kisses, that that embrace would be our last? How could I have guessed that that look of promise and desire he wore on his face as he turned to gaze at me over his shoulder before quitting the caney would be the last time I would set eyes on him on Arawak Island?

For the next day had dawned, clear and bell-like, just as had every other day. The sun had risen far too early, but I was hardly distressed by that fact, given that the day unfurling would inevitably give way to a glorious night. The general marriage celebration was continuing, and Adam and I knew how the day's events would proceed. So we rose from the mats on the floor, having slept little, but *finally* rested for the first time in many weeks. Our preparations to leave the caney were slower this morning, hampered, of course, by the need to touch and kiss and explore, just once more.

But full daylight was almost upon us, and even on the day after a grand festival, Arawak custom did not permit lounging about the caney or daytime social intercourse between women and men. The men had their ceremonial hunting and fishing to do. The women would certainly not be idle.

It was true, of course. We were not. So accustomed was I by then to the rhythm and activity of the women's day in Arawak life that I was not particularly surprised to see The Proud One in and among us that morning—*not*, mind you, that she chose to do any work or make herself at all useful. In all events, my guess was confirmed that honeymoons did not form a part of Arawak marriage ritual.

It was toward midafternoon, I would say, that Sylvia and Rose and I decided to go down to the lovely southern bay to search for shells. (I had had the presence of mind to have presented my friends with their gifts that morning, since I had defaulted on my promise to return to them the evening before. They were highly appreciative, although I do not think they knew what to do with a small hand mirror or an emergency sewing kit. However, they did find the snipping scissors delightfully amusing and thought they could make use of the empty glass bottle in a variety of ways, none of which included its use as a vessel for liquids.) Now, Margaret and Lily were invited to come along, but they dithered over the decision and chose, finally, to stay in town.

So it was, as I have said, near midafternoon that the three of us tripped merrily down the path leading to the sandy sward of land, discussing the events of the preceding days. I was as placid and satisfied as any woman in the world could be. The three of us relived with some relish Blue Eyes's rout of the Spanish, mulled over the ball game on the plaza, detailed the wedding feast, oohed and aahed over the rumbling of the earth. On this last event of nature, their interpretations diverged widely from my own, but I was tactful enough to keep my opinion of their Zemis to myself.

Since it was bright and sunny, I had brought along my parasol. I

was not so lost to the world that I had forgotten about the effects of
the sun on the skin of a redhead. In fact, I do believe that my complexion had improved since living among the Arawak. The women
use extraordinary creams on their faces and hands after every bath.
This cream was green, too, like the shampoo. In any case, Sylvia and
Rose had become accustomed to seeing me with the parasol and had
ceased even to make comments about it, while I never once thought of
the oddity of parading on the island dressed in a pink nagua, my hair
unbound, holding a grey-striped parasol.

On the beach we were busy. We must have collected nearly a hundred shells in several rush baskets. At one point we were kneeling in
the sand, absorbed in sorting the good finds from the bad. My back
was to the south, with the waters of the bay behind me. My parasol
was propped on one shoulder, shielding me from the sun's rays glancing off the waters, but also, and incidentally, shielding my vision from
any activity that might have been going on in the waters behind me. I
had no reason to be concerned about it, after all.

Sylvia, whose head was bent down over our collection, was at one
moment seated facing me and the waters of the bay. The next moment
she was on her feet. She did not say a word but merely stood there,
lifted her arm, and pointed. The look on her face was of undisguised
horror. Then, before I hardly registered her action, Rose had stood as
well and assumed the same position.

Of course, I rose quickly and turned to see what had drawn their
attention. Why, what could have been more amazing to my eyes just
then than a small Johnnie boat in which were seated three men, just
a few yards off shore! These men were hatted and suited in naval blue,
cut and gold-braided in a style that was thoroughly familiar to me—
though, somehow, strangely foreign. Behind them, across the glint of
gently heaving sapphire water of the bay, I saw a stately, red-hulled
frigate with the Union Jack fluttering smartly on the main truck.

I, too, remained motionless and wordless.

One man, slim and fair, typically English, and the youngest of the trio, jumped out of the boat and waded foot-deep in the water to beach the boat. That done, the other two men, one rather old, with a paunch, and heavily decorated, lumbered awkwardly ashore, assisted by the third man, who was well-built, conventionally handsome, and in his middle years. I instantly recognized, in descending order of age and girth and rank, an admiral, a vice admiral, and an ensign.

I shook myself of my surprise and immobility, turned to Sylvia and Rose, and said, in Arawak, "This is entirely unexpected, but I do not see any way around it! I must go to greet these men."

Sylvia had hardly roused herself from her surprise. She said in wooden accents, "Don't, Beauty. Don't do it."

I had to smile. "You don't understand, my dear! These are men of my people."

Sylvia shook her head. "We can run up the path to the town," she said, ignoring my comment. "They'll never find us. They might not even come after us! But if they do, Great Arawak Mother will be there. She'll know what to do."

I seriously doubted that Great Arawak Mother would be more effective than I in dealing with three English officers of the Royal Navy.

"You know, my dear, this situation rather reminds me of the encounter between Blue Eyes and the White Devils," I pointed out quite logically, "only a lot less life-threatening! I feel sure that I am a good deal more capable than anyone else—except perhaps Blue Eyes, who is not with us at the moment, is he?—to send these gentlemen on their way with no questions asked."

It was not until I had articulated my intentions that I realized how very strange they were! A few weeks ago, even only a few days ago, I would have been only too glad to have seen the British flag off shore. Now, however, that Adam and I were about to leave the island on our own terms, I found this naval vessel and its crew rather an annoyance.

Stranger still, I felt a vague hostility toward this intrusion and thought that my dear friends, the Arawak, would be better off without it.

Sylvia still looked doubtful but had adjusted her frown to indicate that she was willing to be persuaded. With a reassuring glance aimed at my two friends, I moved forward to greet the three gentlemen.

I stopped. Something about the strange looks on these three very English faces had halted me. The men were walking toward us, but as they moved, they had bent their heads together to whisper to one another. It was quite irregular behavior, and most offensive. I certainly did not understand it until the words of the vice admiral fell on my ear with rather stunning effect: "Perhaps we can speak with her," he said, his voice wary, measuring.

To which the youngest (the ensign) responded, "Do you think . . . could she possibly be *English*?" he asked in amazed accents.

These blockheads were, of course, referring to me. Surely they did not think Arawak women had red hair and carried parasols!

"Of course I am English," I responded, clearly and unequivocally.

I had quite a lot more to say but was prevented from doing so, since this statement seemed to throw them into unnecessary confusion. The admiral began to bluster impolitely, the vice admiral coughed into his fist, while the ensign's eyes boggled and then fell and stayed on poor Rose, who was unmarried and most shapely by English standards. The stare to which he subjected her was *extremely* rude. No Arawak man would have ever *dared* regard an Arawak woman in such a fashion.

Out of this confusion came one clear statement, and that was from the vice admiral, who had recovered himself first to say, quite properly, "Pray excuse us, ma'am, and our surprise, for how could we have guessed that you were a . . . countrywoman?"

"How, indeed?" I said, and then asked, with what I hoped was a civil smile, "But who, may I ask, might you be, and what has brought you to this island?" I could make allowances for one to show surprise at finding an Englishwoman in a nagua on a remote island in the Caribbean, but I did not think it sufficient excuse for one to entirely forget one's manners.

In response to my question, the vice admiral admirably took the cue. He bowed gracefully, properly lifted his plumed blue bicorn to curl it into the crook of his arm. He wore his own hair, which was a light brown.

"I am Lord Rollo, ma'am, of the service of King James, vice admiral of the *Pride of Devon*," he said, deeply respectful and with an evident reference to the ship in the bay.

I dipped a very brief curtsy in return (a properly wrapped nagua does not permit the full execution of such a movement) and moved my eyes to the admiral, who made a manful attempt to pull himself together.

"Albemarle," this one harumphed by way of introduction, and without the slightest gesture of courtesy toward me. Perhaps he did not wish to doff his hat for fear of spoiling his finely rolled tie wig. "Commander of the same."

"And you, sir?" I demanded of that dolt, the hatless, wigless ensign, who, having managed to tear his eyes away from Rose, proceeded to stare dumbly at me. I stared him down, naturally. His fair skin flushed deep red, and with a great effort, he looked away. He seemed, furthermore, to have lost his power of speech.

Lord Rollo stepped into the breach. "And this, ma'am, is Ensign Pocock—" he said a little sternly (and by way of confirming all of my guesses as to their relative ranks) "— who will recover himself without further delay."

Lord Rollo's words penetrated Ensign Pocock's thick skull. He cleared his throat, straightened, sketched an awkward bow, repeated his name and rank, and fell back a step.

"And you, ma'am?" Lord Rollo continued with another proper bow. "Whom do we have the honor to address?"

Here might have been the moment to have had the wit of Adam Winthrop. However, in that flash of a half second, I was glad that Adam was far off, on the other side of the island, away from the sight of these men. In truth, this question, as natural as it was, caught me slightly off guard.

An infinitesimal pause fell. Lord Rollo continued, "That is, we might like to know your name, ma'am."

That was precisely the problem. *Which* name should I divulge? I was still sensitive to the taint of my father's name. However, I had firmly abandoned Mrs. Lipscomb but could hardly, in any true sense, identify myself as Mrs. Winthrop without implicating Adam in a tangle not of his own making. Then, again in the present context of Arawak Island, it was rather that Adam should have been known as Mr. *Sedgwick*, after all. However, I did not think that these three gentlemen would appreciate the nuances of that explanation.

I recalled having been in this situation before. Honesty had served then. It would serve now.

"I am Miss Sedgwick," I said, without allowing another awkward second to elapse. I again attempted what I could of a curtsy within the graceful confines of the nagua. "Eve Marie Sedgwick of London."

I noticed that Vice Admiral Rollo looked slightly surprised by my identity. However, before he had a chance to respond, the admiral launched into a haphazard jumble of questions and remarks.

"Well, Miss Sedgwick, ma'am," he grumbled, "it's a surprise to us and a wonder that we meet up with you here, don't you know, and wonder how it is that you have come to find yourself on this island. For ourselves, we've been after that Spanish pirate in his ship, the *Cinco Llagas*. We were on our way to Jamaica, don't you know, when that ba—" he made a noise deep in his throat, excused himself, and continued "—when Don Pedro fired on us for no reason at all, save that we were skirting too close! So we decided to give him chase and repay him the favor! He shook our tail off Dominica five days ago, but we have reason to think he was sailing in this direction, only a day or two ahead of us. Rumors of gold, don't you know! Have you seen him, what?"

Honesty had its limits. For a variety of reasons, I did not think it wise to recount the truth of what I knew of Don Pedro and the gold.

"Dear me," I said in the little pause that indicated I was to make some response. Although I have never, as a firm rule, been practiced in the feminine art of simpering stupidity, I hoped that I had schooled my features to a look of maidenly horror during Admiral Albemarle's recital. I attempted to inject fear into my voice. "Pirates?" I said. "Sailing in a ship called *To Sink the Ladies*?"

"Not pirates exactly, ma'am." This from Lord Rollo. "And the ship is called the *Cinco Llagas*," he corrected. "Her captain is one Don Pedro, a full-fledged officer in the Spanish navy, and as wily a sailor as one is bound to meet."

"And you say that they are headed here?" I asked, my eyes wide.

"No," said Lord Rollo, "I say that they should have already been here by now—that is, *if* they were indeed headed here." To this I had absolutely nothing to say. Lord Rollo paused delicately, then said with utmost courtesy, "Pray excuse me, Miss Sedgwick, but I cannot help but inquire after your name. Are you not, perchance, the daughter of the late Major General Jonathan Sedgwick?"

"Sedgwick? Major General Sedgwick?" I heard the admiral mutter under his breath, as if dredging a memory.

I instantly stiffened. I could hardly believe my ears. This encounter was worse than I could have possibly imagined. I believe that I managed a "Yes."

Lord Rollo bowed. "Forgive me, ma'am," he said with great tact, "but you will understand that news of Major General Sedgwick's, ah, difficulties reached the Royal Navy."

Admiral Albemarle suddenly recalled what he had heard. From under upraised brows, his eyes regarded me in a way that I had hoped my departure from England would prevent me from ever receiving again. Apparently I had been wrong.

"Good gad! Sedgwick!" the admiral blustered. "A scandal! The Spanish! Yes, yes, quite!"

With a distinct effort, I replied, "Indeed, there was a scandal. However, my father died of heart failure the week after his denunciation—before he could clear his name. Soon thereafter, I left England."

Lord Rollo's handsome brow furrowed deeply. "Soon thereafter?" he queried. "Then, perhaps, you don't know—that is to say, a thorough investigation was launched of Major General Sedgwick's activities. He had led such an exemplary career, after all! Well, the long and short of it is, ma'am, that I believe his name was cleared."

My heart leapt. Perhaps this was not to be a horrible encounter, after all. "His name cleared?" I echoed.

Lord Rollo stepped back a pace and disclaimed delicately, "I cannot say for sure, ma'am! I am sorry that I did not follow the particulars more closely. However, I believe I heard something to that effect, and now that I think about it, I am not sure that the investigation was pursued to its very end, given that no one seemed to be about who wished to have your father's name cleared publicly—if I do not mistake the matter!"

"But my Uncle Harry—Sedgwick, as well," I said quickly. "Surely he wished to see his brother's name cleared. He, too, is an army man."

Lord Rollo bowed and stated his regret that he was not better informed about the details of the results of the investigation and the subsequent fate of my father's tarnished name. Then, much to my relief, he shifted the discussion most properly, as if we were *not* standing on a remote beach and I were *not* wearing a native nagua: "It is not my intention to refer to events that can only give you pain, although I think you have reason to hope that belief in his guilt is now, in some quarters, quite a thing of the past! However, I believe that we were discussing Don Pedro, the Spanish blackguard. If he and his band had landed here, you would have known it and have been able to tell us about it, would you not?"

My mind was spinning from the news. It was as much from happiness as from a desire to keep the Arawak secrets hidden that I said, honestly, by way of reply, "Well, the island *is* rather out of the way."

"The demmed currents," was Admiral Albemarle's opinion.

"And given that, then, ma'am," Lord Rollo pursued, "I hope that it is not an impertinence to inquire as to how *you* arrived here and came to be so . . . circumstanced?"

"You can easily understand how it was for me after my father's denunciation," I began. "He had booked a passage on a ship, the *Judith*, which was bound for the New World. However, after he was *falsely* accused, and after I suffered other . . . losses, I was persuaded to take his place."

I was now sufficiency in command of myself to be able to give a fluent account of the sinking of the *Judith* and my subsequent arrival on the island. I stressed the friendliness of my hosts, the Arawak. I kept close to the truth, save for two points: I did not mention the presence of Adam Winthrop; and I credited my rather lengthy stay on the island to the fact that I had been gravely ill after my exposure following the shipwreck and needed to be nursed back to health.

The three men marveled over my miraculous survival, asked a few questions, discussed among themselves what they might have heard about the disaster of the *Judith* or her fellow ships. Encouraged by their evident satisfaction with my story, I finished my account by assuring them that the Arawak had not at all kept me captive but were planning to convey me to a European port as soon as possible.

Admiral Albemarle began to protest this, grumbling that he did not think it possible to allow his countrywoman to remain here, alone, when he stood in all readiness to rescue her. It was evident that he had quite a bit more to say in this general vein, but his words were cut off by Lord Rollo, who had taken on a deeply pensive air and who said, as if yet another interesting thought had just occurred to him, "Perhaps *that* is what that poor man has been muttering about all this time!"

Lord Rollo stepped forward then, sweeping the admiral behind him. "We boarded several very ill seamen at Bridgetown, to the south of here," he explained, "who were the survivors of some mishap or another—weeks ago it was! Since we are more or less directly bound for England, it was decided that the *Pride of Devon* take them on to return them to home port. Two are in a coma, but one its partially conscious, although raving. We have not yet been able to understand what he is saying, but I wonder. . . ."

My mind leapt ahead to the possibilities of what he was suggesting. I gave voice to my immediate thought. "Could one of them be named Thomas?" I wondered.

"Thomas, Thomas," Lord Rollo repeated thoughtfully. He turned to Ensign Pocock. "Ensign," he said, "since you have been principally in charge of the men we boarded in Bridgetown—"

"*Yes, sir!*" Ensign Pocock responded immediately, stiffening his back and looking straight ahead at nothing in particular.

"—could one of them be named Thomas, do you know?" Lord Rollo inquired. "Perhaps the one who is partially conscious and rambling?"

My heart had begun to pound irregularly at the thought of survivors from the *Judith*.

"That I do not know, *sir!*" was Ensign Pocock's crisp reply.

"Then, *think*, man!"

"Yes, *sir!* It's possible that one of them was named Thomas, *sir!*" the ensign responded.

Lord Rollo turned back to me, with a smile compounded of inquiry and helplessness. "You see, ma'am?" he said, then paused. "You could assist us—and these poor seamen—if you were to come aboard just now and possibly identify one or more of them."

I hesitated. It seemed unlikely in the extreme that Thomas was lying, semiconscious, in the ship off store. Still, other, equally unlikely events had recently shaped my life, thus making the possibility that I could help him and learn news of the crew and passengers of the *Judith* entirely plausible.

Lord Rollo's next words decided the issue for me. "I do not think, ma'am," he said, quite charmingly, "that in all good conscience I can leave this island without having you see for yourself our three helpless passengers."

It seemed churlish to refuse him the request, especially after the excellent news he had given me about my father. I turned to explain the situation to Sylvia and Rose, who were looking anything but pleased by all of this.

"I shall be back presently," I said to them.

"That's what you said last night," Rose complained.

"Ah, yes," I hedged, looking away, fighting down a slight blush (which is alien to my nature), "but *that* was different."

I informed the admiral that I was ready to cross the bay to the ship.

"But I will expect you to bring me back, of course, once I have determined whether or not I recognize any of the men," I continued quite firmly. "For I think that I must tell you that my Indian hosts on the island have already arranged for my departure, and I would not wish to offend them after they have so kindly taken me in and looked after me!"

The admiral seemed about to protest, but Lord Rollo stepped in again, bowed, and said graciously, "Certainly, ma'am."

I had thought, perhaps, that Ensign Pocock or Vice Admiral Rollo would stay ashore, but such was not the case. With some further words of doubt from Sylvia and Rose and further reassurances on my part, I climbed into the Johnnie boat with the other three men. It was rather cramped and my parasol jostled with their hats. It was only when we were halfway across the bay that I had second thoughts about this plan.

At one moment, Ensign Pocock was regarding me with the stupidest expression on his face. I was very pleased when Lord Rollo, with an effective admixture of cold formality and reproof, brought the ensign to his senses. Lord Rollo, I was beginning to see, was a very proper man.

He continued this propriety when we arrived on deck. Under the wide eyes of an understandably amazed crew, Vice Admiral Rollo escorted me personally to his regally appointed cabin while the hold was being evacuated of men so that I might circulate there without embarrassment when I inspected the three seamen. Within minutes of having been seated in a real chair for the first time in months and offered a tawny wine (which I declined), I was startled to my feet by a great shout which arose above us on deck. Lord Rollo left me alone, closing the door behind himself on a ceremonious bow.

A minute later, I heard shouts above of, "Pirates on the starboard!" and "Spanish!"

Moments later Lord Rollo returned to the cabin to announce that a privateer's ship built on a Spanish model had been sighted to our starboard and would soon be upon us. Without delay, the *Pride of Devon* was weighing anchor, unfurling her sails, and reaming her cannons, readying them to be loaded. There was no further talk of my identifying the ill seamen or of my returning to the tranquil beach where I had been sorting through a harvest of shells with Sylvia and Rose. I was told not to move from the cabin. The door was even locked behind me—for my own protection, of course.

Well. Seated at the portholes of the vice admiral's cabin, looking out, it seemed like no time at all before I lost sight of the lozenge-shaped, sun-drenched gem of an island floating so tranquilly in the limitless ocean, ruffled by the winds of heaven.

In the next couple of nerve-racking days of possible pirate attack, I had ample opportunity to reflect that Great Arawak Mother had been right to be apprehensive about my immediate future. It seemed a great irony that my life was in far greater danger on a ship of the king's navy than it ever had been in Adam Winthrop's company.

Not that I actually saw that ship menacing us from the south and east, but several of our own cannons were fired. I did not know whether they had made their mark or not. Nor did I ever see the three seamen whose existences had been the cause of my coming aboard ship in the first place. By the time the pirates had been outrun, the three seamen had happened to die, one by one, so I was informed by Lord Rollo, and had been given their proper sailor's burial at sea. Under the circumstances, Lord Rollo explained in soothing terms, it was all for the best that I had been rescued from the island.

To which I answered, rather testily and perhaps a little unfairly, for I was *not* pleased with the turn in events, "By a ruse, sir! I never saw the pirate ship, and I never saw the three seamen. I have reason to doubt the existence of both, added to which are my gave doubts about your reasons for having 'rescued' me!"

"Dear lady," Lord Rollo said with a low bow and voice full of hurt and candor, "I deeply regret your doubts, which are entirely un-founded!" He bowed again. "But perhaps I have misunderstood *your* intentions and reasons for wishing to have remained on the island in the company of half-naked savages?"

How could I protest or demand to be taken back to Arawak Island without exposing my relationship to Adam Winthrop—the very rela-tionship it was not my right to make public? Although I felt the tremendous injustice of the situation (and harbored, even more so now, a distinct feeling of having been *cheated*, let us say, of Adam's attentions), I would sustain myself over the next weeks wholly with the feeling of exceeding nobility in not demanding a return to Arawak Island, thereby protecting both Adam Winthrop's and the Arawaks' privacy, neither of whom would benefit from a visit from yet another shipload of White Devils.

Since I was *the sole woman* aboard and had only a pink nagua for dress, I naturally *did not* circulate on deck. I doubt, in any case, that I would have found any pleasure there. Instead, and for company, Lord Rollo was so kind as to visit me every few days for conversation, when he had a moment's respite from his arduous duties on deck. He had given me his luxurious berth and saw to it that I was provided with all varieties of delicate foods and wines to tempt my palate.

Within days we were sailing close to the island of Porto Rico and the port of San Juan. Although the Dutch had successfully stormed and sacked San Juan a half century before, no such attempt by the *Pride of Devon* was made on this pass. This discretion was, perhaps, owing to San Juan's massive bulwarks and its imposing citadel, known as El Morro, which had been built since the Dutch raid, or even, perhaps, to the successive defeats there of Drake and Cumberland nearly a century before, the bloody details of which still grew green in English seamen's minds. Whatever the case, as we skirted provocatively close to the island, the *Pride of Devon* did not do more than fire off a cannon or two, rather aimlessly and without real intent, just to let the Spanish know that we had been by.

Soon thereafter, we arrived at Kingston, Jamaica. Lord Rollo strongly suggested that I not disembark, because there was no passenger ship in the vicinity bound for England any time soon, and none of his officers had the leisure to escort me around town. He did not mention the difficulties that might arise as a result of my unusual dress.

Nagua or no, I tried to escape, of course—several times, in fact, thinking this to be my opportunity to find a way back, alone, to Arawak Island. Although I did not think I was exactly being guarded, I never made it past any one of the officers, who were always so courteous as to redirect me to my quarters, if I was found outside the vice admiral's berth.

What I saw of Kingston, then, I saw from my porthole. I registered in a mechanical sort of way the great stir of life along the quays:

sailors in rough garments and of harsh-sounding, rough speech; stalwart fishwives with baskets on their heads, petticoats hitched up to expose bare legs and bare feet, calling their wares shrilly and almost inarticulately and with Negresses in tow; watermen in caps and loose trousers rolled to the knees; shipwrights and laborers from the dockyards; rat-catchers; water-carriers; planters in wigs and ruffled shirts, carrying walking sticks; and everywhere merchants, buyers, and sellers. They hovered over capacious burlap bags filled with brownish-red coffee beans; piles of great, multifingered hands of green, ripening bananas; golden walls of cane propped against low brick balustrades; teetering towers of tobacco leaves; and auction blocks on which Negroes were sold, minute by minute, black skin glistening in the hot, Caribbean sun.

We spent not more than three days at Kingston. Just before our departure, Lord Rollo was able to procure a suitable dress for me. We took to sea again, this time heading north, navigating between Hispaniola and Cuba. Lord Rollo's visits began to occur daily, and by the time we had reached the Bahamas, from which point we would travel to the Florida coast, where we were to catch the gulf currents, the tenor of his visits had seemed to change from the polite to something friendlier.

He announced himself at my quarters one evening, and since he had been a model of propriety from the first moment I had spoken with him on the beach, I was surprised at his state. Perhaps he had been drinking. Other than the occasional reference to my father, or to the army or navy, our conversations had been strictly impersonal. He had principally asked questions about my life among the Arawak, their customs, details of the island, and such. This evening, he began to probe more into my past, to ask after the events in the days following my father's denunciation and his death.

When I was unresponsive, he changed methods and tactics and reached over to touch the shell necklace at my throat.

"You haven't taken it off," he said, almost puzzled. Then, on a far-away note in his well-bred voice, he added, "I would have thought the savages would have given you a gold one."

I had reassured him on several previous occasions that there was no gold on the island and that the Arawak were as poor and pitiful a people as could possibly be imagined. He seemed to have believed me on those previous occasions, although he did return to the point more than once. Now however, was not the moment to defend the Arawak.

I had recoiled at his touch. I jumped up and reached instinctively for my parasol, which was at hand. I made my feelings about further intimacy known to him by pointing the ferrule at the bottom button of his vest, exposed beneath his loose-cut coat.

He rose as well. He instantly retrieved his propriety. "How you *do* misunderstand me, my dear," he said stiffly to that gesture.

I was unappeased. I shook the business end of my parasol with intention.

His smile was gentle and understanding and handsome on his face. "All I have ever wished to do since seeing you on the beach," he said, "was to rescue you from unpleasant circumstances and protect you from harm. It is my dearest wish to clear your father's name officially, upon our return to London." Then, bowing low and very gracefully, he withdrew. He did not come to visit me again during the rest of the voyage.

Not many days later, we sailed into the teeth of North Atlantic winds. We were bound for England.

CHAPTER 15

e's such a nice man, don't you think, my dear?" Aunt Charlotte said. "And so handsome!"

The words had fallen on my ears, but I did not fully register them. My eye had been caught in the luminous facets of the crystal goblet in my hand. My fingers savored the hard coolness of it. I set it down on a table of highly polished walnut strewn with pewter bowls and plates. I was seated upon a tall, straight-backed chair with straw mesh laddered between twisted columns (nothing like a duho), of which there were several scattered about, all gay with cushions and heavily curved arms and legs. On three of its walls, the room had no less than six high, mullioned windows, hung with stiff brocades of deep red and blue. I looked up at the beamed ceiling and lost my eye in its complications, it was so unlike the simple thatch of a caney. The architecture of this room was thoroughly modern, except for the whimsical minstrel balcony that structured the fourth wall. It was not used for minstrels, as it would have been under the reign of Elizabeth. Rather, the balcony served as a loft where my uncle kept his desk, which was positioned in front of the row of glazed windows that allowed the light of day to stream in and to illuminate balcony and receiving room alike.

Looking down again, I took in the portraits lining the walls, then the cheerful fire which danced on the hearth of the spiral-brick fireplace. Its light, combined with the wan winter sunlight, glanced off metal and glass, and, still-unaccustomed, the effect dazzled my eye. A smooth wooden floor ran beneath my feet, hugged by a woolen carpet from Flanders. I had always loved this room and its warmth, coziness, and light.

"My dear Marie," Aunt Charlotte tried again, "I said, isn't he a nice man, and so handsome, too?"

These words penetrated my abstraction. "Who, Auntie?" I asked.

"Lord Rollo! The man who just left!" she replied, allowing her exasperation to show through. "Are you daydreaming again, Marie?"

"Why, yes, I am afraid I have been," I admitted.

Comfortably ensconced in the comfortable suburb of Islington in the presence of my comfortable Aunt Charlotte, I found it difficult not to compare my life in London to that on Arawak Island. This Aunt Charlotte perceived as daydreaming. I recalled that once, not too many months earlier, it had been my fondest wish to be surrounded by proper furniture. . . .

"Perhaps the shipwreck has affected you more than you realize," Aunt Charlotte broke in to my train of thought, "for you did not used to be that way, my dear. Not that I don't find your somewhat *softer* spirit, shall we say, a bit of an improvement. Before your departure and your father's—er, that is to say, you were always so— But, never mind about that now! It's more to the point to say that I know not how you can have been so *oblivious* to Lord Rollo's presence just now—" the note of censure in her voice was pronounced "—especially after the obliging invitation he came to extend to you, and very prettily said, it was, too, not to mention everything else he has done for you!" She paused, this time in happy reflection. "And so handsome he is, too!"

Almost every chance remark was destined to provoke in me some point of comparison between the two very different lives that I had lived. Lord Rollo, be he never so handsome, was no match for the attractions of a certain half-Arawak warrior I had known.

Although Aunt Charlotte could be counted to hold only the most conventional of conventional ideas and to voice only the most conventional of conventional opinions, in this case, she was right: I had never been in my life dreamy or *mopey*, and I did not suffer such people gladly.

I cast off my memories and smiled. "Yes, indeed," I agreed. "And so kind of him to have paved my return to London. I am indebted to him!"

"Your indebtedness is not what be wants from you," Aunt Charlotte said, "if I do not mistake the matter, my dear Marie!"

"He will have to accept it," I stated, "for, after all, as you say, it was he who cleared Papa's name and took the trouble to go to the Secretariat to speak with Uncle Harry upon our arrival in London."

"And one does not expect such consideration from a navy man," Aunt Charlotte added, "given that the Sedgwicks have been army men their entire lives. And what with all the hubbub swirling about the king's head just now, I am sure that all men of rank and distinction are going quite distracted! Your Uncle Harry does not think that James can outlast the challenge from that foreigner, William, you know—"

(Here I recalled that Adam had said something quite similar on one occasion.)

"—and it's reported that William has just commanded a Dutch fleet to set sail for our shores!" she continued.

I had already reacquainted myself with the rapidly degenerating Stuart affairs of state. "And none too soon, for that complete nincompoop of a monarch," I said, not mincing words, "devout Catholic that he is, is determined, with his whimsical laws, to make life as difficult as he can for his fellow Catholics! You might think that by ordering the bishops of the Church of England to read his latest Order of Indulgence from every church pulpit, he was trying to hurt the Catholic cause, rather than promote it!"

Aunt Charlotte looked rather surprised. "Since when have you been sympathetic to followers of Rome?"

"Since seeing a bit of the world," I said, rather airily. (Here the reminder of Adam Winthrop was strong.)

"The Colonies," Aunt Charlotte muttered darkly, not for the first time since my return. She held fast to the belief that the wild, uncivilized Colonies negatively affected anyone who had the misfortune to visit them, most particularly on the score of religious tolerance, which Aunt Charlotte felt to be vaguely wicked. "However, we were speaking of your feelings toward Lord Rollo—who is a good Anglican, I might add!—and the very evident fact that he wishes more from you than your feeling of indebtedness!"

"Were we?" I countered. "But I am hardly ready to express any other feelings toward him just yet."

"Ah, well, I understand, my dear," she consoled. "But time has moved on, and you are young enough to put that tragic episode of your marriage behind you!"

"But it is too soon!" I protested, involuntarily.

"Your husband has been dead over a six-month now," she said, "and although I know that he was very dear to you—"

"My husband, dead?" I was surprised into saying, rather blankly, my heart plummeting.

She paused, visibly taken aback. "I did not wish to cause you fresh pain, my dear, with my reference to Mr. Lipscomb's very tragic accident!"

"Oh, yes, Edward!" I said, brightening.

"Who did you think I was talking about?"

I had recovered. "Yes, yes, Mr. Lipscomb, of course," I said, hoping to repair the slip.

Aunt Charlotte regarded me with a frown. "The Colonies must have had a very strong effect on you," she said, now in deep disapproval. "Were you among *very* strange people, my dear?"

It was an effort not to laugh at that. Among various other services that Lord Rollo had performed on my behalf upon my return several weeks before, he had determined that the true story of where and how I had come to be a passenger aboard the *Pride of Devon* need not become general knowledge. If the world were told that I had spent the several months after the disastrous shipwreck of the *Judith* in company of a gentle plantation owner and his wife in Jamaica, who would know different? Perceiving the wisdom of this, I had agreed to this story, albeit reluctantly.

It was easy to answer Aunt Charlotte's question honestly. "They *were* very strange at first," I acknowledged, "but I became accustomed to their ways."

"You may promptly forget them, for you are not in the Colonies any longer," she said.

"At least I was not rescued by Puritans," I said, straightfaced, and by way of consolation.

"Yes, wasn't that fortunate!" she replied without a blink. "Nevertheless—and I am sure I need not remind you again—people will be watching you very closely for a while, so you must be on your best behavior, not that you ever gave any consideration to behavior in the past! And speaking of which, don't you think it would be proper for you to undertake a visit to Mr. Lipscomb's family? Do I not remember that he was from Hertfordshire?"

"Yes, he was, but perhaps you had forgotten that his parents died in his earliest adulthood, and so I was never burdened with in-laws. Wasn't *that* fortunate?"

"Eve Marie!" she reproved. (She had always used my full name for emphasis.) "Now, *that* sounds more like you!" she said, not necessarily in the spirit of a compliment. "And that is *exactly* what I am talking about! You may have been, ah, outspoken before, but I do not think such manners will serve you now, for you are still in an early widowhood and must live down the very strange experience of your shipwreck, coupled with your father's scandal, which still lingers in everyone's mind, although that now seems to have been cleared up to everyone's satisfaction! And for having rescued you from both disasters," she continued, coming (again) to her point, "you have Lord Rollo to thank!"

"For which," I repeated, "I am indebted to him!"

Again, Aunt Charlotte was right. Lord Rollo had been responsible for my reestablishment in London. Perhaps I had misjudged him that night on the ship when we had sailed through the waters of the Bahamas. Since that encounter, I must confess that Lord Rollo had handled me with unfailing propriety and delicacy, and he had been prompt in having the case of treason against my father reopened and pursued to its happy conclusion. No less a personage than Sir Stephen Fox himself had reexamined the evidence.

Since, in fact, there was no more evidence now than there had been six months earlier, it was merely a matter of days before the name of Major-General Jonathan Sedgwick was officially cleared by the Army's Office of Ordnance. Before I knew it, I was being ushered up to Aunt Charlotte and Uncle Harry's great stone house, just off the Islington High Street, and being folded into Aunt Charlotte's arms with the little speech, "My dear Marie, what an experience you have had! And to think of all you suffered for . . . for *nothing*! Not that I am not grateful to that lovely family in Jamaica—the Elthams, they are called?—although I am sure I have never heard of them! But I always knew, deep down, that your father was innocent and that he would *never* have stooped—that is to say, that it would all come out right in the end! And now it has! But just let me look at you! Why, you don't look any worse for wear. In fact, one might say that your looks have improved! *I* might say so, in all events! And now I am not at all sorry that we accepted all those boxes of papers and files from your father's library, which your uncle has stored by his desk—for I am sure that no one else would have wished to have had his tainted— er, that is, let me say again how *happy* we are to see you and that everything has turned out for the best!"

After this affecting display, Uncle Harry, with quiet good taste, said little. He hugged me briefly, then looked at me. He had aged. The look in his eye was kindly, yet troubled. He said simply, "You understand, Marie, that I was too close to the situation to untangle it to my—or anyone else's—satisfaction. Lord Rollo has done our family a signal service."

Uncle Harry, incidentally, had been the best of my relatives in the darkest days of my father's disaster and Edward's subsequent death. Of course, this is expected of one's father's brother, but strangely, *he*, of everyone immediately connected to my father, had *not* denounced the accusation. That meant, of course, that he, of everyone, did not have to reverse himself.

Anyone attending closely to my narrative thus far might think that to have found myself back in England, my comfort ensured by the proper furniture and clothing, not to mention a plentiful supply of hair pins, and my father's name cleared, would have been all that I could have wished for. However, those same readers might also easily believe that my strange experiences on Arawak Island might have caused a change in my desires. As for the evolution of those desires, my story is far from over.

It *was* pleasant to be an accepted member of society once again— my *own* society—and the pleasure I felt at my reentry was somewhat akin to the pleasure I had felt strolling through town on Arawak Island the day after Adam had triumphed in the initiation rites. However, and in comparison to that morning's stroll through the village, my whole experience among the Arawak was taking on the quality of a dream, or at least, a significant lapse from my usual behavior in respectable society.

"Now, my dear Marie," Aunt Charlotte was saying in the midst of my reverie this morning after Lord Rollo's latest call, "we must discuss your dress for the Royal Guard ball at Holland House. How wonderful of his lordship to have invited you! Your dress must be something special, but we have no time to lose, for Alice will need to be stitching it this week."

Indeed, it was *very* pleasant to be, once again, an accepted member of society, invited to balls, needing new clothing. I had had, of course, to have an entirely new wardrobe since returning to London. I was able to afford quite an elegant one, and with no financial assistance from my aunt and uncle, for the army had determined to allot me my father's pension, including a rather handsome supplement for all that I had suffered.

About my suffering, I admit to being *mopish* from time to time, but I have long experienced that purposeful activity is a great balm to troubled spirits. This morning, after concluding the discussion of the details of my evening toilette with Aunt Charlotte, I proceeded to continue on with a project that had caught my attention some few days before. I was beginning to throw myself with some zeal into the landscaping at Chelsea Hospital, which was just then being built. I was delighted to have my participation in this project approved with very little persuasion (or bullying) on my part. However, this experience was proving to have its complications.

Through my activities at Chelsea Hospital, I discovered that nothing attracts normally very sober and sedate men (some of them retired *army officers*, no less!) more than the hint of tragedy hovering about a young woman. To be attracted to a member of the opposite sex for this reason alone I find most ridiculous; however, I shall have to save the development of such a theme for an entire future work.

As I was saying, this morning, I had seen that the best cure for my low spirits was a brisk walk to Chelsea (which had come to be considered part of London, everyone will remember, in the wake of the Great Fire a score or so years earlier). Although it was November, I chose to walk, for it was a sunny day. (In very relative terms, that is. London has never seen the sun such as I have seen it.) I chose a grey silk and a heavy grey woolen cloak for the occasion. I had forgotten how *uncomfortable* the boning was in the bodice and the stomacher, and how heavy the cloth was, but I suppose that some concessions are to be made if one is to remain fashionable. On that score, I was pleased to see in the streets of London ever more the appearance of the parasol as an accoutrement of fashion. It flattered me that I had been among the first to launch this feminine mode before my departure last spring.

My eye was, as I traversed the streets of London, caught up in the fashions I beheld, which, as a result of my absence and my experiences, seemed very strange and new to me. The women were not so very different from what I remembered, but the men—I was no longer used to seeing them in so much dress! They wore great perukes with flowing curls and plumed hats. Their mincing steps were offset by ornamental swords carelessly concealed in the ample folds of their circular cloaks of olive-brown worsted, embroidered in silver and gilt. Lace foamed at their necks and wrists; their half-boots were buckled and red-heeled. Even after several weeks among my own countrymen and -women, I found my eye still needed to make adjustments.

Understand that, upon setting foot once again on English soil, I found my perceptions wholly changed. My first impression, to my own surprise, was the general sense I had received of gray and stone and age. After the ever-young, timeless, tradewind-swept islands of the tropics, no contrast could have been more stark, more brutal than that of the low English skies, barren trees, and arctic chill which swirled around my native island, frosting moors and fields and city streets. It was difficult not to miss the jungle and the enchanted glen, with its magical pool; the fruits and the fish; the sun, and rain, and dark, and dawn, and thick brown dirt, so soft and warm beneath one's feet. However, it was not the landscape, or the cold, which most profoundly affected me. It was, rather, my renewed perception of time and history. They were everywhere. They surrounded me, enveloped me, nearly submerged me, at first, in the weight of layers which seemed bulkier to me than the clothes on my back.

On Arawak Island, there was no time. And without time, there could be no history. Each today, hot and slow, was like yesterday. Each yesterday was like the day before. Each tomorrow would be like today. When the day was over, it lost its particularity to drip and blend into the limitless pool of the past that existed only in the memory of one's mother's mother and her mother's mother. There were no moments, no periods, no eras, no ages, no saecula, no cycles, no falls, no rises, no revolutions. However, perhaps, in more recent memory, Arawak time could have been divided into two parts: Before the White Devils Came, and After the White Devils Came.

In the English Islands, each day was dated, each year numbered, each event noted for its day and year, and laid in a neat row. This is called a chronology. Upon my return, I found all numbers and dates quite superfluous. Once I readjusted to English time, I rediscovered how nice it is to know when something happened, to whom, and in relationship to what.

The attentive reader will recall that Adam had once confessed that he did not miss the marking of time. Since London fairly bristles with clock towers, my reminder of him was, as I have said, constant, coming every quarter hour.

My sense of the precise, which had blurred in my timeless time in company of the Arawak, returned to sharp focus. It seemed significant, then, to remember that the exact date of my departure from Portsmouth had been April 27, 1688. My return to England, by way of Southampton, was on October 23, 1688. The date of my "rescue" from Arawak Island was August 11. Adam and I must have washed ashore there somewhere around June 19. That meant that I had spent a mere two months, a scant eight weeks, in Adam's company, which did not seem like much, *if* one wished to reckon by English standards.

If one wished to reckon by Arawak standards, on the other hand, eight weeks had been time enough—certainly time enough for me to get to know the man, his faults, his qualities, and his passion. I had not expected his passion. I had not had the time fully to experience it, either, and I was, in fact, very vexed about it all. On the subject of his passion, I remembered now vividly his enigmatic words from the last time we were together: "I have something to tell you, in the nature of a confession," he had said. "A delicate matter." Then, "I've already decided to tell you—but not here. Not tonight."

What could he have meant other than the implication that, once we left the island, his relationship with me or his responsibility to me or whatever it was that bound us together would stop? The exact content of the confession seemed rather secondary. Perhaps he would explain that he was, first and always, a soldier-sailor-trader, wishing no woman to tie him down to one port. Or, perhaps, he would confess that he was *already* married. Perhaps he would have any number of other things to say, all equally meaningless to me, all directed to the same dreary end.

Although the content of the confession was secondary, I continued to feel—and with a great deal of confidence—that the act of the confession itself was primary. Adam Winthrop owed me that much, after all; and, because of that, I had a great deal of confidence as well that he would make every effort to find me, in order to confess it. In fact, I was beginning to suspect a reason that would soon make it imperative for him to come and find me. I did not suppose that a man of his particular resource and talents would have any difficulty leaving Arawak Island and discovering my whereabouts.

On these various aspects of Adam Winthrop's confession and his need to confess to me, I was to discover, soon enough, that I was both right and wrong—and this condition was one to which I am learning to accustom myself, and which, I have come to believe, since having lived the adventures I have lived, is a condition more common generally than is often supposed. But, again, I anticipate.

Perhaps it was because these particular thoughts were on my mind that, instead of going straight to Chelsea Hospital, I chose a route that would take me down to the River Fleet and the wharves. In the past several weeks, I had already wandered there once or twice, with some vague hope of gathering information. I did not know precisely what information I was seeking, but I was sure that if any were to be had, it would be there.

I am more than well acquainted with the conditions in and around the Fleet. Remember, however, that I have been face-to-face with Arawak warriors bearing spears, and so the terrors of these wharves perceived by most of the population—notably, the feminine half—did not hold any weight with me.

From the street, I surveyed a dismal sight—one that held crumbling banks, rotted wharves which had unfortunately not burned down in the Great Fire, fetid sluiceries where stench and disease mingled easily and the dank waters are clotted with the seepings from butcher's stalls, dung, guts, blood, drowned puppies, stinking sprats all drenched in mud, dead cats, and turnip tops floating sluggishly past.

It boggled my imagination to think of this open sewer, this veritable cloaca, this vast cesspit, existing on Arawak Island.

I did not pursue the thought, for suddenly, the form of a man below on the docks caught my eye. From the back, he looked familiar as he lounged against a stout wooden bollard around which a mooring line was loosely looped.

Raising my skirts fastidiously, parasol in front of me, I descended the rickety wooden steps and made my way across the greenish planks of wood to the man. I gained his attention by the simple expedient of tapping him, once, on the shoulder.

The man turned, fists already raised, ready to do battle with his assailant. At sight of me his face turned ashen, as if he had seen a ghost, and his fists fell to limp balls at his side.

"Well, well!" I said. "How are you, Thomas?"

CHAPTER 16

"Missy!" Thomas exclaimed. He shook his head, and blinked once. "*Missy!*" He gave voice to the thought that evidently possessed his entire being. "We thought you were *dead*!" His voice improbably mixed profound shock and a kind of reverence with a hint of reproach.

Really, I must say that his face and demeanor were most gratifying. "Well, as you can see, I am not," I said, at my most prosaic (I was enjoying this encounter), "and you appear almost happy to see me."

"Happy?" he echoed, unable to clear the cobwebs of disbelief from his mind. "*Happy?*"

"Why, yes, happy," I repeated. I could not resist following this with an innocent, "Are you not?"

"I don't know," he blurted, still attempting to master himself.

I laughed. "That is honest, in all events! But surely, Thomas," I asked slyly, "you don't continue to hold that one, small encounter we had aboard the *Judith* against me, do you?"

From the blank look on his face, Thomas, poor dear, did not have the faintest recollection of what I was talking about. Neither did he care, for he waved away that impertinent question with a pertinent one of his own: "And the master?"

"Ah," I hedged, "I was hoping that *you* might have some news of him, sir."

The faint light of hope that struggled to come to life in the depths of the eyes in his wizened face extinguished. He slid the dirty woolen cap from his head with a mittened hand and said, flatly, "Then, he *is* gone."

I hastened to reassure him. "No, no, Thomas! The last I saw of Adam Winthrop he was very much alive," I said. "It's just that I have not seen him since August, and I am hoping that he is on his way back to England. If he is, I was thinking that perhaps he would come here, or that he might make a point of finding you—"

"He's *alive*?" Thomas broke into this, his wrinkled face crinkling with a happy disbelief which shaded quickly, and subtly, into a rather knowing look. "Haven't seen him since August, eh? Do you mean to tell me all about it?"

"Not all of it," I stated with dignity.

As one can easily imagine, the presence of a well-dressed lady at such a place as the River Fleet wharves at Holborn was remarkable enough to attract the attention of an unsavory, quite noisome, group of Thomas's colleagues. That I should engage him in a discussion which put him through such high flights of emotions was entirely too good to be missed by his fellows.

At this precise juncture, I noticed that we were now surrounded by men who looked and smelled as if they would benefit themselves and the world by a month on Arawak Island, learning proper shaving and bathing practices. Fortunately, I had my parasol and my tongue. I made effective use of both.

When the men did not immediately disperse at my command, Thomas interjected, "Move on, lads. Youse heard the lady!" which he followed with a comment, tinged with apology, "Better do as she says, for she'll not let you do otherwise. You're no match for 'er!"

"So you *do* remember!" I said, rather pleased.

To this, Thomas shrugged and winked. "Now, about the master?" he asked when his cohorts had lounged away from our vicinity.

"We are both alive and of a piece," I replied, "and the survivors of an extraordinary occurrence, which, when I look back upon it, seems the most ordinary thing imaginable!"

Thomas looked interested. "And I will tell you all that you need to know," I continued, "after you have first told *me* of what happened the day after the night that the *Judith* went down!"

Thomas replaced his grubby cap on his wiry hair, but not before giving his scalp a thorough scratching. "We were picked up the next day at sunset," he said, "by the *Minion*, which saw our distress flags. Other than that, the ship and most of her cargo was lost. There was nothing to mourn in the event, excepting the master's loss," he said, then added after a moment, "Yours, too, ma'am, of course."

"Of course," I replied. "So you did not stay in the boats over a day?"

"By sunset the next day, it was, we were saved," he iterated.

"Dear me," was all I could think of to say to this news.

Thomas frowned. "That weren't long, ma'am! No, indeed. In fact, I'm thinking you should think it lucky!"

"I do," I said, recalling just where Adam and I were at sunset of the day after the *Judith*'s sinking, "and I'm thinking that Mr. Winthrop will be none too pleased when he hears of it!"

Thomas cocked an interested brow.

"But it was a rotted ring fitting!" I explained, defending myself. "I made the knots securely—all three of them!—but I did not know that the ring attached to the supply boat was. . . ."

"Like that, was it?" Thomas said. "So, you were together in a Johnnie boat?"

I nodded.

"We didn't know. We thought that you both had gone down with the ship—separate, that is."

"But Mr. Winthrop rowed our Johnnie boat past that first one with the captain and crew and spoke with Captain Hawkins, I believe his name was," I said, "while I was seated not three feet away from Mr. Winthrop in the same boat."

"Well, er, the captain, ma'am, was far cast away by that time," Thomas explained, "along with all the other seamen, and so could not say for a certainty whether he had spoken with Mr. Winthrop or not! As for you—"

I raised my brows in inquiry. "Yes, Thomas?"

Under my quelling eye, Thomas took this fence in a rush. "The fog was thick as soup that night and so no one could recall whether they had seen you—or him, for that matter!— and odds were running even that if he *had* met you on board, he would not have taken you with him!"

"I thank you very much!" I said, my vanity hardly affected by the opinions of very dirty and low-minded seamen. "I'll have you know that by the time our adventure was over, Mr. Winthrop thought very well of me!"

And what adventure might that have been? Thomas was curious to know.

I recounted in accurate, though incomplete terms, the conditions of our capture on Arawak Island. Thomas listened, wide-eyed, as appreciative an audience as I was ever to have, and had the tact to ask no embarrassing questions. I left out the part about the great treasure and the Spanish attempt to claim it. I also left out how I was tricked off the island by unnamed Englishmen. Thomas allowed the change of subject when I demanded, "But tell me what became of the other passengers—Mr. and Mrs. St. Charles, for instance."

Thomas had not paid much attention to the passengers. He gave it as his opinion that they had all arrived at their destinations, as they were supposed to have, and not but a few days off schedule.

"Mrs. Arbuthnot included?" I wanted to know.

When it was clear that Thomas had not the faintest idea who I was talking about, it took only a brief description to identify her to Thomas.

"Ah, the fat, loud one, you mean?" he responded. "Lucky it was for her that the *Minion* came along when it did, for it had already been voted on among the crew that she was to be strangled before the next day dawned!"

"That is not quite what I was asking, sir!" I said to this. "My question was rather to know whether *she*, along with all the other passengers, is comfortable now in Jamaica."

"They all got off at Kingston within a fortnight after the sinking," Thomas informed me.

My hope, of course, was that they had remained in the West Indies, as they had planned to do. Mrs. Arbuthnot was not from London, but Mr. and Mrs. St. Charles were and had known my father and my family. It would be inconvenient, to say the least, if they returned to hear the story that Lord Rollo had put about for my protection. From what I knew of their plans, however, their move to the tropics was intended to be permanent, and so their access to London gossip was extremely limited. I was delighted, of course, to learn that the tragedy of the *Judith* had not also doomed her crew and passengers. It was, in fact, nothing short of miraculous that, after the stormy seas we had passed through, all of us were still alive.

Thomas and I continued to exchange desultory comments about the disaster we had shared and survived, when a positively inspired thought occurred to me. "Perhaps you can tell me, Thomas," I said, "whether or not Mr. Winthrop is married?"

Thomas seemed genuinely nonplussed by the question. He scratched his head. "Married?" He frowned over the word, as if he had never heard it before, and repeated, "Married?"

"Yes—married, sir, as in having a wife!" I said.

"As to that, ma'am, I wouldn't know," Thomas answered.

Perhaps I had misjudged the relationship between Adam and Thomas. "How long have you been with Mr. Winthrop?" I asked.

"Over ten years," Thomas acknowledged, "on and off. We met first in France, then again in the Low Countries, as you might be knowing, where we campaigned together."

Apparently I had *not* been mistaken. "And after ten years of acquaintanceship, you do not know whether he is *married* or not?"

"No."

"Do I take that to mean that he is most likely not married, then?"

"No."

"Good heavens, man! Don't you think it probable that he would have brought up in conversation the existence of a wife at least *once* in ten years?"

To which entirely logical question, Thomas responded again, "No." He explained himself. "You see, ma'am, on a battlefield, or then, after a battle, when the soldiers are, er, seeking their ease around a bottle or . . . or *another* object, it's not likely that one talks about a wife. It just doesn't come up, if you see what I mean. So, he might be having a wife in France or in Spain or in Flanders or in Ireland, or in all four places, for all I am knowing, and my not knowing it wouldn't argue one way or the other about the fact that he is the best man to have on your right when your life is at stake!"

Men! You could not count on them to know anything important! "But, surely," I persisted, "you must know something personal about the man!"

At that, Thomas took deep umbrage. "Haven't you been listening, missy?" he demanded, affronted. "I've been telling you that I know the man as if he were my brother! We've broken bread together and camped together and caroused together. He got me out of more than one scrape alive, I can tell you that, and I can also tell you that it was only fitting when the time came that I returned the favor."

"The Spanish prison?" I queried on a hunch.

"He told you about that, did he?"

"We had a few hours to fill," I explained. If Thomas could not tell me anything really pertinent about Adam Winthrop, I thought that he might at least be able to inform me of the mystery of his release from Don Pedro's tender care. "However, he never did explain how it was he came to be released," I said, and very cleverly appealed to his vanity by adding, in a leading tone of voice, "Do I gather that you were instrumental in obtaining his freedom?"

Thomas looked modestly down at his boots. "I didn't do naught that he wouldn't have done for me!" he disclaimed instantly. "And if you're knowing of his encounter with a certain Don Pedro, it was, then you'll be knowing that it was after a thrilling battle in eighty-five when Brigadier General Winthrop—"

"*Brigadier General* Winthrop?" I broke into this, quite amazed.

"Yes, ma'am, a brigadier general is just below a major general—" he began.

"I am well aware of that!" I snapped.

"It's just that women don't usually have a notion as to what's what in the army, and—"

"I have many notions on that subject!" I broke in again, impatient of twaddle. "What I would like to know is *what* Mr. Winthrop was doing as a brigadier general. I assume that this was in the *English* army?"

"If you have so many notions, missy, then you'd not be asking whether or not it was the *English* army!" Thomas retorted, quite put out himself now. "And as to *what* he was doing, it was receiving better pay. As the quartermaster general he made half the daily pay of a commanding officer and half again as the physician general, which was where he started!"

I reined in all my patience. I enunciated, quite calmly, "I am well aware of pay scales in the army. My point was that I thought that

Mr.—Mr. *Brigadier General* Winthrop had, I think he once called it, an inbred aversion to redcoats."

"That he does," Thomas affirmed, "being born Irish."

This man was impossible. "Then, what, sir," I repeated, "was he doing in the English army?"

"There's no need to take that tone with me, missy! What he was doing was doctoring—to begin with! For the French were run out of Flanders when the English came. Marlborough needed physicians, and Winthrop needed a job, and I see no reason to waste further breath in speaking of what's plain as day!"

"As for tones, my good sir," I replied, "I might point out that yours is below comment! But it would interest me to know how, entering the army as a physician, he suddenly became a brigadier general!"

"As if it's any business of yours!" Thomas retorted. "For if you know so much about it, as you seem to think you do, you could reckon it was on account of his ability to lead the men and his good ideas."

"His good ideas?"

"Aye! His most brilliant being the reverse blockade off Amsterdam, which included the sinking of two or three of the best ships in the Spanish fleet. Now, some might be saying that the excellence of the plan was somewhat spoiled when Don Pedro trapped him on land and took him back to Spain to clap him in irons; but his name was sung among the men for many months to come, and in any case, he and Don Pedro go back a long way. "

"How far back?"

"Some flap over a petticoat," Thomas said. "Years ago already it was."

So, he did know *something* of Adam's amours. "A Doña Domenica?" I hazarded a guess.

"I wouldn't be knowing!" Thomas flashed back. I had apparently surpassed the limits of his ken in this area. "I've told you all I know about such things, missy, *if you'd been listening*. And I'll tell you another thing: I don't have much mind for more! Now, if you'll be on your way, there's a good girl, I'll not have to be calling my friends over to escort you to the street above!"

Rude, *impossible* man. "But his release from prison?" I demanded. "You haven't told me yet!"

"Corruption in a government office, what else? And the right word in the right ear at headquarters! Now, get thee hither, missy, or I'll lose my temper in earnest!"

"But, if he had exposed a corruption, he might have been well promoted after that," I pointed out. "Why did he sell out, as he apparently did?"

"The moment he got out of prison, counteraccusations began to come his way, and the entire affair became too muddied for Winthrop's liking!" Thomas replied hotly, obviously losing the desire to speak with me any further on this, or any other subject. "And the long and short of it was, missy, that he was paid handsomely to keep quiet. With that money he bought the *Judith* and thought himself well quit of the whole!"

I understood many, many things now. Most of all, I understood his desire not to mention his unsavory past—in particular, his army career. I had learned enough of him to know that he was a man of honor, and I could well imagine that he would not have liked to admit to me that he had, in essence, *been paid off*. I would not judge the delicate point of whether he was guilty of some dishonorable action. And as for not having confided in me—well, I had not confided to him the details of my father's fall from grace, either.

Still, something eluded me in this explanation. . . .

Thomas was turning to go. He had told me everything I needed to know—for the moment. "And where might I contact you, if I had need of you?" I asked hastily.

Thomas hesitated. He must have seen the look that crossed my face, for he said hastily, "I'm thinking of safety, missy!"

"No matter what shameful lodging you may have found for yourself, you need not concern yourself for my safety," I replied.

"I wasn't thinking of *yours*!" he answered.

"That does it, sir!" I said, my temper snapping, and opened my mouth to deliver myself of what I thought of him, his manners, his mind, his lineage, his—

He forestalled me by gesturing behind him and muttering, "The Virgin Queen," which was presumably an inn in the neighborhood.

I thanked him and swept off the wharf, my brain seething with conjecture all the way to Chelsea Hospital.

If my interview with Thomas had been as unexpected as it was unsettling, I was afforded a much more satisfying encounter with Julianna Castleragh at the Holland House ball.

Lord Rollo was to call for me in his carriage at seven o'clock the evening of the gala. He had become quite a regular caller at Sedgwick House. Aunt Charlotte was in an increasing tizzy over how to interpret his intentions toward me. On each occasion he came to call, he spent the proper amount of time with Uncle Harry and made discreet, often kind, comments about my father and all that he had suffered. He seemed interested in taking charge of father's files, which were sitting in the corner of the minstrel's balcony. He wished to put them in the War Department, he said, in order to go through them for their military and historical value. He did not press, however, and seemed content to allow Uncle Harry to think the offer over.

Since this evening at Holland House was a gala sponsored by the second Earl of Holland, who had been an army man himself, Aunt Charlotte and Uncle Harry had been invited and, naturally, Lord Rollo had offered to take them with us. It was very kind of his lordship.

Understandably, there had always been something about Lord

Rollo I did not like, and which, no doubt, was the result of my negative association with him and my "rescue" from Arawak Island. As I
am large-minded enough to recognize my own prejudice, I was
attempting to overcome my dislike of Lord Rollo, since he had never
done me any intentional harm and had actually exerted himself to do
for me what he considered to be good. This evening, I was resolved to
receive him cordially.

Alice spent the afternoon in seclusion, putting in place the last
stitches on my gown. Thus, I was somewhat rushed by the time the
clock struck six. Auntie was dressed and waiting in the receiving
room at a quarter to the hour of seven. Knowing Lord Rollo to be a
punctual man, I descended the stairs just as the clock struck the first
of seven strokes and the click of carriage wheels in the street below
came to a halt at our door.

I entered the receiving room to fetch my shawl and mantua, where-
upon Aunt Charlotte took one look at me and exclaimed, "But,
surely, my dear, you are not going abroad in *that*!"

"Why, yes," I said, pulling on my gloves and casting my shawl
about my shoulders. Just then the door bell clanged. "Come along,
Auntie. We should not keep Lord Rollo waiting!"

Aunt Charlotte was paralyzed in her chair. "But your dress," she
gasped, "your dress is *pink*!"

Uncle Harry, who had just entered the room, had a rather milder
reaction. He ran his eye over me and said, in his understated way,
"Unexpected, but very pretty, my child."

I thanked him, returned the compliment, and teased him with the
comment that I hoped my dress would not clash with his very handsome military red.

"No more so than with your hair," Aunt Charlotte said to this but
added, after a moment, "not that that *particular* shade of pink isn't,
oddly, flattering!"

"It's the color of the Caribbean wood flower," I informed her and was prevented from any elaboration by the entrance of Lord Rollo.

Greetings were exchanged all around. I had to admit that Lord Rollo cut a dashing figure in his naval blues, from his thin, handsome face, to the broad set of his shoulders, to his well-turned calf, encased in white silk below the kneebreeches. His low bow over my gloved hand was handsome, too, and when he raised his eyes to mine they held a deep warmth that I had not perceived to that degree before.

His words were prettily said but nothing out of the ordinary, since my aunt and uncle were within earshot and were looking, with evident approval, on our exchange. However, in the brief moment we were alone in the receiving room after my aunt and uncle had preceded us into the foyer, Lord Rollo turned to me and said low, "You look as wild and beautiful and desirable in that dress as the first time I saw you on the beach."

Something in my reaction to that statement caused him to continue, almost immediately, "But I do not wish to rush you, my dear. I know not what you experienced among those savages you lived with for those months, but I know that it must have been something strong. Since rescuing you, I have bent every effort to making you comfortable in your return to England."

"And for that I thank you," I said into the little pause. I willed myself not to remove my hand from the crook of his arm, where he had laid it.

"But your thanks, my dear, are not at all what I want!" he replied to this, as Aunt Charlotte, in all her conventionality, had predicted.

It was fortunate that as we left the room just then, I had to let go of his arm in order to pass through the door. Once out in the foyer where stood my aunt and uncle, no more intimate words, regards, or touches could be exchanged. I felt a vast relief, which was sustained during the carriage ride from Islington to Holland Park by the simple circumstance that Aunt Charlotte and I sat together on one comfortably cushioned seat, while Uncle Harry and Lord Rollo sat facing us. The conversation was unexceptional, except for Lord Rollo's occasional hints that the army and the navy should have closer relations in the future, with expressive glances in my direction.

In time we passed the stone sentry boxes and were bowling into the drive curving around to Holland House with the crunch of gravel under our wheels. The beautiful mansion was alive with lights and activity. So many carriages had jammed the drive that we jostled with the one in front of us and had to wait fully fifteen minutes before a liveried footman had pulled out the carriage steps and held open the door so that we might descend.

Once out of the carriage, I had only the briefest of moments to contemplate the many-turreted outline of the modern mansion before leaning against Lord Rollo's arm and treading the broad, shallow staircase.

At first I was overwhelmed by the size and magnificence of the occasion. There were too many lights, too many people, too many jewels, too many draughts, too many curtsies to make, too many eyes staring, too many names to remember. The earl of Holland and his countess, however, were all that was warm and inviting, and they made just the right little speeches about my return to London and my father's return to grace.

When I stepped into the long, narrow ballroom, whose windows gave out onto the park rolling away from the house, I lost sight of my aunt and uncle, who were swallowed in a throng of some three hundred and more guests. Lord Rollo excused himself from my side for a moment in order to fetch us two glasses. I felt a wave of panic. Horrible memories of a similar occasion crowded in on me, and I would have turned and run from the scene had I been able to command my limbs to move.

Although the ballroom and the occasion were different, the sights, the sounds, even the smell of the wax candles and the heavy wines mingled with perfumes and hair powders, reminded me vividly of the horror and humiliation I had felt at the moment that Commander in Chief Torentson, with his solemn announcement of treason against the Crown, had ruined my father's life. It seemed, at once, both a moment and a lifetime ago.

And now, just as it had happened at my worst moment all those months ago, I suddenly saw before me the sharp, pretty face of Julianna Castleragh swimming before my eyes. Nothing just then could have been better calculated to have restored my spirits to their customary strength and good sense.

Not that I did not have adjustments to make in this encounter. She greeted me with a bright, welcoming, and thoroughly false, "Mrs. Lipscomb! What a pleasure it is to see you again!" At first, I did not know whom she was addressing.

However, I was struck all over again by the uncanny resemblance of her dark, glossy hair and her voice to The Proud One, and that association gave me my opening speech.

"Miss Castleragh," I returned, "it is a great pleasure to return and to see all of my friends." Thinking of the occasion when I had last seen The Proud One, I added, keeping my voice devoid of all expression save that of polite interest, "That is, you *are* still Miss Castleragh, are you not? Or have you, in my absence, made some man exceptionally lucky by changing your name to his?"

At that moment, Lord Rollo returned to my side and placed a goblet of wine in my hand. He raised his brows inquiringly at the woman before me.

Before I had a chance to introduce them, Miss Castleragh answered my question by rolling her dark, *alluring* eyes over to Lord Rollo and saying, "Not yet, but as you've no doubt heard, General Cadogan's son has recently requested permission of my father to pay his addresses to me. Jonathan is a darling, really he is! But he is so doting and so *jealous* that I simply do not know if he is the one for me!"

I had not heard anything about it. However, I did guess, accurately enough, that Julianna Castleragh had only to *look* at a man who was with me to set her sights on him. I had the inspired thought to allow Miss Castleragh to "steal" Lord Rollo away from me. To this end, I took Lord Rollo's arm possessively and glanced up, adoringly, into his eyes.

"Allow me to introduce Lord Rollo to you, Miss Castleragh," I said. The look of surprise and warmth that Lord Rollo returned assured me that my little display of interest was succeeding, perhaps too well. "Lord Rollo, vice admiral in the Royal Navy. Richard, this is Miss Castleragh—Julianna Castleragh—whose father held the commission just below my father's," I continued, then paused to lick my lips for my moment of supreme triumph. I batted my eyelashes delicately up at Lord Rollo before turning to look at Miss Castleragh. "Lord Rollo," I informed her, "was so good, so kind, so *generous* to have gone through all the proper channels to have cleared my father's name. Why, you remember, do you not, Miss Castleragh, that horrible evening at Hounslow Heath when my father was so falsely accused?"

"Oh, yes, my dear, I remember, and I heard last week about Major General Sedgwick's rehabilitation," Miss Castleragh acknowledged. The look on her face and the tone in her voice at having to admit my father's vindication was deeply satisfying to me. Miss Castleragh was always one to recover quickly. She continued, without missing a beat, "And how happy I am for you, my dear! And I *do* think it fortunate that you were not wearing pink that night, for as lovely as you look in it, I am afraid it would have drawn undue attention to you at an embarrassing moment! You will recall how I stood by you and tried to comfort you at your time of need!"

I was now assured that my dress this night was *perfect*, and I recalled precisely how she had stood by me that *other* night.

I straightened up and away from Lord Rollo's side. If she was equal to a display of friendship, then so was I. I grasped her hand warmly and gushed, "I *do* remember, my dear, and I have become very fond of pink lately. I am glad you approve! Now, I know that you are just *dying* to hear the details of my father's vindication from his lordship!" With that, I took her hand and placed it where mine had been on Lord Rollo's arm. "My two dear, *dear* friends!" I breathed, on a low sigh of pleasure. "How happy I am to see you together! And how happy I would be if you, Lord Rollo, would continue your kindness and generosity toward me to recount to my dear friend how you cleared my father's name. Leave no detail out, and don't be modest!"

Lord Rollo was far too proper a man to ogle Julianna Castleragh's neckline, but I was hoping that he would find something in her to interest him for a while so that I could get away from him for a few minutes, at least. As often happens at large, fluid gatherings, Aunt Charlotte approached me at just that moment. She excused me from the company of Miss Castleragh and Lord Rollo, saying, "I shall bring her back to you presently, your lordship, but there is a host of those who wish to greet Marie, and so I must take her away!"

As we left, Aunt Charlotte threw a surreptitious glance over her shoulder and turned back to me to whisper, "But you must have a care, Marie, that Miss Castleragh does not set her desires on his lordship! I recall vividly what she was saying about you and Mr. Lipscomb on the eve of your marriage—but never mind about that now! I am absolutely delighted to tell you that Commander in Chief Torentson is here and has something he *particularly* wishes to say to you!"

The commander in chief's words were gratifying. Although I would learn the very next day that my gratification was premature, hearing

these expressions of regret, condolence, and retribution had a powerful effect on me.

In fact I felt light, as if a great weight had lifted from my shoulders.
I floated through the rest of the evening, greeting and speaking with
whomsoever should wish to welcome me back to London society.
Lord Rollo was at my side, but only intermittently. I supposed that he
had many men with whom he needed to speak, but I did not, in truth,
follow his movements, nor he mine. In a ballroom with three or four
hundred guests, one is not always able to keep one's eye on any individual.

When the twenty-four violins struck up to play, I danced, but not
every set. Lord Rollo invited me to the floor once. I noted that he
invited Miss Castleragh once, as well.

I strolled and wove my way through the throng, most often in company of Aunt Charlotte, who was as eager as I to soak up the approv-
ing words and glances that came our way. The evening was beyond
the halfway point, and the orchestra had stopped in a brief lull, when
I came upon a thick knot of people in animated discussion. My eyes
fell on a man, turned three-quarters away from me, and dressed in full
naval habit. How he was now part of the navy I did not pause to consider. I knew only that my heart—that unanchored organ—flew to
my throat, my temples, then fell to my knees, which wobbled slightly.

I took several steps toward the group. I noted with a part of my
mind that Aunt Charlotte was greeting an acquaintance. When I was
next to the man, I looked up at him. He must have sensed a presence
at his side, for at that very moment, he turned and moved a little away
from the group. When he looked down at me, blue eyes came to sudden life. The deep copper of the Caribbean sun had faded from his
skin somewhat, but his visage was still swart. Focused on the two
points of blue light in his face, all other perceptions of the bright ballroom, the buzz of conversation around us, faded to an indistinct blur.

I whispered in disbelief, "Adam."

"Eve," he replied.

Though the pause of surprise seemed to last forever, I believe it was only a second before I regained my self-possession—not *completely*, however, since my next words were the silliest I had ever uttered in my life.

"I thought I would never see you again," I breathed.

His blue eyes smiled. "How could you have doubted it?"

CHAPTER 17

How could I have doubted it, indeed? Nevertheless, having said the words, I knew that they were true: I had not, deep down, believed I would ever see him again. Although I had not completely known it, my brittle shell of confidence had long since been cracked by my experiences of the past days and weeks and months. In that flash of a moment, I felt it shatter, and I touched for the first time the gelatinous core of my emotional ruin.

The sight of him, the feel of his eyes on me, and the sound of his voice went straight to that indistinct center and gave me back a measure of my strength.

"Although," he said without pausing, "I did not think it would be this easy to find you."

My complete bewilderment must have shown on my face, for as I framed a question, he gave his head a tiny negative shake of warning and asked quickly, "Where are you living?"

"Islington," was the only answer I could think of at the moment. "Not far off the High Street." I blinked, stupidly. "I think."

He nodded, once, in understanding. There was time for no more. Aunt Charlotte had finished her greetings and was turning back to me to draw me into the group of ten or twelve.

In that brief space of private contact with Adam, the world had stood still. Now it was whirling on its axis to make up for lost time. I felt a little giddy as Aunt Charlotte introduced me to a variety of people I supposedly already knew and to whom I made heaven only knows what idiotic rejoinders and clumsy curtsies.

Adam had stepped back to blend, once again, into the group. He was still standing on my right. I could feel his presence, even without looking at him. (I *dared* not look at him for fear of giving myself, and him, away.) It was fortunate that the introductions were made in a circle that began with the guests on my left, so that I had time to recompose myself.

By the time the introductions had gone halfway around the group, I was able to register the names and faces. I even began to understand something of what was going forward at this naval ball. I knew, of course, that King James was being directly threatened by William of Orange and that James had commanded a standing army, largely officered by Roman Catholics, which he believed could repel William's invasion from Holland. However, when the next man was introduced, first to my aunt and then to me, I began to realize how short might be James's reign.

"Is it true you landed your ships at Devon unopposed last week?" someone asked of this man.

Admiral van der Kuylen of the Dutch fleet, sailing under the colors of the House of Orange and the names of William and Mary, was a large, barrel-chested man. His naval-blue suit, encrusted with gold braid, tassels, and medals, did not fully temper the overall impression he gave of redness. His meaty hands were rough-red from the rigors of a seafaring life. His complexion was high and florid. Even the fairness of his Dutch hair had less of yellow and more of strawberry. When the words came out of his mouth, they sounded harsh and red-chapped. However, what he said was really rather jolly.

"Oh, aye, idz true!" Admiral van der Kuylen chuckled. The sound rumbled merrily in his chest. "At Torbay we landed, nod bud four days ago id vhas, and nod a redcoat in sight! Do you subbose ve are velcome?"

He was making a joke. It was a successful one. "Yes, yes!" came the enthusiastic, laughing response.

"Bud not by Chames!" the admiral laughed in response. "Und glad ve are to be zo velcome; oddervise, ve vould nod be at zuch a lofely pardy!"

How stand James's forces at Salisbury? was the next question.

"Dey stand, dey stand!" the admiral replied. "Widdout Chames. Strange notionz he has of leadership, dis one. He fail to leave London to take command of his army. He fail to come to dis lofely pardy. Instead, he try to abbease opinion by refoking zome of his Cadolic abbointmentz! It vill nod vork! Ask my captain!"

With that, Admiral van der Kuylen nodded to Adam, who stepped forward a half pace and bowed.

"Captain Vindrop!" the admiral pronounced proudly. "He is Irish, you zee."

Not everyone saw.

One red-coated army officer, at least, had adjusted to the admiral's accent and his implications. However, he was not quite able to keep the surprise and vague suspicion out of his voice when he ventured, "You are an Irish Catholic, then, Captain Winthrop?"

Adam bowed by way of assent to the officer's question. "But not a fool," he said smoothly, "and I'll not allow my natural Irish sentimentality to stand in the way of my common sense."

Some of the narrow suspicion in the red-coated officer's eyes was replaced by the desire to discover the extent of Captain Winthrop's common sense. "Well said, sir," the officer replied with a slight bow of his own. "And how come you to serve Admiral van der Kuylen rather than George Legge, the Earl of Dartmouth, who is presently commanding James's fleet?" the officer asked.

This question was reasonable enough, under the circumstances. I, too, wished to know the answer to that one. It was the admiral himself who responded. "By no easy meanz, und zo I tell you!" the Dutchman laughed heartily. "Dis man Vindrop vhas in de Nedderlanden yearz ago already! Fighting de Schpanish! Aach! Vat times dey vere!" The admiral's eyes misted over in what was visibly fond reminiscence of the rout of the Spanish in the Netherlands. "Vindrop was in de army then. First in de French serfice, den in de English under Charles—nefer under Chames. He had ideas, dis one! Aach! Many ideas! I remember, in partikular, de days in Den Hague vhen Vindrop first came to my notice. Dis vhas a verrry good idea he had for tricking de Schpanish!"

"And, Irish Catholic or not," Adam interjected at this point, "I reasoned that my service in the campaign against the Spanish would serve me well, should I ever wish to return to England." Adam paused, then added, looking straight at the officer, "Or so it was suggested to me before I joined Admiral van der Kuylen last month."

I was absurdly flattered—I had pointed out such an advantage to him during one of our discussions in the caney. Fortunately, no one was looking at me just then, for I am sure that I flushed.

Then I realized that Adam's comment had been as much to divert attention away from a recital of his exploits in The Hague as to communicate with me; and I could only guess what the idea that had attracted the attention of the admiral had been. Thoughts of Adam's good ideas and the Spanish involuntarily brought to mind the vision of him standing on the ledge of the cliff, wearing nothing but a golden bird's head and a breech cloth. Under my lashes, I glanced speculatively at his fully clothed body. I am quite sure that I flushed again.

Fortunately, once again, no one was attending to me. Instead, the relative merits of James and William were bantered about. It was a family squabble, after all, and although William did not wish to supplant his father-in-law, James, he did wish to make James uphold the less restrictive religious sentiments that had prevailed under Elizabeth, and to call a free Parliament. The representatives of the army and navy assembled at Holland House this night were ready to support William's wishes, even if it meant that his forces would leave the coast to march on London.

"Und dey, too, vill march into London unobbosed!" the admiral predicted with every evidence of good humor.

Adam contributed very little to the discussion—just enough so that he would not draw attention to himself through his silence. I noted that he skillfully deflected any probing into his immediate past, and for this, I was naturally grateful.

I was not surprised by his reticence, but that his return to London should be through military service—of any country, and for any king. I thought that he no longer wished for the life of the soldier or sailor and that, even if he had, the way he had been bought off in the midst of a scandal might have precluded him from any further service. Perhaps Admiral van der Kuylen did not care about Adam's dishonorable past—perhaps he needed every skilled seaman he could find.

Only one ticklish allusion to Adam's recent past arose. That, too, he was able to deflect—*most* outrageously.

Shortly after the admiral had predicted William's imminent success, the fiddlers came back to resume their scraping of German airs. No doubt feeling at home with the music, the admirals thick blond brows rose in an expression of delight, and he declared that he had not come to this "lofely pardy to talk only of bolitics." His feet, he explained, could never rest when good music was being played.

"My Captain Vindrop, howefer," he informed the group, with a broad wink at his captain, "has told me he does nod danz! His feet, dey pain him! A very strange story he tell about it. Verrry strange! A topical disease he call id! Id vhas all I could do to have him come dis efening! He tell me, no boots vould he vear. And no boots vear he on ship, id is true! Bud tonight I tell him, come! Vear your boots! He vear dem, bud he vill nod danz!"

My reaction was immediate. My own feet began to throb in sympathetic pain. I did not look at his boots or think of his poor feet in their leather prisons, for fear that I, myself, might fall.

I had, in fact, no time to dwell on thoughts of Adam's feet, for the admiral continued, almost without pause, "Und at dis lofely pardy, I must ask a lofely woman to danz wid me! Of you, madame, I beg the honor of a danz!"

It took a slight nudge from a delighted Aunt Charlotte to signal that the admiral was addressing me. "Why, my niece would adore to dance with you, Admiral!" she chirped when I did not immediately find my tongue.

"De lofely lady must answer for herself," the admiral said jovially. "Does the lady like my infitation?"

"Yes, yes! A lovely invitation!" I said, flustered, unable to find a better adjective. I laid my hand on the admiral's proffered arm.

We left the group to join in the set of dancers forming in the center of the ballroom, but not before I heard one of the red-coated officers ask, astonished, "A tropical disease that attacks the feet, Captain Winthrop? I've never heard of such!"

"It's nothing," Adam said casually. "Now, my back is quite another story entirely! Since being in the tropics, it itches when I wear a coat. I am hoping to find someone to scratch it."

I could not help myself. I looked over my shoulder at him and found him looking at me. He was assessing me in a way that was positively *indecent*. I saw him shrug and work his back suggestively. Plainly confused, the red-coated officer put his hand up to Adam's back and offered to help.

Adam declined, saying that the cure for his condition was not so simple.

"You acquired a kind of rash?" the officer ventured.

Adam replied, gravely, that he did not think so.

It was *all* I could do to make it through the dance with Admiral van der Kuylen. I believe that I made many terribly stupid responses to his conversational openings—they were so stupid, in fact, that at the end of the dance, he restored me to Aunt Charlotte's side and conveyed to her the impression that I was a perfectly behaved young woman who held all the correct opinions. I must have agreed with him constantly. Aunt Charlotte seemed puzzled, but rather pleased, and said brightly. "Yes, her various tragedies have certainly improved her!"

I really have no idea how the rest of the evening went. By the time Adam had left my side with that most *provocative* remark, the ball was almost over. Which was fortunate, for I was quite, quite distracted. However, it was a most *unfortunate* state of mind to be in, since at the very end of the evening, Lord Rollo asked me to marry him. I am not quite sure how I responded to him when he pulled me into a dimly lit alcove off the main ballroom. I most likely said something like, "Dear me, what a thing to ask me at such a moment!" Men, being the odd creatures that they are, often interpret such responses to mean something like "yes," which, of course, is a great mistake. However, it made no difference what I said or how he interpreted it, for I had no intention of marrying him. Not that I could worry about what my response to Lord Rollo had been, for my mind was filled to exclusion by *other* thoughts. I began to see how it was that a woman could become so flighty, so simpering, so *stupid*, really, when her entire being was *consumed* with thoughts of a man—*not* that I approved of this most unattractive aspect of feminine behavior, but I *was* beginning to understand it.

Somewhere around midnight, Lord Rollo graciously returned Aunt Charlotte, Uncle Harry, and me to our house in Colebrooke Row (*now* I remembered the address!). I believe that he kissed my hand and said something to the effect that I had made him a happy man and that he would come on the morrow to discuss all the particulars with General Sedgwick. I think that I replied quite stupidly to the effect that Major General Sedgwick was dead and had died in disgrace.

Lord Rollo smiled and said, "I know, my dear, and we shall go through your father's papers to clear our minds of all shadow of a doubt! I have already spoken to your uncle, the *general*, about that. I am so happy to have another, happier topic to discuss with him!" His regard was warm; his hand was hot. "Until tomorrow!"

Somehow, I extracted my hand from his and bade him good night. Somehow, I answered all of Aunt Charlotte's conventional questions, mounted the staircase to my bedchamber, undressed my hair, rid myself of Alice, and freed myself of my stays and stomacher. At last comfortable in my nightdress, I was alone with my thoughts in my bedchamber, staring blankly at the fire hissing on the hearth and wondering how I was going to make it through the night.

My thoughts were confused, but consistent and circular: How would Adam find me? Islington was a large village, after all. There were many paths and alleys off the High Street. Could he guess that I was staying with my uncle, whose name was also Sedgwick? Would he make a morning call or wait until the evening? How was I to make it through the night? How would he find me?

I banked the fire and went to bed. I rose, relit the fire and considered again the possibility that Adam would guess that my uncle's name was Sedgwick. I crossed to the window and closed the shutters, which I had inadvertently left open. I recrossed to the fire and stared at it. The shutters banged a little. I had not shut them properly. I crossed, once again, to secure the latch. I returned to the fire. Once again, there was a noise at the shutters—little tapping sounds. It was annoying—really, it was—when I had much more pressing things to think about.

The intermittent tapping persisted. It was as if pebbles were falling on the shutters. Annoying as the sounds were, I had nothing better to do than to adjust my shutters—again. I opened the sash and leaned across the slope of the cold stone window casement in order to catch the latch more securely. The November night air was, of course, damp and cold, and a ghostly mist lay in patches below in the alleyway that ran behind the house. As I reopened the shutters, the better to secure the small iron bar, I thought I heard a voice drift up through the tatters of fog.

"Eve," it called, as if from inside a blanket.

My sensibilities were quite deranged this night, but I did not think that I had reached the state where I would hear imaginary voices. I edged out over the casement and peered down into the alleyway. I thought I saw the figure of a man.

It spoke. "Eve," it said.

The figure moved and emerged from behind a swirl of mist. A haze of moonlight fell on it. I blinked. My heart leapt. "Is that you?"

"Yes."

"What are you doing here?"

"Throwing pebbles at your shutters."

"How did you find me?" I asked, quite astonished.

Adam did not, apparently, think the question worth answering. "I'm coming up," he informed me.

My addled wits were completely restored by this time. It was evidently pointless to mention that midnight had struck and that the door to the house had long since been bolted shut for the night. "How?" I asked.

At that he disappeared again into the fog. I nearly cried out for him to return and to apologize for my stupid question, but did not. I was rewarded for my forbearance by his return a moment later. I noticed that he was carrying what looked to be a heavy loop over his shoulder and under his arm.

"With this," he said, and held up the burden on his shoulder for my inspection. It was a length of rope. "Stand back," he commanded.

As if I would obey him just like that. "What are you planning to do?" I wanted to know.

"There is a weight attached to the end of this rope," he said in a voice I had heard before, "and I am planning on throwing it through your window. I would rather it did not hit you, for as much as my cherished desire to wring your neck has sustained me these past three months, I would still prefer to throttle you while you are conscious! Now, stand back!"

I was not amused, and I thought he was speaking rather loudly. "Shhhhh!" I hissed down. "You'll wake my aunt and uncle."

"Their bedroom is at the end of the other wing of the house," he said, quite accurately.

"How do you know that?" I asked.

"I've already checked the house out. I work fast," he said. There was no end, it seemed, to his talents. Then, apparently tired of the chit-chat, he said, "I mean it! Stand back!"

I did stand back. Fortunately. The next moment, the end of the rope whizzed by the side of my head and fell with a plunk on the wooden floor. I suddenly understood. I leaned back out of the window.

"I see! You are going to climb up!" I exclaimed in low tones. "I shall knot this end to something in my room—a piece of furniture, perhaps. Something heavy, of course."

"I thought you might figure it out. Try the bed," he said. Then after a provocative pause, "I'm not worried about your knots, but is the bed nailed down?"

Of all the—! "No, it is *not* nailed down," I whispered harshly. I leaned out the window to give him a piece of my mind. "However, I hardly expect the bed to become unleashed from the moorings of my bedchamber and end up floating in a current down the Thames! You shall be quite safe!"

"If I were looking for safety, I would not have come," he replied, shedding his coat in preparation for the ascent.

Annoying man! "Do you wish me to tie the rope to the bedpost or not?" I demanded.

He gestured for me to get on with it. I took the weighted end of the rope and knotted it securely, five times, to one of the posts at the foot of the bed, and then wove it through the cords of the bed curtains for good measure.

Almost immediately, I felt a tug at the rope. Then it pulled taut. I went back to the window and saw Adam beginning to climb the back face of the house. Given that events had proven him an unusually agile man, I did not imagine that he would have any difficulty scaling something so mundane as a fifteen-foot wall. In addition, the wall, being of stone, had ample ridges that would serve as footholds.

Thus, I was surprised when, after having hoisted himself up the side of the house about five feet or so, he let go of the rope and slid down to the ground. He shook his head in disgust.

I peered down out of the window. "Are you all right?" I called down softly.

He looked up. "I'm not sure," he said. "Lean out a little more."

I leaned far enough out the window so that my hair was falling about my shoulders. Then I noticed that the bodice of my gown came loose and that Adam had a full view of my breasts.

"Much better!" he called up.

Annoying, *annoying* man! I ducked my head back inside and waited a moment until I saw the cord running past me pull taut again with his weight. When I looked back outside, I saw that he was now scaling the wall quickly, like a cat.

He had taken off his boots and stockings and was climbing barefooted. His head was now just several feet below my window.

Another two or three upward thrusts and he would be safe, at last, in my room.

"*Faith*!" he swore softly under his breath. The next few extraneous and rather profane comments he made informed me that he seemed to have torn his shirt and cut his shoulder on the brace of an old gutter spout which had not been taken down when the gutter trough had, evidently, been rerouted.

By the time he penetrated the window, he was bleeding and shivering from the cold, without coat or footwear, as I was myself from having stood at the open window so long in nothing but a thin chemise. I helped him in, although he hardly needed it, and hastily latched both the shutters and the window behind him.

For my greeting, I moaned, "Your poor feet, and now this! I nodded at the torn skin on his shoulder.

He shook his head. "It's nothing," he dismissed, "but it's true that my feet aren't fit for proper shoes anymore." He added, with disgust, "I should have been able to climb the wall with my boots on."

Before we could do anything else, his wound had to be tended to, for it was flowing quite profusely. I grabbed the nearest piece of white cloth I had at hand and ripped it into strips. He had gone to stand by the fire and had shed his shirt, and was now beginning to mop at the blood ineffectually. I pushed his hand away and began daubing at the ooze myself. When the wound was clean, I fashioned for him a bulky bandage.

My eye fell on the two vertical welts on his chest, just above his heart. I looked up at him. Many, many words had formed on my lips. All of them died a happy death at having him stand before me, coatless and shoeless and bloodied and very, very dear; at having him look down at me, just so, in the light of the whispering fire, all words melting from his mouth, too, when he looked at me, his lips curving up, as if bemused; at seeing his eyes, the blue of tropical waters, stained black with desire; at having him take my head in his hands; at having his face blot out the rest of the world, at having his lips capture mine in a rather fierce embrace.

Still shivering from the damp cold, I was thirsty and felt that I was drinking in great splashes of sunlight. Our kisses flowered like the stars in the Caribbean night and flamed like the fireflies. Yet, the many kisses blended into one that would never really end this night, but would only be interrupted by several intervals when we paused to form our lips around words.

At the first interval, Adam brushed his lips to my ear and said, "We were rudely interrupted."

"About that—" I began, but could get no further.

"Spare me," he said into my ear, "that explanation."

"No, really, let me say—"

"I mean it," he said, a little roughly, into my neck. "Plague take it, woman, I'd rather not think of it just now, so don't insist."

"Were you very shaken by my departure?" I asked, unable to resist the question.

He answered me in a wholly satisfying manner. At the next interval, he said, "But I did not come here for this." He drew back from me a little.

If ever a woman was beguiled by a very thorough kissing, it was I. Unable to stand properly, I swayed against him, like a flame seeking a steady draft to burn straight.

"Or did I?" he asked, with a little inward chuckle.

"You didn't?"

His response, once again, was very reassuring. At length, he raised his head. He put his hands on my shoulders. "No, we've wasted enough time. I came to tell you about myself," he said, "about my past."

"Too late. Among other things, you wish to confess to me that you were a brigadier general in the English army," I said, "although that's not much of a confession."

"Yes, that, among other things," he repeated slowly. His voice was a little surprised, a little wary, his eyes a little shadowed. "And it's not much of a confession, I agree." Standing slightly apart from him now, I felt that strange regret and reluctance struggle inside of him. "But, how did you find out?"

I smiled and answered, "Thomas told me everything."

"You saw Thomas?"

"At the Fleet," I answered. "You haven't?"

"No, I just came into town tonight, with Admiral van der Kuylen, hours before the Holland House ball," he said, "and found you."

"Lucky, aren't you?"

"Very," he agreed. "And what, exactly, did Thomas tell you?"

I, myself, now had a confession. "The rest of the crew and passengers from the *Judith* were rescued the very next evening," I said in a rush, biting my lip.

The wary look vanished from his eyes momentarily and he smiled. "Excellent!"

"You're not angry?"

"A misplaced emotion, given everything," he replied, and returned to a subject that seemed to exercise his mind. "Thomas told you everything?"

I nodded, my own clear eyes on his shadowed ones.

"About how I got out of prison?" he asked.

I nodded again.

"And you understand?" he persisted.

"You thought I would not have approved," I said, almost incredulous that my opinion could have meant so much to him.

He looked at me through narrowed eyes.

"Of course, I do not," I said, "but I've come to see that while I might not approve of something, I am still able to understand it."

The shadows left his eyes, and the regret and reluctance seemed to drain from him. "If that is the case, then you are a woman of large understanding, Eve Marie Sedgwick," he said.

I smiled. My understanding might have been large, but then, so was my desire. I found that my concentration was wavering again, just as was my ability to stand upright. I leaned into his chest again. I felt the beat of his heart against mine and was excited by it.

He took me back in his arms, pleased, even surprised, by my gesture of intimacy. "And I must be sure and thank Thomas next time I see him," he murmured into my hair, "for having explained so admirably and so thoroughly why I had to do what I did."

I began to think that he was teasing me, tantalizing me with his nearness, his conversation that deferred the promise of his kisses.

I, too, was in a teasing mood. "Oh, he did not tell me everything, your Thomas!" I rallied him.

The shadows returned to his eyes. He stepped back from me again.

"He wouldn't tell me a word about Doña Domenica!"

The shadows vanished. His eyes twinkled. "Good man, Thomas! Knows just what to tell and what not to! I've not known him previously to have so much tact."

When he began to kiss me again and with abandon, it was my turn for stalling and deferring. "Oh, no!" I said. "Tell me about her!"

"After you tell me about poor Edward," he replied.

"I have nothing to tell," I protested.

He shook his head, once. "Neither do I."

"I'm glad."

He explained, straight-faced, "She was too tame. She never once cast me adrift in the middle of the Atlantic."

Before I had a chance to protest this most provocative, *unjust* statement, Adam was looking, with interest, beyond my shoulder at the piece of furniture dominating the room.

"A bed," he commented.

Following perfectly the trend of his thoughts, I turned to look over my shoulder at the object in question. Memories of the mat on the caney floor and the soft, damp, green moss of the jungle ground, even the ludicrous passage in the hammock, possessed my thoughts. I looked back at him. "A bed," I confirmed and gave the matter some thought. "I don't know. What do you think?"

He, too, considered the bed for another moment, then said, "I've heard it's very suitable for the purpose."

I could not help laughing. "Have you?" I said. Then, by way of acquiescing, I added brazenly, "Well, if we don't like it, there is always the floor."

Soon we were safe and happily marooned, just the two of us, on the white, wide sea of the bed. The patchwork counterpane was thrown back to the foot, the colors of its diamond-shaped pieces melting into one another to become all one shimmering color, a far-off piece of land. It was the patchwork of colors that Arawak Island had presented to my eye the first time I had seen it, warm and inviting, exotic and terrifying. I remembered how anxious we both had been to reach the island. This night, however, with the land lying just beyond the white swell of sheet, we had no desire to reach the colorful shores just yet.

Only one color, a gaudy spot of red, scarred the blank, innocent sea on which we were floating. When Adam drew me, very tenderly, into his arms, my eye fell on the stain of the bandage at his shoulder. I touched it briefly and looked up at him. He smiled and shook his head, dismissing yet another of his injuries. In the ensuing hours of the night, I was to be reassured of the insignificance of this newest wound, for it was not to inconvenience him in the least.

At first, pressed to his length, my arms and legs felt as limp and clingy as tendrils of Sargasso weed, entwining and trapping both of us in brief, serene, deep, and very dark doldrums of suppressed passion. Then it was as if we were climbing a very lovely tree, broad and leafy and bearing fruit, hugging the rough bark and shimmying past smooth leaves. In the twining, forking, shifting branches, we explored the cool blue shadows of the crook of an arm and the bend of a neck, and we responded to the heat striking up to our bodies through hands and lips and legs. It was a guava tree, perhaps, or a mango tree that we climbed, and every touch, every kiss and breath exchanged, reminded me of the sweet smells and tastes of the tropics. I thought I caught the faintest hint of frangipani in his hair, which I had never liked, but now sought lovingly.

Finally, we were cast out to sea again, exposed to searing heat of direct sunlight, and caught in a current. Together, we sped along in the wide street of swiftly moving water. We were heading not for the tranquil lagoon where we first stepped out onto Arawak Island, but to the rocks at the turning of the land where the mountain thrust its spur into the sea. The stream of water flowed around a rock, smoothly at first, to meet another, then another, and the stream was no longer uniform and unidirectional. It had developed ripples and eddies and splashes and waves folding back over themselves, until at last the water's movement as it broke on the shore was complicated and chaotic and savage and satisfying.

Spent and happy, we dozed and slept and kissed and found the current again. Toward dawn, my head against his chest, his hand idly fondling my breast, Adam said, looking straight up into the brocade canopy of the bed curtains, "What a *lot* of trouble you are to me, Sedgwick."

I felt that the statement called for a response. "Let me explain," I began.

He shook his head "I repeat: spare me that, at least." His voice was laced with irritation and resignation and, as usual, humor.

"No, really, I have quite a logical explana—"

"Logical," he grunted, breaking into this. "You are going to tell me that you were on the beach collecting shells. That much of the story I got. You did not notice a British frigate approaching the bay."

"I didn't!"

"They are small craft, I agree," he replied with a fine irony, "and easily missed. However, neither did you see the landing boat approach. Nor did you think to *get off the beach* when you had an opportunity!"

"It did not seem right," I said.

"Indeed," he said still gazing into the tight gathering of brocade forming the raised center of the bed canopy. "So, when a boatload of strange men set foot on shore, you went to *greet* them."

"That *did* seem right," I defended myself.

"Right and wholly idiotic! Eve! What could you have been thinking?"

"I suppose you might have done better?" I challenged sweetly.

"Faith! Almost anything would have been better than what you did!"

"You weren't there," I said coolly, "and so you do not know just what I did, or how . . . how *natural* and straightforward the encounter seemed at the time!"

"I didn't need be there to guess that you introduced yourself, engaged in a pleasant chat, and, for some reason best known to yourself, allowed yourself to be *tricked into going aboard ship* with the first English sailors to pass by the island!"

"It was not a trick," I said loftily, even though I still harbored the faintest doubt about that attack by Spanish privateers that had caused the *Pride of Devon* to weigh anchor before returning me to shore.

"A landing party of English naval officers encounters a young Englishwoman on a beach in native dress who does not jump at the chance to leave?" he said. "Eve! Think about it! You were tricked!"

"You make it sound so . . . so *obvious* when you put it like that," I said, "but let me tell you that—"

It was on the tip of my tongue to mention that it was perhaps, deep down, Lord Rollo's mention of my father's possible rehabilitation that had made me so amenable to his request to go aboard ship. However, I did not have a chance to go into that long explanation, for Adam interrupted, "Spare me the details! The transparency of it all might drive me to distraction! Never have I met a woman who is so idiotic and—"

Here he searched for words. "Obtuse, perhaps?" I suggested, rather hotly now. "I believe you once called me idiotic and obtuse." Recalling that conversation further, I remembered that he had called me "adorable" as well, but I did not mention it.

"You have hardly given me reason to revise my opinion! And 'idiotic' and 'obtuse' are only the mildest terms I have called you over the past several months!" he said. He turned me around slightly to look at him. "Faith, woman! I've just had to cross half the globe to find you!"

I returned his regard. That admission did somewhat mollify the effect of having been called "idiotic," "obtuse," and worse. Nevertheless, I still felt the need to exonerate myself. "But you don't understand at all!" I said. "Oh, I admit that they did catch me by surprise —Admiral Albemarle, Lord Rollo, and Ensign Pocock."

At that, Adam released me and turned around abruptly to lie on his side. "Who?"

"The *Pride of Devon* was commanded by Admiral Albe—"

"Not him. The next name."

"Lord Rollo?"

"Yes. Lord Rollo," he repeated slowly. Adam's eyes, resting on me, had narrowed. A furrow came to mark the space between his brows.

Thoughts of Lord Rollo and all attendant associations made me sit bolt upright in bed, drenched suddenly in guilt. Full realization of just how I had spent the last several hours flooded in on me. "Good God!" I breathed. "Lord Rollo is coming today to speak to my uncle about —about *marrying* me!"

"*What*?!"

"Well, I have absolutely no intention of marrying him," I said, thinking that Adam did not have to react *quite* so strongly to that.

"I should suppose not!" he said.

That reminded me of something. "By the way, you aren't married, are you?"

"I am," he stated.

I groaned and fell backward on the bed. I held my head. I felt ruined. I felt deranged. I felt as if I had fallen in the worst disrepute and disgrace imaginable.

"And so are you," he continued. "It seems that I arrived none too soon!"

"What—what do you mean?" I asked. Then understanding dawned. "Oh, you mean that you are married to *me*—that *we* are married to each other!" My relief was profound.

"What else could I have meant, you idiot?" he demanded.

"Do you think that counts?" I asked doubtfully. "We weren't ever *really* married, you know."

"A technicality," he replied.

Just then, the clatter of the peat man on his early rounds in the alleyway drifted up to my room.

"And I'm thinking," he said, continuing to look at me meaningfully, "that circumstances will soon make it necessary for us to claim our relationship—if I'm as shrewd an observer as I think I am."

A cryptic remark, if I ever heard one. "Being the shrewd observer you are, you will see the sun squeezing through the shutters just now and should be on your way. Unless you, in turn, wish to be *observed* by the entire neighborhood!" I said. "And, technicality or no, I doubt that we could adequately explain the terms of our marriage to my aunt and uncle if they were to catch us together just now !"

Adam, a man of action, was fully dressed in a matter of minutes. Or partially dressed, since his boots and stockings and coat were outside, below my window. "When's he coming?" Adam asked as he stuffed shirt into knee-breeches.

"Who?" I demanded, quite reasonably.

"Rollo!" he snapped. He unlatched the window and shutter and tested the rope for strength.

"I don't know," I said, rather surprised by this interest. "Later today. Don't worry. I'll refuse him."

Adam looked up, sharply, at that. "I'm wondering, finally, what Thomas told you," he said, on a complete tangent, I thought.

"You know, I understand completely," I said in a soothing spirit. "I might not fully approve of your actions, but, well it might help you to know that my father was an army man himself—but I'll tell you all about that later! More to the point is the fact that I am well aware of—"

"You're in a muddle, Sedgwick," he broke in to this, shaking his head. "I should have known! Let you loose for a couple of months and—and this! *Faith*, woman!"

"Do you mean *ever* to explain yourself to me?" I asked, rather indignant.

"I don't know," he said, still shaking his head. He had the oddest expression on his face, as if he did not know whether to be angry or amused. In his indecision, he reached out to me and kissed me thoroughly, passionately, reassuringly. "Just stall that Rollo fellow until I get there." He shook his head as he jumped up on the window ledge. In a fluid movement he had caught the rope and had begun to rappel down the side of the house. "I'll think of something," he said, as his head jerked below the coping of the window.

The sun was just beginning to pierce the dimness of night. He had to hurry. "I almost forgot!" he said. "Tell me where Thomas is staying."

"The Virgin Queen," I informed him. "Holborn, I believe."

"You are good for something, at least," he grunted to this valuable piece of information. Then he descended easily and without mishap to the ground below. I saw him pull on his boots and shrug into his coat.

This was neither the place nor the moment to argue with him that

I had shown myself good for many, many things, including saving his life on several occasions. Instead, I called down what seemed a more pressing question just then. "Will I be seeing you again today?"

For an answer he said, "Yes, and I hope to have thought of something between now and then! What a muddle you are in! I might have known! But, for now: untie the weight from the bedpost and throw me the rope!"

However, I was unable to untie my five knots. Adam was disgusted and did not seem to think that this fine ability to tie a secure knot should win me any praise. After a minute of trying, we both agreed that with the peat man hovering in the neighborhood and the day dawning, there was no longer time for him to retrieve the rope.

The last I heard him say before he slipped away down the alley was, "You're in a muddle, Sedgwick." Then he was gone.

Hardly knowing what else to do with it, I left the rope attached to the bedpost, slid it under the bedcovers, and hid it in a coil under the bed.

CHAPTER 18

*T*was to learn soon enough the extent of the muddle I was in. Not that I had believed Adam at all, for I had long since learned that he often considered the least threatening of situations in a very dark light. I had also long since learned that I was not likely to win undiluted praise from him, no matter how logical, how sensible, how *reasonable* was the action I might take.

After his departure in the cold, damp morning, I determined on a very reasonable course of action: I returned to bed. It was very early, after all, and I was very tired, and truth to tell, I *was* feeling rather muddled. Strange as it was, I even felt—though the emotion is as alien to my nature as are blushing and simpering—a little weepy.

However, once in semislumber, my weepiness vanished and was replaced by a languor—a kind of muddling, if you will. It was certainly a voluptuous one. I dreamed of white beaches and seared soles upon hot sand, toes dabbling in the frill of water skirting surf's edge, the blue, blue sky, the rustle of the trade winds through the fronds of palm and the thatch of caney, the smell of fresh fish roasting on the spit and the grainy taste of maize and the sweetness of the papaya, the beating of the drums, the promise hidden by the breech cloth, and the subtle stimulation of two diagonal welts of flesh pressed against my breast.

I floundered in these sights, sounds, smells, tastes, and touches for the better part of the morning. When Alice came to the door at ten o'clock to rouse me, I protested. She left. I returned to bed. Several minutes later, however, I rose unrested and unrefreshed and wanted nothing more than for my heavy bones to skim out over the white waves of the sheets and drown in their depths.

But I rose. And dressed myself and my hair. It was not until I had opened the door to my bedchamber and was about to exit to the hallway and greet the world that I stopped to consider the possibly scandalous implications of my behavior the night before. Not that I regretted it, of course. Though tired, I was quite happy this morning. However, I was perplexed about which emotion formed the basis for that happiness just then: was it my desire for respect, which required that I mentally transfer Arawak custom and law to England and consider myself married to Adam? Or was it the delicious, illicit violation of English custom and law, such as I had experienced on Arawak Island when taking the men's path into the jungle with Adam, that had made the encounter so satisfying?

Such indecision was clearly not in my nature. Then, again, neither was my earlier weakness or weepiness. I felt the sudden, unaccustomed wish to run back to my room and bolt the door behind me. I doubt I would have made it down the stairs had it not been for the very bracing thought that occurred to me just then: *And isn't it just like a man to sense and take advantage of my weakness and weepiness, to become suddenly high-handed, to declare me in a muddle, and to express the hope that he must think of something to extract me from it!*

Suddenly hungry and bright-eyed and ready to take on the future, I swept down the stairs. Crossing the black-and-white-tiled foyer to the dining room, I heard evident and unusual activity going forward in the receiving room. I poked my head into this chamber and saw Uncle Harry, in the midst of a great pile of papers littering his minstrel balcony, grunting and groaning over the moving of what looked to be boxes filled with more papers.

"Uncle?" I said. "Good morrow, sir!"

"Ah, Eve Marie, good morrow," he replied and stood up. He abstracted a linen handkerchief, mopped his brow, and dusted his hands. "Just a little housecleaning." He looked discomforted, almost embarrassed, I would have said. "Your father's papers."

"Oh?" I said, curiously.

"Lord Rollo wished to see them, and I am attempting to find some order to them."

Memory returned. So did a vague guilt. I could hardly look Lord Rollo in the eye later today and appear to entertain an offer of marriage, after having just spent the night experiencing amorous bliss (either conjugal or wanton) in the arms of another man.

The complexities of the situation suddenly made me hungrier still. (Or was I suffering from an excess of lingering passion? Even the gnawing in my stomach this morning was difficult to interpret.)

"He did say he was coming, did he not?" I replied, hoping that my voice sounded composed. "Well, if that is the case, I had better get along and take my breakfast."

"Breakfast?" My uncle laughed and said, "Lunch, rather. But I think you've missed that, too." He cast a glance at the encased timepiece against the wall.

"Dear me!" I cried involuntarily when I saw that the afternoon was well advanced. What I had thought was five minutes more sleep must have been hours! "And Aunt Charlotte?" I inquired.

"Out on commissions with Alice," he informed me. "Since it's spitting and threatening to rain, however, I do not expect that they will be gone long."

I noticed then that the normally sunny chamber was a little grey, and its greyness bespoke overcast skies. It had not been raining when Adam had disappeared into the morning mist, and it had not been raining in my reverie. Although a cheerful fire was dancing on the wide hearth, I felt how depressing was this England! How I suddenly longed for Caribbean shores! And how I longed to avoid the meeting with Lord Rollo!

"I shall look for Aunt Charlotte's return," I said simply and excused myself from the room.

For some reason, the imminence of Lord Rollo's visit made me feel slightly panicky, as if the walls were closing in on me. This was entirely irrational. I headed straight for the kitchens to assuage my hunger, and since the hour was so late, I returned to my chambers to change into something more suitable than a morning gown to decline the gentleman's offer of marriage. Thinking that I not need advertise my brazenness, I chose a modest, mist-grey worsted with a parchment lace collar. The dress was drab and prim and entirely right for the occasion.

Some spur prodded me to return to the receiving room without delay to give Uncle Harry a hand at sorting through my father's documents. Why he should have been so intent on doing so before Lord Rollo arrived I could not guess. For whatever reason, he was so engrossed in one piece of paper he was reading that he did not see or hear me until I had crossed the receiving room to the little corkscrew of a stair that rose to the balcony. And when I said in my normal tone, "May I help you, Uncle?" he started, as if caught doing something he should not, and turned to look at me with an expression of fear and something else again that might have been sadness.

He quickly composed himself. "You startled me, my dear," he said. He hesitated, infinitesimally, as if rapidly debating with himself, then invited, with his usual, charming smile, "Yes, do come up. I welcome a helping hand." He held up the paper he had been reading, shook his head, and sighed, as if thoroughly bored. "But it is a tedious business, I warn you!"

Although his words were encouraging, his tone was slightly discouraging, and I wondered if his invitation might not have been due to the fact that I already had one foot on the first step of the stairs and that he could think of no good reason to deny me.

I mounted the eight or nine steps to the landing and crossed the planking of the charming balcony, wading through several waves of yellowed papers that flowed across the floor and up and across the large desk. When I reached my uncle's side, I peered over at the paper he held in his hand. His earlier reluctance or hesitation, if that was what it had truly been, was evidently gone. He held the page up for my inspection, saying, "Nothing of interest here—or anywhere else." Now, I thought I heard relief in his voice.

It was, in truth, an uninteresting document. There were columns of numbers, written in my father's crabbed hand, neatly added and subtracted and balanced. I recognized from several of the entries that this was a portion of the financial record of one of the earliest Spanish campaigns.

He handed it over to me and said that when I was finished with it, I could put it on the stack of papers he was forming to his right. I certainly had no use for it, so I placed it where he said. Then I looked about to see if there were some system to his efforts. I leaned down and reached into a box of papers he had apparently not yet begun to sort. I leafed through them, found them to be as uninteresting as the first page I had seen (I had not expected otherwise), then asked where he would like to me put them.

"The reports from Ostend," I said, holding them up briefly for his inspection.

Uncle scanned the topmost page and nodded. "Some of your father's best work," he commented briefly.

"Yes," I acknowledged, "but if you'll recall, almost immediately thereafter, bad management and a reverse on the battlefield brought near financial disaster to Charles's troops. Even when Father attempted to repair some of the damage out of his own pocket, the losses were not completely mitigated."

"Not exactly out of *his* own pocket," my uncle replied.

I shrugged.

"If it's any consolation to you, my dear," he said, "it was very difficult for your father to have had to use your mother's legacy to you to bail him out of debt. He deeply regretted it."

"I know, but I did not mind at all, as you—and he—well knew," I said, a little stiffly, for the memory of the entire transaction was painful. In it, I had lost my entire inheritance, but was quite willing to do so, given that it had helped Father when he needed it most. Edward, on the other hand, had not been pleased.

Perhaps it was that pain that caused me to burst out of my stiffness with a rather impassioned, "And for his generosity—*his*, not mine!—he was repaid with a charge of treason and the sentence of death!"

"His death was from natural causes," my uncle said quietly.

"You do not believe that any more than I do!" I retorted. "A week in the Tower for a man of his . . . his integrity was as good as a hanging!"

Uncle Harry looked sad. "Yes, well, although at the time it was said that he had died of guilt." He held up his hands in a gesture of helplessness. "It's been a difficult year for our family, although I must say that I have not been badly treated, all in all, by those in command at Hounslow Heath. Perhaps that has been the repayment for your father's longtime loyalty to the Crown. Or perhaps it's a further indication of the disarray that has characterized James's tenure on the throne. Perhaps William will prevail and improve the relations between military and Crown! For myself, I would be just as happy to let sleep the case of your father's guilt or innocence—not that I am not . . . pleased that Lord Rollo has taken an interest in having the entire episode officially cleared, mind you, and all the nooks and crannies of your father's deeds exposed to the bright light of day," he continued, with a distinct lack of enthusiasm, "but I have my doubts about the real good it will do in the end."

"So, why are you spending so much time organizing the papers for Lord Rollo?" I asked, "if you think it such a waste of time."

"Oh, perhaps because the official order for the sequestering of the papers came this morning, and I—"

"The papers are being *sequestered*?" I exclaimed.

"It is normal procedure, if the Royal Navy is to come into possession of them," Uncle Harry answered.

He bent, pointedly, back to his task. I, too, returned to mine. I was not in agreement with my uncle, but for some reason did not voice my opinion. I was highly desirous of seeing Father's files searched, searched again, and searched a third time, if necessary, to assure all concerned that he had been *innocent*. He was owed that much, at least.

Uncle Harry and I remained there on the balcony, silent, slowly working through the files and scattered papers for the better part of an hour. I happened across a box that contained most of Edward's business, which had pertained in large measure to affairs in Spain. Seeing his handwriting, holding those pages he himself had written, caused me some strange moments.

Then, under a haphazard array of sheets and letters and memoranda, my eye caught the corner of a large, flat packet, slightly yellowed now, but with several foreign-looking stamps barely visible from the way the packet was situated in the box. I thought I recognized it. It might have been the packet that Edward had been holding that day—about three weeks before my father's denunciation, it was, if I remembered correctly—standing at the door to my father's library. I had seen that the broad envelope was decorated with a variety of foreign franks, probably Spanish. When I had asked Edward about it, he had answered evasively.

Before my hand even reached down to slide that packet out from under the papers on top of it in order to discover for myself whether that was the same packet or not, a variety of dissonant, conflicting images jostled in my mind. I remembered, first, the moment in its original form.

"Edward, dear," I had said, as I was planning on leaving the house for the afternoon, "what an interesting-looking envelope."

He had turned, rather too hastily, as if he had not known I was behind him. His handsome face, framed by curling blond locks, had betrayed surprise. He denied that the envelope was of any interest.

"But it is foreign," I pursued lightly, donning my gloves and pulling the thong at the end of my parasol over my arm, so that it could dangle from my wrist.

Its foreign character, he determined, was the least interesting aspect of it. Then my father had come to the door, had opened it, had seen Edward, the packet, and me. Before I had an opportunity to register anything, my father had ushered Edward inside and the door had been closed.

"Well, well!" I sniffed. "Men!" Then, I quit the house and promptly forgot all about it.

Standing on the minstrel balcony, in that split second that I reached down to draw the packet from the box, other associations collided with that first memory of Edward. I recalled that trifling incident just moments after my father's denunciation when Julianna Castleragh had been speaking to me. I remembered that this encounter with Miss Castleragh had been uppermost in my thoughts during one of my early encounters with The Proud One. Those memories, furthermore, seemed to crash and slide crazily into all manner of other memories and associations, with one emerging clearly: the sight of Adam Winthrop's highly expressive face and his dry voice saying, within minutes of having first arrived on Arawak Island, "Faith! A chicken cart?"

The envelope was now in my hands. I turned it over and had my finger at the flap to open it. Before I had slid my hand in to withdraw the contents, my attention was completely diverted by the arrival of Aunt Charlotte, who divested herself of her cape and bonnet and handed them to Alice at the same time that she advanced into the room.

"At last you have arisen, my dear!" she said. "Alice tried to wake you at ten o'clock, then tried again around noon, and finally, I said to the silly girl: 'Let my niece sleep! She has had an eventful evening and will have an even more eventful day ahead of her today if my suspicions are correct!'" Here her voice was arch. "And, of course, my suspicions *are* correct, for I am aware that Lord Rollo will be coming to call *any minute* now, and so I wished to be here before his arrival to make sure that you haven't decided to wear something perfectly shocking. Well, you look *charming* in that dress, and let me say that the grey becomes you far, far better than the *bolder* colors that you seem to have taken a liking to—but enough of that! How are you, my dear? And you, Mr. Sedgwick?

Hardly had my aunt made her entrance, than the bell over the door clanged and a new visitor was announced.

I cannot say that I was delighted to see Miss Julianna Castleragh step over the threshold to the receiving room. Nevertheless, I smiled. I knew what was expected of me.

"Miss Castleragh," I said, with every evidence of pleasure. "How kind of you to call on me." Still absently holding the packet in one hand, I crossed the balcony to the steps and, with the other hand, lifted my skirts to descend. With a glance back at my uncle, I said to Miss Castleragh, "You will have to excuse my uncle! He is deeply engaged in a matter of most interest to our family—I am *sure* you will understand—and wishes to continue in his work before the arrival of Lord Rollo, who, I believe, has promised to call before the afternoon has died!"

Uncle Harry, who had properly greeted our guest, looked grateful and continued in this work.

Miss Castleragh replied, "Oh, yes, indeed, he must continue and not allow my little self to distract him! But I could not stay away today, knowing that you have returned to London—and under such auspicious conditions! Why, Lord Rollo did indeed tell me, as you had bade him, of your father's . . . rehabilitation, shall we call it?"

At that moment, we had both walked far enough toward each other to meet and embrace. As I hugged Miss Castleragh lightly to me, I caught sight of Aunt Charlotte just beyond her shoulder. I had to constrain myself not to laugh at the look that crossed Auntie's face. It might as well have had the words emblazoned across it: *Do not let Miss Castleragh steal Lord Rollo away from you!*

I winked audaciously at Aunt Charlotte to inform her that I had received her message, though I had no intention of obeying it. Miss Castleragh broke the embrace, then stepped back from me, attempting at the same time to take both of my hands in hers in a loving, friendly gesture. In this, she was thwarted by the envelope in my hand, which I had forgotten.

"What's this?" she asked, pointing to what I held in my hand.

"Why, nothing at all," I replied, as evasively as Edward had done.

"What funny little franks are upon it," she continued. "I declare that it must be foreign."

"Why, so it is," I agreed placidly.

"But I could not stay away today, and so I have said," she said brightly, "after seeing you looking positively *ravishing* at the ball last night! Are you not quite weary to death from all your traveling and exertions of the last days and weeks?"

From that broad opening, she proceeded to draw me out on the particulars of all my experiences. Aunt Charlotte saw to it that the three of us were seated and provided with refreshments. Fortunately, I had the story of my extraordinary adventure down pat, so that its recital was unexceptionally *ordinary*. During our entire little chat, Miss Castleragh did not take her bright, avid eyes off me. She drank in every word, exclaimed where appropriate, clucked and commiserated, and generally made herself all that was agreeable and friendly.

I did not like the woman. I could not say why I did not like her. I did not think it worth the soul-searching, either. All I knew in those brief minutes, in woman-to-woman socializing with Miss Julianna Castleragh, was that I deeply missed my friends Sylvia, Rose, Lily, and even Margaret (that ninny)—their giggles, their smiles, their concern, their curiosity, their strangeness. As we spoke of all the details of the ball the evening before at Holland House, a part of my mind stood apart. I recalled a dear, dear friend from the years before my marriage to Edward. Catherine was her name. But Catherine had married and gone to live with her husband, in the North. I had seen her only once in four years, when she had come to attend my wedding. I thought, not without great good sense, that the Arawak way of life was far superior to the English, in that dear female friends would always remain together, in the same community.

I must have sighed on the thought, for Miss Castleragh, ever alive to my moods, said, her voice tinkling on a laugh, "Am I tiring you, my dear? Or boring you? Good heavens! I hope not, for I had never thought of myself as a tedious bore, such as one finds in Mrs. Waugh or Mrs. Worth. Such prattleboxes, don't you agree? No? You were never so circumspect before, Mrs. Lipscomb," Miss Castleragh said, leaning over to rap my knuckles archly. "And that tapping of yours! It is quite distracting!"

I had not realized it, but I must have been lightly tapping the corner of the packet absently against the massive arm of the chair in which I was sitting. At her notice of my little tic, I instantly stopped, excused myself, and placed the packet on the table at my side.

"As I was saying," she continued, hardly pausing for breath, "the toilettes—if one could call them such—in which Mrs. Waugh and

Mrs. Worth appeared last night were *appalling*! Not to mention the ways that they had dressed their hair! Ah! I see that you agree with me!"

I had no opinion whatsoever on the dresses that these two maligned ladies wore, and it was most certainly not *their* taste in clothing that I found appalling at just that moment. I am quite sure that Miss Castleragh would have continued on in this most unbecoming style for some more minutes had it not been for the clang of the door bell a second time in this quarter hour.

I knew even before he entered that Lord Rollo had arrived. Sure enough, a moment later, this gentleman was ushered into the receiving room, looking handsome and well turned-out, as was his custom, but also a little harassed, even worried, I would have said.

Miss Castleragh chose that moment to glance over at me in a regard worthy of The Proud One, which seemed to say: *So, it's true what I heard last night about the tragic but rehabilitated widow and the rich and handsome Lord Rollo! I did not come a moment too soon!*

I rose at Lord Rollo's entrance to greet him. Aunt Charlotte and Miss Castleragh remained seated. Uncle Harry had now, perforce, to quit his work, descend from the balcony, and join our group. Greetings all around and bows between the gentlemen were exchanged. Presently the ladies were seated. Lord Rollo, with a quick flick of his hands, lifted his coat tails and scabbard, which held his sword, and sat down with great elegance. Uncle Harry seated himself last. Miss Castleragh's goblet had been refilled, mine had remained largely untouched, while Uncle Harry and Lord Rollo had just been served tawny wine.

I spoke and was spoken to, as a normal person in the conversation, but I could afterward never remember exactly what was said in those first few minutes, for my eye had fallen to the envelope at my right, which I had placed, quite indifferently, address-side up. My eye had been caught by the vivid color of the franks. A red one, in particular, drew me. I suddenly recognized, with an uncomfortable thud of my heart, that the figure it displayed in miniature was the gold-and-crimson crest of Castile. I had seen such a crest several times in my life, of course. The most recent occasion was on Arawak Island, looking through the long glass when I had seen the golden lion rampant on its field of red as the banner attached to the mainmast of Don Pedro's *Cinco Llagas*.

I had the oddest sensation sitting there, quite safe and comfortable in the receiving room of my Uncle Harry's stone house in Islington, that a great evil had entered these four walls. I did not know from which direction it had come. Perhaps it had entered with Miss Castleragh, or with Lord Rollo. Perhaps it had been sleeping for many months in this room, in this envelope, now only inches from my hand. The packet suddenly seemed on fire. I willed myself not to jerk my hand away from its vicinity. I did not wish to attract undue attention to it, to me, to the evil that I now began to suspect it contained.

I was too late. When next I looked up to join in the conversation, I noticed that Lord Rollo's eyes were first on me, then on the envelope at my side. I thought I caught the hint of a narrowness in his eyes, a cold calculation, a malevolence. I was suddenly put in mind of a great similarity between Lord Rollo and The Dissenter, of all people. I was not blinded from perceiving the similarity by Lord Rollo's beautiful tie wig, or his elegant, snow-white cravat, or the deep-blue coat and vest whose lengths were proper and in the mode, or his correctly cut breeches, or his silk stockings, or his buckled shoes with the red heels. All of these contrasted sharply—and superficially—with The Dissenter's essential nakedness. No, I saw clearly now that Lord Rollo intended some harm to me and mine.

I had faced a fierce band of Arawak warriors, thinking that I had breathed my last. I could face Lord Rollo.

I smiled at him—an almost coy, timid, somewhat reassuring smile,

I hoped. The cold narrowness in Lord Rollo's eyes disappeared, to be replaced by something warmer, but equally unattractive to me. A proper man—on the surface at least—Lord Rollo properly shifted his eyes away from me.

I had entered the conversation, which revolved around various aspects of the entertainment the night before. I could not quite enjoy this lively, idle chatter—not while the envelope burned at my side. I caught a look that Lord Rollo exchanged briefly with the greedy, grasping eyes of Miss Castleragh. I easily interpreted it and thought: *And isn't that The Dissenter and The Proud One all over again!* Some things remain constant the world over.

Now, if only Aunt Charlotte had the presence and authority of Great Arawak Mother, the Sedgwick family might just make it through this afternoon with our dignity and reputation intact. However, Aunt Charlotte did not seem to have a thought in her head beyond seeing me married off.

"And the admiral asked her to dance!" Aunt Charlotte said in obvious reference to me—not for the first time, I think, but then, I had not been following the conversation closely. "Was he a good dancer, Marie?"

This, I do believe, was Aunt Charlotte's method of keeping Lord Rollo interested in me. "I don't rightly recall," I answered calmly, "for I had such difficulty keeping up with his speech that it took all my powers of concentration to maintain conversation."

"He said that you were an excellently behaved young lady," she continued, "and expressed every opinion that you ought!"

"A rare lapse," I commented.

Miss Castleragh's irritating laugh trilled out. "Mrs. Lipscomb never used to keep her strong opinions to herself!" (I was quite sure now that Julianna Castleragh knew perfectly well how much the appellation "Mrs. Lipscomb" *grated* on me. Otherwise, she would not have been using it at every opportunity.) "Mayhap tragedy and adventure have improved her!"

This was Miss Castleragh's attempt at a joke. My aunt took it at face value. "The Colonies," she replied to this, but with a little less disapproval than on previous occasions.

Lord Rollo proved himself interested in my dance with Admiral van der Kuylen, but not for the reasons that Aunt Charlotte might have fashioned for herself. After asking me smoothly about the tenor of the conversation I had held with the admiral and expressing his hope (as was now politically favorable to do) that William would indeed march on London and bring a little order back into the government, he inquired of me—blandly, innocently, "Did I hear correctly that the admiral was accompanied by a rather dashing captain last night?"

I saw no reason to dissemble or play dumb. "Yes, he was," I said, quite forthrightly. Although my heart was now thundering away most sickeningly in my breast, I was rather pleased that my voice held the correct mixture of polite interest in the question and indifference to the answer. "I did not catch his name, but I believe the admiral had known him years ago during the Spanish campaign in the Netherlands."

Fortunately and entirely inadvertently, Julianna Castleragh came to my aid, for I did not believe that I could maintain such disaffected discussion of Adam for long. "Captain Winthrop!" she cried brightly. "Oh, yes! I remember meeting him, as well! About midway through the evening! An interesting man," she said speculatively, "and so unobliging not to wish to dance with me." Here, her voice changed to a pout. "Now, the admiral explained the very strange reason why this Captain Winthrop would not dance, but I don't know! He looks to be such an agile, athletic man that I think he was just teasing me!"

I did not care to enlighten her about either his physical abilities or his feet. Lord Rollo seemed somewhat impatient of this digression into Captain Winthrop's dancing abilities, or lack of them. The smile with which he favored Miss Castleragh was one of slight irritation.

"Of course, a man would be rather more interested in the captain's sailing abilities than his dancing steps, given that the admiral has chosen him for a rather important position in a scheme that might provide England with a more stable ruler," Lord Rollo said to her. "Did you discover, perchance, the captain's recent past record which might have prompted the admiral to single him out for distinguished service?"

This answer Miss Castleragh had not discovered.

Into the little pause, Lord Rollo said very smoothly, very silkily "Is this not the same Winthrop who had that . . . unpleasant experience in a Spanish prison in the not too distant past?" He paused and looked around, an inquiring lift to his finely shaped brows. "General Sedgwick, have you heard aught of this?"

Uncle Harry was no fool and would not be drawn. He also turned the conversation to the *real* topic when he said, in response, "The name Winthrop means nothing to me. I would not know, of course, anything about this particular Captain Winthrop or his tenure in the Spanish prison. Peninsular affairs were, as you know, my brother's department."

Lord Rollo betrayed himself (to me, at least) when his eyes slid momentarily, almost involuntarily, I would have said, to the envelope at my side. "And you, Mrs. Lipscomb," he asked, "do you recall hearing anything of this man Winthrop?"

Lord Rollo had, apparently, taken a leaf out of Julianna Castleragh's book. Was his use of my married name a subtle implication that Edward had been involved in whatever it was that swirled so malevolently around in the room just now and hovered, like a negative energy over the envelope? I was put forcibly in mind of the power that had pulled on my eyes and nerves and the pores of my skin as I stood over that deep pit on Arawak Island and stared down into hundreds of thousands of pounds' worth of pure gold.

That image led my thoughts down an unexpected new path. Could

Lord Rollo know that I knew of that gold, of Don Pedro's attempt to claim it, of Adam Winthrop's ruse to preserve it for its rightful owners? No. He could only suspect it. No matter how Adam had criticized my actions that fateful morning on the beach with the *Pride of Devon* anchored off shore, I had been wholly, completely *unequivocally* right to have hidden from the top ranks of the Royal Navy all knowledge of treasure, Don Pedro's visit, and Adam Winthrop's presence on Arawak Island.

Nevertheless, Lord Rollo's implication remained. Had Edward been involved in whatever nasty business I sensed was lurking? Had my father?

I did not allow even a split second to elapse before answering Lord Rollo's question. "Yes, Winthrop *must* have been the name of that poor man with the strange feet!" I said with a very credible (if I do say so myself) mixture of surprise and amusement. "I was so busy adjusting for all of the admiral's other pronunciations that I believe the name 'Vindrop' passed right by me!" I paused, with some artful effect, as if a thought had just occurred to me. (I perceived myself rising to the occasion, painful though it might possibly become for me.) "But, why should I have heard of him, Lord Rollo?" I asked, entirely innocently.

Lord Rollo's smile was all that was evidently kind and condescending. Some sixth sense had warned me so fully against him that I was now able to see behind that smile to the chill and something else again deep inside him. Could it have been fear?

"My dear," he said, and his voice held the surface kindness, as did his smile, "I do not wish to cause you pain. It's just that I do believe this man Winthrop has had a . . . varied career, shall we say, and is not a man of the highest . . . reliability."

So much delicacy! "Do you fear that he will not serve Admiral van der Kuylen reliably?" I asked. "That he will be the cause of a failure of the admiral's fleet to prevail over James's?"

Lord Rollo flicked an invisible speck from his gold-braided sleeve. "This I do not presume to know, of course," he said. When he raised his eyes to look at me, they were peculiarly penetrating. I was certainly proof against his penetration. "It's just that I have reason to believe that this Winthrop was the man who denounced your father so falsely."

This pronouncement, not unnaturally, produced a babble of comment. The exclamations "The blackguard!" "The knave!" "It can't be possible!" "The admiral should dismiss him immediately!" "He should come to stand trial!" and so forth could be heard to fall immediately from the lips of Aunt Charlotte and Miss Castleragh. Uncle Harry, curiously, said nothing.

I received this news with a painful wrench of my heart. I had not expected it, and yet it did not completely jar with the forces I already felt at work in the room. I did not know who needed to be defended just yet—Adam, or my father. Under the weight of this pain, the contemplation of which I would have to defer to much later, I rose to an even greater level of emotional strength.

"Why should a man who looked nothing at all out of the ordinary, save for his apparently very wretched feet, wish to do something so nonsensical as denouncing my father?" I asked, as if I were thoroughly unimpressed by this disclosure.

"Because, my dear," Lord Rollo replied smoothly, "this man Winthrop was languishing in a Spanish prison at the time. A man in prison is often apt to want to get out—by whatever means available to him—even if it means fabricating the most wicked lie imaginable."

I considered this point of view with every evidence of seriousness. "Well," I said. "I own that I could be most annoyed and, yes, even angry with 'this man Winthrop' if he is the source of this vicious rumor that ruined my father's life—" I choked a little over those last words "—but I fear that I must save my very *gravest* censure for those authorities in the Royal Army who allowed those rumors to persist, who *believed* them, and who threw my father in the Tower as a result of them without a thorough investigation. That is, if the source of the rumor were as unreliable as it now appears to be!"

Lord Rollo knew just how to handle this. "You are entirely right, my dear," he said in his most sympathetic voice, "which is why I thought the whole affair would benefit from a thorough public airing. Those directly responsible should be reprimanded! I think we all now who they are. And as for this man Winthrop, I hardly think he should be let off the hook so easily—much less be rewarded by a captaincy in William's navy!"

"His lordship feels just as he ought!" my aunt opined a this point, hardly able to contain herself.

Julianna Castleragh, who was making a meal over this entire conversation and almost smacking her lips with delight, seconded that opinion.

"Just as he ought!" Aunt Charlotte repeated. "And for that we should be thankful, should we not, Mr. Sedgwick?"

Uncle Harry smiled his sad smile at his wife, but when he turned to Lord Rollo, it become one of thoughtful reflection, which held steel. "Indeed, Mrs. Sedgwick," Uncle Harry replied, not taking his eyes off Lord Rollo. "The Sedgwick family is already eternally grateful for the signal honor you have conferred upon us by having begun to have my brother Jonathan's good name cleared! How could I be other than grateful? However, now you allude to a problem that I confess makes me feel ill at ease! I'm afraid that we are wading into muddy waters. Very muddy waters! I do not know where it shall end. With the shakiness of the present regime, and the new one—if new one there is to be—not yet in place, I feel a reluctance to undertake accusations and counteraccusations that might prove, as in my late brother's wretched case, to have been false from the very beginning!"

Lord Rollo knew just how to handle this observation, too. "General Sedgwick, your sensibilities do you credit. I fully appreciate your desire to prevent another man from suffering the wretched fate of your dear brother. However, permit me to dwell on two of the excellent points you have raised. First there could hardly be a better time than now in which to, ah, sweep out the dust and debris of the old administration so that a transition of power might be more smoothly executed. This was precisely the reason why I brought up the past of this man Winthrop, but I will not pain you by insisting just now on what legal action might be most appropriate to take against him! It is only that I feel it most acutely, the navy being, as you know, my own backyard, although I think I heard once something about his having been in the army. But it only goes to show how slippery a character he is." Lord Rollo paused to smooth a crease in his elegant knee-breeches. "And most important, as you so wisely observe, it is *imperative* that no false accusations be made! I insist on the strictest integrity in this! And that is why, dear General Sedgwick, I have wished to have your brother's papers thoroughly investigated."

Sequestered, I believe, was the word Lord Rollo chose when he issued his order from the War Department.

"Investigated," he was continuing without missing a beat, "for clues to the possible conspirators and intriguers in this, a most sordid and unhappy affair."

Uncle Harry bowed his head in acknowledgment of all of Lord Rollo's excellent points.

"You feel just as you ought!" Aunt Charlotte exclaimed after this fluid speech. "*Just* as you ought! And certainly, as you know, my brother-in-law's papers are at your disposal. Why, Mr. Sedgwick and dear Marie have been poring over the documents for the better part of the afternoon, in their attempt to help speed to its happy conclusion this entire *sordid* affair, as you say. And speaking of happiness—" Here, she nodded at me in deepest approval. "—I feel that, in order to speed a future happiness of *a very different sort*, some of us in the room are *de trop*!"

In that moment that Aunt Charlotte had engaged Lord Rollo's attention (and, perforce, Miss Castleragh's lively interest), and they were exchanging a volley of polite nothings on the subject of future happinesses, Uncle Harry bent on me a look that could read as nothing other than: *Be on your guard!*

Aunt Charlotte and Miss Castleragh rose from their chairs. Taking his cue, Uncle Harry rose, as well. Lord Rollo rose, of course, to see the ladies out. Feeling entirely uncomfortable with what I would have to face in my minutes alone with Lord Rollo and wishing only to be in my room to ponder all that I had just heard, I rose, too, in order to bid Miss Castleragh good day.

The five of us were standing in the center of the receiving room, exchanging the blandest pleasantries in the world, when the entire surface calm and politeness of the occasion was rent by the shattering, scattering, sparkling of broken glass from the window lining the minstrel balcony and by a prolonged and blood-curdling cry from deep in the throat of the very strange, two-footed feathered animal that came swinging on a vine through the broken gash of the window. In its airborne journey it crashed, as well, through the banister lining the balcony and landed, sure-footed, amidst splinters of glass and wood on the floor of the receiving room, not five feet in front of us.

CHAPTER 19

The effect of the shuttered peace and glass was as frightful as can be imagined and affected each one of us differently. Were I a woman of lesser fortitude, I am sure that the sight of the wildly painted, befeathered animal who had hurled himself like a savage beast into our receiving room would have caused me to faint on the spot.

I note for the record that Julianna Castleragh did, in fact, swoon into Lord Rollo's arms. Aunt Charlotte was audibly surprised. I cannot describe her verbal emission, except to say that it was more than a shriek. In any case, my uncle, obviously stunned, was in no position to help his afflicted wife overcome her emotions. Instead, he paled and groped both for his handkerchief and for the arm of a chair upon which to lean. When he found them, he sat awkwardly and began to mop his brow.

Lord Rollo's nerves were apparently steelier than my uncle's, his reactions quicker. In the twinkling of an eye, he had neatly disposed Miss Castleragh into the chair she had lately vacated, where she slumped. Without hesitation and in a fluid movement, Lord Rollo then reached for the sword at his side and unsheathed it.

However, the two-footed animal had all the advantage, both in the situation and in his agility. He must have anticipated Lord Rollo's move. With a flick of the extra length of the vine on which he had swung into the room and which he still held in one hand, the animal knocked the sword from Lord Rollo's hand, and it fell onto the ground with a clatter.

That clatter fully restored my senses. Recovering now from my surprise, my first thought was: *I am certainly glad he wore thick-soled boots to protect his poor feet from abuse!* and my second thought was: *If he has attempted to disguise himself as an Arawak Indian, he has thoroughly missed the mark!*

Now, Adam knew as well as I that the Arawak do not wear buckskin shirts and pantaloons decorated with fringe and feathers; they do not paint their faces in such a hideous fashion; they do not knot their hair so that it sticks out all over the head; and they certainly do not wear boots. I could forgive him this last item of costume, but not the others. The moment, however, was not propitious for a discussion of his sartorial solecisms. In any case, events were moving forward rapidly.

Hardly thirty seconds had elapsed from the moment Adam had first crashed through the glass on the upper story and had swung his way through the minstrel balcony to land in front of us, and almost simultaneously, it seemed, to knock the drawn sword from Lord Rollo's hand.

The shrieking continued. I realized quickly enough that the noise was no longer coming from Aunt Charlotte, who had had the good grace to collapse into the chair next to Miss Castleragh. (The afflicted lady was coming around. I did not think Julianna Castleragh would have wanted to have missed much of this quite extraordinary scene.) No, the noise was coming from Adam, loud and high-pitched and in sounds that were vaguely human, perhaps Arawak. I did not immediately understand what he was saying. Neither did he look at me, for that might have given his whole purpose away. (Not that I had any good idea about *what* his purpose conceivably was; only the haziest of suspicions were beginning to take shape in my brain.) Given that I did believe something quite dramatically important was at stake for me in Adam's sudden appearance, I did my best to look suitably stunned and scared at this remarkable intrusion.

And his shrieking continued. In Arawak, I must suppose.

Lord Rollo's wits were fully about him. Not but several moments after he had lost his sword to the two-footed animal's rope vine, the vice admiral in the Royal Navy lunged for the savage beast. The savage beast flicked his rope vine once more, this time letting it tangle around his lordship's ankles, causing him to sprawl, wig-first, across the floor at the beast's feet.

"Why, you—" Lord Rollo began.

The two-footed animal spat down on the human heap at his feet and said, in a really comical attempt at pidgin, "White Devil! White Devil want gold! Gold!"

This pronouncement, not unnaturally, caused an altered charge in the room. No one would have expected Aunt Charlotte or Miss Castleragh (or even myself) to have gone to Lord Rollo's aid. However, Uncle Harry was in a different position. He had risen shakily from his chair, presumably to assist the gallant Lord Rollo in subduing this beast; but as those English words came out of its mouth, I turned toward my uncle and saw him frown, then hesitate, then glance strangely at me.

It seemed to be an important moment.

I tried to communicate that this wild creature was known to me and essentially harmless, but was not sure how one best transmitted such a message solely through the eyes.

Adam was continuing to croon strange Arawak syllables. Suddenly the sounds crossed some barrier of understanding, and I perceived the Arawak words, "Treasure map, Beauty! Treasure map!"

The hazy suspicions took even more definite shape in my brain.

"You cur! You animal!" Lord Rollo ejaculated from the floor. His accents were rather less elegant than those I had heard him use heretofore, thus helping further to make concrete my suspicions.

Uncle Harry had to act. "I say here, you . . . you *beast*," he began, and took a step forward as if to assist Lord Rollo to his feet and to subdue the savage.

"Gold! Gold! White Devils!" Adam chanted to the assembled company, eyeing each in turn with fierce regard. "Treasure map! Treasure map!" he chanted when he came to me.

I had the presence of mind to glance at the large, flat, dangerous packet lying so easily within my reach—and so far from my grasp.

Adam nodded once, then turned back to the pile of elegance rising from the floor, and none too soon. Lord Rollo had already regained his balance. A murderous look was in his eye. My heart flew to my throat when I saw him slip a wicked dagger out of the inner recesses of his capacious coat. I made an involuntary movement forward to check him from stabbing Adam, but Adam was quicker still. He had reached down into his boot and had withdrawn his own dagger. With it, he easily parried Rollo's thrust and disarmed him at the same time.

Lord Rollo, now desperate and cursing audibly, was making a move toward the table next to my hand, where lay the envelope in which I now fully realized reposed an extremely valuable piece of paper.

Adam threw the dagger (missing me by inches). Its point knifed through the center of the envelope, effectively pinning it to the wood of the tabletop.

Then, two things happened at once. Lord Rollo withdrew a small, gold-mounted pistol from his coat—he had certainly come well-armed—and fired at just the same time that Adam took another knife from his other boot and, with a great shriek and a yell, leapt across the room and grabbed me. Thus, Lord Rollo's bullet hit not the savage beast but thin air, and lodged into the wall beside the fireplace. The report had caused Aunt Charlotte, who was just coming around, to fall back into her chair and Miss Castleragh to jump up from hers.

I was now Adam's shield. With his left hand around my neck in a hold that was unnecessarily brutal, I thought, he held the second knife at my throat. (His resources for extricating himself in this situation were, after all, highly limited.) No one moved. Even Lord Rollo was effectively checked. He lowered his pistol—thank God. I hated to imagine what Adam might have been forced to do to make the situation more realistic. From the look on Miss Castleragh's face (Aunt Charlotte was in a swoon), I must have been wearing a wholly convincing look of surprised horror.

In the moments of stillness, Adam took the opportunity to pry loose the knife pinning the envelope to the table. When the packet was free and in his right hand, the venom leapt out of Lord Rollo's eyes and crossed the few feet separating him from Adam. Adam was unshaken. At the barest movement from Lord Rollo in our direction, Adam visibly tightened his hold around my neck and touched the blade of the knife more threateningly against my throat. (It was not all show. It really hurt.)

Aunt Charlotte had revived enough to suffer a relapse at sight of my capture. Even Miss Castleragh, bless her heart, looked manifestly shaken. Uncle Harry and Lord Rollo remained completely motionless, while Adam backed himself and me toward the door to the receiving room that would lead out into the hall.

Now, this was not a particularly good plan of escape—if escape he had, indeed, planned. However, I suppose that, under the circumstances, he could not have expected to leave the receiving room by the same means he had entered it. Although only about a minute or two *at most* had ticked off the clock since the shattering of the glass, and but a few seconds since the pistol shot, there had been time enough for the servants to have been roused from wherever in the house they had been. I could hear the entire household staff converging in the main hallway. They were evidently about to burst into the room.

They were not given the opportunity. Still holding me against him in one hand and the envelope in the other, Adam toed the door to the main hallway open with the tip of his boot. It was at this moment that I fully realized the effectiveness of the old adage: Surprise is the essence of attack. Ten able bodies stood in the hallway—more than enough to have overpowered this extraordinary-looking man-beast and freed me. However, these ten faces registered all the shock and amazement that my Aunt Charlotte, Julianna Castleragh, Lord Rollo, and Uncle Harry had lately experienced, and these ten people were not more capable of responding to this absurd situation than had been the group in the receiving room.

Thus it was that a lone, two-footed animal, painted and befeathered and holding a hostage, was able to cause those ten people to fall back in stunned awe. That action allowed the animal to gain the inestimable advantage of maneuvering himself and me toward the first step of the staircase, his back protectively to the wall. He took the first step up those stairs, backward, with me still in front of him as a shield, the dagger still at my throat.

Then, a wild thumping began at the front door at the moment that Adam and I had reached the first step of the stairs, which coincided with the moment that Lord Rollo and Uncle Harry erupted into the hallway. They ran into the space created by the ten able bodies who were still standing, motionless, in a semi-circle, their wide eyes pinned on me and Adam. Lord Rollo reloaded his pistol and aimed it at us. He did not fire.

The wild thumping at the door continued. My uncle had by this time become fully cognizant of the fact that all was not as it seemed, and if there was strange business afoot, it was not *all* for the bad. He also seemed to realize that I was not in any grave danger—well, not in any immediate danger of having my throat slit.

"Open the door, man!" Uncle Harry commanded of the first footman. "Not the rest of you!" he continued when it seemed as if the other nine were going to spring upon Adam and me. "I believe this— this *man* here is dangerous!"

Adam and i had taken three slow, backwards steps up the stairs.

The door had been opened to reveal the face of Thomas. "There's been a cart turn over in the street just now!" he informed the entire assembly quickly and anxiously. He gestured toward the street and, indeed, the sound of a ruckus of no mean proportion drifted in. "An accident! There's them what's hurt! Hurt bad!" Horses snorted and stamped. Human voices were raised in altercation. Others groaned and cried in pain.

Not a bad diversion, I thought, *Not bad at all.*

For a deliberate man, my uncle suddenly made a series of quick decisions. "You, John! You, James! Out into the street! Go for more help, if necessary! You, Mary! Find out who among the hurt need the most immediate attention!"

As if just gathering his wits, Thomas made some noises in apparent reference to the strange scene he was witnessing in the foyer of this house on Colebrooke Row.

"John, James, Mary—out!" Uncle Harry said, gesturing with head and hands, shooing them toward the door. "We've private business to attend to in here." They obeyed promptly and closed the door on Thomas's creditably bewildered face.

"Good God!" Lord Rollo exclaimed as these three servants left and shut the door behind them. "We need every man we can get just now! Every man and woman!"

"And the last thing we need is some oaf off the street bruiting about what he has seen in here!" was my uncle's cool reply. "Furthermore, sir, be so kind as not to countermand me in my own home!"

"I'll do whatever I damned well please in the name of the Royal Navy!" Lord Rollo retorted, leveling his pistol menacingly.

"God's wounds, man!" my uncle cried. "Are you mad? Put that thing away!"

"I'm not going to shoot—yet," Lord Rollo answered. He had not taken his eyes off me and Adam. "Don't let him get away, Sedgwick!" Lord Rollo commanded. His voice sounded a dire threat.

"There's nowhere for him to go," my uncle returned. "Let him go up those stairs. He's only got the roof as the means of escape."

"That's right," Lord Rollo said, his voice dripping sarcasm. "Inform him of his escape route."

"I inform him of nothing," Uncle Harry replied. "He must have had his rope rigged on the roof to have come in the windows that way. I imagine that he has already devised some way of escape, again by the roof—although he'll have to crawl through the attic now to do it. Besides, that savage can't understand me."

"Savage, my—" Lord Rollo broke off. "That's no savage."

"How can you say so?" my uncle challenged.

Julianna Castleragh was happy to inform him. "Because he has blue eyes," she said, with lively interest. She and Aunt Charlotte had also arrived at the door to the hallway. Aunt Charlotte was gripping the door jamb for support. "He also looks vaguely familiar. . . ."

She did not have time to place the face, for the loud hammering began at the door again. Thomas was playing his part perfectly. He declared that the accident was worse than he had thought. He needed reinforcements. He took only perfunctory notice of the admittedly unusual scene in the foyer of this very correct household. He seemed to know just what to do to stall, to divert, to confuse further an already confused situation.

By then, Adam and I were on about the tenth step of the stairs. My back was molded into his frame, his knife still at my throat, Lord Rollo's gun pointed straight at my breast.

During this diversion, and still facing forward and away from

Adam, I moved my lips imperceptibly in order to whisper, "How are you going to get out of the house?"

His lips were at my ear. "I don't know yet," he admitted. "I left that part of the plan open, depending on the turn of events."

"Oh, this is a *plan*?" I asked, skeptically.

"Almost," he replied.

"That's what I thought, for your costume is *atrocious*," I commented under my breath. "Completely inauthentic."

I did not suppose that he would be abashed by this criticism. He was not. "No worse than yours," he replied. "I thought you had been cured of your taste for grey."

Well, really! "Grey is very proper," I whispered in return, "and becomes me well."

"It's boring and you know it," he returned. "Now, the pink—ahhh, the pink is something else again."

We continued to edge up one more step. "I own that pink on me is in better taste than the horrible way you have painted your face," I said. "Did you think to fool anyone with this costume?"

"Not for long," he returned, "which is why I have had to move fast. That Rollo fellow knew almost from the start that this was a ruse, but he's in no position to show his hand."

It was true. Lord Rollo stood below us in the hallway leveling his pistol at us, unable to shoot in front of so many witnesses, his eyes burning into Adam and the envelope he held in his hand. My uncle's eyes were equally transfixed on us, but a different, knowing look had entered them.

"As for this almost-plan," I said, "I suppose it would have been too simple for you to enter through the front door, announce yourself, and confront Lord Rollo directly?"

"Far too simple," he agreed. "And it seems you're forgetting one or two reasons why I might not have wished to do that."

"Is he speaking to you, Eve Marie?" my uncle called up at me, in a voice that displayed suitable concern. "Are you at your last prayers, my dear? Do not worry, my child! We shall not make any movements that will cause him to harm you! Do I see him talking to you? Can he speak?"

At my uncle's question, Adam halted our progress on the steps. He had to act as if threatened. He readjusted his grip on me to underscore the menacing character of his present actions.

"I . . . I don't know," I replied. My voice trembled. It was quite effective for showing my fear. However, the source of the tremble was hardly fear. I simply did not know whether to laugh or cry at this most absurd and absurdly complicated situation. I *was* in a muddle. I was *not* in a muddle. I felt tired and heavy and happy and light, all at once. "I think this . . . this man is trying to say something to the effect that if a servant were to pounce on us from above, I would suffer. He said, 'White Devil. White Devil. Up, bad. No up, good. Ugh. Ugh.'" My voice trembled wildly now. "Is there, perchance, any servant left upstairs who might happen upon us, inadvertently?"

"No, no, my dear," Uncle Harry reassured. "I believe they have all assembled here, except for the ones who have gone outside to assist with the accident just now."

In other words, Adam's way was clear. We continued our ascent and were but a step or two from the landing.

"White Devil! White Devil!" Adam hurled down, needing to keep up the effect. "White Devil want gold!"

"Don't let him get away, Sedgwick," Lord Rollo continued to threaten malevolently. "It will be your career, man!"

"You can't imagine that I am worried about my career at the moment, sir!" my uncle snapped back without hesitation. "Not when my niece—my brother's only child—is in grave danger!" Then, to me, "Don't fret, Eve Marie, dear. Don't fret, child."

"Perhaps his lordship could lower his pistol," I suggested, my voice still trembling. "I believe that it makes this . . . this man nervous."

Under the circumstances, Lord Rollo had no choice but to do as I asked. "It's a ruse! It's a ruse!" he cried out in his frustration, unable to contain himself.

"It's the most exciting event I have ever witnessed," confessed Julianna Castleragh, also apparently unable to contain herself.

Aunt Charlotte had arrived at the door to the foyer. At sight of what was going forward, she well and truly collapsed. She began to slide down the door jamb. Alice, who had been lurking in a corner of the foyer, rushed across the flags to save her mistress before she fell in an ignominious heap on the floor. That action created enough of a diversion for Adam, once he had one foot on the landing, to whirl me up and around the banister, out of immediate sight of the foyer.

And not a moment too soon. Seeing Adam slip out of view, Lord Rollo had raised his pistol and fired—once again, into the wall. Aunt Charlotte must have revived again, for I heard her moan, "My child! My baby! My darling niece! Is she still alive? I cannot bear to look!" Alice calmed her with soothing words.

Julianna Castleragh pointed out quite rightly, with a mixture of awe and relish and censure, "You might have hit Mrs. Lipscomb, your lordship!"

He might well have hit me, I realized, so crazed was he now with anger and frustration and greed and whatever else it was that motivated him. He was ready to bound up the stairs after us, but my uncle must have momentarily barred his passage, for I heard him say, "Everyone outside! You, too, Rollo!"

Then, "Out of my way, you fool! You're in this with them! It's a ruse!" This from Lord Rollo.

Adam and I were running down the hallway to my bedchamber.

"I'll challenge you on that later," I heard my uncle say sharply, "but for now, I'm more interested in my niece's safety than my honor. Now, everyone outside! I think the man must be planning his escape by the roof!"

My uncle must have run outside, the servants following, as Adam quietly closed the bedchamber door behind us.

"You're trapped!" I moaned.

He did not reply. Instead, he handed me the fateful envelope and began shoving the bed against the door. "I'm not, if the rope is still attached to the post," he said.

"It is!" I cried low. "It is! You're saved!"

He merely grunted in reply.

By then, Lord Rollo had bounded up the stairs and was pounding on all the doors leading off the hallway, attempting to discover which room we were in. When he came to mine and the door did not cede to his violence, he began cursing all manner of obscenities and directives to *Open up! Open up in the name of the Royal Navy!* He paused, as if listening. We made no noise. The next moment, he continued on down the hall, pounding on every door, yelling crazily. By the sounds that came next from the hallway, Lord Rollo must have found the door to the attic stairs and clambered up them.

Adam had already opened the window and was uncoiling the rope to propel himself out into the cold, grey rain of dusk. He untangled four of the five knots I had made and tested the last one's strength with all his weight. It held.

"When I reach the ground, unknot the rest of the rope and throw it down to me. I don't want you implicated in this in any way."

"But how will I say that you escaped?" I asked, reasonably.

"Tell them I flew," he tossed off with a shrug, "or jumped, or whatever you want. I'm a savage beast, remember?"

He crossed to the window and prepared to leave my bedchamber the same way he had entered it a few hours earlier. Lord Rollo's footsteps resounded above us, stalking about in the attic. He fired several times in the darkness. The man was mad.

I became aware of the envelope in my hand. "What of this?" I asked, holding it up to him.

"It's yours to keep," he stated. His voice was flat, emotionless.

"Mine?"

We stared at each other a long moment. We heard Lord Rollo descend the attic stairs, travel down the hallway past my bedchamber, back down the main flight of stairs to the foyer, still yelling wildly. Muffled by the distance and the closed door of my bedchamber, a scuffle seemed to be taking place in the foyer. Lord Rollo had apparently run, quite literally, into Thomas, who was crying out, "Begging your pardon, sir! Begging your pardon!" with his lordship barking, "Out of my way, you idiot! Out of my way! It's a ruse! A damned ruse!"

I almost smiled, but the entire episode was too serious to admit of humor. "He knows about the treasure of Arawak Island?" I ventured, gesturing with my head toward the door, referring to Lord Rollo.

Adam's eyes were grave. He nodded at the envelope in my hand. "So it would seem."

I held his eyes a moment longer. "Go," I said. "They'll be looking for you."

He shook his head, infinitesimally. "Thomas will take care of them the next few minutes. Your uncle seems to have diverted everyone to the roof." A pause. "Do you understand now?"

I certainly understood that regret and reluctance I had felt on so many occasions with him on Arawak Island. I certainly understood what it was that he had wanted to confess to me.

"I'm not sure I want this," I said, tapping the envelope against the palm of one hand.

"I'm not sure you do," he agreed.

"You'd better go," I insisted.

Into the smallest of silences, he said, almost in a rush, "You'll come with me? We can escape together. The boat is waiting."

"The boat?" I echoed

"I can hardly stay in England after today," he answered.

"You can't?"

He shook his head. "It would only be a matter of time before I'd find myself in prison again."

"But you have evidence," I said. "In here." I held up the envelope.

"*You* have the evidence," he replied.

I could only frame one, comprehensive question. "Why?" My voice sounded small and plaintive and even a little whiny.

"I exposed your father once," he said. His voice was matter-of-fact. "His name has been cleared now—at least to the world at large. My freedom, if I were to remain in England, can only be bought now at the expense of exposing him a second time." He smiled, with faint relish, "Along with Rollo, of course." He shrugged. "I'm prepared to forgo that pleasure, however."

"I doubt that Lord Rollo is prepared to forgo the pleasure of doing you harm. He knows you're involved, and he knows you were at the ball last night," I said, "and I would venture that he knows it's you in that . . . most *ridiculous* costume."

"As for this costume, Rollo can only suspect me," Adam said. "He's on tricky ground himself, now that he's tipped his hand to your uncle's viewing."

Masculine voices on the roof drifted in through the open window of my bedchamber. Adam did not move.

I wanted to laugh. I wanted to cry. I wanted to throw my arms around him. I wanted to push him to the window so that he could escape before it was too late. I had the worst feeling that he would do something noble for me—like remain silent to protect my father's restored name, and allow himself to be imprisoned, if Lord Rollo should catch him now.

"Go!" I implored.

He nodded, once, and hopped agilely upon the window sill, rope in hand. He paused, yet again. He gestured, minimally. "You won't reconsider and come with me?" The gleam in his eye was all that was attractive and provocative. "I carried you safely down a rope once before, if you'll recall. I didn't drop you then, and I won't drop you now."

It was all I could do to say, "I can't." I choked over the words. "You understand."

His answer was a lop-sided smile. He did not kiss me goodbye. He jumped out the window, straining the rope and causing the bed to hop with his weight.

"The gutter prong!" I cried low. "Don't cut yourself."

"I won't."

"Your boots!" I cried out again. "Can you make it in your boots?"

"It's easier sliding down in them than climbing up," he answered.

His head was about two feet below the window. I turned away to be ready to unknot the last knot so that I could throw the rope to him. A second later, however, his face reappeared at the window.

"Only with you, Sedgwick," he said. I whirled at the sound of his voice. It was laced with wistful humor. "Only with you would I go on a treasure hunt in reverse. First, we find the treasure. Then, we find the map." He smiled, as if at a lovely memory, and shook his head. "You'll know what to do with it," he said, in obvious reference to the map. Then his face slipped below the sill.

Within seconds, I heard his feet hit the ground, and I winced at the thought of the pain he must have felt. I untied the last knot and threw the rope down to him. I could hardly see the ground through the rain and the mist, but I knew that within seconds of catching the rope, he had vanished in the alleyway.

I had the space of a heart beat to touch, with trembling fingers, the piece of parchment that lay within the envelope. It slid out with no resistance. It was a simple, innocent piece of parchment, containing no life of its own. Even without candles, I could see in the dim light of the grey, rainy evening what it was. My heart did not leave its accustomed place in my breast. It did not flip. It did not race. It did not stop. It behaved as any heart in the face of sure knowledge. It beat regularly, steadily, faithfully, as my eyes registered, without the hint of possible mistake, that I was looking at a perfect map of Arawak Island and that X marked the spot of the Arawak treasure.

The conclusion was unavoidable. This map had been in my father's possession. My father had received it, most probably through some envoy of Don Pedro, as his payment for having sold English military secrets to Spain. He had booked his passage on the *Judith* all those months ago in anticipation of going to the New World to claim his reward. This map explained why he had committed high treason and why no one had, until today, been able to prove it. Adam and I were the only ones in the world who knew it for a certainty.

It was a bitter pill for me to swallow. I was quite sure that my father had wished to restore to me my inheritance, which he had lost in earlier military campaigns. It was somewhat noble of him, but mostly stupid, and very unworthy of him. He had paid a high price for this stupidity—a very high price for this wish which was never realized.

So, too, had I paid dearly: once with the loss of my inheritance; twice, with my father's death; three times with Edward's death.

Now, there were shouts on the roof. Confusion sounded from the foyer. "Where are they? He's gone! The beast is gone! Disappeared!"

Now I had lost four times, for I would never see Adam again.

"Eve Marie! Eve Marie!" hallooed a voice from the foyer. It was my uncle. "Where are you? Where are you, child? Are you hurt? Speak!"

I quickly ripped the map into as many pieces as I could, then slipped the shreds and the envelope between the mattress and the bed frame. I would burn the whole at the earliest opportunity. Then I shoved the bed back from my chamber door and pulled my dressing gown from my clothespress. I unlatched the bedchamber door.

"I'm here, Uncle!" I called out to him just as he was mounting the last step to the hallway. "The . . . the beast had bound my mouth and hands with this," I said holding up the cloth, "and got out the window of my bedchamber."

"Your bedchamber?" he said, suitably amazed. "Here we were the whole time thinking he had taken you on the roof. Never would I have guessed—"

Our eyes met. I understood two things very well in that moment of contact: that my uncle had been nearly certain of my father's guilt, and that he was fully prepared to protect the Sedgwick family from searching questions and eyes.

I nodded, once. I knew he would back up whatever story I could concoct to account for the disappearance of the savage beast and the mysterious envelope. Sounds of servants and Julianna Castleragh and Aunt Charlotte and Lord Rollo trailing up the stairs caused me and my uncle to turn around before we had exchanged any other words.

I knew another thing just then: that I would not find decent rest this night or, perhaps, for many nights to come.

CHAPTER 20

*A*fter Uncle Harry found me, Julianna Castleragh was the next to reach my side in the wake of the man-beast's disappearance, followed by Aunt Charlotte, and a close third by Lord Rollo. They were immediately swallowed in the ensuing wave of servants who came running through the house now, checking and checking again every nook, every crook. Soon the hallway was swarming with so many bodies and eyes and questions and shouts and tensions and relief that the strange and contradictory feeling of lightness and heaviness almost overcame me and I nearly *fainted*.

I do not believe that I had ever before experienced how very *useful* is fainting in a difficult situation. I was simply unable to answer the anxious questions and to remain stable on my own two feet at the same time. This unfeigned inability turned the trick perfectly. Lord Rollo and even Julianna Castleragh were compelled to acquiesce to the authority—that is to say, wishes—of a female in distress who is on the verge of a swoon; and it was my distinct wish *not* to speak of that horrible man-beast, *not* to relive the most awful, most terrifying, most life-threatening situation that a woman of my genteel breeding and character had ever been in. (The reader might infer from the effectiveness of this ploy to avoid specific discussion of Adam and the mysterious envelope that I am recommending, as a kind of preliminary moral to my story, the cultivation of artificial displays of feminine weakness. I am advocating nothing of the kind *as a general rule*.)

So, my uncle saw to it that I was brought tenderly down to the receiving room and provided with restorative food and drink. I was entirely correct in my surmise that he was prepared to protect me from too many probing questions and to back up whatever story I offered for the disappearance of the man-beast and the envelope. Lord Rollo stayed only long enough to ascertain that the man-beast still did have the envelope in his possession, by what means he had left the house, and in which direction he had fled.

Lord Rollo had recovered himself sufficiently to have put a strong guard on his tongue and to have behaved in a far more solicitous manner toward me and my uncle than he had been disposed to display in the heat of the action. He accepted without a blink my account of how the man-beast had flown from my bedchamber window and landed on the ground fifteen feet below without difficulty. With a certain measure of dignity, Lord Rollo then collected his sword and his dagger, along with his hat and cape, and quit the receiving room with the assurance that he would do all in his power to catch that fellow and retrieve for us the paper which the man-beast had stolen. Lord Rollo said that he did not doubt that it was most valuable, and he said that it had confirmed all his suspicions that something most irregular was afoot concerning the reopening of my father's case. On a bow, Lord Rollo also extended to my uncle the services of his personal plasterers and woodworkers to repair the two bullet holes that he had caused in the walls.

My uncle reciprocated the excruciating cordiality of this ritual of departure. I was serene in the knowledge that, even with a spare five minutes' head start, which was all the time *at most* that had elapsed since Adam had disappeared into the alleyway behind Colebrooke Row, the man-beast would outmaneuver Lord Rollo in a game of cat-and-mouse in the back streets of London.

When his lordship had gone, Miss Castleragh exclaimed, "But how very odd was his behavior!'

"How so, Miss Castlergh?" my uncle inquired. "It was quite natural of his lordship to wish to repair the damage he had done to our home."

"No, I mean his behavior *during* the episode!" she said, apparently unable to notice when a subject was being turned. "It was quite extraordinarily unlike him! He was . . . yes, he was almost raving!"

"Nonsense, my dear!" my uncle replied with a kindly smile. "It was the situation that was quite extraordinary, not Lord Rollo's behavior! I believe that your sensibilities were as deranged as everyone else's to single *his* out for comment! No, no, I found no fault with him."

"One would not have said you thought so at the time, General Sedgwick," Miss Castleragh pursued. "If I recall rightly, you were highly critical of—"

"But then, my sensibilities were as affected as everyone else's," my uncle broke into this, "and, now that we have had a moment to cool our passions, we can surely see that all of our thoughts and desires were directed toward achieving the same goals—that of saving our poor, dear Eve Marie from harm and stopping that man-beast from escape. I am profoundly relieved—as I am sure we all are—that the first of the goals was achieved! We may count on Lord Rollo, I am sure, to do everything in his power to secure the second goal!"

Uncle Harry continued with a rather gentle flow of similar remarks and persuasions until, at last, all of Miss Castleragh's perceptions had been "improved"—that is to say, conformed to whatever official version of the incident Uncle Harry was planning to offer for public consumption. Uncle Harry had risen to the occasion, and I believed that he was fully equal to the task of establishing proper terms with Lord Rollo when next he met him.

My uncle, in short, was a prince, and I loved him in those brief hours as I never had before.

I was also proven correct on the subject of my sleepless night. Unlike my luxurious dreams of that very morning, my dreams this night were of desire and despair. I was alone. I was on board a rudderless craft, with no goal in mind, no shore in sight, my dreaming self struggling helplessly for consciousness. When, however, the next day dawned, I was hardly happier, for I awoke awash in misery and self-pity.

I will not dwell on that.

I will not dwell on that, because I *need* not dwell on it, quite apart from the fact that it is in excessively bad taste. Although this particular dream does still recur on occasion, it no longer has the power that it had that first night after Adam had left my life and England.

Now, here is precisely the place where I had made a wrong conjecture, which was entirely the result of *having been on the wrong path* (metaphorically speaking, of course). As I have said, I awoke the next morning at an emotional nadir, worse even than the pain and humiliation I had felt at my father's denunciation. My only act of will this morning was the burning of all the evidence of my father's treason, which I retrieved from under the mattress. Then I dressed by habit. I cast a shawl about my shoulders absent-mindedly. I descended the stairs mechanically. I sat at the breakfast table. I cannot remember whether or not I ate anything. My aunt and uncle cosseted and cajoled and were very, very dear, but their efforts fell woefully short of being able to touch, much less soothe, the pain in my breast. At dreary length, we repaired to the receiving room. The glaziers, two of them, were already on the minstrel balcony, chipping away at the fragments of glass that had remained in the casing after Adam's smashing entrance. New panes were propped against the wall, waiting to be cut, fitted, and leaded.

The door bell clanged. Uncle opined that it was Lord Rollo, who had promised to return to us in the morning with "news." Perhaps he had brought with him the plasterers and woodworkers. Aunt gave it as her opinion that it was that tattle-tale Julianna Castleragh, come to gather "news." I frankly did not care which one it was.

Thus, to my deep surprise, in strolled Adam Winthrop. He was looking fit and relaxed and very comfortable with himself and the world. He was not in naval uniform but dressed as a gentleman, neither fancy nor unassuming, mind you, but very well. It had been a long time since I had seen him looking thus.

Suddenly everything made wonderful sense. In the face of all conflict and adversity, he had devised a plan. I went misty on the spot.

He bowed and introduced himself. "Mrs. Sedgwick, General Sedgwick," he said, businesslike but still affable, to my aunt and uncle. Then, to me, he bowed again, "Mrs. Lipscomb."

I did not know what to say. I smiled—broadly.

My uncle invited Adam Winthrop to sit. He did so. Preliminary civilities were exchanged. Points of contact were established. Adam remembered the pleasure of two evenings before in meeting General Sedgwick's wife and niece. My uncle was regarding Adam keenly, questioningly, and finally, rather benevolently. Aunt Charlotte was visibly agitated, not knowing what to think or how to take the intrusion into her house of a beastly man by the name of Winthrop who, if the upstanding and righteous Lord Rollo was right (which she did not doubt for a moment), had been the direct cause of all the Sedgwick family misfortunes.

Within the proper amount of time, Adam came to the point of his visit. "One of the reasons I have come today," he began, his voice hovering between serious concern and direct matter-of-factness, "was because an infamous rumor has come to my ears linking my name with your family in a rather tragic—"

The door bell clanged.

All of Adam's casual unconcern fled. His face and body and every faculty were suddenly alert.

In case any doubt about the unseasonal caller's identity might have remained in anyone's mind, Aunt Charlotte cleared it up by saying anxiously, "Oh dear, I believe that must be Lord Rollo."

My uncle and Adam exchanged a brief but very deep regard. After the barest moment, Adam said, a little curtly, "Stall him."

My uncle rose swiftly and crossed the room. "I believe that Lord Rollo and I must first give our most urgent attention to the bullet hole in the upstairs hallway," he said. On an inspired thought, Uncle Harry reminded Aunt Charlotte that she had important business to engage herself with in the nether regions of the house. Aunt Charlotte did not protest.

When they had left, Adam rose from his chair and came to stand in front of me. His hands were outstretched.

"Eve?" he asked. It was a most loving sound.

At first I did not answer. (I was completely besotted.)

"Eve?" he asked again, his hand still outstretched.

"Yes?" I managed, uncomprehending.

"Are you coming?"

Then I understood that he was issuing me an invitation of some sort. "Where?" I asked.

"Out the back door," he replied, then, looking up at the minstrel balcony where the glaziers were hard at work, "or out the open window to the roof."

Comprehension came slowly. "You mean . . . abscond?"

"In a word, yes," was his answer.

"I thought you had come with a plan," I said, "a plan to make everything right."

"I did come with one," he said.

"I thought you had figured out a way to . . . to *resolve* everything," I persisted.

His brows rose in mild inquiry.

"I mean, when I saw you come in these few minutes ago," I began, "that is, when I saw you *walk through the door* like an ordinary man, I thought you had discovered a way to clear yourself and bring Lord Rollo to book, all the while still preserving my father's good name!"

"My entrance appealed to you, did it?" He looked rather pleased with himself. "Yes, I do enter rooms through doors on occasion. It was even my intention today to *leave* by the door—preferably the front door! It seems now that only the first part of the plan can be successfully accomplished. And if we wait any longer, I *will* be leaving again by the front door—only, not of my own volition."

"No plan?" My voice choked. I may have been on the verge of tears. The world had taken on a darker hue. I was back in my rudderless, dream-tossed world, struggling to awaken. "But I had hoped—I had hardly *dared* hope for a happy ending. You see, I was thinking that if William of Orange were to prevail over James—"

"He's bound to prevail."

"Yes, of course," I said, very mechanically, "and with your record in the Spanish Netherlands, and given Admiral van der Kuylen's esteem for you and his friendship, I thought—ideally, of course, in my heart of hearts!—that a way could be found to . . . that a place could be made for you here in the coming government."

He shook his head. "I have discovered no plan where you could have it all ways. I cannot openly accuse Rollo and protect your father at the same time. Besides, Rollo has the entire administration of the English navy behind him. Now, as for Admiral van der Kuylen, he has agreed not to notice if a small sloop should edge her way out of London harbor tonight." He shook his head again. "But I have no plan where I could be absolutely certain of convincing the highest ranks of the military of Rollo's guilt in your father's affair. I cannot be absolutely certain that, if I chose to stay in England now, I could stay out of prison on the charge of a false accusation against your father. Surely you can see that, Eve?"

I could not. Not yet. What was more, we were at the heart of the matter. Adam Winthrop had been my father's accuser. This circumstance seemed the deepest, darkest obstacle that lay between us, after all. Adam's actions of the day before had preserved the present rehabilitation of my father's name. Nevertheless—

"You don't even have a plan to dissolve the horrible knot that lies between you and me—and my father?"

He looked down at me. It was a kindly, indulgent smile. "I cannot undo what another man has done in the past."

Again he paused. "I will not undo—or repent—what *I* have done in the past."

"But . . . but," I protested. I was struggling to consciousness. It was disorienting and unpleasant, but I wanted to see the light. "When you walked in here, I suddenly thought that everything would turn out right—that there would be a perfect end for me, for us, for our story."

Adam smiled again, this time provocatively, irresistibly. "A perfect end?" he rebuked lightly. "This from you, my dear Eve Marie? I know you rather better than that! My wits have failed, as you see, to devise the perfect end. I was depending on *you*, rather, to supply a moral for the story."

I awoke. I saw the light. I rose from my chair and accepted his outstretched hands in mine. I had imagined that Adam would, somehow, wave a magic wand that would dispel my father's crime, as well as the realities of the entire English military, just as he had waved the golden scepter that made the Spanish disappear from Arawak Island.

Of course, he had devised no such plan. No man could make the imperfections of the world go away. I had been greedy to think that I could have it all my own way, and I had cherished tidiness over all other considerations. I saw exactly *where I had gone wrong*: I had wanted no loose ends. The moral of the story came to me, instantly and effortlessly. It is that *the sins of the father are* not necessarily *visited on the children.*

Yes, *that* is the moral of the story—that and no other. It is not a perfect moral, but a happy one, and doubtless extremely unsatisfying to those readers whose temperaments demand that the just be rewarded and the unjust be punished, or who, as I did before I got on the right path, prize neatness and tidiness and just plain *repetition* over messiness and loose ends and *new beginnings.*

I have come to see that most of this world's misery is the fruit not, as the priests would have it, of wickedness, but of stupidity. Of all the stupidities, I have come to consider greed the most deplorable, followed closely by blind adherence to convention. And if any good man of the cloth should read these lines—be he Anglican, Dissenter, or Catholic— let me tell him that he would do the world and himself a lot of good by meditating on the moral to my story.

I was free. I was free *not* to follow in my father's footsteps. I was free *not* to repeat his errors and stupidities. I was free *not* to fight his false battles, nor accept his enmities as my own. I was free *not* to bind myself to impossible resolutions and tidy endings.

Once having cut the ties that bind, it was perfectly logical that I would be left with a handful of loose ends.

"And my uncle?" I said into the small space of silence.

"Do you fear he'll not be able to understand?" Adam asked.

"I think he'll *try*," was my answer.

"Do you think he'll suffer consequences if you suddenly disappear?"

I shook my head. "I think he could devise a story plausible enough to account for my disappearance." I paused, an almost satisfying thought crossing my mind. "Lord Rollo doesn't *dare* push him too far these days, I think."

Of course, escape was the only course of action open to us. My new, untidy self was not disposed to conventional entrances and departures. I had had quite enough of doors to last me a lifetime. Looking up at Adam, I smiled and answered the question he had originally put to me. "Out the window," I said, squeezing his hands.

We ran across the short space of the receiving room to the minstrel balcony. The glaziers had already replaced several of the panels Adam had smashed, but a lovely square opening in the wall remained—the perfect space for us to get through. Now, in the perfect happy ending, we should have been able to step through this open space of the window and fly off into the great beyond.

This did not happen. Instead, we had to pick our way among the shards of glass and to contend with the very indignant glaziers who objected in rather vulgar terms to our desire to invade their working space and disrupt their labors.

Adam slipped several hefty coins into the palms of both with the words, "Don't tell the fancy gentleman that we have left by the roof."

"What fancy gentleman?" one of the glass cutters was moved to inquire.

"The one who is about to burst into this room in a frenzy of anger," Adam informed him. "General Sedgwick, on the other hand, may be told of the means of our departure after the fancy gentleman has left—as he no doubt will within a moment or two of entering the room."

Understandably the glaziers looked blank, but compliant.

In a perfect happy ending, the sun would be shining. This morning it was most certainly not shining. It was misty and cold and damp, and I had no coat, only my shawl. Neither did we fly off anywhere. The eaves, which looked very broad from the street below, narrowed considerably when one had to hop across them. (Adam and I seem to have difficulty, when we are together, keeping our feet on *terra firma*.)

The dignity of our journey across the roofs and back alleyways of London was not improved by the fact that only seconds after our escape through the window onto the roof, we heard Lord Rollo enter the receiving room raving, "Quit stalling, Sedgwick! Damn the bullet holes! I know he's here! You're in this with him! I'll prove it! Where is he? Where is that blackguard? I had guards posted the night through at your house in order to catch that lying, thieving cheat! What? *What*? You *dare* threaten me, Sedgwick? I have done nothing against the law to put your house under watch! You, there! Man! On the balcony! Where is he? Where is that scoundrel?"

Adam and I naturally did not wait to discover how the glaziers answered. However, from the circumstance that Lord Rollo did not immediately erupt onto the roof in hot pursuit of us, and from the sounds of his booming, half-crazed voice, which receded, we assumed that Lord Rollo had been sent in the direction opposite from the one we were taking. Nevertheless, since we knew that he was very close behind us and doubtless had mobilized a significant number of military men to help him, the pursuit was warm enough. Adam and I were forced to take the least scenic route through London in order to arrive at the wharves, where a boat was waiting for us. It is hardly necessary for me to describe in detail this crossing of London. The reader will fully comprehend the implications of "the least scenic route" if I mention that it included several passages through the sewers.

Not that Adam was particularly apologetic about this journey. I was prepared for messy loose ends, but this was a bit much! We had taken a slight breather from running. Only once, after a long argument about who should wear his coat, which he won, did he make anything nearing an expression of regret. He said, "The mother of my child shall not go cold in a sewer."

I had hardly admitted to myself that I was pregnant. It went a long way toward explaining my unaccustomed feeling of combined lightness and heaviness. It was a lovely feeling, really, and the look in Adam's eyes and the sound of his voice when he said "mother of my child" had the most romantic effect imaginable, despite the fact that the walls around us were crawling with life I do not even care to describe.

"How did you know?" I asked dreamily.

"Your eyes," he said. "The whites are almost blue. I have never seen them like that. In addition—"

His contemplation of the bodily clues to my delicate condition led his thoughts down other directions—well, we *were* in a sewer.

"Adam!" I said astringently, recalling his wandering attention. "Never mind that now! Tell me instead what you would have told my uncle had not Lord Rollo interrupted you. I thought then that you had perhaps hit on the perfect way to extricate yourself from my father's demise."

"Yes, I had, really," he acknowledged. "I was going to lie through my teeth." He laughed, unashamed, at my expression. "What, Sedgwick, you don't approve?"

I could not say that I *did* approve of such fundamental dishonesty. I was about to say that—

But, no. I held my tongue. Getting on the right path had been the inspiration of the moment. *Staying* on the right path, I was beginning to discover, was going to require more than my usual fortitude, and Adam Winthrop is a *most* unreformed character.

"Sedgwick, you're too much," he declared after a small pause. His voice still held laughter.

That did it. "I?" I echoed ominously. "I am too much? Let me tell you that—"

"Shall we stay and discuss it?" he broke into this, quite politely. "Or go?"

I strove for self-possession. "We may save this discussion for later," I said no less politely, though a little coldly, "and depart on the instant!"

My decision at just that moment was prompted not only by the impasse in the conversation but also by the shouts in the street above. It sounded as if there might be a contingent of men out looking for us. Adam proceeded to pick his way through the sewers, and I really did not care to learn just how he had come to know these subterranean passages so well.

To make a rather long and hair-raising and *very* untidy story short, we made it to our boat with several extremely narrow escapes from the long arm of Lord Rollo's law and order. Within a matter of hours we were free of the sight of London and practically given a naval escort down the Thames in the shadow of one of Admiral van der Kuylen's vessels. Within days we were on the high seas.

I must say that life on board ship suits me down to the ground, so to speak. Thomas is not yet of the same mind as I. Yes, Thomas is with us, along with a small, ragtag crew for whom I have great hopes of reform. I will tolerate messy loose ends only in the grand outlines of my life, not in my day-to-day existence. Thomas and the rest of the crew shall be convinced of the error of their unregenerate ways by the time we reach the coast of Africa.

About those loose ends and my ability to adapt to the less-than-perfect world, I still cherish the notion that Adam will be rewarded for his deeds. I am not sure how he shall be rewarded for having saved the Arawak treasure without also exposing the existence of the Arawak treasure, and I am not sure how he shall be rewarded for having preserved my father's good name without also exposing the fact that my father was guilty; nevertheless, such is my turn of mind.

Since leaving England, we have heard that William of Orange has taken London in a bloodless revolution. I have discussed with Adam on occasion the possibility that he will be awarded a governorship— in Jamaica, perhaps. Adam is of the opinion that if we continue in our present style of existence, he shall be happy merely to escape the prison and the gallows while Lord Rollo is still alive. I am practical.

I have pointed out that Lord Rollo may have the great good taste to die.

In addition to the pleasures that I have rediscovered being on board ship, I have found that the activity of putting pen to paper also suits me well. It has provided me with great entertainment and a way to mourn my father. My grief is finding fresh outlets, my understanding of him changing, growing, and finally, incorporating forgiveness, though perhaps not forgetfulness. It is, when all is said, such a *relief* to speak one's mind.

With pen in hand, I feel happy, almost complete. Words spring to its tip, sentences roll off it, truths and insights are inscribed with it onto paper. My story is told. The relationships have been laid bare, and it occurs to me, as I think back over my love for Adam and the intertwined coincidences that brought us together and nearly drove us apart, that a final, anticlimactic moral to this story might be the observation that the *absence* of amazing coincidence in one's life might very well prove to be the most amazing circumstance!

About that pen, Adam is inclined to tease. He often hovers and interrupts, as he is doing now.

"But, Adam, I am not yet finished, my dear! Give me a moment. Just one more thought. What are you doing? Adam? Give me that pen. What do you have in mind? Oh—! Give me that pen, Adam. No. You shall *not* make me laugh! Give me that pen! Oh—!"

Julie Tetel Andresen brings the historical novel to life. Blending adventure, mystery, and romance, she takes her readers on absorbing journeys into periods as diverse as the Middle Ages and the Wild West. After establishing a following in the commercial marketplace, Julie has been finding a growing audience among discerning readers who appreciate her well-researched history, high style, subtle humor, complex characters, and grand love stories.

Julie is from the Chicago suburb of Glenview, Illinois. Since 1975 she has lived in Durham, North Carolina with her husband and two sons. For information on where to obtain her other titles, write her at: 97354 Duke Station, Durham, NC 27708-7354 or at jtetel@acpub.duke.edu. Her Web Page is under construction.